In a Milk and Honeyed Land

In a Milk and Honeyed Land

Richard Abbott

ISBN: 978-0993-1684-2-0 (softcover)
ISBN: 978-0993-1684-3-7 (ebook format)

Matteh Publications

Contact:
Web: http://mattehpublications.datascenesdev.com/
Email: matteh@datascenesdev.com

For Roselyn, for family

Contents

Also by the Author

Historical Fiction

Novels:

Scenes from a Life
The Flame Before Us

Short stories:

The Lady of the Lions
The Man in the Cistern

Science Fiction

Novels:

Far from the Spaceports

Cover information

Original Matteh Publications logo drawn by Jackie Morgan.

Maps

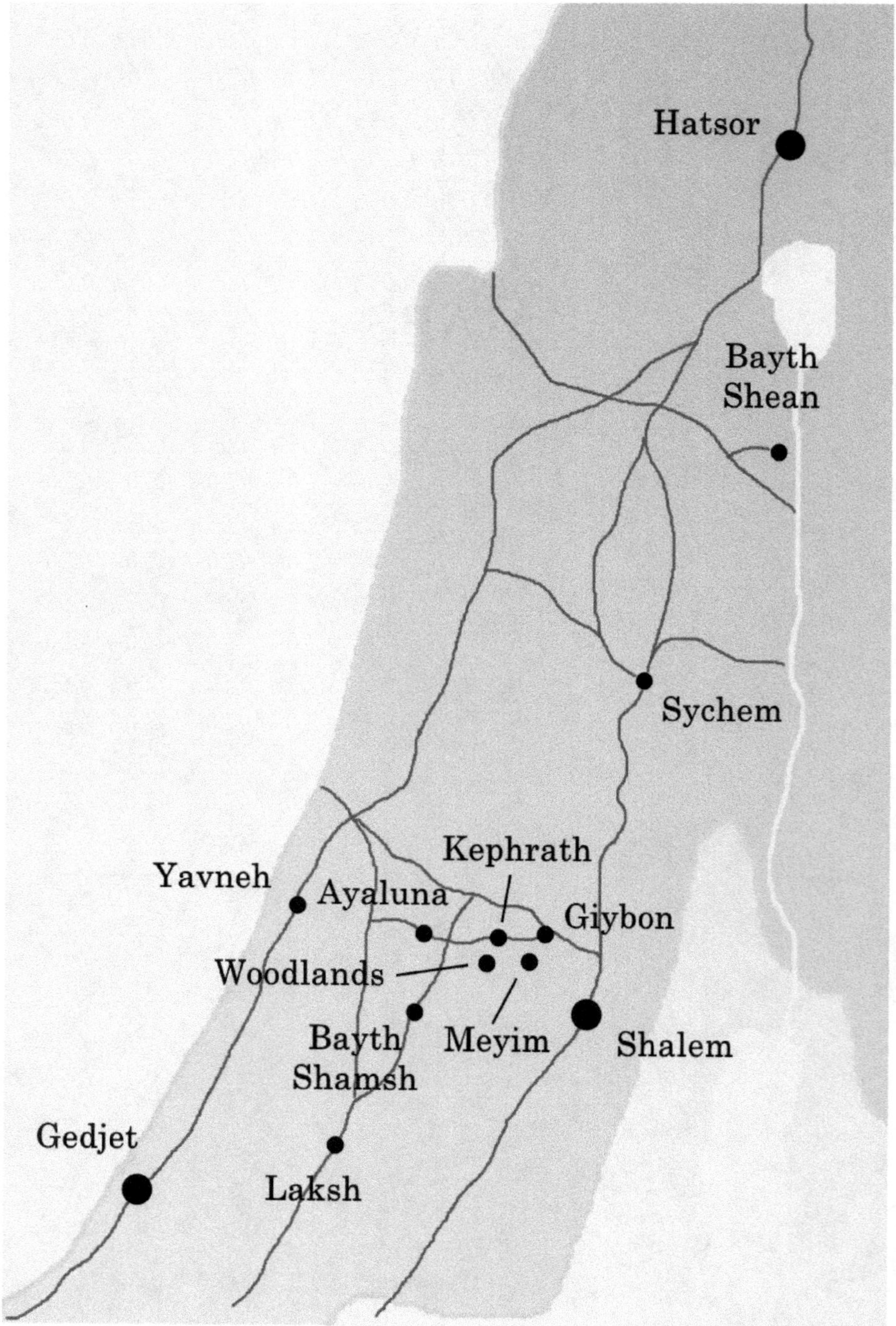
Hatsor
Bayth
Shean
Sychem
Kephrath
Yavneh
Ayaluna
Giybon
Woodlands
Bayth
Shamsh
Meyim
Shalem
Gedjet
Laksh

The Region

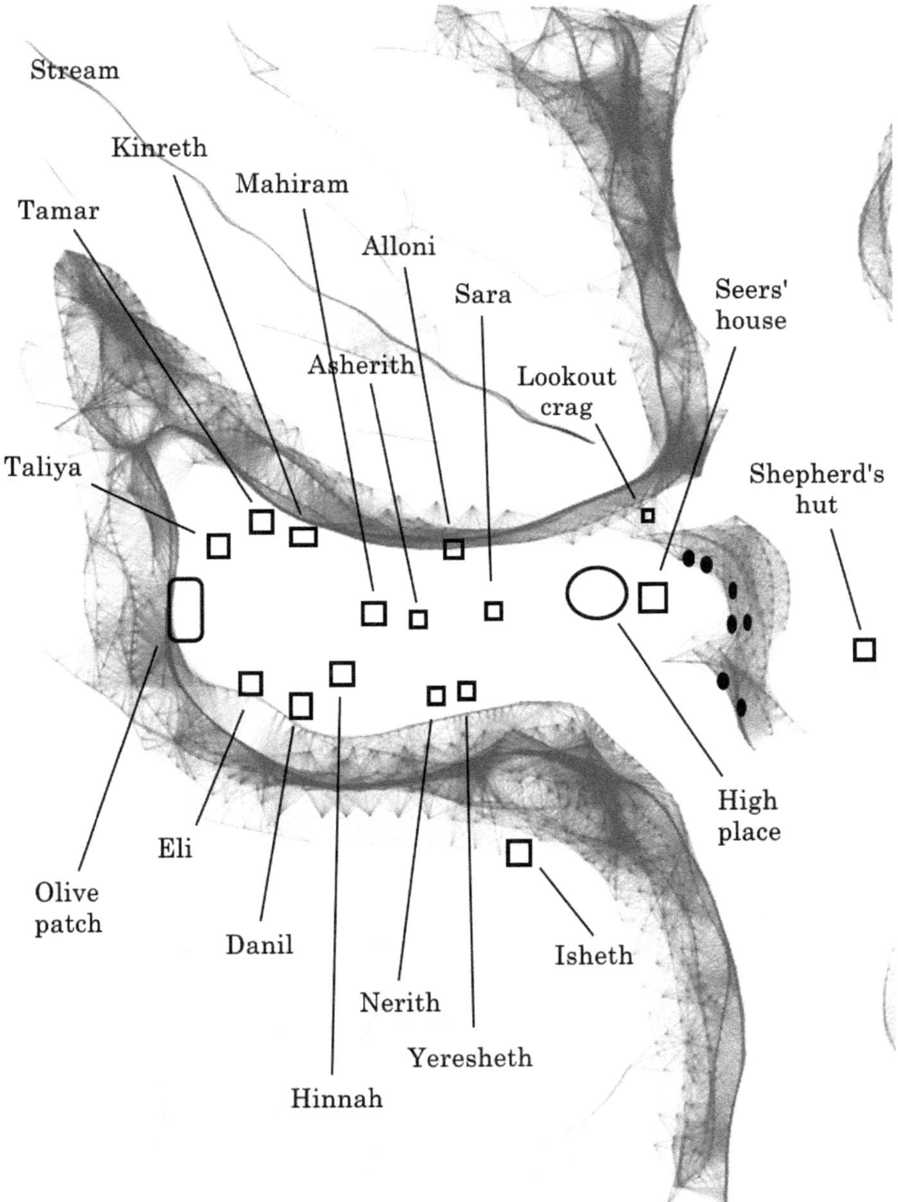

The Town of Kephrath

Prelude

THERE WERE FOUR CHILDREN of the god that year. I remember hearing that, many times over, through all my growing years, though it was a long time before I understood what it meant. That year was a unique year, a unique time to be alive. There were more of us then than any other year, before or since. Perhaps such a year will never come again, not now the hill country is changing and the new houses are leaping up in little clearings everywhere. Indeed the whole land is changing. Had I wanted, they would have built for me one of these houses in whatever village I chose, as a reward for all my efforts. Some would once have said that this would have been the reward for betrayal rather than the wages of labour.

But even these newcomers could see that my place was in the great house beside the high place of Kephrath, among the families of my birth. The place where I lived and laboured, loved and learned loss. So, whether through gratitude or pity, here I live still. I am at home among my people to be sure, but I am also a stranger in the eyes of these strangers. They even tie their kefs differently to us, bundled oddly around their head. I have not troubled to learn their style. I am strange here to them, though I have lived here my whole life, and the land is becoming strange to me, though I know every hill and valley in it. They still need us to uphold the new alliances, but the need sits uncomfortably with some of them.

I feel, however, some kinship with them. They have had something of an uncertain, shifting childhood, and have chosen to be here, to live here in this place that is beautiful but not overflowing with wealth. They have been brought up singing one song, and then have tried to learn another. They have found themselves willing to unite with people who they had not planned to meet, and who they came upon by chance. Though their customs are odd, their yearning is not. They feel, like me and like my own people, the hunger that comes with displacement, and the thirst that impels one to find a home.

Prelude

This story tells of we three who lived past infancy, and the things that we did and said in those days. Although there were four of us born, Mahur was a sickly boy who died before the year of his birth had turned. Then there were three, for a little while. Then there were only two. We were the linen sashes that tied up all the leather-bundled tales of our village life.

I remember those bundles that were carried on the backs of the Mitsriy scribes. They still travel the roads down near the coast, still with their escort of bowmen, but they have not come up this way now for many years. The traders who brought little caravans of donkeys up and down the great ridgeway road, or across the rough hillside tracks, still come to us, but less often now, and at erratic intervals instead of every season.

I have been seer to my people, and sung the songs of the great cycle around the stones of the high place. Now I tell tales. I have watched over the threshold that divides the living and the dead, and although I am still doorkeeper in my own house, it is becoming a different house, a different life.

There were four children of the god that year. We were reckoned as once-orphaned, living each in the house of our mothers, brought up as foster child by their husbands, with half-brothers and half-sisters according to the overflow of life in that family. We did not understand what it was to be a child of the god for many years – the words that had meant so much to empty wombs passed us by in the silent air.

The words meant nothing, but some of us grew familiar with estrangement as we grew up, looks of darkness and rejection from unwilling surrogate fathers, a sense of displacement amongst our peers, mixed pride and disdain. Others found happy acceptance. We still clung to each other. This is our story.

Alph

Kiraru Year 7 – Etanim Year 10

I WAS IN DELIGHT all those days,
  playing in his presence all the time,
playing in the places where we live,
delighting with the children of the land.

CHILDHOOD IN THE HILL COUNTRY was an ever-changing round. Damariel ran with the other children to the little stream and splashed in it, all of them naked minnows together in the noisy water. It was the end of a cloudless Kiraru day, and was very hot outside the dappled shade of the short trees, their leaves faded and slightly shrivelled as they waited for the autumn rains.

Several of the village women did aunt-duty from a vantage point off to one side, shaded out of the sun under a rocky outcrop. Long strands of creeper hung down from the top, reaching almost down to the head of the tallest woman. Like the rest, she wore a married woman's kef, with blue borders and diagonal weave.

Damariel stopped knee-deep in the stream for a moment, watching her adjust the way her kef draped over her left shoulder and then retie it. He was suddenly caught by how the trailing greenery itself looked like the fringes of a kef, with the blue embroidery of the women's headscarves like flowers budding at the ends of the tassels.

He turned to one of the other children nearby, excited and wanting to share this new insight into his world, but as he turned around a water fight started and the air was loud with shouts and laughter. He saw his two younger brothers in the middle of it, jumping up and down together to make their waves bigger. His friend Kothar was off to one side, calling out loudly, getting everyone involved except himself. Nobody was interested in vines that hung like a kef over a rock.

His brothers were both summer babies, born almost exactly a year apart, and very alike in looks and temperament. They had dark hair, starting to wave like their father's. Damariel had something of his mother Yeresheth's face, so he was told, but, of course, looked quite different from Baruk and Bashur. They looked like their father Shomal. He didn't.

Their little sister Sosanneth was too young yet to venture into the stream, and she sat with open mouth on one of the women's laps and pointed at the medley in front of her.

She saw Damariel looking at her, waved her arms, and laughed, but all at once the fighting caught up with him and he was toppled into the water. He gasped and scrambled to the edge, running up the bank to Sosanneth who held out her arms as he approached. He picked her up awkwardly and dabbled her feet in a quieter part of the stream, a little away from the others.

The sun dipped behind a tree on the ridge above them and the women got up, calling and corralling their charges into some order, carrying the younger ones and leading the rest back up to the village houses, where the sun would linger some while longer. Qetirah's mother Kinreth was carrying Sosanneth on one hip and Qetirah's younger sister Laylah on the other. Qetirah and Damariel followed along behind. The minnow children went back inside by twos and threes, dried off and were made to wear at least some clothing.

Damariel hung back from following his brothers into their house, and waited until Kinreth had set Sosanneth and Laylah down on the ground. Taking their hands, with Qetirah on the other side, he helped them across the door lintel, passing under the branches and bright flowers of the mimosa tree rooted beside the door post, draped amply above their heads.

They went into the house. Damariel's mother was in the final stage of preparing bread, and a bean sauce simmered to one side. The two women talked for a while across the open kitchen space as Baruk and Bashur ran about, Sosanneth and Laylah giggled as they watched them, and the older two children began shaping the dough into flat circles on the griddle.

The village houses were all much of a pattern. The door led into a broad room running front to back. In here was a place to cook, some storage jars for water or foodstuffs sunk into the floor, stools and a table to eat at. On either side, left and right, were smaller rooms, mostly for sleeping places, or set aside for indoor work such as weaving, carpentry, or repairs.

Some houses had another room or two tacked on to the long side, usually for some particular purpose; Qetirah's father Caleb used his for metal-work. Many of the extra rooms had been added when a daughter married, so bringing an extra man into the household. Ideally the house never really stopped being extended in this way, though in practice few houses had added more than a couple of rooms for this purpose.

Outside there might be a wooden or stone lean-to, or a small shelter for livestock. Most households used the flat roof area as extra living space, at least in the summer months, with a wide diversity of walls or windbreaks approached by means of a ladder outside or steep stair inside. The largest house in the village belonged to the seer and his wife, but Damariel had never been inside it and had no idea how it was arranged.

Damariel did not know it then, but that summer was the last time he and all his year would play naked together in the stream. When the springtime came again, the girls of his age had been separated out and seemed to move around only in close-knit, slightly intimidating groups, wrapped carefully in their plain white adolescent kefs. They had learned to tie these in the upland style, covering all their hair, tied below their chin, and lying loosely at shoulder-length over smock or dress. The boys spent most of the day working with the older youths and men. For them, a kef was more of a practical thing, convenient for keeping sweat out of the eyes.

Shomal was quite particular about his sons wearing their kefs all through the waking hours, especially out of the house, but some of the other fathers were less strict. Walking around the village and the adjoining strips of cultivation you might see all manner of variations of style and habit for the men's headwear. The women were altogether more consistent and discreet.

For the meantime, however, Damariel's attention was focused on making the bread into even shapes. The two women finished talking, and Qetirah, Laylah, and their mother left for their own house.

Qetirah lived a little further down the ridge and off to the northern side. Her father worked with metal, mostly bronze but some silver when he could get hold of it, and Qetirah often wore a little brooch he had made once from a small piece of scrap metal. She lived near to Kothar, Damariel's closest friend. Kothar was bold and outspoken, and Damariel felt rather in awe of him on some days and quite shocked on others. However, he knew without a doubt that in difficulty, Kothar would be loyal and confident.

But just over the ridge from Qetirah's house, and a little to the west, stood two or three houses belonging to a family Yeresheth thought little of and spoke out against. Damariel was discouraged from making friendships with the children of these households, though the reason for this was never very clear to him.

Yeresheth's house was also on the southern side of the village, a little way down the ridge from the high place. Her sister Nerith lived in the house across the narrow alleyway with her husband and two children, a bright yellow rock-rose bush adorning her door. There was an uncle, too, but he had moved away to one of the larger towns along the distant coast before Damariel had been born, and he had never met him.

Damariel had been told that his mother's mother used to live in Yeresheth's house, which of course had been her house in former years. But with Baruk and Bashur being born only a year apart, and Sosanneth born less than two years later, she had moved in with Nerith. He vaguely remembered her being in the house long ago, but for most of his life she had been a remote, rather shrunken figure who he saw only occasionally.

Shomal, Yeresheth's husband, had no living relatives, and the house he had grown up in had been taken over by another family in exchange for a field with some olive trees at the extreme western end of the ridge, where it caught the setting sun and the fluttering wind blowing up from the coast.

The village relied on several different means of support. Most families had an area of cultivation – some, like Shomal, grew mainly olives or other fruit or nut bearing trees, while others mostly tended vegetables and other crops. Many mixed the two in one measure or another. Alloni cultivated a wide stretch of land that was perfect for grape-vines: it had belonged to his mother long ago, but as she had had no daughters it had passed to him and his wife to be tended.

Either side of the central ridge, following the contours down a little way amongst the short trees and scrub, were terraced strips with grain and beans. Along with the crops, a few households had decent-sized flocks of sheep or goats. These were mostly pastured in groups during the day a little way off, north or south along the hillside, or else taken off all together for a few weeks at a time. Small noisy groups of chickens strutted around most of the houses.

The surrounding countryside was another source of food, and almost all the women knew where to find wild berries and green herbs in season. A few of the men, like Kothar's father Labayu, hunted or trapped game as it roamed, regularly bringing rabbit and hare in numbers down to the village, with occasional deer for the festivals and other special occasions.

The lowlands off to the west were much more generous, with large herds scattered in the denser vegetation, but the main targets down in the valleys were the storehouses of the villages there. Danil led a group of five or ten other men in infrequent raids to secure easy bags of supplies. They went armed, and spoke as though they were warriors, but rarely saw real danger. Stealth and speed of movement were the tactics of choice, and a real pitched fight with weapons could mean disaster for both communities.

There were a few craftsmen and women in the community, like Issi the potter, Caleb the metal-worker, or Shelomith-Rahmay whose embroidery could be found in most of the village kefs. Most of these people's work stayed within the village and was exchanged for other goods, but some of it went up the hill to Giybon to be traded further afield, supervised and organised by the chief.

Sometimes of an evening Yeresheth would recall for them the names of her ancestors, her mother and mother's mother, the men they had married, back as far as she could remember and the children retained interest. Damariel had stayed awake a few times when she had told the list of names back to the time when the whole community had moved south, south out of the mountainous regions well to the north, where the winters were so much colder than here and the living was harder. He was never quite certain of the sequence when he woke up the next morning, and was convinced that she did not always tell the names in the same order. The names got stranger as they came from longer ago: names from the north that only a few in the village used any more, and nobody in Damariel's family. These were names like Daduya and Perizzi, Putiheba and Erwina-Teshub, and the oldness of them rolled around his heart as he slipped into sleep.

At the top of the village, serving as the spiritual and social heart of the community, was the high place, with its arc of standing stones nearly joining in a circle, leaving an open gap looking out towards the north. Beside the stones stood the altar stone, and the house of the village seer and his wife Qerith. Iqnu had been seer and priest much longer than Damariel had been alive, and Damariel only ever encountered him as a slightly vague, slightly fatherly figure at a distance. He heard him speak only at the opening of the great summer and winter festivals in which young children were involved. Next year he would be allowed to stay longer at these, and take part in the autumn and spring festivals as well. He was dimly aware that Yeresheth and Shomal had quite different opinions about Iqnu, and that Shomal usually changed the subject when the seer's name was mentioned.

The meal was ready, and before long Shomal returned from his field, his tunic speckled with olive twigs and leaf-dust, a bundle of tools gathered in one hand and a small bag of vegetables in the other. The children alighted around the food. Sosanneth was nearly asleep already, and managed only a little bread and a few spoons of stew before being settled in the sleeping room.

Shomal talked at some length to Baruk and Bashur about the day just past, more briefly to Yeresheth, and finally to Damariel. Shortly after, the three boys joined the sleeping Sosanneth and spread out their own sleeping rolls from where they had been bundled against the side of the little room. As Damariel fell asleep, his inner sight still full of a rock wearing a kef, he heard the adults' voices quiet in the next room.

Outside, the village of Kephrath clustered along the backbone of the ridge. There were about a hundred houses straddled across the crest as it ran down from the high place and its stones towards the setting sun, spilling a little down either side into the valleys below. Households of clan-related families tended to cluster together to form islands in the community. Yeresheth would tell them that originally, generations before, the division into clans had been cleaner, stricter, but as the years had gone by the lines had blurred. Intermarriage was quite common, as was exchange of property as family wealth ebbed and flowed. The clan islands were no longer so distinct, but extended encroaching swirls into one another like cream being stirred into porridge.

Perhaps twenty houses now stood empty and unused. The older inhabitants spoke of how this family and that had moved towards the coast, or how this family and that had merged with another and left their home vacant. Nobody remembered a day when all the houses had been full, but the stories that had been passed down spoke of such a time, when even the several ruined, roofless houses up the ridge from the high place had echoed with occupancy, along the track towards Giybon. But in some of these houses, even the door plants of the women had died back and withered.

Straddling the track up towards Giybon was the town gate. The gate stood on its own, not connected to a wall or any other building. It was ceremonial rather than practical; trade was conducted here, or formal decisions on behalf of the community, and it served more to represent the boundary between the village and the outside world than to divide or protect. The Mitsriy, who had governed the region for many years now, would not let walls be built in defence in most towns, and only those few who retained their older defences, with steep slopes and large stone blocks, were allowed to keep them. This gate was not a defence, but a gathering place.

Two summers later they mourned Yeresheth's mother and placed her in the family tomb. Damariel remembered the day as a very solemn one, with his mother and aunt supporting each other up by the stones as her body went into a dark cave. A group of men had rolled a great stone back across the entrance, and Iqnu had carried out some kind of ritual. A spatter of unseasonable rain had pattered across the group of villagers stood around, and that, together with the scudding wind, had prevented him hearing most of what was said. Afterwards, life continued in much the same way as it had before.

But the following year he had cause to think again about the number of people living in Kephrath. On this particular day he first saw the man who was the chief of the four towns, Yad-Nesherim. Yad-Nesherim lived up at Giybon, which therefore, just for now, was the head of the four towns. It had not always been this way: Yad-Nesherim's father, while still a young man, had wrested the chiefdom away from a family in Jarrar's town, Woodlands.

That had been achieved without too much conflict, since the previous chief, Kabkabim, had become greedy and inept. Even the people of his own town had wanted him gone in the end, as his steady accumulation of wealth, his increasingly obstinate demands, and his refusal to be lavish with gifts and favours had settled opinion forcefully against him. He had been the fourth son of his line to hold the chiefdom, and the older stories never spoke well of such long lineages holding power. Two or three generations worked, but often after that the seed grew weak and the growth was twisted.

Once, many generations ago, two chiefs had come out of Kephrath, and a woman who had written on behalf of the whole community to the Mitsriy governor, but not since. A couple of families, such as that of Shelomith-Rahmay, still asserted a lingering status through descent from a former chief. The family still held good standing in the community, but the link was reckoned by most to have grown tenuous.

Other families now held – or at least claimed – more sway and influence, such as Issi the potter and his wife Asherith, whose children Saphiret and Yusuf seemed intent on gaining status. But the rivalry for the privilege of chiefdom was between Giybon and Jarrar's town. They were larger than Kephrath or the fourth town, Meyim, and power seemed to follow size these days. Meyim was smallest, and had never yet produced a chief. Damariel had heard it said that Giybon, with the largest and most important high place of the four towns, was most deserving of having the chiefdom as well, but he had also heard others argue against this in the cool of the evening when wine was being shared.

From time to time Shomal spoke about the chief and his family with a mixture of envy and derision. The envy was focused on the undeniable fact of their wealth and influence, and the derision on their apparent complete ignorance of what went on in Kephrath. It was said that Yad-Nesherim visited Woodlands every month, Kephrath twice a year, and Meyim only once. Damariel wasn't sure about this, as he couldn't remember the chief appearing more than once a year, usually at one of the festivals when food, wine, and pleasure flowed very freely. But if Yad-Nesherim only put in a personal appearance once a year, his influence was much more overt.

Every half year some of his men arrived in the village with a row of donkeys, to collect pannier loads of grain, wine and dried fruit to take back to Giybon. Twice a year half a dozen of the village men had to go and work on the chief's land, his buildings, or the trackways leading north and south for a few weeks. Trade was largely conducted through his hands and his network of contacts, and townspeople were discouraged from trying to negotiate their own deals. Instead, those who had craft or skill were supposed to take their goods up the track to Giybon for him to manage; frequently some covert dealing took place outside of this official policy.

Yad-Nesherim also maintained favour with the Mitsriy, personally providing them with the tribute owed. Small groups of Mitsriy soldiers might pass along the track, but did not stop in Kephrath to harass or threaten.

Yad-Nesherim was also diligent in cultivating good relations with the communities. Most families had at one time or another received some little gift or favour to acknowledge service or loyalty. Once when Shomal had been called to work duty in a particularly hot summer, he came home again with a sack of grain and a leg of venison across the donkey's back. Kothar's family kept on their wall a small Mitsriy amulet given to them by Yad-Nesherim's father one winter. Most of Damariel's friends could tell similar stories.

To Damariel's eyes, it all worked like a larger version of village life; very little silver changed hands, but gifts of one thing or another passed around from house to house, and from town to town. So long as the chief maintained a flow of generosity out to the four towns, as well as collecting goods in from them, people remained reasonably happy. Other than raids down into the lowlands, there was no threat serious enough to need warrior-like skill.

The real stability was in the hands of the seers, a man and wife at each of the four towns, binding the parts together into a whole. The chief had no say in who was to be the next seer, but the seers provided the means to validate and support the chief. At the transition of power, it was they who anointed the new leader. In principle they could challenge as well as support, though this was rarely put to the test.

They met as a group when and where they pleased, and had their own plans and purposes. In name, and in speaking their mind on a matter, they were held equal, but the high place up at Giybon was the largest. It also was the location of the great flat stone that, from time to time, people slept on to seek a prophetic dream. The clarity of these dreams, and the foresight they gave, was renowned. Occasionally people would travel from far away, well outside the four towns, to see if the other world truly was closer here than in their own home.

To find their own apprentices, and to train up the next generation were parts of the seer's job. Only small parts, though, and their main task was to hold together the links connecting this world to the next. They stood among and between the living and the dead, among and between humankind and the gods, and were apparently only tangentially interested in matters of the chiefdom. Damariel had never met any of the other seers or spoken with them, but had seen them from time to time when one or other came down to Iqnu, sometimes alone, sometimes in groups, men and women with a sure sense of their own purpose.

On this particular day then, Yad-Nesherim arrived in Kephrath with his son, Mahur-Baal, a youth enough older than Damariel to carry weapons with the fighting men, and Ben-bamah, the man who led the raiding parties from Giybon. They brought with them two other men from Giybon who participated in the raids, a Mitsriy scribe leading a loaded donkey, and a squad of half a dozen Mitsriy soldiers, all except their officer armed with bow and short sword. The officer carried a staff of office instead of a bow, but one of the other squad members served as his weapon-carrier.

Iqnu met Yad-Nesherim and the others at the standing stones and greeted them courteously, especially the scribe, who although bald seemed to Damariel to be quite young. The group were shown around the town, looked into houses, counted fruit trees and flocks, metal tools, jars of oil and wine.

Qetirah told him later that in her mother's house, they had tallied all the finished and part-finished pieces of metal work Caleb was working on, and weighed all the spare amounts of bronze and silver scrap in the house that were not already accounted. Her father had spent considerable time moving things back into their right place out of the neat scribal piles where they had been counted.

By late morning they were done. Iqnu took Yad-Nesherim, Mahur-Baal and the Mitsriy officer into his house. The other soldiers, Mitsriy and Kinahny, went down to Danil's house and sat outside, sharing jugs of wine and weapon tales. Danil knew Ben-bamah and the others well, though each village conducted its own raids and rarely collaborated on them. The scribe sat on one of the stones at the edge of the high place, in the shade of one of the other stones, and busied himself working on a large leather roll stretched over a wooden frame. Damariel went closer to see; he was writing careful characters into ruled columns, copying across from rough marks on some spare sherds of pottery.

The scribe looked up suddenly and saw Damariel watching him. He wiped his forehead and said something that Damariel did not understand. Seeing the boy's blank look he switched to a thick but comprehensible version of Kinahny that Damariel was later to think of as a southern accent.

"Hello, boy. What do you want? Well, look, see the other men, the soldiers are down there if you want."

He pointed down the hill to where a burst of male laughter sounded from outside Danil's house.

"Yes, they are, great lord, but I wanted to see what you were doing."

"I'm doing hot work. If you bring me a thing to drink, well, I can show you these things, see."

Damariel ran off, begged a small jug of watered-down wine from his mother on the grounds that the seer's guest needed it, picked up a handful of raisins while her back was turned, and ran back up the hill. The scribe finished another column of marks and ran his finger slowly down a column of marks as though checking something. That done, he grunted with satisfaction at the provisions, and moved slightly to one side so Damariel could sit beside him. He looked up and down the marks that the scribe had made on the leather roll and pointed to the most recent column of signs.

"What are these, great lord?"

The man smiled a little at the title and moved his hand across the columns.

"Look, this says how many houses in your little village, and this how many men, how many women, this, how many olives, and so on."

Damariel pointed at one of the signs.

"But this is not a man, sir. It is a hoop like the little ones we use to keep the trailing vegetables off the ground."

"A hoop means ten. A coil like this, with a tail off to one side, means one hundred, so ten lots of ten. At the top here, this is a man, you can see that easily, there he is sitting with one hand raised. And this is a woman, here in her long dress. This one means tree, see, it is like a branch. This roll here", and he pulled a second strip of leather from his bag, unrolled it, and held it up for Damariel to see, "this is the counts for your neighbour village Merom."

"Meyim", said Damariel without thinking, and suddenly jumped up with his hand over his mouth. "Great lord, I did not mean that you had spoken wrong."

The man laughed. "If I have written it wrong, well, it must be changed. So let me change it now. Look how easy it is."

He took out a sharp knife, scratched out the first two of the four signs and carefully wrote two more in place. When he finished he pointed to the signs, one after another, and repeated "Meyim." Damariel had sat down again to watch, and shook his head.

"Great lord, why must you count so many things?"

"Well, so that your chief can pay the right taxes to the great king who is the sun of all the earth. He should pay neither too little nor too much. Look, these columns are the tally from last time, ten years ago, when I suppose you were very small. Perhaps you were not even a baby, growing as an egg inside your mother. Who can say? Your chief has said to the official who governs from Gedjet that he should pay less now, and I have come to see if he is right or he is wrong."

"Which is it?"

The scribe gestured up and down the columns of figures.

"Well, there are fewer people but more trees, fewer flocks but more metal work. Fewer houses that are lived in. I think your chief may be right, but before I know for sure I must get the full total."

"It doesn't seem so difficult that it needs a great lord like you?"

"How do you mean, boy?"

"Sir, those men, the soldiers, they will do what you say. Just now they drink and laugh with Hannah Taliy's father, who leads our own raids, but if you commanded, they would come up here and do whatever you said."

"Yes, that's quite right, boy. You have it just right. They think that because they have weapons and know how to use them, well, that makes them more important. But you are quite right. It is not like that. Look at this."

He took another drink from the jug, bent to pull something else out of his bag, and as he straightened, moved a little to stay in the shade of the tall stone beside him. It was a roll of a much thinner, more delicate stuff that crackled slightly as he unrolled it.

Damariel had never seen anything like it. It was covered with little characters, mostly black but with a few here and there picked out in red. He kept hold of it and moved it away as Damariel reached out to touch it, but lifted it up so he could see it clearly. There was a pause, then Damariel shook his head.

"Lord, I cannot understand it. But the marks are not the same as the leather ones." He pointed. "This one here is like that one there, but this one, and this, they are quite different. What is it, great lord? Why are they different?"

"Well, this leather one is for the records of the great king, may he live in prosperity and health. He is the sun at whose feet people from every land bow down seven times and seven times again. As of course do you, boy."

He glanced at Damariel, who nodded seriously.

"Even your chief who you call victorious in battle and glorious over his enemies must do this."

He laughed a little, not unkindly.

"So it must be written as befits a record of the king. But this one is the way a scribe writes to another scribe, or to other men or women who can read. A friend gave me this just before I left the Beloved Land. It is a copy of a piece he himself was given by a friend who owed him a favour. What it is, is advice written to a young man choosing his life's work. Look here, here it says do not be a farmer, because the work is hard and nothing grows properly, and here, do not be a soldier, because the life is dangerous and miserable, and everyone orders you about. But here. . . " and Damariel's eyes followed the pointing finger as it skimmed over the lines of markings.

"Here it says to be a scribe, because a scribe is a fine profession in which you walk freely, and you account for the offerings to the gods, and inspect fine monuments, and live in beautiful houses with the best of all women to be your wife, and have all manner of men and women servants to serve your every need. And in your eternal house, your name will be remembered because of the writing, even if, and may all the gods forbid, your family should neglect you or forget to carry out the offerings for you. Your name will live on forever in the writing you have made."

There was a pause. Damariel looked to and fro along the rows of signs and pictures, seeing little stylised gods and men, birds and animals, things of nature and things made by the hand of man. The scribe finished all but two of the raisins and gave the last ones to Damariel.

"Do you write, boy? I have also learned the Kinahny signs you are now using among yourselves. What is your name?"

Damariel shook his head.

"Damariel, sir. Not really. But our seer who lives just there in the house with the oldest vine, the lord Iqnu, he showed me how to write my own name, and the names of my brothers and sister, and for a while I wrote 'this belongs to Damariel', or to Baruk, and the others, all over things in the house until my mother's husband got cross about it and made me stop. So now I just mark on trees and stones when I am away from the house."

The scribe laughed and pulled out a flat lidded box with sand in it. He bent down and found a sharp twig.

"Here, show me. I shall be pleased to see your name just here."

Damariel took the twig from him, bent over the tray in concentration, and scratched out his name slowly.

"Very good, boy. Now, in my writing it would look like this."

Just below Damariel's marks he scratched, very neatly but quickly, four signs from right to left. Damariel looked at them, very solemnly.

"Is that how I would be written in your land, then, great lord?"

"Yes, except that we would give you a proper Mitsriy name. You would not be called Damariel, but we would call you, oh, Nehem-Meri-Amun, I think. Then we would write it like this."

He made another series of marks, longer, with a seated god-figure at the start.

"My name would grow longer in your country, then?"

The scribe looked directly at him quite suddenly, an odd expression on his face.

"Well, I think it could, yes. Would you like it to?"

The door to Iqnu's house opened, and Iqnu himself brought the group out into the sunshine, through the dappled shade of the leaves of the old vine that clung to the house walls and crowned the entrance. Qerith stayed back in the shadows of the door. Yad-Nesherim led Mahur-Baal and the Mitsriy officer towards where the other men were resting.

Iqnu walked over towards the scribe, looking curiously at Damariel sitting beside him. Damariel stood as the seer approached and looked at the ground, but the Mitsriy remained seated, gathering his belongings together, collecting writing instruments, leather, and pottery pieces into his bag.

"Sir, I hope the boy has not troubled you."

"Not at all, seer. It has been pleasant talking with him and hearing what you have taught him until now. You should teach him more."

"Of course, sir, if you say so."

"I do."

"Well, Damariel, thank you for entertaining our guest so well. Now, run along to your home. We are all done here."

Damariel turned obediently to go, but the scribe caught his arm, saying, "Wait a moment." He bent over something in his lap, then stood up and handed a small pottery sherd to Damariel. On it he had marked in black ink the two sets of signs for Damariel's name, one longer than the other. "Here, keep this, boy. May your name grow ever longer, Damariel."

Damariel looked down at the piece of clay in his hand and nodded silently, his heart full of a passion he could not voice. He clutched the piece of writing tightly and held it against his heart. Then without looking back he ran off down the hill. He passed the group of Mitsriy and Kinahny soldiers, passed Issi the potter's house within earshot of the Mitsriy officer calling one of his men away from talking to Saphiret, Yusuf's older sister, burst back into his house hearing his mother and Sosanneth in the side room, and hid the pottery sherd that held his name in amongst his most precious personal things, where his brothers would not find it, where he could keep it safe.

He came out of the house again. The visitors had gone. Shomal and his sons were coming back from Danil's house. Shomal had a wine-flushed look and seemed very pleased with himself. Baruk and Bashur were chattering with excitement, and ran on to join Damariel when they saw him.

"Damariel, where have you been? You should have been with us. We've been in Danil's house, we were allowed to stay with the men and hear the Mitsriy soldiers talk and one of them passed round his bow and I held it and Danil says we can be in the raiding parties as soon as we're old enough. Wherever were you, you should have been with us and seen all of it."

Shomal had gone past them inside the house. Yeresheth appeared a few moments later, looking flustered, holding Sosanneth tightly so she could not get away. She looked at the three boys. "You three, go and tidy up in the olive field."

"Mother, why? Can't we stay here? What is there to do?"

"I don't know. The wall needs fixing. It always needs fixing, you know that. Scare the birds away. Go on now. Start clearing the area at the far end where you might plant some vegetables. Go on now Baruk, Bashur, it's what your father wants. Damariel, just go with them, now, go along." Nerith had come to her door at the sound of the voices. Yeresheth put Sosanneth's hand in hers. "Nerith, look after Sannah, will you. Shomal says he wants to talk."

She glanced briefly at the children, at Sosanneth looking cross but holding her aunt's hand now, and the three boys now running down the hill towards the olives. The two women looked at each other for a long moment. Nerith put her head on one side and pursed her lips. Yeresheth shrugged and then went back into the house, closing the door behind her.

Shomal was in a good mood at the meal that evening, leaning against the wall and watching Yeresheth as she moved around the room, his eyes clinging to her. He was full of words.

"We certainly pulled the kef over the eyes of those prying Mitsriy today. I bet they only saw half what we've got. They never even knew about my olives. Old Nawar now, he made sure they never saw it, led them all up and down this place and got them right confused. Yeresheth, sweetie, we must give him a jar of good oil this season, one of the bigger ones. And chief Yad-Nesherim will be really pleased with us, he won't have to pay nearly so much tribute these next few years and it will all be thanks to us here in Kephrath. Those blabbermouths up at Jarrar's town didn't hide anything, so all the credit's ours. Baruk, Bashur, well done for being at Danil's house with the soldiers. That's how to get yourself noticed, be right in the middle of it. You learn what you can from them, even if they are Mitsriy."

He paused. "Even you, Damariel, they tell me you spent time up with that scribe of theirs so he never moved from the high place. Good plan that, well thought of, you make sure Iqnu knows it was you."

Damariel nodded but said nothing, remembering the afternoon differently. Bashur nudged Baruk and whispered, "Ask him". Baruk cleared his throat, looked around at the others and sat up very straight.

"Father, sir, Danil said we could go out with the raiders before too long. Is that so?"

Yeresheth looked up from the pot she was stirring and began to speak, but Shomal was quicker and louder.

"Of course, son, you and Bashur too, both of you. But only when you've both learned some skills. Not for a few years yet. But keep putting yourself in front of Danil, he's the one you have to persuade in the end, what with him leading the raids and all. Make sure he knows who you are and what you want, so there's no doubt in his mind. Today was good for you."

"Father, was our work in the field good too?"

Shomal looked momentarily puzzled, and then laughed. He was leaning back against the wall and looking very expansive.

"Oh, yes, the field. Yes Baruk, I'm certainly very pleased you went down there to work this afternoon. Tell me what you did."

The three boys took turns to describe what they had done, but Shomal was not really listening. He rubbed his hands together and tried to catch Yeresheth's eye, but her head was bent over the cooking area and the fringe of her kef defeated him. In the pause at the end Sosanneth spoke.

"Why did I have to go and be with Aunty Nerith? I was helping mummy do mending of shirts and dresses."

Again Shomal overrode Yeresheth's attempt to speak.

"Now, my pretty daughter, it's good for you to be spending time with the other women. Your Aunty Nerith has lots of things she can show you."

"But I like being with mummy."

"Ah, so do I, Sannah. But you're of an age to be with other girls, other women. You can't have her all to yourself, you know."

Yeresheth clattered the loud clay pots together, and began to gather the empty bowls into a pile. Her movements were very tight, very precise, and she was concentrating fiercely on the task in front of her. Shomal leaned back again and watched her indolently. Eventually she let her eyes meet her husband's. There was a cold hostility in them. He shrugged and chuckled. "What?"

"So can I help you now, mummy?"

"No, Sannah. Go up to the roof and make up your beds. All four of you, go on now."

The children climbed up and began arranging bedding in the warm evening air. Like most of the other houses, a small part of their upper floor had its own roof, but most was open to the elements for warm-weather use with only a light cloth stretched across wooden poles over their heads. Even though the nights had turned a little longer than the days, they were still up in the open part. A few weeks more, and they would be back inside, all four children sharing one of the rooms. One or two houses had an actual room on the upper floor, but this was rare.

The night breezes and scents reached them up on the roof, and the freshness was pleasant. The sun was low on the horizon away in the west. Sosanneth was already yawning, but Baruk and Bashur began talking again about the time in

Danil's house. Downstairs, Yeresheth's voice had suddenly become angry. They paused to listen, but could make out nothing except the word "boasting". Shomal didn't seem to be replying, but once or twice they heard him laughing.

Beth

ETANIM YEAR 12 – MEPAGH YEAR 13

O DRY-BONED LADY let me pour your last libation,
oil and wine to cleanse this buried room,
light little lamps beside your gilded bracelets,
shake once more your timbrel's lonely bells.

TWO YEARS LATER, it was late evening in another Etanim day, and the days were unseasonably hot. The family had eaten, and the full moon had risen a short way above the eastern trees. The house was hot and airless, and Damariel, seeing his father's heated mood, began to consider how best to make himself scarce. His younger brothers were loud in the corner, and Sosanneth was sulking having been told that her years of being a child at the stream were now over. His mother spoke.

"Nobody has gone to pour water at the tomb of my family this month."

She looked around the room. Baruk and Bashur glanced at each other, then at their father. There was a little silence, filled by Damariel.

"I'll go, mother."

Shomal frowned.

"Someone must pad down the roof. Someone must carry up the bedding and the screens. Someone must help me with the tools. Someone must gather the hens."

"I can do them, father, all of them."

Baruk had spoken from his place in the corner, and Bashur nodded and stood up beside him.

"I can help him, father."

Shomal nodded and waved his hand at Damariel in dismissal.

"You go and see to the dead, then. My sons will help me here. Take whatever your mother has prepared for the offering."

A little later Damariel walked out into the night air and turned up the ridge towards the high place and the seer's house. He passed between two of the stones and left several flat bread rounds and some onions on the doorstep. There was an oil lamp flickering in one of the windows, and he stopped for a moment to look at it. The house was large, with an extensive enclosed and roofed area on the upper floor as well as an open hot weather area.

Behind the vine with its dangling bunches of grapes above the door frame, the central area rose up into a little lath tower standing higher than the rest. Attached to this, a carved wooden panel faced him. The reliefs shone silver in the moonlight, and Damariel looked up at them, trying to puzzle out which parts of the carving were pictures and which were writing.

As he stood there, the seer's wife Qerith suddenly appeared from behind the upper room and the carving, carrying a bed roll and a bundle of sheets. He smiled and thought of his brothers doing the same at his own house, well able to imagine Baruk taking the lead over his brother.

Qerith bent to pick up some stray wind-blown leaves from the flat roof and tossed them over the edge. As they fluttered down she saw Damariel and lifted her hand in greeting. She was not wearing a kef, and her unbound hair spilled over her shoulders. Embarrassed, he lowered his eyes and carried on across the crown of the hill. He heard her call after him, once, twice, but the night air swallowed her words and he carried on.

He went down the next part of the ridge and then up a little to the caves, the part of the town where the dead lived. He was well aware that they also lived around his house. He had helped his mother three summers ago to dig a little hole in the hard-packed kitchen clay, and put some of her mother's hair there. As woman of the house, his mother was responsible also for the monthly prayers for the dead, and until Sosanneth was of an age to take the responsibility on, Damariel was called to help. This was where the dead all rested; this is where they were gathered. This was their domain.

He thought back to the day that his mother's mother had been set to rest here, the whole village gathered to lament and honour her, even the households that as a rule kept themselves apart from the family. He could remember very little except for a shower of sudden rain. He wondered briefly how many generations lay here, what they spoke of in the whispering dark, whether they were pleased with him and his family, whether they were able to commune with their remote ancestors buried so far to the north. How much did they see of what their descendants were doing, and how far were they really still interested?

He scrambled up beside the great rock that closed off the entrance, past the crag that jutted out like a tower, to the little fissure behind it that led back down into the body of the tomb. The fissure itself was small, too small for his hand, but the top part had been flattened by former generations into a shallow bowl, chiselled out and then smoothed to receive offerings.

He retied his plain white kef into the solemn pattern, covering his mouth and nose as well as his hair leaving only his eyes exposed. He sat cross-legged beside the little bowl. He poured some water and a little mixed oil and wine into the crevice, then scattered some crushed spice and barley seed into it, and finished with another splash of water. The liquid stain was dark on the stone bowl, and he thought how the mixture was trickling through the rocky channel and dripping into the echoing vault below. The liquid and its seed was working its way through the little channels, he felt sure, and he wondered what fruit it would bear in the earth's silent belly.

He sat back and recited as many of the names of his ancestors as he could remember, starting with his grandmother and working back. He recalled his mother's brother who had fallen in the mountains, then Kunor's wife Kalit, and the child Walud who had died with her during the birth, through to others who were only names to him, empty of living details. Then he turned to the north and called on the kings of the dead to protect them all, and finally sat watching the moon for a while, huge over the highland hills.

He loosened his kef back into its normal pattern. A breeze had sprung up from the west, cool on his side, and he sat for a while enjoying it, leaning against the rock pillar at his side, in no hurry to make his way back home. Eventually he rose, clambered back down to the ground, brushed the worst of the dust from his smock, and set off.

He did not want to go near the seer's house again, nor to venture too close at this hour to the households that his mother disliked, so he headed a little south, to his left, skirting the hill's crown, away from any of the houses. At first he was among low scrub, fragrant with juniper and rosemary. Little night animal noises rustled around him, and cicadas sang in the brush to either side, falling silent as he came near and resuming once he had passed.

He crossed over a small dry wadi, heavy with herbed scents, and paused on the other side to gather his bearings. Lost in his thoughts, he had wandered a little too far to the south, and he angled slightly right to pass by the house of Ethan the shepherd, who was away with the flocks up in the higher ridges for another few weeks.

He stopped abruptly. Ethan's door had opened and voices came from inside. A woman laughed softly and then spoke. He could not hear the words, but heard her voice lift up in question. It was Isheth, Ethan's wife. Damariel moved a little to one side, into the shadow of a cypress, as a man came out of the door and paused by the trunk of Isheth's snowbell tree. The two embraced and kissed, until the man turned, their lingering hands keeping contact as he stepped away.

He came towards Damariel, wrapping a particularly large kef over his head and shoulders. Damariel realised with sudden insight that it was Iqnu the seer who was approaching. He caught his breath, and some dry twigs under his feet crackled and snapped. The village priest gave a great start.

"Who is that? Come out of the shadows, you, come here. Who is there?"

Damariel, heart pounding and speechless, took a few steps away from the tree into the moonlight. He pushed his kef back from his forehead so the older man could see him clearly.

"Damariel! It's you! Well, lad, it is too long since we talked. How long have you been there? How long, I wonder?"

Damariel shook his head and stammered in reply, "Not long, great sir. Not very long to be sure. I just came down from the chamber of my mother's ancestors, up there by the crag. Mother sent me there to pay our respects and give our gifts."

He waved behind him. The other man nodded and looked at him for a long moment, hands on hips. "How long, then? You know that I must be out at night for the sake of the village. Did you see where I came from?"

Damariel looked up at him, and then across at the shepherd's house. The door was shut again, and there was no light at the window. He thought about Ethan and his wife Isheth, thought briefly about the things that his mother had said about that household, and then said, quite slowly, "Honoured sir, I am not very sure what I did see now. The night is dark. Perhaps you would help me remember what happened?"

The seer laughed a little and then put his hand on Damariel's shoulder.

"Come up and sit with me on the ridge, lad. Sit with me for a while. I think a lot about you, all of you, of course, Qetirah and Kothar too, and little Mahur who passed beyond. And Galmet, and little Yad-Shalim since then. But just now, most of all you. It is past time I did more for you. I wonder what you should most like? They tell me you like to sing?"

"Yes indeed, great sir, and I have made up some words myself. Mostly though I listen around the fire and try to remember and sing again what I have heard the next day."

The two sat side by side on the pine scented ridge. In the distance a stag called out.

"I think it is time you learned more, lad. You should learn it from me, it is me you should be listening to about such things. Don't get involved in little tales. So many people will just tell you anything. But you can trust what I tell you: you understand that, don't you? Come to me every month, on this full moon night, and I can teach you the singer's art. How should you like that?"

His eyes were very intent on Damariel, and a great desire clutched at his heart, but the picture of Shomal's stern look drifted through his mind.

"Sir, I do not think that my father will allow it."

The seer laughed again, differently this time, and put his arm around Damariel's shoulders as he replied.

"Your father, hey? I don't suppose Shomal would allow it without some inducement. But let me speak with him about the matter. I may well be able to persuade him. Your mother, now she will certainly agree. But you now, Damariel: what should you like?"

Damariel paused, thinking a while, and before he could speak the other man went on in a great rush of words.

"It's not just singing, you know. Let me teach you other things. And perhaps we should meet twice a month, not once. There's all kinds of things I could tell you. Do you know how we remember the way north from here to Damaseq, or down south through the Nagb to the border forts of the Mitsriy?"

He shook his head, intrigued. He only knew of the local tracks and their destinations just a short distance away, the four towns themselves, and in more general terms the whereabouts of their immediate clan allies and neighbours.

The seer nodded.

"Let it be settled, then. Come to my house tomorrow around sunset, and we shall make a start. No sense waiting for next month, we must make a start right away."

He stood and held out a hand to help Damariel, facing him and suddenly quite serious.

"As for tonight, you know, I was up on the northern fell and found one of Ethan's chickens. I took it back to his house. That was all. No need to tell anyone, no need to remember it, is there? People will talk about all sorts of things, and there's no need to listen to them. Just a lost chicken. Is that clear?"

Damariel thought of the couple coming out of the house door, the kiss shared in the moonlight, the lingering hands, the lack of chickens, and weighed it all against poems and journeys to distant places. He nodded, took the older man's hand, and stood up.

"Surely it is as you say, honoured one. I am sure I can remember it as you say."

"Good. Then speak no more of it. Just think of all the things I can teach you. Now, go home, greet your family from me, and tell them I shall visit tomorrow, in the middle of the afternoon."

He started up the ridge towards the high place, and after a few moments Damariel continued his own journey, round the edge of the hill and past a few outbuildings to go between his aunt's house and his mother's. Baruk and Bashur were both up on the roof, arranging the wicker screens and bedding. Inside, Sosanneth was asleep on her mother's lap. Shomal looked up at him as he pushed the door open. The cross edge had faded a little from his voice, but still hovered in the background. Damariel closed the door quietly, warily.

"All done? You were gone a long time?"

"I met the seer on the way back, just down below the high place. He says he will visit tomorrow in the middle of the afternoon."

Shomal and Yeresheth looked at each other across Sosanneth's sleeping body, then Yeresheth looked down and brushed the girl's hair back from her face. Shomal stood up and rearranged his tools in the corner, facing away from the others. In the silence the voices of the two brothers could be heard from the roof.

"Did he say why? What did he say?"

"No, mother, he did not say all that was on his heart. He said he had not seen as much of me, all of us I mean, as he would wish. Surely he will tell you rather than me?"

Yeresheth looked up at him again, her eyes suddenly moist and sparkling in the oil light's flame. Shomal seemed finally satisfied with his tools and sat down again.

"Of course he will. Do we have something to set in front of him when he comes?"

His wife glanced around at the kitchen stocks and nodded, and he stood up again, restless and impatient.

"Make sure that he feels welcome here, Yeresheth. That should certainly be easy enough for you. Damariel, tell your brothers he is coming and get them to bed. You as well, get to bed. Here, take Sannah with you."

There was bustle for a few moments. Sosanneth woke at the movement and cried in protest until Damariel settled with her on the roof and rocked to and fro with her while speaking to the brothers.

All four children settled down to sleep. Parental voices drifted up from the main body of the house. He strained to hear but could not make out the words. Shomal was doing most of the talking, long trails of speech mostly ending in questions. Yeresheth was quieter and shorter in her replies.

Shomal came up first, and with a wordless heavy sigh unrolled his bedding and lay down. Much later Yeresheth came up. She bent down by Damariel as she passed, and kissed his cheek softly before moving further on to lie down near Shomal.

Damariel looked up at the moon through the woven screen branches and wondered what had happened.

Iqnu came down the next day in the late afternoon. At the time, Shomal was down at his olive trees with Baruk. Bashur, under protest, had been inside watching Sosanneth while Yeresheth baked some bread rolls with honey. Damariel was outside the house moving the chickens around so he could search for stray eggs and clean their area, but hearing the seer's voice he straightened up, abruptly noticing the straw and feathers scattered across his smock.

Iqnu nodded to him gravely and went to the door. As Yeresheth noticed him, she smiled, warmly, a little shyly, brushed her hands clean of flour, and then kissed him on both cheeks.

Bashur was sent running to fetch Shomal, and Damariel hurried to finish his work, aware that the two adults were watching him as he did so. Yeresheth had her hand on Iqnu's arm and leaned in to him as she talked, so Damariel could not hear her words. Iqnu shook his head and laughed aloud, and she smoothed back her kef and smiled happily. Looking up, Damariel saw that Shomal was outside, about to arrive, and was frowning heavily at the sound of Iqnu's laughter. Yeresheth moved quickly away from the seer and tended to the bread buns as her husband turned the corner of the wall and came across the open area to the door. He looked impatiently at Damariel.

"Leave that now, lad, leave it till later. Get yourself cleaned up and join us."

When Damariel joined them he found the three adults sitting on stools. Sosanneth was out of sight in the side room. Catching his mother's signal, he picked up the tray of warm bread pieces and served them to the seated adults. Looking around, he gauged that he was not supposed to eat any himself, so stood by the door and waited. Shomal had just finished formally welcoming the seer to Yeresheth's house. Iqnu, seeing he had finished, thanked him properly and then gestured at Damariel.

"Your boy is a credit to your household."

Yeresheth smiled. Shomal said, "As are my other two sons, sir."

"Of course. But for today I am thinking of Damariel. I have a mind that he should learn something of the work of a singer. You know that the son born to Qerith soon after our marriage was taken by sickness three years ago."

He paused, and there was a moment of silent remembering prayer.

"And our daughter Asherith is now married to Mahur-Baal, first son of the great chief Yad-Nesherim, victorious over his enemies and glorious in battle. She now lives up at Giybon and has chosen not to walk our path. So I have nobody here to assist me and Qerith with the songs, and we have a duty to find those who are able. I have heard that Damariel has a talent, and I wish to train him in it. Who can say where that might lead?"

Shomal looked at Damariel, then back at Iqnu.

"It is a great honour, sir, but you must know how useful the lad is. He works here and down at the olive patch. I am not sure how we could manage without his help. Perhaps some times of the year, but surely not at harvest."

Yeresheth made as if to speak, but Iqnu made a little movement of his hand and she remained silent. Shomal saw the exchange, and his eyes narrowed a little.

"Of course, I understand how much you need him. But Shomal, we are not talking about him coming to be with me every day. To begin with, one day each month, or perhaps two at most. Sometimes just evenings as the light fades. Of course he would be free to work with you at other times. If he shows he has talent, perhaps I could apprentice him in time, but he must be proved first. And then we would come to some proper form of arrangement. Shomal, if you were willing to do this, I think you would find me extremely grateful to you. Very grateful indeed. Now, I think you have a dispute with Emeq about where the wall should go around your olives? For a start, then, I could smooth things with Emeq, talk to him, help him to see your side of things. Perhaps you would find my gratitude more useful than a few hours work from Damariel."

Shomal put on an expression as though thinking carefully, but all of them, including Damariel, had seen the quick look of satisfaction that crossed his features.

"Ah, well sir, though it will be hard to lose Damariel for those hours, I see that your need of assistance is greater than mine." He paused, and the silence stretched a little in the house. "Yes, I agree to this. Let it happen as you say."

Yeresheth had been looking at him with a careful lack of expression, and in the little pause before his final words she glanced at Damariel and rolled her eyes a little in exasperation. Damariel kept himself from smiling, feeling conspiratorial. Iqnu nodded expansively and looked at Damariel.

"So, lad, it seems that the arrangement is acceptable to Shomal. And, no doubt, to your mother. Are you still content with it?"

"Yes indeed, great sir, with all my heart."

"Excellent. Be up at the high place just before sunset tomorrow and we shall make a start."

He rose, accepted farewell blessings from the house, took one more of the bread buns, and left. Damariel kept quiet, seeing the look on Shomal's face. He picked up a broom and began to sweep the doorway. Yeresheth had busied herself in putting cooking equipment away. Shomal shook his head.

"Speaks as though he owns the boy. Throws me little bits and pieces to make up. Not that I don't appreciate the help with Emeq. Of course I do. But in this very room to put me in a corner like that. It's not right."

Yeresheth stopped working, glanced briefly at Damariel and then turned to Shomal.

"Perhaps Damariel could fetch his brothers while we talk about this, Shomal? I expect you left them working down at the olive field?"

"That's where my sons work, to be sure. Yes, Damariel, go and fetch them back here."

Damariel turned to go, but Shomal continued, "But make sure you've cleaned everything there before you leave. Close it all down for the night properly. I don't want to have to go back down myself."

By the time the three boys got back a meal was nearly ready. Sosanneth had woken up and was putting bread on the plates. Shomal was doing something noisily up on the roof. Yeresheth's face was very red and her expression very set. She hugged the three boys as they arrived, and sent Bashur up the stairs to fetch Shomal. When he came in, he exchanged glances with Yeresheth, sat down on a stool near the door, and then called Damariel to him.

"Learn what you can from the seer, lad. Make us proud of you. Just make sure it does not get in the way of your work for me."

Baruk and Bashur looked at each other. Baruk spoke first.

"What's this, Damari? Father, what's this talk about the seer?"

"The seer wants Damariel to learn some of his songs and what have you. One or two evenings a month he's to go to the high place and learn all that."

Baruk clapped his older brother on the shoulder. "That's wonderful, Damari." But Bashur pulled a face. "How come he gets to do that? What about his work here? Will we have to do that for him?"

Shomal turned to Bashur and sat him on his knee.

"Nothing unfair will happen to you because of this, son. Damariel knows that he must do his share. I'll see to it that the work is shared out fairly."

Sosanneth was watching the four of them, clearly not very sure what was happening or why. Yeresheth put an arm round her and sat her down before ladling stew onto the plates. Baruk started to ask Damariel what he would be learning, but in truth Damariel had no very clear idea, and Shomal started talking at length about what the olives would need in the next few months. Much later, as they settled for sleep on the roof, Baruk asked him again. The two boys spoke for a few minutes until Bashur started to complain at the noise they were making, and their mother came up from the room below to make sure they were settled.

Damariel found, month after month as he spent time with Iqnu, that the seer was well intentioned, and diligent so long as the effort did not take him out of his way, but was inclined to make large promises that he had no intention of keeping. That very first evening, the day after Iqnu had been to their house, he spoke to Damariel of the lands and peoples living nearby. Damariel listened with fascination at the size of the world and its variety, though Iqnu seemed to have actually visited very little of it. Seeing Damariel's open mouth, Iqnu laughed and said that by the next spring, if Damariel would learn the way-list, he would take him down to Shalem and show him the great high place there, or maybe they would go beyond that to follow the desert trails down to the Mitsriy home land.

Every night through the winter, Damariel recited the route names to himself as he fell asleep, strange places that had no meaning to him but spoke of lakes and ruins, hills and clefts, an exotic terrain inhabited by strangers. His dreams kept him wandering all around these distant places, where people spoke in a way he could not understand.

The spring came, and there were reasons why they could not go. In time Damariel became used to the offer of promise, the failure to deliver. But the learning itself, the songs and the poems, the reading and the writing, the glimpses into other places and other times; all this he loved, and revelled in the expanding sense of his place in a mighty world.

By careful choice of words over a few months, he had managed to persuade Iqnu to see him regularly twice a month instead of erratically. Iqnu in turn had persuaded Shomal that his gratitude was worth the absence of Damariel on these evenings.

The weeks skipped past, with Damariel impatient for the passing of time in between the evenings with the seer. They always met at the high place, or in a rough lean-to shelter near the caves of the ancestors if the weather was poor, never in the seer's house. Damariel hardly ever met Qerith, hardly even remembered that Iqnu had a wife.

During this time, Damariel became acutely aware of isolation. His younger brothers, especially Baruk, seemed to find it easy to win acceptance from most of the other families. For his own part, especially with households linked more closely to Shomal than Yeresheth, or which for some reason were at odds with Iqnu the seer, he experienced a hesitation, a blockage in the easy flow of community life. It was never an overt rejection, more of a withholding or drawing aside.

He found himself spending increasing amounts of time with Qetirah and Kothar, who found the same difficulty of relationship. It was as though these two were more truly his family than Baruk and Bashur, and their company was more satisfying than that of the others of his own age.

Sometimes these others, or more commonly their parents, would treat them with a kind of awe. But more often there was a faint sense of being made fun of, of words spoken behind their back that they could not comprehend.

The three friends could no longer meet and play down at the stream, but they found other ways to be with each other as often as they could. Damariel also found that their households were places where he found peace more easily than his own. Yeresheth clearly loved him deeply, but Shomal's mood and attitude were unpredictable.

In contrast, Kothar's parents, Labayu and Tamar, made him as welcome as if he was Kothar's own brother. Labayu tried for a time to teach them both skills of hunting and trapping, but while Kothar absorbed them with ease, Damariel fumbled in the making of traps and snares.

They had no other children, and from time to time Damariel and Kothar would come in from outside to find their mothers in close conversation, with Tamar's eyes intent, fixed brightly on Sosanneth as she moved about the kitchen area.

The two boys grew very close at this time, until Damariel felt that he had three brothers rather than two. But one of the three was his own age, and felt with something of the same intensity as himself the isolation of being a child of the god, and Damariel found himself naturally gravitating more into his company. As time went by, Kothar developed his own strategies for dealing with the situation, cultivating a rather bold and brash exterior.

So Damariel spent a great deal of time at Tamar's house, enjoying the easy company of an adult man who welcomed him around the table instead of seeing his presence as criticism. He had less opportunity to go into Qetirah's home, but when he did Caleb would usually invite him into the long extra room that contained his little smelting furnace. There he would see scraps of metal melting in the heat and transmuting into a multitude of shapes – brooches and animal traps, tools and arrowheads.

Caleb and Kinreth were both as deeply attached to Qetirah as to their joint daughter Laylah, and Damariel never once heard issues of birth held up between them. Then he would go back to Yeresheth's house, and feel all over again the difference that lineage could make.

By the time late spring was turning into early summer, Damariel realised with absolute certainty that Iqnu was not even going to take him to Shalem, such a short way along the track. He also started to notice that life at home was deteriorating. During the summer Yeresheth started to talk to him how in the autumn he would be declared a boy no longer, but rather a young man. Baruk wanted to listen in, as he was only a year and a half younger. Then Bashur would want to be part of the conversation, and complain loudly to Shomal if not accommodated.

Before long, Yeresheth began to find places and times to talk to Damariel outside the house, on the way to and from the high place, or in Nerith's house across the way. Bashur tried then to find covert ways to listen in, and reported back to Shomal what was said. Several times a month the children would try to settle to sleep against a background of raised voices and anger. Yeresheth's face was more often tinged with red, and her lips more often pursed with frustration.

In conversation, Yeresheth would support Damariel and Sosanneth, while Bashur could always be expected to side with Shomal. Baruk was in an uneasy middle ground, drawn towards both sides for different reasons, and an object of competition and intense diplomacy. More often than not he would find himself yielding to Bashur's sibling pressure.

There was a time late the following summer, when the festival of the new wine was only days away and the community was preparing itself for the celebration, that Damariel later looked back on as a turning point. It was one of the preparation days, a day of fasting followed by a gathering of the whole community up at the high place. There had been a sacrifice of a pigeon with some oil and wine, and then a time of singing.

In an unusual time of family togetherness, all six had sat listening while several different people had stood to offer contributions, and then Iqnu and Qerith had related one of the stories from the dawn of the world.

Away from your word the oceans fled back –
from the voice of your thunder they hurried away –
up over the mountains down into the valleys,
back into the place you established for them.

By the end, the sea had been tamed by the lord of all the earth, and tied back within its shores as a mother would swaddle her baby. There it could froth and roar, but no longer spill over the tops of the hills.

At the end there was an appreciative clamour; whatever other opinions people held of the seer, all agreed that he and Qerith were excellent at delivering the songs. After that someone called out from the circle.

"Seer, tell us how we came to be living in these hills."

Iqnu turned to acknowledge the speaker, and then stood up to look round at all of the assembled people.

"I could tell that story, Issi, but tonight I am not the one who should be recounting it to you all. There is someone here who has a better right to tell that story than I. It is Mahiram, father of Danil, if he is willing. Mahiram, honoured in years, will you speak to us of that story tonight?"

Mahiram, sitting off to one side, looked up and nodded. There was a pause while Danil helped his elderly father forward. He sat on one of the stones, leaning on his staff, and there was an expectant silence around the gathered people. Damariel had seen the old man a few times before, but had never heard him speak more than a few words. To his surprise Mahiram's voice, though quavering from time to time, carried strongly around the circle, was confident in the thread of the story.

There was a holy silence as he prayed aloud, before launching into the tale, speaking it instead of singing. It was one that Damariel had heard before from Iqnu, and in simplified form from his own mother, but on this occasion there was a great deal more to hear. Mahiram spoke as though he had himself been one of the settlers that came down from the northern hills, surviving marauders and the winter cold to found the four towns here in these happy hills.

He knew that, in fact, the migration had been at least four generations before the old man's time, perhaps more, that Mahiram was as much a native of the hill country as he was himself. But during the telling Damariel was caught up in the movement of his people as though he held his own mother's hand on the mountain passes, gathered food with his brothers, carried his sister as she slept, and waited hungry in the camp while his father hunted for game with the other men.

When he had finished there was a long, profoundly appreciative silence. Sosanneth had in fact fallen asleep, although in this world she was on Yeresheth's lap. As Mahiram moved slowly back to his place in the circle, before the next recitation started, Shomal picked Sosanneth up and chivvied the other children along.

They went back to their house down the path, with Baruk and Bashur running ahead, racing to see who would arrive first. There was a bustle of activity, and as Damariel settled to sleep he heard Shomal go out again, back up to the celebration.

The next day started slowly, and all four children were up and about well before either of the adults. They began making noise, so Yeresheth gave them some food and water, and then sent them away down to the olive field with some instructions how to spend their time usefully.

They ran about for a while in the sunshine, deciding that was the best way to scare birds, then started to fit some of the loose dry stones back into place in the low surrounding wall where they had become dislodged over the summer.

After a while Baruk, who was in charge of the water skin, called a halt and they all sat leaning against the wall of the little hut.

They started talking about the celebration of the previous night. After a while, Baruk suddenly turned to Damariel.

"Look, Damari, you've been learning all this time with the seer. When are they going to get you doing something?"

Damariel shook his head.

"It's not like that, Baruk. Not yet. Maybe if he takes me on properly as his apprentice some time. But just now he won't let me, I know he won't. He'll say I don't know enough to do it right."

"But that's not fair. I bet you'd do it better than some of them. That Pirizzi, now, he was really boring."

They all laughed.

Bashur broke in, "What else would you expect from someone from that family. Mum always says they're no good".

He pulled a face that was just remotely like the expression Pirizzi had had as he had been singing last night, and they laughed some more.

"Alright, Bashur, he surely was boring. Truly. But that old man, now, Hanna Taliy's grandfather, he was really good."

They nodded, each remembering the old man telling the migration story. Baruk spoke first again after the memory-filled pause.

"What did the seer mean when he said he shouldn't be the one telling that story? Why did Hanna's grandfather get to do it?"

"Well, you see, in the circle like that then the one who everyone agrees knows most about the story gets to tell it. If the seer had started to tell it himself, lots of them would have disapproved. So he avoided that by looking around for someone he knew would tell it better than he would."

Sosanneth looked at him with wide eyes.

"What do you mean, disapproved? Would they all have got up and shouted at him to make him stop?"

"Oh no, Sannah. Nothing like that. But they'd have showed him he'd done wrong to tell it himself. Maybe some would have wandered off before he finished. Or maybe they'd just listen badly by laughing at the wrong time, or something. He'd know what they meant. He knows that the best person should always be the one to tell the story."

"Are you best at telling any stories?"

Damariel shook his head.

"Not yet, Sannah. Maybe one day. But not yet, not in a circle when the whole village is gathered together."

Baruk jumped up with excitement.

"Damari, look, you'd be best at telling stories here, just with us four. We don't know anything like that. Tell us something you've been learning."

Damariel looked at him. "Well, I suppose so. I don't know. The seer hasn't said anything about that."

Bashur shook his head. "I don't think it's right, Baruk. Dad hasn't said anything to any of us about this. Even if the seer had said something, we can't just do it. I mean, he isn't our father, is he? He can't tell us what to do on dad's land, it's not his place to do that at all." Sosanneth looked up at him. "But it's mummy's house, isn't it, not daddy's?"

Bashur looked annoyed with her. "That's not the point. The seer can't say what we should do here. I don't think Damari should do this, Baruk."

"Well, I do. Come on, Damari, tell us something. You've got to do it better than Pirizzi did last night. What do you say, Sannah?"

Sosanneth nodded, looking from one brother to another in turn. Damariel scratched his head, wondering what, in fact, he did know well enough to tell them. Deciding on something suitable, he sat up in readiness. Bashur stood up.

"Don't you dare. If you do, I'm going to get dad. He'll stop you."

Damariel and Sosanneth looked at each other, then back at Baruk. They knew that he was the only one with any chance of changing Bashur's mind. Baruk held out the water skin to Bashur.

"Come on, Bashur, just for a few minutes until we start the next job mother told us. She'd want us to have a break sometimes. We've already scared off the birds and fixed those bits of the wall. The next thing is gathering up the fallen bits of wood and that won't take us long. We'll all do that together after Damari has told us something."

Bashur sat down again, refusing the water. He said nothing, but he looked unhappy and made sure he was facing angled away from the others. Damariel launched into the story of how the first man and woman were made in the meadow of flowers, how they walked together in the morning and named the beasts as the gods paraded each of them in turn. He knew there were parts of the story that Iqnu had never taught him, would not tell him until he was older, but he knew enough to make it sound complete in itself. He did not try to sing it, but kept something of the great rhythms alive in his words.

The others were listening closely to him – even Bashur was leaning in to catch the unfolding drama – when they heard Shomal's voice calling to them as he approached. Bashur jumped up and ran round the corner of the little hut towards him. Damariel and Baruk looked at each other, wondering what he would say, but they heard only normal happy greetings. Hastily, before Shomal came into view, they both retied their kefs into a fashion he would consider decent. Sosanneth ran after Bashur, and the older boys collected the water skin and tools and followed her. Shomal had picked up Sosanneth and was holding her over his head. He was obviously in a good mood.

"Ah, my pretty Sannah's here as well. How's my most beautiful daughter?"

He lowered her to the ground again and saw the boys coming. He glanced around here and there, saw some places where the wall had been fixed and nodded approvingly at them all.

"You've been working well, I see. Just having a rest were you? That's what your mother and I have been doing, having a rest."

"Yes, father," chorused the children together, and Bashur added, "but Damari was doing some song that he heard from the honoured seer. I didn't know if we ought to be doing that."

Shomal shrugged.

"No harm done, so long as you've done the work first. It's only a bit of fun. Nothing serious. You were right to tell me, though, Bashur. Good boy."

Baruk and Damariel exchanged quick glances, relieved at the outcome, though Damariel had inwardly seethed at the dismissal of the sacred memory of the community. Bashur grinned at them both. Then Shomal sat in the shade of the hut while the four children collected twigs and larger pieces of fallen wood and piled them together.

Much later they all walked back up towards the house. As usual, Baruk and Bashur ran on ahead. Sosanneth held Shomal's hand as they climbed the ridge; Damariel walked a couple of paces behind. Before they were in sight of the house, Shomal stopped and turned to Damariel.

"Look, lad, I know you're doing this with the seer. That's fine, he's seen to it that I don't lose out because of it. Quite useful, in fact. But I don't want you getting my boys all mixed up with that. They're going to do a proper day's work on my land, or learn a skill. A trade of some sort. It's all right for you to do these songs and all that. But don't you get my boys all confused. That's not the road I want my sons to walk. Do you understand?"

Damariel could do nothing but nod in reply. Sosanneth, who had let go of Shomal's hand when they stopped, took hold of Damariel instead as they went the last few steps up the track to the house. Back indoors, Baruk and Bashur were reciting a long catalogue of all the work they had done in the olive field to Yeresheth, who was sitting mending some clothes of Shomal's while the bread finished baking. They paused after a while, trying to think what else to weave into the telling, when Sosanneth suddenly spoke up.

"Mummy, then we all sat together and had a drink of water and Damari told us a story about how people first happened that the seer had taught him and Bashur didn't like it and then we came back here and daddy said Damari mustn't tell things like that any more because it would mean Baruk and Bashur wouldn't do jobs he wanted them to do when they grow up. But I liked it and Damari was good."

Yeresheth looked at Shomal. He shook his head.

"Yeresheth, it wasn't like that."

Sosanneth went over to Yeresheth and sat on her lap, looking up at Shomal.

"But daddy, you said to Damari that he could sing with the seer but you didn't want your sons getting all mixed up in it because you had other work for them."

Yeresheth smoothed Sosanneth's hair behind the ribbon she still wore sometimes in and around the house instead of a proper kef. "All right, Sannah, hush now." She put the needlework down beside her and glanced briefly at Bashur, who stood off to one side, watching her.

"All four of my children will do me honour in their own way. All four of them will use the talents they were given when the Seven Ladies watched over their birth. I'll not hear that one of them is more blessed than another, or of more value to the village."

She held Bashur's gaze until he nodded once, and then looked at the others in the room in turn, ending with Shomal. "I'll not hear that from anyone."

She sat Sosanneth beside her and turned to look at the bread in the oven. There was a little silence in the room, until Shomal noisily rearranged some tools in one corner, saying something under his breath about believing a daughter who was barely able to talk, instead of a husband who could speak for himself. Bashur went over to help him, and they moved some things outside and some other things in. Yeresheth ignored the whole burst of activity, told Baruk and Damariel to clean and flatten the roof where the wind had caught it during the night, and showed Sosanneth how to recognise when the bread was cooked.

On the roof, Baruk glanced over into the courtyard where Shomal and Bashur were sharpening some of the tools, then came back to Damariel before speaking.

"Look, Damari, I don't know what's going on. What's got into mum and dad?"

Damariel, feeling wise with the benefit of his extra eighteen months, shrugged and packed down some of the loose roofing.

"Mum likes what I do. Dad doesn't. He says I'm not really his son, that you should have the rights of being his firstborn. So really he doesn't want anything to do with me. The only reason he lets me go to the seer at all is so he can get better deals for his olives, or get someone else to give him something for nothing."

Baruk sat beside him and helped work some loose straw back into place where the wind and weather had teased it away from the rest.

"I've heard that from some of the older boys. You and Qetirah and Kothar, all the same, they say. And Galmet. And that younger boy, what's he called."

"Yad-Shalim."

"Yes, him. What is it about you all? "

"I don't know, Baruk. They won't tell me. But you see it, don't you? And the others in the town too. Mostly they don't talk about it at all. Then if it comes up they either back away and go all strange, or they make fun of us."

Baruk nodded, and after a brief pause continued.

"But you are my brother, Damari, aren't you?"

Damariel carefully let go of the springy wooden lath and made sure it stayed in place.

"Yes I am, Baruk. But by mum, not dad, if I've heard people right. He never forgets it, won't let her forget it either. It's different for Qetirah and Kothar, both their dads are pleased with it."

"How come? Weren't they..." he paused and looked cautiously about, dropping his voice even quieter, "weren't they married when they had you? But so what? That girl up the street, Niri-Shadday, you know she's about to have a baby and everyone says it was Nesher, but they've never been married up at the stones."

He glanced round briefly, left and right.

"Have you heard what some of the other lads were saying about her, you know, like Yusuf?"

Damariel nodded quickly, and the two brothers grinned at each other before Damariel sobered again.

"I don't know, Baruk. I asked the seer once but he wouldn't tell me. Said I could know when I was older. They all say that. Same with some of the songs, Iqnu won't teach me some of them yet. Keeps saying I have to wait until I'm older to get to do them. I hope they're worth the wait. But I feel like I have nothing to do with Shomal at all, like he's just some kind of uncle or something. The older I get, the worse I think it gets. Look, Baruk, you and Bashur look like him, same hair, same eyes, same hands, whatever. Sosanneth has a bit of him, even if she's more like mum. But I don't. It's like every time he looks at me he sees a foreigner."

"Like one of those Mitsriy we saw last year?"

His eyes widened.

"You don't think that mum, I mean, maybe she… Before she married dad, I mean, maybe, do you think…?"

He trailed off as Damariel put a finger to his lips.

"Baruk, don't even think of saying that downstairs. Especially not to Bashur, he'll just tattle it to someone else and who knows what will happen. Anyway, I don't think that's it at all. I just don't know. Nobody ever tells me. Look, we have to go down or he'll think I'm teaching you something I shouldn't. Baruk, look, thank you. But you need to keep with Bashur when he's around. Don't get into trouble because of me."

Baruk pursed his lips, then finally nodded. They went back down, to where Yeresheth had baked bread and gathered them all around the little table to eat.

Gaml

IBALATU YEAR 15 – BUL YEAR 16

REFRESHING LIKE RAIN are my words,
distilling like dew is my speech,
like cloudbursts upon the grassland,
or rainfall upon the young crops.

BARUK CAME OUT OF DANIL'S HOUSE and set off across the ridge towards home. After completing his childhood and passing through the ceremonies to be counted as a young man of the community, he had deliberately set out to be noticed by Danil and the others of the raiding party. So far he had not succeeded in being really included in that group, and Danil's own son was too different in age from him to make anything to his advantage out of a potential friendship, but he entertained hopes. Bashur, almost the same height despite their year separation in age, followed him as closely as possible and was clearly attempting to make every available use of the sibling relationship.

Today, Baruk had managed to spend time with Danil without his brother. He smiled to himself as he joined the main track down from the high place. He was genuinely fond of Bashur, for all his over-close attachment, and most of the time was happy that he was there with him like a shadow. Though they were not twins, they understood each other's moods and feelings better than most brothers or friends, even when they disagreed over their thoughts and opinions. Mostly, he appreciated Bashur's presence nearby. Some days, though, it was good to go on his own.

He heard his name being called, and turned to see Damariel hurrying down towards him from the high place. He waited until he caught up with him.

"Just going home?"

"Yes. Dad let me off some time in the olive field this afternoon. Reckoned we'd done enough for the day or something. So I took the chance to spend a bit of that time with Danil."

"That went well?"

"Yes. He's always helpful, whenever I ask he's happy to talk to me about how the raids are done. I'm learning a lot. There's not so many of them go regularly, never quite enough for what they want to bring back. So I think I can talk my way into going with them if they think I'm keen. Well, and if I know what I'm doing."

They walked a bit further in silence together.

"Been up with the seer, then, Damari?"

Damariel nodded.

"And what did you learn today?"

"He's been teaching me these last months how to read not just our own writing, but the older stuff too. Like they used way back before our time. Actually they still do in the big towns, and if you have to write to the Mitsriy ever."

Baruk nodded, not especially interested yet in the topic, but before he could speak, Damariel rushed on with enthusiasm.

"Baruk, I never knew before today that a woman from here, from our own town, wrote to the Mitsriy governor once."

"Oh yes? What did she say?"

"Nothing much, really, just warning him about a big raid between two of the nearby towns. The usual double-dealing and trickery they do in those other places. But she wrote to them, Baruk, and they took notice. She called herself the lady lioness and they thought she was like our queen."

Baruk laughed.

"They didn't know much about us, then. Though the lion bit wasn't far off."

Damariel joined in the humour.

"No, I suppose not. But they took notice of her all the same. Respected her."

"She can't have been from mum's family or we'd have heard about her years ago. If there was anything like that in her ancestors she'd have told us."

"That's true. I don't know if she was a chief's wife or the seer at the time, or even just one of the village women who could write. But I saw the copy of what she wrote and have been puzzling over it all morning."

At that point they both stopped and looked back up the hill. A sudden shouting had started somewhere up near the high place, men's voices raised in fierce anger. Baruk took a step or two back up the hill, but Damariel stopped him.

"Do you think we ought to?"

"Don't be ridiculous, Damariel. Whatever it is, I'm not going to miss it."

They set off again along the ridge, and started running as the shouting began to grow louder. Like them, others were coming out of houses, looking, and starting to gather together up at the heart of the community. At the stones, Ethan the shepherd, his large face red and his large fists clenched, was being held away from Iqnu by three of the other men. Qerith had pulled her kef down over her face and was facing away from them off to one side, leaning on the wall of the seer's house, her expression completely hidden.

The two boys joined the gathering circle of villagers, Baruk pushing through to the front so he could see, and Damariel following. Ethan took a breath and shouted something incoherent at Iqnu; the only words they could make out in the whole tirade were "Isheth" and "while I was away". Beside him, Baruk heard Damariel gasp.

"What is it, Damari? What's this about?"

Damariel shook his head, his eyes fixed on Iqnu who was looking around at the ring of villagers, clearly trying to elicit sympathy or help from the assembly. One of the older lads nearby heard the question.

"Ethan says the seer took his woman for himself. While he was away up along the ridge with the flocks. Just before you came he was saying she confessed it all to him when he got back today. Over a year all told they've been at it with each other, so he says. Not just once, you know. All while he was away with the flocks. And in her own house, too. Not like it was somewhere else."

"Is it true?"

"No idea. But Ethan's all a sweat. Look at him. He's called the seer both thief and liar, and the seer hasn't said anything back."

"Where's Isheth? What does she say?"

The other shrugged.

"Never seen her yet. Maybe she's got a tale to tell too, but right now she's not here to tell it."

Ethan's parents, Hinnah and Nawar, had arrived. Nawar went over to his son and gripped his arms, waving away the men who had been holding him away from Iqnu. Hinnah went off with Danil's wife Rivkah towards Isheth's house. In the sudden quiet they heard Ethan's voice as he spoke to Nawar. Most of what he said was indistinct, but every so often one word or other would burst out loud. Nawar listened without comment for some time, still keeping hold of his son as though he might burst away at any moment.

Qerith moved away from the house to one side and sat on one of the flat stones, her face still covered. Shelomith-Rahmay went and sat with her. Nawar looked very sombre as he turned towards Iqnu, who glanced around the circle again, still trying to gauge whether the mood of the community was for or against him. But before Nawar could speak, Rivkah came running in, across to where Qerith and Shelomith sat, her kef all awry and blood on the sleeve of her smock.

"He's tried to kill her. Beaten her something terrible. But she's not yet gone across, not yet. Lady, she needs someone who can heal. Lady, please come and do what you can for her."

She knelt in front of Qerith, but there was no reply. After a long pause her veiled, hidden head shook once. Shelomith stood up slowly, looking suddenly much older than her years, beckoned to one of the other women to take her place with Qerith, and went off with Rivkah. Someone on the other side of the circle pushed their way through to the front.

"Her brother lives up at Woodlands. Azziy, they call him. Someone should get him. If Ethan's killed her he'll want to know about it. The whole family will. It'll be a matter of honour."

Nawar thought about it for a long moment, several different emotions playing across his face as he inclined his head reluctantly. But before he could speak, Mahiram's older voice broke in.

"Hear me now, there's more involved than the honour of two families. It's a seer's matter and we need a seer to judge on it now. So yes, send a boy up to Woodlands by all means, but send one up to Giybon as well to get a seer down here to tell us how both Iqnu and Ethan are to be treated. They'll be here tomorrow. If I'm heard there'll be no judgement upon anyone's family before then."

There was a murmur of acceptance, approval around the circle. Two lads were sent off in different directions up the ridge. Debate began then as to where Ethan and Iqnu should be kept while they waited for others to arrive, but before this could be resolved Rivkah and Shelomith returned with Hinnah, all with torn kef and dust on their head and shoulders. Isheth had not been able to bear her injuries and had gone across.

Ethan said nothing, did nothing, but looked away into the distance with no expression on his face. Iqnu grimaced, made as if to tear his own kef but then stopped. Nawar shook his head and sat on one of the nearby stones, head in hands. Qerith shook off the hands of the woman who had been sitting with her, took off her sandals, walked across to Iqnu and slapped him across his face with them, twice, side-to-side, before turning and walking away down the hill. Shelomith went with her.

It was as though Qerith's actions stirred the community into action, as though they were like a judgement on the case. Two of the men nearby took Iqnu's arms and led him into his own house. They shut his door and at Mahiram's word, pushed a boulder against the door so it could not be opened. Ethan turned as though to go with Nawar, but he shook his head and turned away. Ethan stopped short, clearly shocked at his father's response, and hung his head, speechless. Nawar walked away without turning. Hinnah wavered, looking this way and that between the two men, but eventually, with an anguished look at her son, followed her husband down the hill.

Ethan was taken away to a hut adjoining one of the empty, unfamilied houses and put inside it, with a boulder against the door just as they had done with Iqnu. The group began to disperse, a buzz of conversation flowing like streams into the tracks and pathways, flooding into the doorways and filling up the individual houses.

The next morning the door of the hut Ethan had been placed in had been broken open from the inside, and the stone outside the seer's house tossed to one side. Neither Ethan nor Iqnu were there. By the time Azziy arrived from Woodlands, Iqnu's body had been found at the base of a low cliff just west of the village. He had died in the end from the fall, but before that had clearly been roughly treated.

Ethan was nowhere to be found, but a group of the men who went hunting soon found the place where his tracks led away down into the valley, heading north-west towards the lowlands. They followed the trail for a few dozens of paces but then turned back to the village rather than go on. There seemed little point: the trail was perfectly clear but Ethan was not stopping for anything and had several hours start. When Qerith was told she made no reply, but simply moved back from Shelomith's home into the great house by the stones and waited for the seer to arrive from Giybon.

In fact they came not from Giybon, but from Meyim, a married couple called Saniyahu and Halith. Halith went in to be with Qerith, while Saniyahu called a meeting of the whole adult community beside the town gate and heard the whole tale told. Baruk was not there, nor Damariel, as their adolescent status did not qualify them as part of the formal assembly, but they heard of it later.

Ethan was publicly declared no longer welcome in the village, though there seemed little chance he would attempt a return. Iqnu, though already dead, was proclaimed no longer a seer among the four towns, and denied any rights to a burial on their land or with his family. Azziy accepted the sum of four times the bride price that had been paid, renounced any further claim that there might be on Nawar's family, and took Ishesth's body to rest with her ancestors.

Nawar had remained silent as he had weighed out the sum in silver and other goods in front of them all. The house that Isheth had shared with Ethan was to be pulled down and the stones scattered here and there around the village field walls and terraces, and such possessions as were in it would be given to widows and orphans. Only the foundations and a few of the bigger wall-stones would be left to mark the place in the community memory.

Saniyahu and Halith were to take up the duty of town ministry themselves, starting right away, that very day. The seers had already met and decided the matter in an all-night vigil of talk and prayer. A younger couple, not long past apprenticeship, were to take their place at Meyim, releasing them to begin at Kephrath. Qerith, still veiled and silent, speaking only with Shelomith and Halith, packed her few belongings and moved back to be near family just past Shalem.

That night Shomal held forth at considerable length about the greedy and untrustworthy nature of seers in general and Iqnu in particular. The whole episode had, it seemed, confirmed all his opinions. Yeresheth kept silent during all this, and at length his whole speech dwindled away and they settled to sleep. She knelt down beside Damariel briefly at one point and whispered to him, "Whatever else you think, and whatever else is said, remember he was good to you sometimes".

A week passed, and the open wounds of the community began to heal towards rough scars. On the third day, when Shomal had started to talk again about the way a seer could betray the trust of others, Yeresheth had stood up and declared that from that day forward, so long as it was her house, there would be no more such talk. Shomal, taken aback at the interruption, stopped, but not before a look of anger and frustration had gripped his features. From then on the talk stopped inside the house, but not outside.

Gaml

Life and work went on. As he approached the house one evening, Baruk saw a group of the young men and women, all a few years older than himself, talking together in a wider space of ground between some of the houses. Issi's son Yusuf was there, and Kalita, the rather intimidating eldest daughter of the Kephrath family who had last provided the chief of the four towns. Several others had formed into a little constellation grouped around their centre. Tentatively he crossed to join them, and found a space among them. Kunor was speaking, but Baruk missed the start of what he had to say.

"So that Iqnu, I reckon he saw a good chance."

Yusuf laughed. "I never thought being a seer was any good. But maybe there's all sorts of opportunities."

Nikkallia, a northern-named girl who Baruk hardly knew, spoke up suddenly.

"I suppose you get to know all kinds of things about people that most of us don't hear. Or anyway you find things out much sooner. Like you say, opportunities. I wouldn't mind finding some opportunities like that, whether it's with the seer or anyone else." She glanced towards Kalita. "Since it's one of the other towns that's giving us the chief just now."

Yusuf nodded.

"I heard that they're saying now that Ethan never touched her like a wife anyway. Even when he was in the house, let alone being away half the time. I reckon she got bored waiting. Iqnu must have known that."

Kalita nodded, pushing her kef back a little from her forehead so that dark waves of hair showed in a little fringe.

"I wouldn't put up with a man like that. If I wasn't satisfied I'd find another in no time. If someone's going to share my house they'll have to look after me nicely. Why else should I let them stay there?"

One of the other boys, Qeren, shook his head.

"Easy to say, but I'm not so sure. He was out all weathers working for her. Kept her house comfortable and she was never in want for food, clothes, anything. She should have stayed faithful to him."

Kalita tossed her head and smoothed the front of her smock. "Well, see if you can guess which one of you I'll be wanting to keep me company then, Qeren."

Before Qeren could say anything, Ayala broke in.

"There's Qerith too. Nobody takes her side in all this. Someone should speak up for her. She trusted him."

Kalita shook her head. "Well, she can't have kept Iqnu very interested. I mean, can she now? Why just let him roam off like that and do nothing? Or maybe he was very good at pretence. I'm just not going to put up with that. And there's another thing too. I wouldn't wait for any man to push me around in my own house or down some cliff outside. Plenty of ways a woman can see a man away first if she finds a need to."

Ayala and one of the other girls made a point of adjusting their own kefs into their place and walked off together. Kalita laughed and looked around provocatively at the others.

"And what do you think about it, Baruk? Do you think maybe you could look after me nicely?"

Baruk, caught by surprise and lost for an answer, felt himself starting to flush as she looked appraisingly at him. Qeren spoke before he could think of anything. "Leave him alone, Kalita. Pick someone your own age to tease," and Yusuf carried on, "Yes, Kalita, let's leave these little ones to their own games."

Kalita laughed and strolled slowly off, deliberately passing very close to Baruk so that the edge of her smock trailed along his arm. Yusuf and several of the others went with her. Baruk took a deep breath, grinned and nodded his thanks to Qeren, and turned away to the track leading home.

Approaching the house, he glanced up and saw Damariel sitting on the edge of the roof, looking out westward past the house of their aunt and across to the wooded ridge that rose on the other side of the valley. He had a broom in his hand, the bundled bristle of twigs resting on the rooftop, but was not working at anything.

Baruk slipped past the mimosa and the open door without being noticed from inside and went up the ladder that was propped up against the wall nearby, ending up just in front of Damariel. His brother, a little startled by his sudden appearance, half got up and then relaxed again. Baruk grinned.

"Not quite finished your work yet?"

Damariel shook his head and, without getting up, pushed at a few nearby leaves with the end of the broom.

"There now, look, that's a bit more done."

Baruk laughed and sat beside him, swinging his legs over the edge of the roof and tapping with his heels on the wall.

"So what is it, Damari? You've been sitting around like this for days."

Damariel sighed.

"It's since it all happened with Iqnu. You know, Baruk, I was with him a lot, all the times I was learning from him. Maybe they think I had something to do with all that. What will I do then? They might drive me out. They won't let me go on learning. Not as if I ever got to be properly apprenticed to him. I've got no standing there to protect me. I don't know this new seer or his wife. Maybe they think they don't owe me anything. What if they don't even want to know me? I don't want a life just fiddling with the olive trees."

"Just go and see them, then, Damari, just as soon as you want. They've settled in now up by the stones. Let them know who you are and what you've done so far. There's nobody else in the town who can say that. They'll want to meet you. Anyway, you didn't have anything to do with Isheth and all that, did you?"

There was a silence that drew out rather too long. After a few moments Baruk looked up in surprise and caught his brother's eye.

"Well, you didn't, did you?"

Eventually Damariel shook his head.

"No, not really. No of course not, not so's anyone could say for sure. But I don't know, Baruk. Maybe he just picked times to see me so I could be, I don't know, like the brushwood or undergrowth that he could hide in. It was always so vague, so..." He waved his hands. "I don't know. All always on his terms. Maybe he covered my eyes like he covered everyone else's. Then there's something else."

Baruk nodded, but said nothing, and Damariel continued after a pause.

"And then you know, sometimes I think maybe Ethan is going to come back one night and do to me what he did both to Isheth and Iqnu himself, if he thinks I was part of it all."

He looked almost defiantly at Baruk for a moment before sighing and pushing some more leaves around with the broom. "Do you think he would?"

Baruk shook his head and took the broom from him to sweep some dust off the edge of the roof.

"Ethan's gone forever, we'll not see him again around here. As if he would risk it all to come back all the way up here especially for you. But if he does come, I reckon that that Azziy will take care of him. He looked like he could take care of himself quite nicely."

"But that's another thing, Baruk. He might have appealed to the old northern ways and claimed the right to extract whatever vengeance he wanted on any woman of Ethan's family. Anything. In exchange for Isheth, you know."

Baruk stopped sweeping again and looked at him.

"Anything?"

Damariel nodded.

"Anything at all. No limits at all. Seeing as how Isheth had been killed like that. Out east they'd still do that now, but we stopped all that since coming down here. But maybe Azziy might have tried to go back to that."

"So that was why Nawar paid up that huge amount so quickly?"

"That's right. Hinnah is the only woman left of the family that Azziy might have come after. Did you see Nawar's face when they first talked about getting Azziy along? That was why. He just didn't know what might come of it if he got involved. But now, you see, what if Azziy decides he didn't get enough recompense on the day? I haven't got silver to buy him off. I've got nothing. But I suppose you think I'm being ridiculous."

"Yes, completely. Why would Azziy come back for you? He's probably never heard of you. Anyway the seers would have something to say about it now the agreement has been sworn. So yes, you are indeed being ridiculous."

They both laughed.

"That's good, then."

For a while they worked together at the more untidy parts of the roof. Down below they could hear their mother teaching Sosanneth a song. Baruk looked around at the result and nodded.

"That'll do. Tell you what though, Damari. I think I'm well in with Danil and the others."

"You are?"

"I am. I think they'll let me go with them soon. Maybe next time they go, or the time after. Or maybe into next year. Soon though. It's taken a bit of time but I'm nearly in with them."
"That's good. But mum won't like it."

Baruk shrugged.

"She'll be alright."

Down the track they could hear Shomal approaching with Bashur.

"We'd better go down. But look, Damari, I could probably get you in as well if you wanted. That might do you good."

Damariel laughed.

"You can't really see me going out with you on that, can you? You go and maybe I'll sing you a song when you get back. That would be more fitting to my talents than heading off down to the lowlands with you lot and starting to wave a sling and a knife around. More likely I'd do myself an injury, or else one of Danil's crew, rather than some lowlander."

"Right, a song! I'll keep you to that. I'll go down with them, and you sing the song afterwards. That'll get you noticed as well. Come on, let's seal the bargain."

They clasped hands and embraced, the way they had seen some of the traders do, and went down together into the main part of the house.

A week later they had been down at the olive patch all afternoon. Shomal had talked about a plan to clear out one corner where some brambles were encroaching, and put in a fig tree instead. So they had cut off shoots and dug out roots, pulled out stones and used them to build up the perimeter wall where it had become sparse and ragged, and finally smoothed over the soil with hoes. Shomal had been pleased with the work and had sent the boys off to do as they wished for a time, while he stayed sitting in the doorway of the hut looking at the outcome.

Bashur had run off home. Baruk and Damariel wandered down to the stream and dipped hot hands and faces into the flow, then leaned back against one of the boulders lining the steep side to the south of the water. A short distance uphill they could hear the sounds of childhood play.

"Hardly seems any time since I was up there with all the others."

Damariel laughed and threw a dry seed case at him. "Well, it's not. You're barely past being a baby, you know."

"Old man."

They sat with their feet in the stream.

"Do you think dad will get a fig tree in there?"

Damariel pulled a face.

"No more than he got the vine up against the hut last year, or the vegetable area planted out the year before. Good ideas but never finished off. Why do you think I want to get away from all that?"

"If only he'd let us do it for real, we could get it all done. He only ever lets us do scrappy things while he decides what to do next."

"And then watches while we do it."

"And then changes his mind anyway. You know, I wish he'd just hand the olive patch over to me to work on it. Of course I'd check things out with him, or mum, whoever, but I know I'd get more done there than he does. There really would be a fig tree, and a vegetable plot, whatever, neat as anything. It could really be something special if only he'd let me do that. Even mum would get to see it as a blessing to us all, and not just somewhere he goes off to in order to get out of doing things in the house. I could do that, you know. I think I could do that really well."

"I think you could, too. You've got hands that make it all work out there. Real skill at it. Maybe raise it up it as an idea with him some time soon. Give him a year or so to think about it so it doesn't all come out on one day. You're good at these plans that take a long time to come to fruit. Especially when it comes to working with the land."

They were silent for a few minutes. From their vantage point they could see some way downstream, to where the undergrowth swept back in a clearing either side of the water. Suddenly Kalita emerged from the side away from the village, ducking under the last overhanging branches and stepping neatly across the stream at a narrow place where two rocks leaned towards each other. Glancing once over her shoulder, she went up the rise directly towards the nearest houses. The two boys leaned further back into the bushes as, shortly after, Yusuf followed her out of the woods, turning away from them to make a longer swing into the houses around the western end of the ridge. Damariel laughed.

"Well now, there's a coincidence, Yusuf turning up so soon after Kalita. And from the same part of the woods too."

Baruk missed the irony in his voice and started to reply seriously. "Oh, but you see they do know each other. They were both together in a group talking together the other day." He glanced at Damariel and realised.

"Oh yes. I see. You know that."

"Of course I do. And I think that maybe they know just a little bit more of each other now. But Yusuf needs to watch out, she'll not be a good one to get on your wrong side. He could find himself in a lot of trouble with her. Like in the story where the fox tried to take a ride on a lion." He suddenly laughed. "Or perhaps in this case the fox who tried to ride a lioness." Baruk remembered how he had been so easily discomforted by Kalita, and how Qeren had helped him. He shook his head. "So, Damari, have you been up to the high place to see the new seers yet?"

"Well, yes I have. The evening before yesterday."

"And?"

"I think they will carry on with me. I told them what sort of things I did with Iqnu, how I wanted to go on. I thought it sounded a lot when I listed it all out, that they'd be quite impressed. But then they asked me about all kinds of things that he never taught me at all. Baruk, I had no idea about so much of it. They were very kind to me about that. And of course it was him, Iqnu, who decided what he would teach me, how was I to know? But now I know there was a very great deal he never did tell me. I think I must have missed out so much they reckon that I should have known. But I think it will be alright. They say they're going to think and pray about it, that it's not something they can just say yes or no on the spot like that."

"Is that how Iqnu began with you?"

"No, no, not at all. One day we just started. Well, to be fair maybe he did think and pray on his own but he never told me about that side of it. Turns out there was a lot he didn't tell me. But at the time he was quite motivated to make a quick start."

"What do you mean?"

Damariel shrugged, and after a moment Baruk carried on.

"But they will take you on?"

"I think so. I hope so. We just have to wait and see. They said to come back in a week or so to see them again. It all seems quite serious for them. I just nodded as though it was what I expected and came away again. What else could I do?"

"Don't they have children of their own to take up their trade?"

"Of course they have children, everyone does pretty much, don't they, but they've moved away from here. One works up and down the coast roads as a trader, the other married a man from Sychem and lives up there now, has done for several years. Neither of them wanted to follow on as seers. The way they told it to me, it doesn't run in families. Not like a normal craft. So right now they don't have anyone with them as apprentice."

"And with all the business about Iqnu they must be short of people. This has to be a good time for you, Damari."

Damariel glanced at him and pursed his lips.

"I suppose so."

"Look, Damari, there's something you can do for me."

Damariel looked quizzically at him. Baruk looked down and traced some lines in a bare patch of soil with a convenient twig.

"Well, I was talking with Alloni about working the land. You know, he has all those vines and they really flourish. There's someone with real talent."

Damariel nodded, wondering what his brother was leading towards.

"Well, you see, he was telling me about a saying they have about the year's working on the land. Of course it starts in autumn, with two months of gathering olives. Then there's two months of sowing. A month, no, two months of - oh, I can't remember now. But it goes all around the year and ends up with a month of gathering in the summer fruit."

Damariel nodded.

"It will start at the feast of the new wine."

"That's it, yes. Well, I was wondering, if I learn it right from Alloni, would you write it for me on something, then I can put it up in the olive patch somewhere. It would be like, I don't know, like a good luck thing. Like people wear amulets with prayers in them that a seer has written out for them."

Damariel nodded again, clearly very moved by the request.

"Of course, Baruk, I'll be very glad to do that for you. Just tell me the proper order when you've learned it from Alloni and I'll write it. On a piece of pottery, or a wooden board, whatever you want most. Pottery or stone lasts longer but I always think the wooden ones look better as you walk by them. Just tell me when, and I'll be very happy to do that for you. Every time you walk by it you can think of me."

Summer turned to autumn. Damariel had started seeing Saniyahu and Halith once a week, for a few hours in the afternoon or evening, but whenever Baruk asked him about the future he said that he felt that he was still on probation with them. He was still not sure whether they would take him on as a full apprentice. He did not really know what they were waiting for, or looking for. On good days he felt optimistic about the matter, but their approach to being a seer was quite different from that of Iqnu, and sometimes he felt like someone lost in the woods. Baruk had, for his own part, very slowly started to try to talk about the olive patch with Shomal. So far he did not feel that he had made much progress.

Today the idea had turned against him, and so, later than he had planned, Baruk ran up the ridge to Danil's house. Shomal had kept him working in the olive field rather longer than he had expected or hoped, and he was late. Then, right at the end of the day when Baruk had thought all was done, he had started to explain to Baruk how the old plan to grow a grape vine against one side of the hut was completely wrong, and how it would be so much better to train it along the boundary wall.

Baruk had wanted to listen, and wanted to make suggestions, and wanted to get away, all at the same time, and was not sure he had handled it well. As it was now, the sun had not only touched the trees on the western horizon, but had already dipped below their crowns by some margin. He was late.

He had not wanted to be late, but rather he had wanted to impress Danil and his fellow raiders with his eagerness and diligence. As he approached the door he heard the men's voices sounding from inside - the mixture of humour, boasting, teasing and mutual appreciation that he longed to participate in. He hesitated at the door, his hand resting lightly on the grained wood, taking a series of deep breaths to calm himself down. Then, calling out to Danil, he pushed the door open and stepped inside without waiting for an answer.

The group of men looked at him as he entered, nodded, then shifted here and there to make a space for him. He sat down, and Tamguta, to his left, nudged him, passed him a beaker of the thin beer they were sharing, and said,

"So why are you so late, Baruk? Been cooking a dove out in the woods somewhere?"

Baruk smiled vaguely, not sure how to respond, when Danil across the circle from him caught his eye and winked suggestively. Suddenly full of realisation, he grinned more broadly and looked around at the others.

"Oh yes, that's right. I was cooking that dove very nicely. Oh yes. But then I had to leave the dove out by the fire so I could get back here with you all."

"Now, Baruk, it doesn't do to leave a dove half-cooked, you know."

"Oh, there's no danger of that."

When there was a general ripple of laughter around the group, he felt he had pitched the answer right; he was accepted among them. The conversation turned to some practical details of when and where the next raid would take place, who had what ideas to offer for success. Baruk felt himself on the verge of contributing several times, but the moment never quite seemed right. His words were never spoken, his voice never quite able to break in.

Much sooner than he had wanted, his time together with them wore to an end. The men finished, with no obvious signal Baruk could see, stood up, and began getting ready to go off to their wives' homes. Baruk stood as well, not sure of the etiquette, and a little unsteady after the several refills of beer he had accepted. Danil nodded and clasped his shoulder.

"You're alright, Baruk. Don't worry. Now go off back to your mother's house before she thinks I've got you killed or something."

Baruk took a deep breath and opened the door. Turning at the threshold, he looked back at the others.

"I'm ready to go out with you all. You know that, don't you? Take me with you next time you go down there. Just you say the word and I'll go down into the lowlands with you. I'm ready now."

Danil looked surprised, then put both hands on his hips.

"I don't know, Baruk. What about that brother of yours?"

"Let him come too. With me, I mean. I'll look after him, I'll promise you he'll stay right beside me. Go on, Danil, please."

The older man looked slightly flustered at the repeated request. He took a breath, and was about to speak when Tamguta intervened.

"Danil, it's too soon for them. They can wait a while. Better for all of us that they wait a bit longer."

Danil stopped what he was about to say and looked around at the others. There were a few cautious glances, a shrug, a generally hesitant air.

"Not long, Baruk. Wait until next year and that brother of yours might be ready to come along too. We'd need you to keep an eye on him down there. But we'd need the word from your family too, what with you not quite being of an age yet. Now go home and make sure you get there safely or Yeresheth will let me know about it."

Baruk grinned and nodded, before going out beneath the branches of Rivkah's honeysuckle tree and turning down past the potter's house towards home. As he got near to the house, he saw Damariel sitting on the wall outside the house, looking out across the wooded ridges, outlined vaguely in the light of the half moon. Kothar was just standing up when Baruk first saw him, clearly on the point of going, and as Baruk approached he nodded to him and set off towards his family home. In the moonlight Baruk could see the large-boned frame he shared with his mother Tamar, but with his straight dark hair and stubby fingers he looked more like Damariel.

Once he had gone, Baruk stopped beside Damariel and put his hand on his older brother's shoulder. Damariel nodded absently, still looking away towards the trees, and leaned against him before looking suddenly up into his face.

"You smell of beer."

Baruk nodded and replied quite carefully, "Yes, I have been up at Danil's house with his raiders."

Damariel nodded. "And did that go well?"

"Damari, I'm in with them for sure now. Just a little while to wait. I'd almost got Danil to agree to take me next time. You know what he's like, he'd agree to anything if you put it firmly in front of him."

Damariel nodded.

"Well, the others there, they stopped him this time. But it'll be just a few more months to wait now. Then they'll take me. And someone, mum or dad, has to give their word too. But I reckon next spring and I'll be away with them when they go. And Bashur too, they'll take us both so long as I promise to watch over him. Danil himself said as much. He did."

"Will you tell him? Bashur, I mean."

At that moment the noise of Shomal and Yeresheth arguing came from the house, and as Baruk watched Damariel's face he realised that he had been sitting on the wall to avoid the situation inside, and that Kothar had come along after he had gone outside, not before. Bashur appeared on the roof with Sosanneth and the two of them started arranging the bedding.

"Come on, let's join them up on top. I'll tell him now, that'll cheer him up."

They climbed up the outside ladder and for a few minutes the four were busy laying out the sleeping area. Sosanneth, hearing more angry words rising up from the main part of the house, curled up in her sleeping roll and turned away. From across the way, Nerith appeared outside her door for a brief moment, then seeing the four children up on the roof she went back in again. The three boys sat together in the moonlight while Baruk told Bashur what Danil had said. As he had expected, the news brightened Bashur considerably, and Baruk found himself having to repeat details several times over.

"But look, Bashur, right now you mustn't talk it over with mum or dad. Let Danil do that when the time's right. He'll be much better at it than any of us. If you or I try it now we might miss the chance for a long time."

Bashur nodded.

"It's all right, Baruk, I do understand. I want this to come out right as much as you do." He paused and thought about it. "Next year, then. We can wait that long. It's not long, really." He paused again. "Damari, what about you?"

"Damari's going to wait here and make up a song for when we get back. I've already asked him about that."

Bashur looked at Damariel, then grinned. Damariel nodded.

"Well, make sure it's a good one then. Something that people will remember."

The three boys laughed together and settled down in a row near Sosanneth.

Dalth

Matan Year 17

Baruk, Bashur– brothers in life
and in death now together –
swifter than eagles,
bolder than lions.

IT WAS JUST BEFORE NOON, on a bright day at the end of Matan, when the barley had been gathered and the early fruit was ripening, that Baruk and Bashur were brought back dead. The previous day they had pressured Shomal to let them join a raid for livestock into the lowland villages, protesting loudly of their talent with sword and sling. Later that evening, when Danil had called the men together to plan the raid, Shomal had gone along for once to accompany his sons. Baruk had used the persuasive way he had with the older men to further his plea. After all Baruk's months of steady preparation for this moment, Danil had agreed provided that the others going were content, and that Shomal consented.

Shomal had kept silent at first while the men were deciding, but when the debate had dipped down in uncertainty, led by a token voice of opposition, he had spoken up for them. His word on the matter swayed the final decision. The boys were of an age to choose, and if Shomal was not going to object to them going, then who else should?

The talk around the group that evening had then gone as it always did, with arguments about how many men should go, which path down was best to avoid being seen, which of the lowland villages was wealthiest and least guarded, how best to withdraw into underbrush after the raid. As always, the talk went on for too long, and all of these things had been said before. Danil listened to all of them, gave every appearance of considering carefully, and made the choices they all knew he would.

Afterwards, back at home, Shomal and the two boys had given the other family members the news together. Baruk and Bashur would be going on the raid, and they would be carrying the family name for him. Yeresheth kept very quiet as they talked, her busy hands mending small tears in the boys' clothing. When they had done she spoke, rather uncertainly, of her pride in them and her fears about the whole raiding business, but in the end gave them her maternal blessing for their success.

Her last words as they set off in the morning, laughing as they joined the eight other men, were to describe the jewellery she wanted. They all laughed together: the village they were raiding would not have storehouses full of armbands and earrings, belts and brooches of gold and lapis lazuli. Bashur turned as they set off down the track, seeing Damariel watching them from the village gate.

"Make up a song for us for when we get back, Damari, or you won't have any share in our exploits!"

Baruk waved as well, brandishing his staff over his head.

"Start making it up now, Damari, 'Brave Baruk and bold Bashur went down the hill with sword and sling!' Make us famous! Sing a song for us!"

Then they were gone, out of sight amongst the low trees where the path followed the stream valley for a while before joining a larger road used by traders going north and south.

The men came back too soon, much too soon, following Danil up the track with fourteen goats, a woman some five or so years older than Damariel, some bags of provisions taken from a shed amongst the fruit trees, and the bodies of Baruk and Bashur.

Only two of the other men were even slightly wounded, and they stood in an uncertain, shifting circle around the bodies, near the priest's house. The news was rippling urgently through the community, household to household calling out to each other. As Saniyahu opened the door, one of the wounded men, hearing Yeresheth come running, wailing, pulled Bashur's kef down to hide a jagged wound across his neck and shoulder.

Yeresheth stopped, hands at her mouth, a tearing shriek coming out of her as she looked down at the bodies of her sons. Sosanneth was now at the edge of the circle as it filled with women coming out of the nearby houses. One of the older women caught her hand as she stared with wide eyes at her howling mother. Yeresheth looked at the man closest to her, walked unsteadily to him and took the bronze knife from his belt. Sosanneth tried to pull away and run to her, her voice clutching in her throat, but the holding woman wrapped big arms around her and kept her in a tight embrace.

Yeresheth took the knife, and in the dead silence cut a gash down each of her cheeks, the blood running down her face, down the knife-blade. She took the collars of her smock and tore it in half away from her body, letting the rags fall to the ground and standing half-naked in the sudden gaze of the crowd. Shomal joined the group, running up the hill from his olives. He pushed his way through the gathering people as Yeresheth took the knife again slowly, deliberately in her right hand. His voice came out more breathless, high-pitched, less powerful than he had wished.

"Yeresheth, stop!"

She stared proudly, defiantly at him and then at the knife's owner who had taken a half step towards her, hand lifted. She stared at them both until they dropped their eyes, then traced the knife blade down both arms, left and right, so a thin track of blood ran from shoulder to elbow. She cut another gash across the top of her breasts, then dropped the knife and threw herself full-length in the dust between the bodies of the two boys, an arm around each, her body shaking with great sobs.

Sosanneth, released at last, ran and knelt by her mother's head, her hands dabbing slightly at the disarrayed, dust-filled hair where it spilled out in a dark flood from under her kef, then bent over and kissed the top of her head. The two remained like that for a long moment.

Then Yeresheth gripped Sosanneth's hands and slowly rose to her knees. She gathered her daughter into her arms for a fierce embrace and the two women stood up. Sosanneth's face was marked with tears, blood and dust from her mother, and her own smock was stained where the two had held each other.

The effort of standing had opened the wound across Yeresheth's chest, which the dust of the earth had smeared shut, and as she walked over to Damariel it seemed to him as if great red rivers of blood were running down her body, blood pooling and dripping where once her milk had nourished her children. She stood in front of him, and he forced his gaze up from the blood on her body to meet her soiled, wounded look.

"You must bury them. You must sing their lament."

Off to one side, Saniyahu moved restively.

"Him, seer, I want him to do it, honoured one. Him. You teach him the words."

Without waiting for an answer she turned to put her bloodied arm around Sosanneth's shoulder, and the two, clutching each other, moved off toward their home. Halith glanced at her husband and then set off after them, walking quickly so as to catch up with them just behind the first houses.

All eyes turned to Shomal, who shrugged slightly, uneasy at being the focus of attention. He squatted briefly in the dust where his wife had lain headlong, briefly touched each boy's arm and then stood up, swaying briefly. He looked at Danil, off to his right, away from Damariel.

"It was their choice to go. Took my place, they did, they wanted it. Told them it was their choice, wouldn't have it any other way. She could have stopped them, she could if she'd wanted. She could. No blame on you."

The circle of people parted in front of him as he started back again towards his olives, his steps halting and uncertain, his eyes cast down. Some of the men picked up the bodies to move them up to the village high place. The priest called to Damariel to come with him.

The crowd began to disperse, leaving the provision bags, the fourteen goats, and the young woman suddenly conspicuous in the open space. Danil looked at them with frustration and anger. He slung the bags on his shoulder, divided the goats among the men who had gone out, and contemplated the woman, his hands on his hips.

Her headscarf had slipped during the journey back, exposing black hair to the right of her face. She had a bruise on her face and a graze across one wrist. She kept her eyes down, avoiding his look even when he pushed her chin back with one hand to look more closely at her. He called out to the priest, who with Damariel was now at the door of his house. Saniyahu turned, looked at the woman and then briefly at the remaining townspeople to gather their mood.

"Take her to Yeresheth", and then as Danil started to lead her away along the track after Shomal, "No, not Shomal in his field. Hear what I said. Take her to the women and let them decide. Give them the food as well, all of it. Only the goats for the rest."

As Danil turned again to go, he continued, "And no returning down the hill for revenge, Danil. Enough has happened. No blame, no fault. Hear me on this."

Damariel went into the seer's house, half-listening to Danil setting off with the girl, swearing emptily as he moved away. Saniyahu took him through to the large room which he had hardly ever seen in all the hours with Iqnu. Before they began, he poured them both some wine from a jug and insisted Damariel drank it. Damariel hardly tasted it, was hardly aware of it passing into his body.

He was filled with a sense of unreality. Baruk and Bashur would be home soon, they were just out in the woods, in the olive patch, by the stream. He had just imagined seeing them lying in the dust. He was going to sing them a victory song just as they had asked as they set off. Then he realised Saniyahu was looking at him across the room, and the songs he had to learn were not of victory.

Saniyahu tutored Damariel all through the rest of that long afternoon, drilling him most thoroughly what to say, where to stand, what to wear, when to sing the lament for the lives of his brothers. He absolutely refused to let him perform the sacrifices, or to speak the invocation to the spirits when the bodies were sent into the tomb. No argument, no debate was allowed on this, and indeed Damariel had little heart to argue for it. He made a token objection out of duty to his mother's words, as he had understood them, but then sat forward and learned what he must. He practiced over and over again, to Saniyahu and, later, to Halith after she had come back to the house, her face set and expressionless.

Finally, as the summer sun settled, Saniyahu stared across the reddened ridges and grimaced at the lowlands which had already fallen into shadow. He sent Damariel back to his mother's house then, since when darkness fell he would sit in vigil over the corpses. Halith reached out and hugged Damariel to her as he passed, staying awkwardly close to him as she retied his kef into the mourning pattern, tight across his forehead and draped ragged past his shoulders. He looked away from her, unable to meet her eyes and abruptly uneasy at the able touch of her hands as she smoothed a crease from the cloth across his forehead.

As he crossed the track to his house, his mother's voice, raised in anger, not quite coherent, pushed out though the door at him. He stopped, his hand flat against the wood, taking deep breaths before going in. There was a sudden silence as he pushed the door open and stepped in.

Yeresheth was sitting at her wooden table, some sewing in front of her, untouched. Her face was still covered in dust and streaked with blood, and the cuts on her cheeks were undressed. She had put another smock on since he last saw her outside the priest's house, but the arms and chest were already badly bloodstained. He realised she had no intention of washing or caring for herself until after the burial. She looked at him and nodded as he walked in, but her eyes were hard and her features set with anger.

Shomal sat across the room from her on a stool, his face red and his lips tight together, unrelenting. Sosanneth seemed to have started unpacking the provision bags brought back from the foray, as some of the contents were around her or placed up on shelves against the wall, but had never finished. She looked frightened and haunted, her hands pressed against her sides as she looked at Damariel and made an abrupt jerk of her head to him.

The lowland girl was standing near the door to the room where he and his sister slept in the winter, where all four children had once slept. She had another bruise across her mouth, a scratch down her left arm, and she was holding the torn parts of her kef in one hand. She had clearly been crying but now stood rigid with tension, avoiding everyone's look. Shomal spoke, obviously continuing with whatever had been said before.

"So what do you want me to do, wife? They won't be coming back again. They ran off all the way down the hill, and who is there now to work my field?"

"All you think about is your wretched field. My children are not even gathered to their ancestors and you think of your field. Last night you were keen enough for them to go. Shame on you for despising their memory."

"I would have more memories if you had not driven them out of this house and down the hill to fight. That was you did that. You said you were proud of them, you blessed them as they went. That was you. Not me. They wanted to go. I missed a place with Danil for them. I might have gone myself. If only they hadn't gone. I would have help with the harvest. I would have more hands to repair the walls. I would have more generations to look at when I am old. I let them go because of you. You forced them out of here. You never liked them working for me. You'll miss them when the olives need picking. Not even as if you could have more children now. I might still, but not you. I'll have more sons. But you're all dried up now."

His hands clenched as she stood up, her breath coming in short gasps.

"You disgusting man. I raised those boys while you were playing dice and drinking with the other men. You gave them your place on that wicked raid. You wanted them to go, with all your talk about getting Danil to take notice of them. And I have more children, a better future than your olives. Olives? Filthy things. That's all you have left. But these here are my children too."

He stood up and took a step towards her, but before he could make a reply, there was the sound of footsteps in the stony path outside, and then the voice of Danil calling to them. Shomal and Yeresheth looked at each other but said nothing, so after a little pause when Danil did not enter, Damariel went and opened the door to him. Danil was breathing hard and smelled a little of last year's wine, but he clapped Damariel on the shoulder cheerily and entered the room before seeing the occupants in their strained, harsh positions. He faltered a little but carried on resolutely.

"I came to, well, offer my respects for, ah, your loss today. They were good lads, both of them, would have been happy to have them with me any time. Shomal, you and I have done this sort of thing before, you know quality when you see it, even if it is, well, was, unskilled. They were doing well, until, well. . . " He trailed off as neither parent responded, looked around the room, and moved his hands vaguely.

"I see you found a home for that lowland girl here, that's good then. All for the best."

He turned to Damariel, who was still standing beside him at the doorway.

"The priest tells me you learned those words well, you'll do your brothers proud, I'm sure. I'll enjoy listening to you. Mind you sing it well. I'll be going now and see you all tomorrow. May the sun rising bring you all peace, now. Fresh morning, fresh news, fresh blessing, that's what they say."

He smiled aimlessly round the room, waved a hand, patted Damariel on the shoulder, and slipped out through the door. There was a little silence, as though even the memory of his coming was being cast away. Shomal sat down again and glanced around the room pointedly.

"Your children, you were saying. None of the village boys looks at that girl much yet. I suppose she'll do in a few years when she does some growing here and there. Then we'll have some more help around here. Another man to live with us, at least, to help me work the land."

Yeresheth beckoned to Sosanneth, who tucked herself under her mother's arm and hid her face from the others.

"She's my daughter and she will honour me. My Damari too."

"Oh well, fine, but he's not my son. He came out of you by that priest of yours, but he is not mine and never will be. In my house he is always second."

"This is my holy child. He opened my womb by the favour of the gods when your seed could do nothing. Worthless. I'd still be waiting yet for a child if I'd placed my hope in what you could manage. He is my firstborn, and I still have my first and my last left to me, no thanks to you. Don't you dare speak this way about my children."

She seemed at that moment to expand and fill more of the little room with her presence than Damariel had thought possible. As Shomal opened his mouth to say something else, she drew herself up like a queen, or a lioness, and forestalled him. "And this is not your house. It was my mother's, and her mother's before her. You came into my house when we married, and you can be put outside it again if I wish it. I am mistress here, and I will decide."

He stopped, looking narrowly at her as though trying to assess her resolve, and then shrugged a little, yielding the ground to her. "I'll not sleep here tonight, at any rate. Don't try to stop me, woman." He picked up his tools from near the door and started out into the night air. Holding it open, he turned again and spoke to the other girl while looking at Yeresheth. "You come with me. I want you: come with me."

Startled, she looked up at Yeresheth, meeting her eyes for the first time. A look of anxiety, perhaps horror, crossed her face as, still without speaking, she tried to find some kind of recognition or rescue. Yeresheth looked away from her, ignoring the mute appeal and stroking Sosanneth's hair. Shomal beckoned again to her jerkily, forcefully, and then slammed the door behind the two of them as he pulled her out into the night.

Yeresheth looked at the door for a long moment, her face without expression, then stood with a heavy sigh. Damariel started to speak, but at the sight of her closed expression stopped. Sosanneth moved as though to carry on unpacking the provisions, but Yeresheth took them out of her hands and began rearranging the figs and barley, the lentils and the grapes.

Damariel and Sosanneth, made redundant in the room, moved away to their sleeping place. Neither wanted to go up to the roof. The evening had grown suddenly dark, and the moon could not be seen from that side of the house.

They got ready to sleep without speaking, the slow noise of their mother's work covering the awkward silence. As they lay there in the night-filled room, Damariel realised his sister was crying. He lay on his back and listened to her, empty and drained of feeling for his own part.

After a long time their mother came in and lay between them, an arm around each, holding them to her through the long hours. For a long time both children lay awake, trying not to move, listening to her heavy, drawn-out breathing. Their minds were full of remembered blood, wounds and gashes, words made weighty and irrevocable with passion.

Finally Damariel forced his thoughts back to the session with the seer in the afternoon.

Suddenly alarmed that he had forgotten all the words, he rehearsed them right through in his heart, start to finish, and finding himself at the end, with the bodies about to be sent into the darkness, he shivered suddenly. Up at the high place, amongst the ring of stones, Saniyahu would be sitting beside the two corpses, waiting for the morning star to rise on the day of their burial.

Damariel was abruptly seized with curiosity. Was the night silent and dark around him? Did little night-owls and fire-flies cluster round him as he sat between one world and the next? What night-visions were stirring in his heart as he watched over the departed? What whistling spirits were trying to slip back in the other way, back into the warmth and life of the village? Would his half-brothers be held safe until their burial rites were done? He shivered again, listening to the two women breathing in the room beside him, and gradually fell into sleep.

He woke early in the morning, to the sound of flour being ground from the barley grains. Sosanneth was still asleep, one hand tucked under her head and the other splayed out, palm upwards, to her left. He got up and went unsteadily into the main room where Yeresheth was kneeling and turning the grindstone.

A clay bowl beside her was already half-full of flour, with a scattering of raisins, and Damariel realised bleakly she was making flat cakes to leave with the bodies. She looked up as he crossed to her and squatted beside her, and she put one arm round him while carrying on the steady rotation of the stone with the other.

The wounds on her face and arms were red, dirty, untended. Neither said anything while she milled the kernels and poured the pale meal into the bowl. Then she sat back with a sigh, and he realised how little sleep she must have had.

He felt a sudden swell of guilt roll across him for the hours of his own slumber, and got up to bring her the pitcher of milk. She mixed the thick batter and set the bowl off to one side. Catching his look into the room where she normally slept in with Shomal, she grimaced slightly and spoke before he did.

"Did you learn all that you needed from the seer? Will you be ready?"

He nodded, and she went on in a rush to stop him talking.

"I wanted there to be more time last night, I wanted you to tell me everything he taught you to do. The other women will be here soon, there's no time now. No reason for you to have heard all that last night. All lies what that man said, take no notice. Don't ever name him again in this house. Never, do you hear? Look, Damari, you must carry on learning from the seer, from Saniyahu. Halith too. Everyone trusts them now, even if they're still new to this village. They've brought households together that have been at odds for years. Don't take notice of anyone who says you can't do it, shouldn't do it. Do it for me. Sing your songs and see your visions. Make my household proud of you. My mother's mother danced among the stones at the festivals, all around the high place, she'll be looking back at you. They say she was splendid to see. Make her proud of what you do. Don't you take notice of those who say else."

Her words came out all in a rush, as though they had been kept rolled behind a stone all night and were now let out into the light of day. He gazed at her with wide eyes, never having known her be so urgent and pressing.

"Promise me," she continued, "swear by our ancestors you'll not turn away from this. Swear to me now. Right now. Here."

Tongue-tied, he knelt in front of her, bowed his head to the ground, and put his hands on her knees. She rested her own hands briefly on his head in blessing, and he felt a great stillness come over him into the midst of his aching soul. Tears filled his eyes, and he stayed bowed in front of her for a long time. Then Sosanneth came to the door, and as she saw him crouched there, her voice came shrill, uneasy, frightened.

"What's happened? Damari? What's happened to you now? Mother? What's wrong with him? Are you alright?"

He got up quickly and went over to her, holding one hand as she rubbed sleep out of her eyes with the other.

"Nothing, Sannah, nothing, it's all all right. I'm fine, Mother is fine."

She held on to him, looking past him at Yeresheth who had started spooning the dough mixture out into round cakes on a griddle, already hot from the fire. Voices, women's voices, came from outside, and she gestured the two back into the other room.

"Keep out of sight for the moment, just get yourselves ready. Sannah, I will need you soon, get ready and come back out to me before these cakes are done."

She started heating the griddle over the fire as the women's voices came up to the door, calling to her, starting to fill the little house with female company. Sosanneth pulled the cloth drape over the doorway as the others arrived. They helped each other get ready, arranged each other's clothes, tied each other's kefs, avoided making eye contact, and then Sosanneth slipped out past the curtain to join Yeresheth and the other women of the village. Damariel sat in one corner of the room, rehearsing the words and the lament in his mind, only half aware of the talk and bustle in the other room.

After a long time there came complete silence. He looked up at the drape, wondering what was happening. Then Yeresheth's voice came again, raised high, wailing for the dead, and the others joined her, woman after woman. Damariel felt himself shake, transfixed to the spot with tears in his eyes as the sound slowly swelled and then faded as they left the house. He sat there for a few moments, letting the death moment build in his mind as the keening had done. Then he got up, straightened his clothes, and left the house, walking blindly up to the high place.

He went by the shortest route, past silent household doors each draped with their own garlands of leaf or flower. He was aware of the sound of women mourning across to the west of the village and knew the men would be gathering to the east. He came into the open space above the last house, seeing Saniyahu there alone with the bodies. He had cleaned the wounds, arranged the limbs in the proper way, and dressed both boys in white tunics tied with a rope belt. They lay across one of the stones, stretched out like a sacrifice, each on a wicker bier.

Saniyahu himself was in his full regalia, with long embroidered gown, wide sash, and an elaborate kef tied into a tower on his head, clothing Damariel had seen only twice before. He was briefly dazzled as the low sun threw golden reflections into his eyes from the thick bands at the seer's throat and groin. He felt shabby beside him, and then saw that the older man was holding something out. He blinked the brightness away and realised it was a woven shawl and sash. He wrapped and tied them to the priest's satisfaction and drew himself up, feeling able now to play his part in the ceremony.

There was no time now, and Damariel stood where the older man told him, to the left of the bodies, just behind the seer, looking towards the sacred north. The sound of the women grew closer from his left, and he knew without looking that Yeresheth and Sosanneth would be leading the rest. To his right, the men approached in a silent group. He tried to see if Shomal was there out of the corners of his eyes, not wanting to turn his head, knowing that to do that he would have to look over the stone with the bodies. He did not trust himself to do that without being overcome with emotion. The women's wailing seemed to go on for ever, treading endlessly up the rising ground towards him. Then it stopped, and there was only the sound of the day breeze whispering in smock and tunic.

Until some years later, when Damariel was himself responsible for such an event, he never knew how long they all stood there to help Baruk and Bashur make their passage to the land of the dead. Looking back, he knew it could not be long, but on that day it seemed an age of the world, as the preparatory words of the seer flowed across the empty space between the stones, between this world and the next, between the men and the women of the village standing either side of the empty space and the two bodies. The words he had to say kept rolling around his mind in rehearsal as he listened to Saniyahu working through the liturgy.

He heard the priest ask where the bodies were to be laid, and heard Yeresheth step forward and offer the chamber of her ancestors and the little flat cakes she had made that morning. He heard him accept the place, and then ask what gifts were to be sent on with them. He saw Sosanneth, her face pinched tight, lay a spinning top beside them for their childhood. He saw Danil step forward with a short knife for each of them for their manhood, which had never been, and place it on their chests, tucking it under the loose cords they wore for belts. He saw Shomal put a nail and trowel between them for their place in the community. Saniyahu nodded and stepped back, and it was time for Damariel to sing.

He stepped up to the two bodies, his eyes fixed in the north, watching the far away cloud shapes like temples or palaces piled on the hilltops, with roofs open wide to the sight of the endless sun, and he sang as he bloomed in the sun, in the wind, in the sight of all those who were living and singing on high. The words Saniyahu had taught him all poured from his mouth just like showers in the spring or like streams in the desert, his word and his song springing out from his soul, washing over the village and filling the high place, poised there between sky and earth.

He forgot the people standing there listening, he forgot the two bodies at his feet, and felt something opening inside him, as though he was being swept along on the current of a song that had started long before him, melody and poetry that flowed round the homes of mortals and gods to inspire them all. It was him, then, him who stood for the whole community, who stood between the living and the dead and sang to both, and he felt all their eyes on him as he did so.

He finished, the moment passed, and after all that he was still Damariel, and he had still lost both his brothers in a single day.

Let them be welcomed within,
Let them rest in their pavilions

So proclaimed most mighty El,
So spoke the lord of the earth:
His judgement is true.

He stepped back again, feeling Saniyahu's hand firm on his shoulder, and looked around. Shomal was a face in the crowd of men, looking somewhere into the valley. Yeresheth was kneeling in front of the other women, looking at nothing but the bodies, with Sosanneth's hand in hers . But Qetirah had her eyes full of the day's brightness as she looked back at him, and Damariel felt a different kind of future stirring in him as she kept his eyes for a long moment until the deeper voice of the seer came across them all, releasing the boys to go on to their ancestors and calling on the dead who had gone before to accept them. It was a bargain on the part of the village, a promise to keep tending the burial caves in exchange for peace and rest for living and dead. The bargain required another death, and a chicken from the family flock sufficed.

After the dying noise of the bird had faded there was a pause, and then several of the nearest men picked up the two wickerwork trellises and carried them the short distance across the hill, outside the boundary of the living, to Yeresheth's family cave. Several more rolled the stone away from the entrance, and then Yeresheth went in with Shomal and the priest and the bodies.

Damariel tried to look in, as he had never seen the inside before in all his visits to make offering, but the darkness of the interior defeated his sunlit eyes. He heard Saniyahu's voice saying something indistinct, and there was a scraping sound as the bones of the last burial were swept to the sides. He realised it would be the body of Yeresheth's mother, and that the tomb had not been opened since then. He wondered what her body looked like, now it was only bone.

The men carried the bodies in, and emerged a few minutes later with the empty biers. Shomal and Saniyahu came out, and last of all Yeresheth. With a heavy sound, the stone was back across the entrance, and Yeresheth walked away without looking back. Several women moved towards her, but Halith waved them aside and followed her alone. The two disappeared into the trees a short distance away. Saniyahu was marking the top and sides of the stone with blood and grease from the chicken, and setting a fire to burn the carcass. The rest of the group started to disperse.

Ordinary conversation was starting again – when the summer fruit would be ready, whose flocks had lambed best this year, whether there would be drought. Low voices were starting again, the ordinary chatter of the village. A few people spoke to Damariel with approval or comfort as he stood there, not knowing what to do next, but he never could remember what they said, or what he said in reply. He took off the sash and shawl and left them both folded nearly on a stubby outcrop near the priest, not wanting to disturb him or speak to him just then. He started back towards his house, not knowing who he would find there, and realised that Qetirah had stayed when the others left, and was waiting for him.

The two of them walked along the ridge away from the village, briefly down and then up onto the craggy outcrops that overlooked the town from the side. Sitting on one of the boulders, they looked down on the little group of houses in the clearing. The high place and standing stones were off to their left, but, to his relief, the burial caves were out of sight. They sat there for a long time, alternately talking and silent, easy with one another. During one of the silences they watched Saniyahu return to his house, and they saw him glance up to their perch once before he went inside and closed the door behind him.

"Will you go and live with him now?"

Damariel was taken aback at her question.

"What are you talking about, Ketty? Why would I do that? Mother will need me in the house. Sannah will need me. I can't just go and move in with him and Halith. What makes you say that?"

"Look Damari, nobody else in this place sings like that. I saw how he looked at you earlier. Who else would he even allow to do what you did? You spent all that time with the old seer Iqnu when you were younger, too. Before all that business. And your mother, she wants you to, you told me that. She'll have you out of that house and out of Shomal's olives soon as anything. Won't she?"

He paused, realising he had no idea what had happened between Shomal and Yeresheth since the burial, since last night. Had there been any time for them to meet and become reconciled? Surely not yet, but perhaps later in the day?

"I don't know, Ketty. They said things to each other last night, mad things, dark hasty things in the grip of all that had happened. Both of them gone, I mean. Sannah was frightened of it all, I was frightened. I don't know where it will end. She might need me around. Both of them, but especially mother."

"I heard some of the other women talking, she won't have him taking up with that new girl, the one they brought back. That's what they're all saying, and a lot more besides. About him and her, I mean. What he was doing in the night. How he just took her off right out of your mother's house."

He looked at her curiously, seeing her slightly redden in the afternoon light but keep a look of determination. She took his hand suddenly, and her skin was warm to him.

"Ask her, Damari, see what she wants. We'll go together, if you want."

He shook his head but kept hold of her hand, enjoying the slightly fierce sound of her voice as well as the contact.

"Not today, Ketty. I don't think today is best for that. I'm all stretched thin by today and she must be worse. Anyway, she's most likely with Halith still. The two of them went off right after the stone went across."

"I know, I saw that. Halith will have got her washed up and cleaned, talked with her all this time. She'll be alright now. Don't just let this one go, Damari. Don't let Shomal just drag you down to those stupid olives."

In her urgency she had put her other hand on his shoulder, and as he looked into her face he realised how very close to him she was, how the edge of her smock was fluttering against his bare arm, how she was turned almost completely to face him. He felt slightly dizzy with her nearness, and couldn't reply. Catching something of the look in his eyes, she pulled away again, shy, and with her olive cheeks flushing.

He wondered if the shades of his brothers would be offended or amused by his being swayed by desire on the day of their burial. Perhaps they would be too busy engaging with their ancestors, taking their place in the community of the dead. Qetirah was standing up, looking down into the village. The moment had passed.

"There she is now, look Damari, there she is with Halith. It's like I said, she's all cleaned up now. You should go to her now, her and Sosanneth, I mean."

He stood beside her, watching his mother embrace Halith for a long moment and then start slowly down the short hill to her house. He nodded and turned to come off the outcrop. He climbed down and then held out his hand to steady her, but didn't move on for a moment.

"Look Ketty, I think you're right, I will talk to the seer. But look now..."

He stumbled a little on the words. "Look, look, I want to be with you, talk with you again. Up here, maybe, on this rock, or somewhere anyway. You're a good friend to me, and I want, well, I want to do this again."

She nodded, not sure about speaking, and the two held hands before going on down the hill. They parted at the first ring of houses and went their separate ways.

As Damariel arrived home he noticed that his mother had changed her clothes. The wounds on her body were clean now, but still angry and sore. She looked very weary, but rose from where she had been sitting with Sosanneth near the cooking fire. The three clung together for a long moment. Damariel looked around for Shomal, but seeing Sosanneth's warning look and quick shake of the head said nothing. He was nowhere in the house, it seemed.

"Mother, I think I should, I mean I think it's best I learn from the seer. Like you said earlier. I think you were right."

She nodded sadly and stroked his hair. "If he'll have you, you must live in his house now. I talked to Halith earlier. She and I, we talked... Well, you must ask him if you can live there. She'll put in a good word for you, but it's not her house like this is mine, it belongs to them both, with them being seers. Not like here."

"What about you and Sosanneth? I can't just leave you to manage on your own. Not now there's all this. What about..."

He stopped again, aware of Sosanneth making a little jerky shaking movement of her head. His mother had a cold air about her.

"We will manage, son. We have skill, your sister and I. We will make a living. And we have friends, other family to help out. But you will bring us, bring me and my household, more honour if you do this than if you stay here. I know you'll care for us when we need it. But this you must do. You must. Ask him today. Go on, go now while we finish preparing the meal."

She pushed him towards the door, gently but with determination, but then caught his hand as he turned to go.

"I was so proud of you today. Baruk and Bashur will rest easy because of you. I know", she hesitated as tears filled her eyes, but stumbled on, "I know you never felt of them as true kin, but you've done right by them today. My ancestors will welcome them because of you."

And so it was that Damariel moved in to the little room behind the seer's house. It was not really part of the house itself, and at first he had to share the room with some of the priest's clothing and vessels, but it was a place of his own. For all that it was small, for all that he could nearly touch both sides of the room at the same time, for all the difficult feelings circling around leaving his home, leaving Sosanneth and his mother alone, he found the freedom exhilarating.

He was acutely aware that few other men of his age could do anything other than live in their mother's home, and for the first few days an erratic string of young men of varying degrees of friendship came to see what joys came with such freedom. But as he settled in, and as he spent more time with the seer learning the songs and the sacrifices, the seasonal rhythms that governed village life and the spiritual laws that linked the two worlds, these visits grew less frequent. He had a new life, and a new sense of purpose.

Haw

DABAH YEAR 17

LIKE RUSHING TORRENTS swelling the fruit,
like orchards astride a stream,
like cardamoms planted for fragrance:
like cedars shading the waters.

DAMARIEL'S FIRST MONTHS in his new home were indeed an introduction to happiness for him. The space was small and cramped, until Saniyahu made time to move out the garments and other oddments, and organise them better inside the house. His new home had originally been just a lean-to, a little larger than the one he had used with Iqnu before, but over the years had grown slightly in comfort as one villager or another had put effort into it as part of their devotion. It had been built out from the main house and shared one wall with it. One branch of the household vine drooped towards the door.

When he moved in, it was all one space, but he had turned it into two rooms by using a cloth drape to divide sleeping quarters from a place to cook, eat, and learn as an apprentice. The two rooms were his: the entire space was his to close out the community if he wished. From time to time he did so wish, just for the novelty, but most days he preferred company. He learned too that there was never a shortage of food and drink, and that when he was not eating with Saniyahu and Halith, he was expected to take for his needs from the little piles of produce left outside the priest's house most evenings.

He also had ample time to sing, to learn the vocation of seer, and to enter into adult life. He found that the proportion of the time he spent reading, learning, and writing out the sacred songs and prayers was rather less than he had expected. Indeed, a good part of his time was devoted not to matters of the spirit, but to building up knowledge of the laws and customs that bound the village together, and bound Kephrath to the other three towns. This was not just a matter of how things were done now, but also how things had been done before the community migrated south, and the range of expectations and presumptions that the members of the towns carried into their everyday lives.

The most obvious divide was between the families that had kept northern names and those who had adopted the style of their new home, but there were other, less obvious distinctions. He was to strive to understand the needs and aspirations of every household in the village. He also became familiar, somewhat to his discomfort, with the practical skills of fasting and prayer, and made a start on the technicalities of making and repairing the musical instruments that were used.

They began to teach him, too, how to recognise when feelings, words or images drifting up in his mind at the regular worship around the stones might not just be his own thoughts, but glimpses into the world beyond. He started to learn when to voice those insights and when to remain silent and wait. There were, they assured him, always others who would speak if he was silent.

More than that, he sat by Saniyahu and Halith during the services, the short weekly gatherings and the longer celebrations for the new moons, listening to one or other of the townspeople as they would pray around the circle, or call out words they thought might come from the other side. The seer and his wife would discern which were true insights and which were not, and whether they were words for the whole community or words for just a single person or family.

Afterwards, back in the great house under the vine, the three of them would sit together and try to tease out why a choice had been made one way or another. They spent hours in prayer with each other, calling on the world beyond this one to confirm Damariel's calling. There came a time, about half a year after he began learning with them, that for the first time at the celebration he felt a little gush of new words deep within him, like a fountain opening up, and he sat there speechless with the amazement of it. This was all material that Iqnu had never introduced him to, not even hinted at, and Damariel found it both inspiring and difficult. In short, he was learning how to minister as a seer and not just sing as a minstrel, and the transition was not easy.

Saniyahu and Halith would teach him anything he wanted to learn, with no reservations about his age. It was exhilarating. It was also disturbing at times, as when he learned the full tale of his own parentage. On this particular day he had heard how Yeresheth had been barren until she lay with Iqnu at the great summer festival and conceived with the seed of the gods. Qetirah and Kothar crossed his mind, children of a mixed inheritance even as he was. Galmet and Yad-Shalim too, though he hardly knew them. He remembered Baruk on the roof of their house, wondering if Damariel had a Mitsriy father. His brother had, it seemed, not been so very far from the truth after all.

Without thinking, looking down and frowning as he absorbed the idea, he said, "Sir, have you ever done that?" and all at once remembered Halith was there with them both. He clapped his hand to his mouth and stared at her, turning red with embarrassment.

"Three times, Damariel, and Halith knows about and consented to all of them. Each time while we were serving across at Meyim. We were most particular to ensure that everyone involved, man and woman alike, knew and approved. In fact none of the children of Meyim have sprung from those unions. Iqnu practiced that particular rite rather more often than is wise for a seer in these days. And he was quite reckless in his habits, sometimes going without the knowledge or willingness of husbands and parents. As you know from the way he left this life, and perhaps from other things you have heard."

Some of Shomal's words leapt back into acute focus in Damariel's mind as he heard this.

"They say that in former generations it was a common thing at every festival, summer and winter alike, but no longer. Iqnu left behind him eight children of the gods from such alliances. Five of you are still alive, with three of you born in the same year. None of the other three towns has such a legacy, nor has done since the time of our great-grandparents."

He paused, and Damariel looked up at him in the silence which followed.

"Was this never spoken of in your house?"

Damariel shrugged.

"Not in so many words. No never, not really. All of us children knew something was different. I think now that my mother was always happier about it than Shomal."

Saniyahu nodded, and talked about the depth of feelings that could be aroused. It was as he had said to Baruk all those months ago - the old customs that might well have sanctioned the public rape and humiliation of one woman in payment for the consenting act of another had long been abandoned, but the reaction of any given family to the act could be unpredictable.

Concerning his own parentage, his mother had steadfastly maintained he was a child of the gods, a true divine gift into her closed womb that had opened the way for Baruk, Bashur and Sosanneth to follow after. But now, for the first time, he found himself wondering whether Shomal was right to see it simply as an opportunity for Iqnu to lie with a different woman. Who, after all, counted as his father? Whose family did he belong to?

After a while they went back to talking about the proper songs to be sung at each of the festivals. It became a more normal day again, except when Damariel went back in his mind to thinking about his conception. Then it was as though he had gone astray in a vast and empty space, unsure how to find a way. His imagination baulked at the thought of his mother and Iqnu lying in union at the summer festival. He had known for years that he was called child of the gods, and had never had to consider what that meant. He had tried to call Shomal "father" all his life, but the gap of alien origins had so often gaped between them.

Where did that place him in relation to Iqnu? Casual affairs happened from time to time between townspeople, especially around the times of the great festivals, and from time to time a child would be born who uneasily straddled two families: Tagi, for instance, who he knew only very vaguely. Village reputations could rise or fall depending how others around responded to the event. A man or woman might find themselves beaten, or applauded, or ostracised for a season, or held in caring sympathy. A reaction of Ethan's magnitude was extremely rare.

But, given what Saniyahu had said, he himself was not the fruit of a casual night's passion. Rather, he was the result of premeditation. But what kind of premeditation? Yeresheth had believed it was a holy act; Shomal that it was simply an abuse of the seer's office.

The main house, where they often sat if it was wet or windy, was indeed large, larger than any other house in the village, and when he had first gone into it Damariel had looked in fascination at the cluster of seven rooms that seemed to extend forever. Little pillared halls made divisions along the whole length, and white drapes could be drawn to separate one chamber from another, or else tied back to create open areas for meeting, for music or the dance. The central room was taller, extending up above the roofline of the others and rising into the decorated panels he had often looked at from the outside.

He discovered early on that the wall he shared with the couple was at one end of their bedroom. He had never in his life slept in a house on his own, and the knowledge of their closeness reassured him. With eyes shut in the quiet night he could imagine them all sharing the same living space, and the intermittent noise of voice or laughter through the wall made it a homely place. He also found, contrary to his expectation of the marital life of seers, that their relationship was lively and energetic, not at all like the static roles taken up by Iqnu and Qerith. Evenings were often marked by noisy dispute or noisy reconciliation.

The first time he heard this, half a month after moving in, he lay fearful in the dark, memories of the last time he had seen Shomal and Yeresheth together filling his heart with anxiety. He fell asleep only after long hours of straining to hear what was happening, and woke several times before the morning came, disturbed by some distant cry of owl or fox on a raid. When he went in to Saniyahu to begin lessons the next day, he had no recollection of yesterday's song, the plans Hadad, lord of the earth, was making for his palace.

The seer stopped him, and within a few minutes had found out about his anxieties. The two had been sitting that day just inside the open door in the warm morning sunshine. Saniyahu shook his head, with fondness rather than exasperation, and calling out to Halith led him through to the next room, which looked southward and was bright and airy.

She was sitting on a stool tuning a four-string lyre. She looked up from her work as the two men entered, and Damariel realised with a sudden surge of embarrassment that she had no kef on her head, and was wearing only a short linen shift that left her legs bare and her knees exposed. He felt himself blushing as he repeated in erratic fashion what he had told Saniyahu outside.

As he told the story a second time, the fears of the night seemed remote and improbable, and he felt disoriented by her as she sat listening quietly. He stumbled to the end of his explanation, feeling off balance and acutely clumsy, ready to leave the breathless room and get back into the open air. They would not let him leave, but made him talk through what had happened in Yeresheth's home, what he feared, where Shomal was living, how he had lain awake for so long in the anxious darkness.

He said most of it looking out of the window to the distant south, unable to see his former home and unwilling to look at his new hosts. At last there seemed nothing more to say, and he dragged his eyes back into the house again. There was a pause, and then Halith spoke.

"He must go and see them today. Both of them. Go to both houses. Look now, he should not learn anything today."

The seer laughed a little.

"Halith, I don't think he can learn anything today, nor remember what we all talked about together at sunset last night. Better he leaves it alone for today."

Damariel started to voice a protest. He was eager enough to see his mother, and his sister, to take them something out of his abundance, but he felt a deep unease about going to Shomal's olive field. He opened his mouth, but looking up from the floor past Halith's bare legs to the look of absolute decision on her face, framed by her dark hair, he fell silent again, and after a pause nodded.

He went to his mother's house first, taking a small collection of grain and fruit with him. Sosanneth rushed out of the door as she heard him calling, and wrapped herself around him in delight. Yeresheth came to the door, her hands covered with flour, pleasure lighting up her face. She let Damariel kiss her and then laughed as Sosanneth tried to brush off the flour dust from his smock. He looked at her, seeing how the wounds on face and arms, though healing well, were left as scars. She lifted her head slightly, aware of his scrutiny and unashamed, and the three went inside.

The women had rearranged the house inside, he realised. The room that he had shared in colder weather with the other children was now clear and nearly empty, with pieces of cloth and some weaving work in orderly piles. In the main living space the cooking area was now beside the door, with the row of storage jars along the opposite wall.

He sat on one of the stools and glanced in to the third room, seeing Sosanneth's bedding rolled up alongside Yeresheth's. Then Sosanneth was sitting beside him, leaning companionably up against him, and for a second he was back at home as he had always been, with familiar sights and smells around him. He took a long breath, happy in their company.

They shared some of the fruit, and Yeresheth added some flat rounds of bread baked that morning. Damariel left half the food in the cloth carrier, and neither of the women asked about it. Sosanneth talked eagerly about her weaving, pulling little bits of fabric and finished garments from the other room and pressing them into his hands so he could see what she meant.

He could see that she was improving rapidly, and the most recent work was of good quality. They had managed to get some dyed material from someone in the village, a friend of Nerith's, and had plans to trade some pieces up at Meyim or Giybon before the winter. Yeresheth sat back, quiet and reserved as her daughter spoke on. Eventually Sosanneth ran out of pieces of clothing and cloth, bundled them all back in the side room, and sat holding his hand again. As she had talked, he had come to realise that she was unsettled.

Damariel told them about the rhythm of life at the seer's house, of the journeys he had already made up to Jarrar's town, of times when he had to fast, or arise while it was still dark, of learning songs and poems. He said how Saniyahu gave more generously than he had promised. He started to say how different he was to Iqnu, but then could not decide how to talk about the old seer tactfully. Closing his eyes to remember, he recited for them the route from the copper mines south of the Salt Sea, up the Valley and through to Damaseq.

Then he too ran out of new things to say, since after all it was still only a few days that he had been living there. Yeresheth asked what life was like, what he ate, how much time he shared with the seer and his wife, pulling little details from him that he had not realised that he knew.

He was part way through answering her when one of the other women called from the door. Yeresheth stood up and went outside to see what she wanted. After a second she pulled the door closed behind her, and the two children could not quite hear what was being said. He put an arm round his sister and rocked her slightly.

"Sannah, what's wrong?"

She shook her head, brushed some stray threads from her sleeve, and looked away from him. He squeezed her shoulder.

"Come on, Sannah, what is it?"

"Damari, everything will work out, I'm sure."

"Maybe so, but something's not right. Sannah, what is it?"

She looked embarrassed, stared across at the room opposite with the bedding rolled up against one wall, then looked back at him rather defiantly.

"Look, Damari, I love being here with mother. We are doing so much now, you've seen it all."

He nodded and was about to reply when she hurried on. "But, Damari, she's not always so easy to live with, you know. Some days she's really angry about what happened, some days she's very cold, others it's all fine. I just never know. Can't tell. And look, Damari, we've got no men around. Father left, you left. Baruk and Bashur, well you know what happened."

She stopped, wiped her eyes with the edge of her kef, and leaned her head against his shoulder.

"You know that. I know you do, I'm just saying it again. Anyway, all in a single day there's no men around, just us two. I don't like that, I miss you all. I think we need a man to be with us here. I need, I need, oh, I don't know what I need."

He sat silent, not knowing how to reply. She suddenly looked up into his face.

"But don't you ever think of coming back. Not even for a moment. She's so proud of you being up there with the seer, talks about it to everyone who comes. I'm proud of you too. We're good really, most of the time. Just every so often I think about needing a man around the house."

They heard Yeresheth outside bidding farewell to her visitor, the cluck and rustle of the hens moving out of her way as she came back towards the door. Sosanneth gripped his arm very fiercely. "Don't you dare say a word to her about this. It's between you and me."

He shook his head and spoke quickly as the door opened.

"Look, Sannah, there's something I need to talk about with you. But we've no time now, it'll have to wait, but remind me soon."

She nodded, puzzled, as Yeresheth came back in. Sosanneth stood up and poured some water for them all. They settled back again to talking.

Much later that morning he left again, heading further down the ridge to Shomal's field and the small hut in one corner of it. As he approached, he saw Shomal working up in one of the trees. The small field was neatly kept, but plain, ordinary, unadorned, uninspired. A handful of goats were grazing lazily in a roped area to one side. He called out. Shomal turned towards him, then nodded, climbed down and came to the dry stone wall to meet him. They clasped hands briefly and Shomal nodded, shading his eyes against the sun.

"I think I might terrace that end of the field, lad, the soil is better there and I'll be able to grow onions and some green stuff. Looks alright, doesn't it? Best thing I ever did, taking these trees on. That bit of land was what that old seer Iqnu, your friend, you know, he got that for me from Emeq. Something good he did, once, hey? Next year, you'll see, I'll have this all clear. I might even get a cow from Yaraq up at Giybon. I might. What do you think? Has that priest taught you about cows yet?"

He laughed shortly and put out a hand to help Damariel over the wall, showing him where the stones were most steady. He took the bag Damariel handed him, looked inside and grunted with appreciation.

"He's looking after you then? Good on you for moving out when you did. About the only thing you've ever done to copy me, eh?"

He moved towards the hut without giving Damariel any chance to reply, and led him in. As his eyes adjusted to the dim interior, Damariel saw it was like the orchard: sparsely arranged and adequately looked after, but empty of beauty or inspiration. There was a clear area near the door, and a bed pallet and cooking area at the other end.

With sudden surprise he saw that the girl from the lowland raid was there, kneeling at the back of the room grinding flour.

As he entered she straightened her kef, stood up, and looked down at the floor. Shomal tossed the bag of produce to her without speaking and pulled two stools up near the door so the men could look out.

Damariel realised, for the first time, what a spectacular view the hut had, west of south down the valley across long ridges of short trees and bushes. He had often come down here with Baruk and Bashur to tend the trees or the goats, tackle the chores, fix the wall, but had never noticed the panorama before. Shomal saw his astonished gaze and laughed. With the benefit of recent lessons, he knew that the track down to Ayaluna and the Sea Road was in that direction, hidden by a fold in the land. From there he could recount the whole trail down to the border forts of the Mitsriy.

"Yes, it's a fine place. But you never saw that before, did you. Always rushing off somewhere again. Not like my sons."

He half-turned his head towards the girl in the shadows.

"Drinks for the two of us, and some of that bread from this morning. Oil as well. And some salt."

They sat in silence until the girl brought the little meal. Damariel tried to thank her as she turned away again, but she made no response and Shomal made an impatient gesture with his hand.

"No need for that. Fine manners, hey? If she needs a name, I call her Amat. It's what she is: it's what she does. But you came here to talk to me, not her. She won't need a name if you don't talk to her. What do you think of the place, then?"

"It is good, very good. I am very glad to have seen it, and you too. Father." He stumbled a little over the last word, and Shomal laughed shortly.

"You never could get that word out straight. I don't suppose you've come to help me out here?"

Damariel looked across the rolling waves of trees while he thought about his answer.

"No, I have not. I am apprenticed to the seer now, my time is his. If you need a pair of hands come harvest, I will ask, but my day's work is up there." He pointed up the ridge towards where the stones of the high place were standing out of sight. He paused briefly to gather some courage.

"Father, I was at my mother's house just now. I went to see her before I came down here."

The noise of flour grinding had suddenly gone quiet behind him. Shomal looked sideways at him with some suspicion, but spoke first into the back of the room.

"Finished all that barley, have you? There's plenty more yet. Look behind the basket there." He shook his head. "And how is my daughter? How's my Sannah?"

"Well enough. She is learning to weave, has some skill, I think, from what she showed me. She's doing well. I think she would be glad enough to see you."

"She knows the way down here. She could do her weaving bits down here too. I could build another room on the side, look, there, along that flat stretch. Plenty of building stones if I wanted. Keep her stuff dry, and it's a bit nearer the stream. I might do it anyway, don't you think? Be worth making this place bigger."

Damariel felt that the conversation was escaping him.

"She'll not want to leave our mother. She's happy there, and they work well together. All the weaving and making clothes they've started. She's only young still, she'll not be wanting to leave home yet. Or at all. That house is her future."

"So why isn't this place home for her?"

He waved away Damariel's words before he could speak.

"Oh, I know, that is her mother's house, and her mother's before that, and so on through eight generations or whatever it is. Oh, I heard that one enough times. Lost count of it all. Good for you to get out now and make something new, even if it is singing and all that. How long do you have to do that? Priest's work gets to be man's work, doesn't it? When will you be meeting our chieftain and getting him to do things differently? Has the seer taken you to meet the chief yet? You want to get in with him now, you know, to get things done differently. Or the other seers? And you'll get all the other benefits you might want. Sure you will."

He laughed uneasily, rather harshly, looking out towards the horizon, and there was a long pause before he continued.

"No shortage of benefits for the likes of you, you can just have whatever you want. Walk along Iqnu's path if you want."

He turned again to look at the girl, finishing pouring barley flour into a clay jar and then pulling a small sack of whole grains towards the pair of stones to start on the next batch. He grinned.

"She does all right here, you know. Keeps me happy, has the place to herself most days. Knows her way round the housework alright. And other things. Still my house, though, Nobody else's."

He laughed shortly, then turned back and looked straight at Damariel.

"Did she, you know, that woman, your mother, did she send you down here to get me back?"

Damariel shook his head, taken aback at the suggestion.

"No, not at all. Look, sir, Sannah misses you. I don't know what happened that day. I had wicked dreams last night, all from under the earth, all of them. Bad dreams half the night, and when I was awake all I could hear was you two arguing all those many times. Especially that last night. I don't know what you can do to make it right, but mother isn't coming down here any time soon. You have to do it, you have to go back up there, you, not her. To make things right with Sannah, at least."

There was silence in the little house, a long silence in which some distant crows could be heard complaining at the noise of children playing in the stream. Damariel could see Amat absolutely still at the back of the house, her hand frozen pulling the barley sack across the floor. In the end Shomal spoke.

"Next time you come, maybe you could bring some dried fruit. See if that priest has some. I have a mind I could make good wine this autumn. Her there can pick some berries and I'll put grapes with them. Maybe I'll put in some fruit bushes in that corner there. Gets the sun most of the day. No fruit this year of course, but they'll do well next summer. I know bushes north of here along the old track that'll do me this year. Bring me some raisins, if you can, they'll help it along. You know, I think I'm going to do a wood store along that other wall when the olives are all in. See those stones over there? They'll be my wood store for when the winter comes. I'll make it soon, you'll see next time you come. If Baruk was here he'd have done it. I know he would. He had all kinds of ideas. Never had the chance."

The grind-stone had begun to circle again over the barley. Damariel bowed his head, feeling defeated and sorrowful concerning his brothers.

"Of course I will bring the fruit. If there is any. I won't know until the day. With your leave, I must go now."

"Still early?"

He could see his father beginning the formal motions of bidding farewell, and with an inner ache he replied in kind.

"I have been honoured. Peace and blessings on the house."

"The honour is mine."

Damariel trudged back along the ridge to his new home, his thoughts as scattered as the swallows flitting high above. Halith was sitting outside the house finishing some cross-stitching on a long sash. He looked at it curiously, seeing the pattern of yellow and blue thread running along the length. She was working on a little stylised lioness at one end of the sash. Its partner was already in place at the other, complete with a goddess standing on its back, arms raised high over her head. Qedeshet, he thought, looking at the design and matching it in his mind with the image on the necklace that Halith wore sometimes.

She looked up as his shadow crossed the path ahead of her, smiled up at him and held the needle in place while she dragged another stool across beside hers. He looked inside the open door as she sat again on her stool, just inside the shade of the roof.

"Is Saniyahu here? I wanted to, well, I could do some of that lesson now. I'd like to make up the time from this morning."

She finished a series of gold stitches down the animal's back and cast the thread off.

"He's gone up the track to Jarrar's town. He won't be back until tomorrow."

"I didn't know he was going. I would, I mean I could have gone with him."

"A runner came down from Jarrar's seer this morning after you left, wanted him up there to talk. Something urgent. One of us went and the other stayed." She saw his disappointment, and stood up again. "Come on, I've done all I want to do to this for today. The lord Hadad's palace, wasn't it, you were doing last night? Had he made his opening in the roof beams yet?"

She laughed at his expression.

"Did you think all I did was dance to his singing? I know the songs as well as he does, some of them a whole lot better. Of course you must learn from him when he's here, but for today you and I can sing together."

She led him in to the house, where she had tied all the drapes back to let the light breeze blow coolness through the rooms. She picked up a timbrel from a table and sat facing him on a stool, and he started to learn the song again to the pattern of her percussion. Gradually he lost his sense of strangeness as the two of them sang through the whole cycle, from the start up to yesterday's lesson.

She carried on for a few verses after he stopped. Her singing voice was higher than her speaking voice, and he leaned back enjoying her melody running like a river as her hand rippled across the timbrel. He realised her eyes had closed as she sang and played, so she was slow to notice he had stopped. She stopped, and laughed a little.

"I need to move about. You play this and sing from the start. I'm going to dance."

"I've never played one of these before."

She frowned and pushed it into his hands.

"Just play it anyway, just hold it here, like this in your left hand and keep a simple beat going with the right. Use the palm of your hand here, your fingers there. Nothing too fancy, you can learn that later. You can call this your lesson for the day, if you like. First steps in timbrel playing."

She picked up two long ribbons from the table, slipped off her sandals, and looked at him. He took a deep breath and started the song, trying to maintain a steady rhythm and remember the words at the same time. She paused, hands high in the air and the ribbons at her side like Qedeshet on the lion's back, until he had got past the first words of invocation and settled into the song's body. Then she was moving like a bird, like one of the swallows he had seen earlier, and the white ribbons were her wings, filling the room with lightness caught from the open windows. He watched in wonder, barely able to keep singing as she danced the song around him through the pillared house.

He stopped again where his knowledge drew to a close, and the skin of the timbrel eased into silence. She stopped too after a few steps more, off to one side, her wings fluttering down through the sunlit air to alight in little curls around her.

She was breathing quickly, her face a little flushed with exertion and her feet dusty from the dry floor. Her eyes were unfocused, gazing somewhere beyond the room. He could think of nothing to say, until all at once she was back inside herself, and she looked at him, seeing him there once again.

"That is so much better. Lovely, thank you."

She rolled up the long ribbons, and put them and the timbrel back in their places. She was breathing normally again, and she laughed as she straightened her kef where her hair had escaped during the dance and tightened her sash a little.

"I'm going down to the stream to bathe my feet. Are you coming, Damari?"

He shook his head, suddenly feeling afraid of the intimacy, deciding that foot washing should be a private matter. Surely he would be out of place there. She bent to pick up her sandals and then went, leaving him sitting in the corner of the room. He sat there for a few moments, and then, as he often did given the chance, wandered from room to room, revelling in the spaciousness of the house. He was never wholly sure if all of the rooms were permitted to him, but neither the seer nor his wife had ever spoken of this, so he went from storage room to shrine to bedroom to kitchen with no sense of hesitation.

Upstairs was the big room where, so he had been told, the four seers and their wives met and stayed overnight all together when they came down the hill. He climbed part-way up the ladder and looked in before scrambling down again. At length he found himself outside again, where Halith's needlework still waited on the stool. He opened the door to his own rooms to let the air circulate, and stood outside them, on his own and with no task to perform. He paused, uncertain, until drawn by happy memory he went up onto the lookout crag above the settlement and lay down in the shade of one of the juniper trees. There he dozed in the dreamy afternoon, drifting away with slow, aimless summer thoughts.

A few nights later there was a feast, a celebration for the short nights of summer. The village at work during the day became more and more light-hearted, turning into the village at play. Heaps of food began to gather at the high place. Men who had been away on the ridges with flocks or to hunt came back early, began roasting three gazelles that had been caught. Women abandoned the routine tasks of the day, and children dashed in great groups here and there, swarming with borrowed energy and gathering flowers to lay in heaps.

Saniyahu and Halith went to four or five houses and gathered some men to play the stringed instruments, some women to play the timbrel and hand-drum. Damariel gave up pretending to learn one of the ritual prayers and helped here and there as he could. Two years ago he had first been allowed to take part in this feast, but that year and last year he had just eaten and drifted off with the other boys. This year was different. This year there was Qetirah to think of.

The sun was low in the sky, hanging like a great red fruit in the western sky, when Saniyahu took up a ram's horn and blew a long blast on it. A cheer went up from the people surrounding him, shrieks of delight from the children. As the sound died away the group of musicians started to play. People gathered round the flat stones and the piles of food among the garlands of flowers. Damariel saw Qetirah on the other side of the clearing beside her parents, her hair just visible along the rim of her creamy white kef, her little bronze brooch pinned onto her smock. He started to work his way round the people and stones towards her, when Kothar suddenly caught his arm.

"Damari, I need your help."

For a brief moment Damariel thought about refusing his friend and carrying on round to Qetirah, but at that moment some of the other young women came up to her and she turned half away from him. He wasn't even sure she had seen him heading towards her, so he sighed and turned to Kothar.

"What is it, then, Kothar?"

"Look, Damari, you know Shaharti?"

"You mean Emeq and Ayala's daughter, Uzziel's younger sister?"

"Yes, yes, that's the girl I mean. Give you half a chance and you'll be telling me all her ancestry. But look now, I want to get some time with her tonight, slip off out of the circle with her for a while."

He grinned expansively.

Damariel looked at him.

"And so? What, you need me to hold your hand?"

Kothar laughed in his rather superior way.

"No, hardly! But look now, you can be sure that Uzziel will be watching her, as it's her first year here. I don't want him holding my hand either. I need you to distract him, talk to him about something, I don't know what. Just keep him busy when I give you the nod."

Damariel spread out his hands. "No promises, Kothar. It all depends how vigilant he is. But look, if you want to distract him, you'd be better off talking to Gazala, Kunor's sister. He's more likely to want to talk with her than me."

Kothar nodded slowly. "Gazala, eh? I didn't know that. Thanks, Damari, Kunor owes me a favour from the spring."

He turned and started to work his way back again through the crowds. Damariel looked about for Qetirah, and saw she was amongst a group of the younger women, forming into a circle to dance. The music changed into a dance rhythm for them, and he saw Halith slipping between groups of people to join the women's circle.

Someone caught his hand from behind, and he turned to find that Yeresheth and Sosanneth had arrived. He hugged them both, and Sosanneth ran off to join Gazala in the circle, vivid, alive with excitement, a bright red sash belted tightly round her waist gathering her smock together. Yeresheth hung back, but Nerith caught sight of her, came over, took her hands and drew her into a circle of older women that was forming.

He leaned back against one of the upright stones, watching as three circles of women danced in the central area, hands linked, weaving around the four flat stones in the middle. Halith was in the middle of all of them, dancing among the stones, keeping time with a little hand drum. She was calling out the words of one of the old songs, line by line, with the other women echoing after her. Some of the men started gathering off to one side and clapping with her drum-beat, gradually gathering more in as they noticed.

Damariel went over to join them, and suddenly saw Shomal briefly in the shadows behind one of the nearby houses. He stood there for a few heartbeats, half hidden behind the wall, then turned and went away again down the hill. Damariel thought briefly about following him, but Kothar called out and waved from where he was standing near Kunor, and instead he went to join them.

The men were forming their own circles now, and started their own dance, energetic and loud, hands raised, with white cloths like little banners in their hands waving here and there. They circled one way and the other, arms across each others shoulders, getting steadily faster as they circled until the musicians could no longer keep up. Damariel found himself laughing helplessly beside Kothar as the circles dissolved. The musicians took a break, and Damariel went to get himself some fruit and wine. Kothar had moved across to be near Shaharti, but Uzziel was standing between the two of them. Damariel looked around for Qetirah but could not see her.

The moon, almost full, had risen over the hills east of the village, and the red western sky was fading. Some torches were lit here and there. The younger children were gathered off towards homes as darkness fell. Damariel watched Sosanneth and Yeresheth talking: saw his sister's anxious, stubborn expression relaxing as Yeresheth nodded.

In the quieter lull after the first dancing, Halith moved out again to the stones, with a double pipe in her hands. She had taken her kef off and unbound her hair, and as she moved through the grass in bare feet, Damariel thought she looked as the Lady Taliy must have looked, rising like the dew to moisten the hard and barren land on the first morning of the world.

She played a slow, haunting piece that drifted around the high place like the primordial mist. There was a little collective sigh as she finished, the top of the ridge quite dark now, lit by the fires where the gazelles had roasted, by the flickering torches, and by the moon.

Damariel leaned against one of the taller stones, watching the people flow around him, watching little groups talking, romancing pairs slipping into the shadowed edges of the circle.

Sosanneth, her red sash throwing back the firelight, was with a friend in the middle of a group of the younger men: Uzziel, he noticed, was not with them, but was off to one side talking closely with Gazala. Kothar and Shaharti were nowhere in sight, and he laughed to himself. He heard quick footsteps behind him, and turned to find Qetirah there.

He took her hand and stepped round behind the nearest of the stones. They were out of the firelight, and her face was lit only by the moon. Halith had not looked so lovely when she came out to play her pipes: surely even Taliy had not looked like this. He opened his mouth to say something, when they heard voices approaching the stone from the other side. Quickly they slipped further out of the circle, further into the friendly shadows, across to the rocky outcrop they had climbed on the day Baruk and Bashur were buried, scrambled up it onto the grassy top.

They sat together there in silence for a while, looking down into the high place where little groups of dancers were reforming now. Their shoulders touched, and cautiously he put his arm around her. She leaned into him and sighed.

"I've not got long, Damari. My parents will see I'm gone before too long, then I'll have to go back home and look after our Laylah for them while they stay out."

He nodded, rested his head on top of hers where she was tucked into the curve of his shoulder.

"I wish we could just stay here."

She squeezed his hand, then suddenly sat up.

"Look, isn't that your sister there, with the wood-worker's son Qeren? Do you think she likes him? You don't think there's something there now?"

He shook his head and circled her with his arm again.

"I don't think so, Ketty, they've known each other since they were babies, been good friends a long time. That's more like a brother-sister dance, nothing more special."

She half-turned her head towards him, her dark eyes large below the edge of the creamy kef.

"We've known each other since we were babies. Are we like brother and sister too?"

He shook his head and touched her cheek where a wisp of hair had drifted out from below the kef. Her face was very close to his, her eyes wide. She moved a little closer, and they kissed. The kiss seemed to go on for a very long time, when suddenly they heard Kinreth's voice calling from nearby. Qetirah pulled away and straightened her smock, looking annoyed.

"Oh, that's mother. Now I shall have to go and look after Laylah. And she'll be asleep and never know if I'm there or not. Oh, it's not fair. She really doesn't need me."

She moved towards the edge of the rock to climb down, and he started to follow her.

"No, Damari, no, she mustn't know about you just now. You stay here until I've gone away with her. Just stay here and she'll not know we were together."

She turned, started to scramble down the side of the outcrop, then stopped and reached out her hand to him. They held hands briefly before she continued on down. He moved away from the rock edge and heard her scurrying round the base of the crag before calling out.

"Over here, mother, I'm just coming. Behind you. Oh look, is it time already for me to look after Laylah, then? Surely it's not so late as that?"

Their voices faded to one side, and peeping over the edge Damariel watched Kinreth go a short distance down the hill towards their house, then stand and wait while Qetirah carried on alone. Then Kinreth turned, picked up the hem of her long skirt and ran eagerly back up towards the high place, legs and feet flickering pale in the light of the moon through the summer trees.

Damariel ducked down again as she passed near him, then turned over on his back and looked up at the stars. He heard the music change again, recognising Saniyahu's touch on the lyre with only a little drum beat accompanying.

He looked over the rock edge, seeing little groups of dancers moving to and fro. He caught a glimpse of Sosanneth's red sash in one of the groups, saw Kinreth join Caleb and put her arm round him. He couldn't see his mother. Halith was back in the middle of the stones, dancing like silver in the moonlight with the timbrel held high above her head. He sighed and looked away again. He did not want to go back into the crowds of people, but wanted to stay just where he had kissed Qetirah.

The next day he woke late. He had not bothered to pull his door properly shut, and there was a bright pool of sunlight angled onto the floor. He got up, splashed water over himself, and ate a piece of bread with some of yesterday's fruit. There was no sound from Saniyahu and Halith, and he realised he had no idea when they had got back to their house.

He pulled a stool out into the sunlight and began copying a poem from a very worn clay tablet onto a wooden frame. The work was absorbing, and quite difficult, but he was still aware of people starting to come and go about the village as the day, very slowly, got under way. Before long Kothar came walking up the main track towards him. He put the frame down, stretched, and got up to meet his friend, who had a pleased air about him.

"You were absolutely right about Gazala, Damari. Worked like a dream."

"So you made yourself time with Shaharti, then? How was that? What happened?"

He regretted the question as soon as he had spoken, and Kothar laughed.

"Who's asking? Are you her father or something? What's it to you?"

Damariel laughed a little awkwardly. They sat down together. Kothar looked briefly at the wooden frame but was not very interested. Instead he talked about how he was going down the ridge with some of the older men to catch game later that day, where they would set traps, what bait they would use. Damariel was only pretending to listen, his thoughts elsewhere, when he realised Kothar had just spoken Caleb's name. He replied without thinking.

"Ketty's father, you mean? I didn't know he hunted. She hasn't talked about that."

Kothar looked at him quizzically.

"No, Damari, I was saying he had given us some metal clasps for the trap, not that he'd be coming with us. What tree were you climbing just now?" Suddenly he slapped his hand on his knee. "Of course, you've been after Qetirah, haven't you now? How did that go last night? I lost track of you, had other things to think about."

Damariel laughed uneasily, thought for a moment, unwilling to talk to Kothar about their kiss, and then said, "Well, so are you her father now?"

Kothar slapped his shoulder and leaned back against the wall.

"Ah me, Damari, that's good, coming from you. Good answer, and I deserved every word of it. Well, it's your secret, then. But look now, if I was Sosanneth's brother I'd be keeping a watch out for her. "

"What do you mean?"

Kothar looked at him oddly.

"Didn't you see her last night? Mixing with some of the older lads? She stayed on after your mother went home." He paused. "Well, it's nothing to do with me, of course. I'm just saying that you don't know who she's talking to."

"Someone like you, I suppose?"

"Come on, Damari, I'm trying to help you out here. Shomal wasn't there, was he, he wasn't looking out for her. You'd disappeared, to who knows where. She was there on her own."

Damariel sighed.

"But nothing happened, right? She's fine."

"Yes she is. Danced a bit, flirted with some of the boys, drank more wine than she's used to. Anyway, when I got back a bit later she was sitting off to one side so I sat with her for a bit. Took her down to your mother's house when she got tired. Made sure she got in home alright. She's fine. I'm just saying to you, that's all. You might keep more of an eye on your sister."

"Kothar, you're good to us. I do appreciate it, really. Thank you. I'll talk to mother sometime when she's not around. But really, I think you're looking for squirrels in the clouds. She's alright. It was her first summer dance. Of course she was excited. She'd made mother promise she could stay late. Had that new red sash and all. Kothar, she really needs something just now to make her feel good, what with Shomal taking up with that lowland girl."

At that point Saniyahu emerged from the door of the main house and greeted the two boys. He looked around at the untidiness lying still all around the sacred stones of the high place, shrugged, and sat down with them in the patch of sunshine just outside the shade of the vine leaves. They could hear Halith inside clattering some pots and putting some water to boil. Kothar, slightly abashed to be with the seer, answered a few questions in short, halting sentences, and before long made an excuse to go. Saniyahu watched him amble away through the houses as Halith brought three bowls of herb infusion out and sat with them to drink.

"Damariel, now that the summer dance is over, I think you could come with me up past Sychem towards Hermon. North, quite a long way. We'll be gone quite a few nights, half a month maybe, so pack for a long trip and tell your family you'll be away. On the way I'll take you to the three towns so you can meet the other seers properly. We'll make a good trip of it. I'm not needed back here now until, oh, until the night of the new moon."

Damariel nodded and spilled some of the drink as he began to get excited about the trip. Saniyahu looked at him curiously.

"Didn't Iqnu ever take you up that way? He told me once he meant to."

"No, never. One day he said he'd take me to Hatsor for one of the feasts. He used to talk about going up to one of the big pilgrimage sites every so often, but we never did that either. He did take me to Giybon once for the day, but no further. Oh yes, and he did make me learn all the routes for when we would make the journey. Maybe they'll come in useful now after all?"

"They certainly will. May this your first real journey be the first of many."

The three of them touched the drinking bowls and drank together. Life was buoyant.

Waw

Merap Year 17

Like a lily seen among the brambles,
so I see my delight among the daughters.
Like an apricot found in the wide woodland,
so I find my sweetheart among the sons.

DAMARIEL AND QETIRAH had been up on their lookout rock since the late afternoon. He had been away with Saniyahu for a week, down the trail this time to Bayth Shamsh and beyond instead of northward, and he had been telling her all about the journey.

She had never been further than Woodlands, and wanted to hear much more detail than he could remember about the town. He described what he could of the houses, how they differed from the familiar ones of Kephrath, the market area that stretched further in one direction than their whole village, the shrines laid out here and there.

It was good to be spending the time together, here in the homely place where they had first enjoyed mid-summer kisses. They were also both very nervous, because of their plans for the night, and were filling in time with idle conversation.

Qetirah had just made Damariel recite the route list from Bayth Shamsh down to Gedjet by way of the coast road, and then had tried to remember all of the stages to repeat back to him. She had finally arrived at Gedjet, albeit by a most unusual route weaving to and fro across the coastal plain. He had then gone over the list again, together with the extra details that helped the memory by breathing life into the empty names themselves.

There was a chill in the Merap air, and the days had been shorter than the nights for some weeks. This place had become like a second home for them, a shared home since the kiss, and today, like so many other days, they had brought some bread and olives to eat together in the setting sunlight.

Damariel was sitting near the edge of the rock, and Qetirah lay on her side facing him, arranging olive stones in little groups with a serious expression, like a miniature high place looking down over the great stones below. The olives themselves had long gone.

The sun was setting now, the evening breeze was beginning to strengthen, and he watched the fringe on her kef ripple in little waves around her face. The light was fading fast. She looked up at him and stretched out a hand towards him. He took a deep breath.

"Ketty, look, I think we could go on down now. The light will be gone soon."

He found his mouth suddenly dry as he reached out to take her hand. It was cool in the breeze, and she gripped him tightly, urgently.

"Don't look so serious, Damari."

He laughed a little nervously, and ducked as she threw an olive stone at him with her free hand. He squeezed her hand and they stood up together. Her dress fluttered in a sudden gust of the west wind, and she tightened the sash at her waist.

An anxious expression crossed her own face, then smoothed away as he cupped his hand round her cheek. She took his hand in hers and pressed it against her body. They helped each other down the craggy edges of the rock, then kissed where the rock hid them from the houses.

The light was fading rapidly, but once they had clambered down from the top, the path was easy to follow. They did not go back the direct route towards her house, across the high place and through between some of the village houses, but circled round the edge of the ridge to the north amongst the low scrub.

Nobody would see them together on that path. No other house overlooked the track. The door was on the western side of the house, away from the next house. It was like their own secret path leading them among the hills, a way to follow, their own personal route list. It was sure to get them unseen all the way from their lookout rock round the outskirts of the village to her house, all the way into her room, into her bed.

Qetirah's parents were both away. Caleb was away with the chief, trading small metalwork up at Sychem, and Kinreth was visiting a cousin with little Laylah.

Her house was empty. Her room would be empty just now, until they went together to fill it. They held hands on the way from the rocky outcrop round the gulley and then the short distance up to her house from the far side, hearts beating, wordless.

At the door, she held back a trailing sprig of her mother's hibiscus plant, reached her hand into the recess in the doorframe and released the latch. She went in and then turned, looking rather formal, one hand straightening her kef as she invited him into her house, a princess within her palace.

He accepted the invitation and crossed the threshold, his head brushing the last red flowers clinging to the branches. Other late petals, already fallen, lay here and there in odd angles of the walls, and little seed-pods, mostly split open, were scattered about.

The sky above them was shining, intensely blue still, even though the sun had now gone behind the western horizon and the ground around them was dark. In the east, stars were beginning to show against the darker sky, and a part moon was emerging brighter as the daylight faded.

Inside, the house looked much like his mother's, with a different collection of cooking vessels, and pieces of metal work instead of fabric, but immediately homely. It was familiar; he had often seen the house before, but it had never seemed so vivid, so immediately pressing on his senses.

He glanced around the main area, seeing some tools and other equipment, one room opening to his left, and a second one ahead separated with a long drape. Remembering earlier times in the house, he knew it concealed the extra room with Caleb's furnace.

To his right was another room, this one with several kefs belonging to Qetirah and Laylah hanging from a peg beside the door frame. Qetirah saw him looking around and nodded shyly.

"That's where I, that's where we, well, that's my room."

He nodded, unsure what to say, and she busied herself with some clay pots.

"Look, mother left some bread and stew here. I'll heat it up for us."

He nodded again, this time on safer ground, and held out the little bag he had brought from the seer's house.

"Here, Ketty, some fresh figs and dried dates for after."

She took the bag and piled the fruit into a clay bowl nearby. For a while they were busy with domesticity, and the smell of hot bread, beans and herbs filled the little room like incense. They ate sitting down on stools that Qetirah gathered from the side room from among the tools, leaning against the wall beside the door to her room, shoulders touching, talking about this and that.

Their conversation began to ebb a little as the meal drew to a close. The last spoons of stew, the last morsels of bread, seemed to take an age to complete. There was no more to eat. Damariel took the plates and put them beside the kitchen fire, making sure it was covered over.

Qetirah poured them each a little red wine from a stoppered jar. They drank it very solemnly, eyes fixed on one another. She took one of the figs and pulled it in two, giving half to Damariel. He held the fruit in his hand briefly, caught by the dark flesh speckled with seeds. When they had finished he took another fig and did the same, this time keeping hold of it for her to eat, feeling her lips against his fingers.

Then they were kissing again, and the sweetness of the figs and the wine was shared on the breath between them. Their kissing grew more urgent, until she pulled away, stood up, and held back the cloth draped across her door. He held her hand, took a deep breath, and the two went into her room.

The room was small and quite plain, with a single window looking out northward over the distant hills. A pale light still hung in the western sky, but the brighter arc of the moon now reigned without equal among the stars. The moonlight picked out the tree branches, mostly bare, some few leaves still clinging here and there. He turned away from the view outside and looked at Qetirah.

She was standing in the middle of the room, clear in the pale light of the window, standing quite still beside her unrolled bedding, with her hands at her sides. Another bedroll, Laylah's, he supposed, was still rolled up against another wall. He took a step towards her and then stopped, entranced at the sight of her.

As he paused she slowly, deliberately untied the knot of her kef where it rested on her left shoulder, unwound it from her throat, lifted it from her head, and draped the empty white cloth across a wicker basket beside the bedclothes.

Released, untied, her dark hair hung loosely at her shoulders. Damariel gazed at her. He had not seen her bare-headed since they had played together with all the other naked children in the stream when they were five years old. He was wordless, and took another step towards her.

She smiled, a little shyly at the eager passion in his face, and lifted up her face to catch the light as he stepped closer again. She ran her hands loosely through her hair, and then reached out to him. Hesitantly he took his own kef off and laid it alongside hers on the basket, where they lay draped together, touching here and there. He took her hands, drew her closer to him, held her against him.

They kissed again, delicately and softly at first, but with increasing ardour. Then somehow her sash came loose and the fastenings of her dress were undone, and the curves of her body were pressing against him, like silver in the moonlight from the window.

She put her hand between them, against his mouth, and stood quite still for a moment. Then she moved lithely out of his arms, wriggled the last wrappings of cloth from her waist and thighs, and slipped partly under the blanket.

The moon cast shadow-branches from the tree outside, dancing like fingers across her breasts as she held out her arms to him in invitation.

He stripped the last of his own clothes away, lifted the blanket and settled into her bed beside her, holding her close against him. His heart was pounding with desire, his lips were full of her sweetness.

They lay side by side for what seemed a long while, enjoying each other's kisses and caresses, and then she rolled onto her back, there was a moment's uncertainty, and then their delight, their union, became complete.

The light of the moon edged round away from the window. Qetirah was in his arms, wrapped closely against him, her eyes a little moist. In the darkening room it was becoming harder to see each other. He kissed her forehead.

"Shall I get a lamp?"

"No, let me go, it'll be easier for me to find it."

She got up, picked up her kef to hold against her, moved by some sudden impulse of modesty, and went to the kitchen area. He heard her moving things about, a rattle of pottery, and then saw the light of a flame strengthen on the other side of the door frame.

She walked carefully back in and set the lamp on a stool to one side before slipping back naked beside him under the blanket. He watched the flame shiver in a light breeze from the window, cast shifting shadows across her bare arms. She touched his face.

"Damari, what will we do if I have a baby?"

He caressed her cheek.

"Not much chance."

"Tagi down the track is pregnant, and she says she only went with Dadua the one time. Well, so she says."

He hugged her.

"Then I'd marry you before anyone realised. You'd know before anyone else, wouldn't you, and we could get it all arranged. Nobody would know."

She laughed a little, but a note of anxiety underlay her tone.

"Damari, people can count, you know. I don't think we'd fool anyone about that. But see, would you come and live here then? Not just one night, I mean. Always."

He stopped and thought about it before answering quite slowly.

"Well, I don't know what Saniyahu and Halith would say. I suppose, well, I suppose I would answer to them about that now. Not mother any more. Maybe you would be able to live up at the house by the high place."

He became more enthusiastic, caressed her cheek.

"That's a better idea. There's ever so many rooms up there, you know. I'm sure they'd give us one if we were together up there. Maybe two. I could move in with you from the little outside room. I'm sure they'd do that for us."

She was silent, looking up at the stars outside the window.

"I wonder what mother would say? I mean, if you weren't apprenticed to them then she would first have to agree to it, to us I mean, and then you would move in here with me. Into this room. We'd find somewhere for Laylah. Our two mothers would sort something out between our families. You know how it all works. But you see, she's been talking to me about me being the daughter of the house since I was ever so little. It's like she had her heart set on me following on after her. What would happen about all that? If I was living up there with you, could I still be mother of the house? Of this house?"

Her expression was very serious. Damariel shook his head slowly.

"I just don't know, Ketty. Never thought about it before. I never had too, and I never heard anyone talking about it. No reason they would talk about it, I suppose. Do you want me to talk to Saniyahu and Halith? They'd know."

"What, and tell them just exactly what we've been doing tonight? I don't think so, I don't think they should know just yet."

She laughed and ran her hand down his arm, then suddenly stopped and half sat up in bed, looking at him.

"Damari, you don't have to tell him, do you, with them teaching you and all? It's not something they would make you talk about even if you didn't want to? Like some sort of confession or something that you have to do."

He shook his head and she settled back again.

He thought about her words.

"Ketty, are you ashamed?"

"No, not at all, not here with you. But look, I don't want everyone talking about it all around the town and in the streets. This is for us, not for gossip around the well."

"Well, I don't have to tell them anything I don't want to. I mean, that you don't want me to. It's up to me. But they might guess, Halith especially, it's hard keeping anything from her. But even if they do work it out, they won't tell anyone."

She nodded, accepting his answer, and after a while he nudged her and spoke again.

"Look, Ketty, have we really only got one night here like this?"

"Oh yes. Father won't be back for two or even three days, but mother and Laylah will be here mid-morning tomorrow. Anyway, you have to go before the proper light comes tomorrow, round the back again like how we came here. Not up the main street where everyone will see you."

"I know. I can do that. But what about after tonight? Could you come up to the great house by the stones sometime when Saniyahu and Halith go to see one of the other seers? They do that quite often, at least once a month, sometimes more."

"I can't come up to the house by the high place just like that. In the evening, with them away at one of the other towns and just you there? Someone would be sure to see me coming or going. We might as well just tell everyone now. That won't work at all. Hardly private, is it?"

He lay back, looking up at the ceiling.

"Well, then we'll have to meet somewhere else for a while. Look, I know. Kothar was telling me about a little hut the shepherds used to use a few years ago. The pasturing is not so good there any more, so the hut is never lived in now. It's not far along the track, following the ridge south from here. I could show you where, it would be our own private place, nobody else would know about it. We could take some bits and pieces along with us to make it more comfortable."

"As long as we don't meet your friend Kothar there. Not so private then."

"What do you mean?"

She giggled and turned on her side towards him. He caught his breath as she squeezed his hand and her body brushed against him.

"Well, perhaps I shouldn't say, you being his good friend and all."

He looked at her quizzically, and she continued.

"Well, I've been spending a lot of time with Shaharti recently. You know, Uzziel's sister. Now, according to her, Kothar wanted to take her up to an old shepherd's hut. On her own. I'm sure you can guess what he had in mind for the two of them. Well, that's what she thought, anyway, when he talked about it. It has to be the same place. This was a week or so ago, maybe she's gone along with his persuasion by now, who knows?"

"But he can't be there every day."

"Don't you dare arrange something with him about who's going when. That's a sure way to make sure the whole village knows. Anyway, what I was going to say was that Shaharti wasn't sure about going with him. She just doesn't know whether she'd be the only girl he took along there. You know what he can be like."

She caressed his face teasingly and wriggled closer to him, sensuous and eager.

"You wouldn't know about that, would you, so I could set her heart at ease? You might know all kinds of things like that."

Damariel thought about Kothar and smiled, enjoying the intimacy, delaying his reply for a while so he could feel her pressed against him.

"I'm sure I couldn't say. But he has been talking about Shaharti for quite a long time now, ever since that dance where we first kissed each other. He wanted me to organise something for him with her then. That was the first time I heard him talking about her. What do you think? You don't think he'd be faithful to her?"

"I'm just saying what she thought. She said she wouldn't mind going with him, you know, she thought she'd like that and that he'd be good to her. But she didn't want to think he'd be there with someone else a few days later."

"I really don't know, Ketty, sorry. He just told me about this place, he never said he's been there with anyone himself. Even if he has, he's not likely to tell me about it. But look, I started talking about it because it's somewhere that we could go to, not anyone else. I want there to be somewhere we can go once tonight is over."

The night passed. Neither slept very much, and both were caught up in a feeling that this precious time together should not be wasted. Damariel woke suddenly to see the first grey light starting to slip into the sky outside the window. The branches of the tree were beginning to show against the paler background.

He nudged Qetirah awake, and they found time for one last, urgent expression of passion before he scrambled from the bed and started to gather his clothes together. She sat up in bed watching him dress, leaning against the wall beside her. Glancing hastily out of the window at the steadily increasing daylight, he got his kef completely muddled and gave up.

He knelt beside her, kissed her one last time, and then slipped out of the door and back around by the path through the scrub, back along the route they had chosen.

She was looking down at him, framed by the window overlooking the path, her own kef draped elegantly across her bare shoulders, and he waved as he ran back towards the high place. Nobody saw him, though morning village noises were starting to emerge from some of the houses, and a dog barked once, off to his right.

As he rounded the house by the high place he heard Saniyahu and Halith talking from their kitchen area. Very quietly, trying to avoid the noisy stones on the path up to their door, he went past the front of the house and along the side wall back to his room. He couldn't hear their conversation, but he thought he went by them without them noticing. He opened and closed his door very quietly, and lay down on his own bed, daydreaming with memories of the night.

He emerged again after a while, trying to look as though he had just woken. He felt extremely weary, and extremely happy. The sky was clear, invigorating and bright with the morning sunshine. The village had come alive while he had been inside, and men and women were out and about their work.

Halith was outside the door of the house working on cross-stitch patterns across the shoulders of a tunic. The sash with its pair of lion-riding goddesses, which she had finished a few months ago, was across her lap so she could match the pattern. Seeing him, she called Saniyahu, who emerged from inside with an old clay tablet and a freshly waxed writing frame. Damariel looked at it blankly.

"You don't remember, do you?"

Damariel shook his head, unable to remember anything at all from before the previous afternoon.

"You're going to copy out part of the story of Kirtu. And then we were going to talk about it when you were done."

The memory returned, rather sluggishly. Damariel took the items, sat near Halith in the sunshine, and started work. The little letters on the clay tablet were very small, and had not been well-formed by the writer. He peered at the start of the text and began to write in the wax, trying to keep his own letters clear and large. But the sun was getting quite warm, and he found his eyes kept closing of their own accord.

He persevered for a while as the day grew warmer, and then caught himself with a jerk as his eyes closed and his head started drooping over the frame. He looked around to see if anyone had noticed. Halith had stopped sewing and was watching him. Saniyahu was over near one of the stones trimming a piece of hide for a drum-head.

"Are you well, Damariel?"

He nodded.

"Oh yes. Very well indeed. I just didn't sleep very well last night."

Saniyahu had heard the conversation and walked over.

"Not bad dreams again, I hope, Damari?"

He shook his head, trying to think of a sensible reason. He looked down at the writing frame, and realised that his letters were scrawled, and the lines he meant to be straight had wandered rather aimlessly up and down. The letters he had intended to be large and clear were random and spidery.

The end result was substantially worse than the original he had looked critically at. He frowned at the writing, wondering how it had turned out so untidily.

"No, I just, well, I didn't sleep very much. No reason really."

Halith touched his shoulder.

"Maybe you ate something. You were up on the rock with Qetirah yesterday afternoon, weren't you? I wonder how she slept?"

Damariel gave a little start, avoided her eyes and shook his head, bending down over the writing frame in an attempt to thwart the conversation. Saniyahu laughed suddenly.

"Oh, that's why you were outside so early."

Halith looked at him.

"Was he? I didn't know that. What's that got to do with it?"

"Come on, Halith. It's all so clear now. He was with Qetirah last night, down at her house. They lay together. That's why he didn't sleep so well. I don't expect she did either. Not a lot to do with anything they ate."

Damariel looked at him, mouth open.

"Saniyahu, sir, I promised Ketty I wouldn't tell you. Anyone, I mean, not just you two. She doesn't want anyone to know about this yet. I promised her. Please don't tell anyone else. Especially not her family. I promised."

Saniyahu nodded.

"Nor did you tell us. You have not broken your promise. And as you should know, we hear a great many things that are never told to others."

Damariel felt a great wash of relief, followed by a great feeling of pride. He grinned at Saniyahu and Halith in a slightly foolish way, suddenly feeling a kinship and sense of equality with them that had not been his before. They were also lovers, and knew what it was like to lie with another. Saniyahu laughed.

"You still have to work on that tablet. Now we know you're not ill, go and dip your head in the stream a few times to wake up properly. Then heat up that wax, get rid of all those ridiculous letter shapes you've done so far and start again. I want the whole lot finished before the evening comes."

About a week later, Damariel and Qetirah found their way to the shepherd's hut Kothar had talked about. Feeling conspiratorial, they had set off from the village separately, along different paths, and only met up once they were out of sight of the last houses. Qetirah had brought some fruit, Damariel a blanket.

The little hut, which Damariel had approached very cautiously while Qetirah stayed back in the scrub out of sight, was quite empty, though there were signs that others had been there in recent weeks. The door had been neatly tied back with some twine, and the final approach path was clear of weeds and stray bramble limbs. Perhaps, after all, it was not so private as he had imagined.

At his signal, she ran the last distance up to the house and joined him inside. There it was warm and cosy, even comfortable where others had padded some of the gaps in the walls, levelled the rough places in the floor, or left little signs of prior occupation. Although shepherds might not have been there for some time, it was hardly derelict and abandoned.

Qetirah insisted that they pushed a table against the door once they were in, clearly anxious that someone else, some other couple, might arrive at any time. That done, they abandoned the outside and explored their own internal land of intimacy, which was still a new world of unexplored pathways. The dry stone walls of the hut faded away as they turned inward towards each other.

Afterwards, they lay beside each other and talked about the future. Qetirah absolutely refused to come to the hut any more. It was, she thought now that she had seen it, far too public, and brought with it too much risk of discovery.

Damariel, rather shamefaced, told Qetirah how Saniyahu had guessed about their liaison within such a short time of seeing him, but that as village seers they were both as committed to silence on the matter as Qetirah could possibly want. Qetirah had become angry at first, thinking he had been recklessly indiscrete, but then settled down again as he continued.

"Look, Ketty, why don't you come and talk to them yourself? Then you'd be sure they mean what they say about it."

She turned towards him.

"Do you think they would mind?"

"Of course not. And it's the middle of the day, so nobody can possibly think badly of you for going up to the high place now."

She thought about it for a short time as she lay beside him, then suddenly brushed her hair back from her face and sat up, pushing the blanket away.

"All right. Let's go now."

"Now?"

She laughed at the disappointment in his voice and reached over to one side for her bundle of clothes.

"Yes, now. Before we get involved in something else. Let's see them now."

They went back separately again to the village, Damariel circling round to the east so they would arrive along different paths. He got to the house first and had just asked Saniyahu to come in from the stones to talk to him with Halith, when Qetirah arrived, calling out uncertainly at the door. Halith went over, opened the door, invited her in, and then embraced her warmly.

Qetirah looked a little shy at the reception, and held out a hand to Damariel for support. Saniyahu brought a small plate with some sweetened bread and they sat together in one of the rooms. For a while they just talked of regular village matters: Saniyahu and Halith seemed quite content just to talk about anything in order to set Qetirah at her ease. But eventually she eased the conversation around to matters of more importance.

“Sir, lady, look, you know, I’m sure you do, that Damariel and I, well, we want to be together.”

Halith smiled a little and nodded.

“Yes, we know that. Go on.”

“Well, you see I was wondering, with Damariel being apprenticed here to you two, not living in his mother’s home, well, what would happen if we wanted to get married sometime? Would he come down to our house or what?”

The seer and his wife exchanged glances.

“Is there a need to get married very soon?”

Qetirah shook her head, and then suddenly realising the import of the question, flushed a little.

“Not in any haste, no. But we were just wondering.”

Saniyahu and Halith looked at each other again. There was no obvious signal that Damariel could see, but Saniyahu took up the thread.

“Qetirah, that is a wise question. And no, Damariel would not come down to your mother’s house. If he is apprenticed to us, then he lives here with us, and the woman that chooses him as husband will live here with us as well.”

Qetirah looked at him in surprise, her voice faltering.

"So if he lives here, then I must live here too? What will my mother do?"

Halith took her hand and held it in both of hers.

"Qetirah, if you marry Damari you will live here with him. On the day you marry, you leave your mother's home and enter this one. I did this when I married Saniyahu. But I was a younger sister, so my mother's household did not change very greatly. You are the oldest sister in your house. Things will be very different for you, and for Kinreth and Laylah as well, if you two marry." Qetirah shook her head.

"You mean Laylah would inherit in time to come?"

"Yes, she will. It has to be this way, Qetirah. We who are the seers of the four towns cannot also share in the normal life of the households. Nor indeed in the life of the chiefs. Everything will change for you if you make this choice."

Qetirah stayed silent for a long moment, looking intently at Halith as though studying her for the truth of the matter. She started to say something once, twice, but did not complete the words. Damariel sat very still, hoping and not hoping that she would look at him, ask him something. Eventually she looked down at the floor and sighed with great feeling.

"I don't know what to think. I never knew this."

She glanced briefly at Damariel in a way that he could not fathom. He wondered for a heart-rending moment if she regretted all that had happened in the last week between them; for a brief moment he even wondered if he regretted it on her behalf before discarding the thought. They all waited for her to speak.

"Well, well, I don't know."

She looked again at Damariel and tried to smile.

"Don't look so anxious, Damari. What's done is done, and happily done as well. But now this is a new thing for me. And you. This is like another new hillside we have come to on our journey. We have to decide what we are going to do next."

"Will you tell Kinreth yet?"

Qetirah put her head to one side and thought.

"Do you think I should tell mother?"

"At some time you must tell her. Especially if the two of you marry: we have never yet married a couple where it was kept secret from the households." Qetirah tried to smile at his words. "You must choose when."

She took a deep breath. Damariel caressed her hand.

"Ketty, we don't have to say anything yet, not until you're sure about this. We two can talk about it over the next little while until we know for sure what to do. Saniyahu and Halith can help us."

"Look, Damari, it's not that simple. I just don't want to keep going with you up to..." she broke off suddenly and looked away from him at the other two. "Well, I'm not sure we should be together like that when we're not sure there's a future. I don't want it unless I know it will last for us. You know what I mean."

Damariel blinked in surprise. It seemed such a short time since they had lain together up at the shepherd's hut, and the prospect of future meetings seemed suddenly to be receding from him.

"Well then, we must make our minds up very soon. I don't want to just keep drifting along without knowing when we'll be together. Not now."

Qetirah turned fully towards him and touched his face.

"Oh, Damari, don't be anxious. We'll work something out. Soon. Anyway, I can't come to be with you next week anyway. Or the week after. We have to wait for a short while. We have plenty of time to think." She put a finger on his mouth to stop him speaking as he opened it in question, a puzzled look on his features, and turned back to Halith. "Lady, I think I would like to come and talk with you very soon about this. I need advice, and you are the best person to give that."

Halith nodded.

"Qetirah, come tomorrow. Saniyahu and Damariel have to go up the track to Jarrar's town anyway, and I shall be on my own from just before noon."

Damariel never did discover what was said on that afternoon. Saniyahu kept him busy with one task and another, and the two of them stayed overnight with Adonibaal, the seer at that town. Every now and again Damariel tried to manoeuvre the conversation around to the subject of Qetirah, and what Halith might be saying to her, but Saniyahu refused to be drawn out on that matter.

Damariel felt himself torn into two places, and wished more than anything he could be in the same room with them.

The time at Woodlands passed very slowly, especially the night. He lay awake stretched out on his bedroll, in the upstairs chamber of the seer's house. Saniyahu had fallen asleep almost at once, and Damariel felt very alone. After a while he got up, crept out to the open space and looked out at the stars for a time, until the cold air started to make him shiver. Eventually he fell asleep, but found himself awake over and over again during the night. He was very anxious.

On the way back along the ridge he asked Saniyahu how Halith had felt at leaving her household when they married. He had heard the bare details of their meeting before, but this time around he wanted to know if the choice had been easy or hard.

To his dismay, it had been hard. Saniyahu had waited a long time for her decision. Her family had not been sure of the choice at first and had spent a long time considering the matter. Hearing this, Damariel wondered how much sleep he would lose by the time Qetirah had made her own choice.

Back home again, he quizzed Halith, who absolutely refused to tell him anything about the time she had spent with Qetirah. Qetirah herself was at her mother's house, of course, and Damariel did not feel able to go down there just yet. Instead he fretted about the situation and found a place up the ridge above the high place where he could see the roof of her house.

When that became too frustrating, he went back to his little room and tried to occupy himself copying the next part of the song of Kirtu. His heart was not really in the work, but at least the letters were straighter and more regular than they had been a week ago, after their first night. Perhaps there would be no other days and nights together.

The next day he persuaded Saniyahu to give him an errand that would take him up to one of the other towns. Anything. After some thought, the seer gave him some of Halith's needlework and a new blank wax writing frame to take across to Meyim. Damariel went gladly; of all the towns it was the one he visited least often, and he felt good about seeing it again. It was only after he set out that he realised the track went past the shepherd's hut.

On his way there he caught up with Kothar, who had been sitting on a large rock by the path eating some olives. He greeted him happily, but Kothar was clearly not in a mood to converse. As they talked, he glanced quite often back towards the village. Realising why his friend was there, Damariel decided that the kindest thing to do was bid a quick farewell.

He hurried off along the path, wondering who Kothar was meeting. He hoped it would be Shaharti, and thought about making a covert attempt to see who would be there. Then he would have an excuse to see Qetirah and, perhaps, would have news she wanted to hear. But the idea of creeping back and trying to remain unseen seemed distasteful, and he could not imagine any way in which it would help his friendship with Kothar.

He quickened his pace and moved on along the side of the ridge. Being by then quite close to the hut, he tried not to remember the brief time he had spent there with Qetirah. He stayed overnight in Meyim, helped out with one or two tasks in the village, and then wandered back in the late evening of the next day.

He had missed Qetirah. Halith had been cleaning and overhauling the musical instruments since late afternoon. Qetirah had come up to the house a little while ago, stayed for a short time, and then gone back to her home.

"Halith, do you think I should go and see her?"

"Of course. Why ever not?"

"I don't know what her mother thinks about me. Or what she knows by now about where we have been. Don't you think it will be awkward going into her house, seeing as how Ketty and I were, well, that we... "

He stopped abruptly. She looked up from one the timbrels and gave it a slight shake so the ribbons fluttered in the light breeze and the little metal rings jingled.

"Don't you think Ketty has had to face that sooner than you?

Damariel flushed with embarrassment. There was no good answer to that, and rather than try to find one he turned and set off down the hill, approaching the house this time down the main path and directly up to the front door.

The door was open, and as he approached he could hear Qetirah talking with her mother. There was a noise of a metal file from further inside, Caleb at work. He called out and waited a few heartbeats for Qetirah to come to the doorway. She smiled happily and took him in to the house.

Kinreth was pouring some grain from a large container onto a plate beside the family grindstone. He glanced into Qetirah's room. Laylah was sitting on her bed sorting out a bundle of clothes and thread to be mended. He turned to smile with fond memories to Qetirah, but she frowned and nodded her head to where her mother was just finishing with the grain and standing up. He sobered at once.

She came over to him and looked at him as though studying him for the first time, rather than seeing someone she had known since birth. He tried to remain calm under the scrutiny, and waited for her to speak. Caleb had stopped working in the other room and now stood in the doorway to his workshop. Laylah, curious at the pause in conversation, looked up from the bedroom. He felt as though whole generations of the family were inspecting him. There was a little silence, broken eventually by Kinreth.

"So, Damari, I hear you have become even more fond of my daughter. Let me hear you talk about the future you think you see for her, so I can think about it. Come here and let us sit down. I need to know if I should be talking with Yeresheth or with Halith if this is to proceed."

He took a deep breath, glanced once at Qetirah, and began.

Zayn

MATAN – ETANIM YEAR 18

ALL GLORIOUS is the daughter who marries today –
like plaited gold are her garments,
in embroidery dressed for her man:
they are come to their bridal home.

IT WAS MATAN AGAIN. Tomorrow it would be a year since her brothers had been killed, a year since the man that had been her father had abandoned her mother and taken up with the lowland girl down among the olives.

Sosanneth sat alone with her mother through the long evening. Damariel had been with them for part of the time, and would return in the morning. Nerith had brought them some food for an evening meal, and helped Yeresheth pick the two best sprays of mimosa flowers from above the door to place in a tall beaker by the door. Now it was just the two of them.

After Nerith had left they had worked together to finish a piece of weaving promised to Gazala's mother. Then as the sun set, the two of them had made their way to the cave where their ancestors were buried, and had poured some oil and a little wine, some seeds and spices into the fissure above the entrance. It had pooled like blood in the little bowl and then dripped slowly through into the empty space below.

They had stayed there a long time, watching the little puddle sink into the ground, the last remains drying in the gloomy wind pushing up from the lowlands. Eventually, clinging to one another in the last of the fading light, they had made their way back down to their empty house.

Now they sat together, in a loose embrace, in the dusk, neither wanting to light the oil lamp, letting sparse threads of conversation work their way in and out of the gaps in the room.

Little village noises came and went through the window without intruding, and after a while Sosanneth could see the edge of the part-moon high up in a sky with some wispy clouds. Yeresheth sighed, and Sosanneth hugged her a little more tightly.

"Sannah, we should sleep. Nothing more for tonight."

Sosanneth nodded, stood up, and leant down to help her mother. As Yeresheth stood up, suddenly they could hear voices approaching the house, in the lane outside the front door: Damariel and Halith.

The two women looked at each other, puzzled, and then Sosanneth went across and opened the door to them. Damariel was standing back a little way from the door, looking irresolute. Halith was a little closer, but to one side, giving Damariel precedence. Sosanneth went and hugged her brother, and heard Yeresheth speaking from behind her in the doorway.

"Dear son, what a surprise. I thought we were not going to see you again until the morning. And Halith too. What pleasure to find you a guest, but I have nothing to put in front of you. The fire is out and the water is cold."

Halith shook her head.

"Think nothing of that, lady. We wanted to come down tonight to see you, as a matter of importance tonight."

She paused, and looked at Damariel, who had let go of his sister, but stood there, saying nothing still, not looking at anyone in particular. Nerith's face appeared briefly at her window across the way.

"Damari? What is it?"

He still stood there, unmoving, until Halith took a step forward and said, with a certain degree of urgency, "Lady, perhaps we could come inside?"

Yeresheth held on to the door frame, glanced at Sosanneth, and then without speaking stood back inside the door and gestured for the others to come in. As her daughter came past she caught anxiously at her hand. Once they were all inside, Halith and Yeresheth sat on stools while the two children stood. Yeresheth had her hands clenched tightly.

"Tell me, one of you, please, what has happened? Damariel, are you well?"

Halith glanced up at Damariel, waited a few breaths, sighed when he still remained silent, and replied.

"Lady, for your hospitality, blessings and thanks. Your son is well, and a credit to you and your household. I know tonight is not a good night for news, but we felt, all of us, my husband too, that this should not wait. Perhaps in the morning you would hear by another means, and that would be wrong."

She stopped again and turned pointedly to Damariel. Sosanneth felt as though her heart would burst out of her body if she had to wait longer, and pulled urgently at her brother's hand.

"Damari, tell us, what is it? Is Qetirah well?"

Damariel shook his head rapidly, as though to clear it.

"Of course, of course, she's well, we're all fine, it's nothing at all the matter with any of us."

He looked around, pulled up a stool from near the cooking area and sat down beside Halith. Glancing at each in turn, gathering resolve, he suddenly held his head up again and looked at Yeresheth.

"Well, mother, look, the lowland girl that lives with. . . "

He paused, seeing a dangerous look come over her features.

"Well, the lowland girl who came to the village and now lives down at the olive patch. You know who I mean. Well, she is pregnant now. She will have her baby as autumn turns to winter."

He paused, waiting for a response. Sosanneth put one hand to her mouth and held on to her mother with the other. Yeresheth was completely expressionless, but glanced quickly at Halith as though to confirm the news. There was a little silence before she spoke.

"I don't suppose there's any doubt about the father. Not as if she only came here a few weeks ago. Who else could it possibly be?"

She stopped herself, stood up and paced around the little room. Quite suddenly, without any warning, she picked up one of the pottery plates from a pile on a shelf and threw it against a wall.

She laughed loudly, rather shrill and ragged. Sosanneth ran over to her and put her arms round her.

"I think that might have been one he used to use. No use to anyone keeping that now, not now, oh no. Sannah, dear, can you see anything else we might have missed?"

Sosanneth shook her head, eyes wide, and looked with mute appeal to Halith, but Damariel spoke before she could.

"Look, mother, I wish I had other news for you. I do. But we had to tell you."

Yeresheth trod deliberately on a shard of the broken plate and scraped it across the floor, satisfied by the grinding sound it made, then sat down again and held Sosanneth against her side.

"Of course, dear, of course you did. You were quite right."

She had become very calm and offhand. Sosanneth's hands had started to shake a little, and she took them in her own and stroked them with a steady movement.

"Ah well, just you and I now, Sannah. Nothing much more, is there. I should have expected it before now, really. He might well get something out of her, but what is there left to come out of me now? And after all I had so hoped."

Sosanneth met her brother's gaze over Yeresheth's head, bent down now with the fringe of her kef hiding any expression. There was a little silence, before Halith spoke to Yeresheth again.

"Lady, I am sorry again that we have to bear this news to you tonight. Is there anything I can do for you?"

Yeresheth shook her head heavily, then looked up at her and shook it again.

"No, not at all. You have been kind to us both by telling us now, though my heart has been cast down very low by your kindness. What else could you have done? I think you could leave us now, though."

Halith nodded, walked over to her, placed both hands on the crown of her head and was silent for a short time before turning towards the door. There was a little sigh in the room as she finished praying over Yeresheth. Then Damariel went with Halith, opened the door for her and left with her, his face held very tense and rigid. Sosanneth stayed by her mother for a few seconds after the door closed, realising that she had started to cry very quietly.

They heard Halith and Damariel speaking outside, their voices dying away as they moved off. Sosanneth stroked her mother's forehead where some of her hair had slipped out from under the kef. Yeresheth sniffed, straightened a little and rearranged her own hair.

"Ah, Sannah, daughter, you're too young and I'm too old for this. Too old, old, old by half again. Whatever shall we do? What will become of my family?"

Sosanneth shook her head and knelt in front of her mother.

"Look, mother, something will work out. He's just ruining everything. Again. Just like before. But you mustn't let him do this to you. You're not old."

Yeresheth smiled slightly, shook her head, and stood up very slowly and heavily, leaning a little on her daughter as she picked up a little broom. She started sweeping up the broken pieces of plate together. Sosanneth stayed kneeling on the floor, and when Yeresheth had finished she came to sit beside her again.

She began to speak, when all of a sudden the door opened and Damariel came back in. Sosanneth turned, and the two women looked up at him.

"Look, mother, Sannah, I thought, Halith agrees, I thought I should stay here tonight with you both, just for the one night. No point you two being here and me up there on my own."

He gestured up the hill and waited for a reply. There was a little pause, and then the three joined together in a long embrace. There was a flurry of activity, getting a spare bedroll out and putting it alongside the others. Then it was all done, and there did not seem anything else to say. There was an awkward pause. Yeresheth spoke.

"Now, you two, I am going out for a short time, up to the high place one last time tonight. No, I don't want either of you with me. Let me do this alone."

She refused to be swayed on the matter, and left the house soon after. Damariel and Sosanneth left the oil lamp burning in the main room and made do with the borrowed light in the sleeping room.

To fill the sudden silence, Damariel started to tell his sister how Saniyahu and Halith had met with the other seers and formally accepted Qetirah as apprentice alongside him. She had not the benefit of any earlier training, not even the slightly haphazard instruction he had received from Iqnu, so Halith would be spending a very great deal of time with her over the months before and after their wedding. She was soaking in the new life quickly, but the demands on their time were difficult.

Sosanneth had listened, somewhat absently, without comment. Now, in the quiet room, she took off her kef and tossed it into a corner, shaking her hair loose to hang around her shoulders. She sat on her part of the bedding with her head on her knees, obviously lost somewhere in thought. Damariel nudged her.

"What is it, Sannah?"

"Oh, Damari, it's not that I don't want to hear about all that to do with Ketty. I do, really. I'm glad for her and you. But just not tonight. While mum's out we need to talk about something. Listen now."

She looked up at him rather defiantly.

"Look now, Damari, our mother's all upset. No, listen to me, let me finish. Of course she's upset about our brothers, today of all days, but there's more. She thinks her whole family's finished now, she's the end of it, all those generations. You know how she used to tell them all to us going back all those years. We all used to laugh at her back then, but now I agree with her, I think it's important too. Well, she thinks it's over now, and it's her fault."

Damariel shook his head.

"She surely can't think that. What makes you think that's in her heart?"

"Oh, things she said just before you came back. And other things before today. She's frightened now that her name will be only ever remembered by generations to come as the woman who was the last of her whole lineage. The last one in the story with nobody to carry the name on afterwards. I'm quite certain of it, there's no doubt at all. But don't argue, listen. What she most needs is to know the family is going to carry on. Especially now with today's news. It's a big blow to her, what that man's gone and done, curse him. She thinks she's too old herself now, so she's looking to us to help her out. Even if she doesn't ask in so many words. We have to do this for her, Damari. We have to."

Damariel took off his own kef, folded it near the top of the bedroll, and leaned back against the wall.

"How do you mean?"

"Come on, Damari, it's so obvious. We have to give her children."

"Well, fine, Sannah, it'll just take time. Ketty and I are getting married just after midsummer, in Kiraru. You know that."

"Look, Damari, you two must have been together already? You and Ketty? Well, you know? You must have, you know, been together properly by now? Don't tell me otherwise. Why are you talking about the summer?"

Damariel sat up again and looked at her quizzically without saying anything. She had no idea what he was thinking, and persisted stubbornly.

"Look, you've been planning to get married a good time now. You must have lain together. Like you were married already, I mean."

She flushed slightly as he kept looking at her without saying anything, not helping her at all to find any words. Abruptly she turned away, loosened her belt, and slipped her sandals off to lie down on top of the bedding.

"Well, you should do something. One of us has to do something. She needs us to be helping her now, right now, not in the summer. You know what I'm saying even if you won't talk about it with me. We owe that to her after everything. Nobody would mind if Ketty got pregnant now even if you've not been through the ceremony. Not like it would be a surprise, not to anyone in the village. I don't know why you don't see this as clearly as I do."

There was a long pause, until they found something else to talk about, trying to disrupt the awkward silence of the room. Soon after, Yeresheth came back. They heard her talking with Nerith, broken sentences, just before the door swung open.

She closed the door, picked up the oil lamp from the main room, looked briefly around to make sure the house was settled, and then joined the others.

By unspoken agreement they settled themselves for sleep the same way as they had a year ago, with Yeresheth in the middle and the children either side of her. Damariel snuffed out the lamp and the darkness of the spring night settled quietly around them all. Sosanneth lay awake in the darkness a long time after the other two had fallen asleep, thinking and planning new futures for herself.

Two months after that day had passed, Damariel married Qetirah. It was high summer, and hot, and where the tree cover was sparse, the grass on the bare ground was already turning brown.

Sosanneth was sitting beside Nerith in the shadow of one of the stones at the high place, holding a bunch of her own mimosa flowers and Nerith's rock-rose, looking across at where her mother stood with Kinreth and Halith beside the tallest stone. She noticed idly that Yeresheth had become anxious and fidgety.

Halith glanced at her, squeezed her hand and then put an arm round her shoulders. Yeresheth leaned in towards her and for a second the two women touched heads. The fringes of their kefs tangled in the slight breeze, and Yeresheth took several long breaths before nodding and straightening again. Nerith waved to her, a little flutter of fingers across the gap between them.

Damariel was in the sunlight in front of them, the afternoon light dappled by the high clouds clear on his back and head. He was wearing his old kef, the one he had worn as a boy, and it looked old and much too small on him compared with the one he usually wore as Saniyahu's apprentice.

He was also looking quite anxious to Sosanneth's practiced eye, and the over-small kef did not help. Over his left arm, folded neatly, another kef was draped.

In ones and twos at first, and then in a sudden flurry, other villagers gathered at the high place, slipping here and there into a loose ring around it, leaving a gap where the main track came up from the houses.

Gazala came and sat beside Sosanneth, a sprig from her mother's myrtle tree tied loosely to the front of her smock, and the two talked for a while. Her brother Kunor was around on the other side of the circle with some friends.

Suddenly there was a stir from the people nearest to the village, and everyone stood up around the circle. There was a pause, and then Qetirah appeared, with Caleb and Saniyahu either side of her.

She was dressed in an embroidered smock that had been passed down through several generations of women in the family, and a long skirt, and like Damariel was wearing her plain white childhood kef. Her approach was to Damariel's left, and Sosanneth smiled to see the radiant look on his face as he watched her walk slowly, steadily towards him.

She stopped two paces away and they faced each other.

Yeresheth moved beside her son; Caleb, Kinreth, and Laylah stood beside Qetirah, with Saniyahu and Halith between facing into the sun. Gazala whispered urgently to Sosanneth.

"Sannah, shouldn't you be up there too?"

"No, wait, you'll see. They don't need me just now. They only need Laylah for a while, then she'll sit back like me."

"But about your father? Shouldn't he be here too?"

"Don't you dare mention him, Gazala. I don't even call him father any more, never again, not after the way he treated mother. I'd spit on him if he turned up now. He should have been here all this last year. It's too late for him now. Especially after what happened in the spring. Nobody wants him around right now. I don't even know if he's heard this is happening."

There was silence around the circle. Halith spoke.

"Kinreth, your daughter Qetirah will marry today, but not so as to remain in your household. She will not take up the role of a daughter. She will not live in the house of your mothers. She will live in this house just as I live in it, but not as my daughter. I live here as a stranger, and this house is only a tent. If Qetirah marries Damariel today she will live here as a stranger, and this house will be only a tent for her too. Are you willing for this to happen to your daughter?"

Kinreth stood in the afternoon light and closed her eyes.

"I am willing."

Halith turned to Qetirah.

"Qetirah, if you marry Damariel here today you will leave the household of your mother. You will no longer inherit as a daughter. You will live here in this house as a stranger, as I live in it, and this house will only be a tent. Are you willing for this to happen?"

Qetirah bent her white-crowned head, her voice too quiet to be heard from where Sosanneth sat. Halith heard, though, and continued.

"Qetirah will not inherit as your daughter, Kinreth, but you have another daughter with you here. Laylah will be the daughter who inherits the house, and the daughter who will choose who lives in it when the time comes. Are you, Kinreth, and you, Laylah, willing for this to happen?"

They both nodded. Halith took one step back as Saniyahu stepped forward, his voice carrying around the circle. In the pause, Laylah turned and ran to sit back in the circle.

"Does any man or woman here today not accept this marriage as a true union, worthy of blessing and acceptable in the sight of both worlds?"

There was silence. Saniyahu and Halith looked around before he continued.

"This ceremony today is not just a wedding of a man and a woman from among our people. It is more than that, because Damariel is apprenticed to me and to Halith, and as she is marrying him, Qetirah is also apprenticed to Halith and to me. They are learning to serve this world and the other world, those who are here and those who are there. In time, and if the people and the gods are willing, they will become seers and priests for you all. They will stand in the place between. They will serve you. I am willing for this to happen, and Halith is willing. Are you all willing for these two to marry and serve you all in this way?"

A great, many-voiced affirmation rippled around the high place like the wind or the rain, and Sosanneth, even as her own voice joined the rest in saying "Yes", caught her breath at the expression of unity. Damariel glanced around the hilltop, catching a person's eye here, responding to a smile there. Qetirah had her hand to her mouth. Saniyahu smiled.

"Qetirah, daughter of Kinreth, give me the kef you wore as a girl."

Qetirah fumbled slightly with the knot on her shoulder, then slipped the kef off away from her head. Her uncovered hair, dark and startling in the sun, moved slightly in the light breeze. A cluster of hibiscus petals from her mother's home-plant were tied in a loop above her forehead.

Saniyahu held up the kef so everyone could see it around the circle of the sacred stones, and then tore it, top to bottom, in one quick move. He gave the torn halves to Damariel.

"Qetirah, from today you are a girl no longer, but a woman, and a wife. Be dressed as a wife now for all to see."

Damariel took the folded kef from over his arm, shook it open, and tied it, slightly awkwardly, around and over Qetirah's head, smoothing the blue bridal edging to the curve of her face and onto her shoulders. The hibiscus flowers, knocked away from their place as he fumbled with the material of the new kef, fluttered away across the ground, chased by one of the children.

The wedding went on. Damariel took his own kef off. Halith tied it in a bundle with Qetirah's and buried them both in a hollow in the rocks. Qetirah tied her new husband's kef around him. But Sosanneth was watching Yeresheth, standing alone in her own wife's kef, crying slightly, the tears in the sunshine highlighting the scars of Baruk and Bashur.

Qetirah and Damariel knelt in front of the great stone, in front of Saniyahu and Halith, while the other family members slipped away into the circle of the community.

There were prayers for blessings for fruit of the breast and the womb, prayers for safety through the passage of childbirth and the other travails of life, little drinks of sour and sweet wine for the couple, small pieces of dry bread and honey.

There was a short silence, and then this person or that from the encircling people called out blessings. Sosanneth heard Kothar's voice across on the other side of the ring, Nerith's beside her, and a few others. Glancing up, she suddenly saw Shomal standing off to one side, mostly hidden behind a building. He was watching Damariel, and did not realise she had seen him at first.

Becoming abruptly aware of her look, he lifted a hand in a partial greeting, but she looked firmly away from him. A few minutes later, when she made herself look again, he had gone.

There was silence around the stones. Saniyahu looked carefully around the circle, decided that all had been said that needed to be said, and held up his hands. Damariel and Qetirah stood and looked uncertainly at him. He smiled and said something to them, and with a great surge of movement towards each other they kissed in the sunlight in the middle of the circle.

A shout of approval and delight rippled around the top of the hill, and the assembly suddenly dissolved into little groups talking to each other, laughing, bringing food and drink in from where it had been kept away to the sides.

People clustered around the new couple, and even came up to her as well, saying happy things, hugging her, laughing. She made her way through the little groups to Qetirah, flushed with excitement and holding this person's hand or that, letting them touch the new wife's embroidery on her kef. Sosanneth hugged her and then found Damariel before moving across to Yeresheth. They held each other in a long embrace.

"Well, mother, it's only you and me now."

"Sannah, it has been for ages. So it shall be until you bring a man into the house."

Sosanneth stood back a little.

"It's not the time to plan a wedding for me, mother."

Yeresheth shook her head.

"Never, not ever, not until you find the person you want so I can invite him into the house. But sit with me for the feast, Sannah."

"Yes, I will, but I want to see my friends first."

Some time later, with the sound of celebration loud on the hill, Sosanneth worked her way back to the main group. Yeresheth waved when she saw her, and gestured to a place saved beside her.

They were part of a large group near Damariel, and Sosanneth squeezed in between her mother and Kothar. He was obviously hugely enjoying himself, with a twig of Shaharti's mother's almond tucked behind his ear, a jug of wine in one hand and a torn off piece of honeyed bread in the other. He moved a little sideways to make more room for Sosanneth, and then leaned back companionably against her arm.

"And how's my best friend's favourite sister?"

She laughed, put on a teasing expression, and kissed him on the cheek.

"Happy that her brother's best friend's favourite lady is at the same table. Who knows what might happen otherwise?"

He nodded and laughed at the retort, and waved happily to Shaharti, sitting a little further away around the circle.

Yeresheth plucked her arm.

"Sannah, do be careful what you say."

"Oh mother, nobody minds at a wedding. Don't be silly."

Kothar had turned the other way, towards Damariel.

"Damari, are you really going to take Ketty back to that tiny little shed of yours? Is that all she's worth to you?"

Damariel shook his head and held Qetirah's hand.

"Saniyahu and Halith are giving us half of their house. From tonight even. And they're going up to Woodlands after this has finished so we'll have the whole place to ourselves until the day after tomorrow. And after that several rooms of our own. We'll be living in a bigger house than you ever dreamed of. Maybe I'll invite you in one day and lose you somewhere in one of the rooms. We won't see you for months while you find your way out again."

Kothar raised his wine jug.

"At least you won't have to go off for walks in the woods now to get the lovely Qetirah on her own."

Qetirah glanced at her mother, sitting on her other side, who put her arm around her daughter's shoulders.

"Well now, and for sure I thought you were out there getting herbs and berries for me all that time."

"But I was, mother."

Caleb lifted his own beaker of wine.

"And from now on may all the fruit of every blossoming hillside in the whole land be yours to taste forever."

Kothar took another drink and opened his mouth to say something else, when Damariel turned to him.

"Kothar, why don't you get those musicians organised. I want to dance with my wife, and I can't do that without music."

His friend nodded and clambered heavily to his feet, moving away to the other groups and calling to this person or that. Shaharti leaned towards Kinreth.

"Lady, I am sorry if Kothar offended you."

She shook her head.

"Not at all, Shaharti, though it's sweet of you to say so. I knew all about my Ketty's little excursions, so I did. She's not the first woman in the family to go gathering fruit in the woods."

Caleb leaned forward and kissed her cheek, winking at Shaharti. Sosanneth watched the play between them, looking very thoughtful, not hearing Yeresheth speaking to her, not hearing what she said. Off to one side there came a sudden sound of musical instruments starting to play together: pipes, a lyre, and several timbrels, wedding music. Kothar's loud voice was calling for a faster beat.

Damariel stood up, bowed to Qetirah and took her hand as they went over to the clear area in the centre of the stones. They started to dance together, and little by little the whole community joined, men, women and children laughing and dancing.

The wedding dances were for the whole community to pair in dancing as they pleased, like the great summer festival but unlike the regular feast-days where men and women formed their own separate circles.

Sosanneth waited until Nerith had persuaded Yeresheth to join her, then loosened her kef a little so some strands of dark hair wisped out from under the hem, and started to dance with a mixed group a year or two older than herself. After a while Damariel and Qetirah separated from each other, dancing first with their own family members and then moving out from person to person until eventually the new couple had partnered everyone.

There was a breathless pause, and then the whole town made a double row stretching like an aisle from the centre of the high place to the door of the seer's house. Yeresheth and Sosanneth took Damariel's hands, Caleb and Kinreth took Qetirah with Laylah behind them. Together in procession they led the new husband and wife to the door of the house, embraced them in a final hug, and then pushed them over the threshold and closed the door.

A great cheer and rattle of timbrels shook across the crown of the hill like spring rain on the waiting fields.

Outside the house, the noise and the party and the dancing continued through the late afternoon into the evening, until in ones and twos, quite late, the people let the hilltop and its stones fall silent. Saniyahu and Halith had left to go up the track to Woodlands in the early evening. Sosanneth noticed that Yeresheth also left the celebration early and made a solitary way down the hill towards her house. She herself stayed out much later with her friends, until there were very few people left on the crown of the hill.

As she finally left the stones, she stopped by the door of the seer's house and placed a curious hand flat against the grain of the wooden frame for a little while, before turning to start on down the familiar path to her home. Then she heard a soft voice calling to her from off to one side, and turned to see Qeren there. She went over part of the way towards him.

"Qeren? I thought you left with Yusuf and the others?"

"I did, but I came back again, Sannah."

She tilted her head, and the white kef shone in the moonlight.

"Oh yes? Why was that?"

He made a vague movement of one hand.

"Well, I wanted to make sure you were all right. I suddenly thought we'd just left you up here. On your own, you know."

"Oh, well in that case you had better make sure I get home safely, I live all the way down there, you know, Qeren."

She pointed down the hill and waited for him to come over to her.

"I know that." He looked around, hesitant, and she tucked her arm into his and squeezed it against her side. "Well, then, you'd better make sure I get all the way home safely. You never know what might happen. This way."

He laughed suddenly, nervously, and they set off towards her house. Outside, soon after, they stood out of the moonlight, under the mimosa tree.

"My mother's inside already."

He nodded but said nothing.

"You know, one day this house will be mine. Mother shares looking after it with me already, so it's almost mine now."

He nodded again, but she could not read his expression. She sighed, then reached up above her head to pick two mimosa flowers. She kissed one of them and gave it to him, then pushed back her kef so she could tuck the other stem into her hair.

"Here, I'll have one and you keep the other. We can swap back again when we next meet each other. I'd like that. Would you?"

He nodded a third time, but then turned quickly and went off up the hill. She shook her head, frowned a little, opened the door, and went in.

The month of Kiraru had gone, and Tsah, and Mepagh turned to Etanim. Sosanneth was helping Yeresheth finish the edge-work on a winter shawl promised to the chief's family up at Giybon.

The news had come down the hill nearly a month ago that the old chief Yad-Nesherim, victorious over his enemies and glorious in battle, had died, and his son Mahur-Baal had taken up the position unchallenged. Mahur-Baal had had this proclaimed immediately after the ceremony where Yad-Nesherim was gathered to his ancestors, an event that Saniyahu and Halith, Damariel and Qetirah had attended to represent the community.

That done, he lost little time in visiting each of the four towns in turn, to collect his dues and listen to renewed pledges of loyalty, and to bestow little gifts here and there among the houses. Gazala's father had received a little pottery bowl from somewhere across the Valley, and Danil a sheath with silver edging for his dagger to confirm his place as raid-leader. He had given some grain to two women who had been recently widowed. There was general satisfaction at the range of gifts, along with grudging acceptance that the next work-party of men would be required before long.

Sosanneth had managed to get him interested in their weaving work, and by promising a shawl for an elderly aunt, had secured his word that he would consider adding some pieces of their making when he travelled north to the area around Sychem to arrange the trade dealings later in the autumn. It would be quicker than waiting for a trader to come to the town gate, though they would not get such a good return for themselves.

So this particular piece had to be finished just right, and the two women had spent rather longer on it than they normally would. They were pleased with the result.

Indeed, Sosanneth was happy in several ways that day. Since the summer festival she had spent rather more time out of the house with friends, and in consequence less time with her mother. She had started to feel that she had grown away from her, and although that had been desirable at first, it had become a source of frustration and sadness to her shortly before news of the old chief's death had reached them.

She had found herself craving a sense of womanly comradeship with Yeresheth, and had made much greater efforts to be with her in the last few weeks. The two of them had started working quietly and companionably together again. They had both enjoyed the experience, and Sosanneth had been glad of the proximity to Yeresheth.

Today, however, Sosanneth was feeling quite unwell; she was introspective in mood and felt distinctly queasy. Yeresheth looked at her across the stretched-out shawl between them in the afternoon sun.

"What is it, Sannah? You're not looking well?"

Sosanneth shook her head.

"Oh, I don't know. Something's not right."

Her mother nodded.

"Your stitching has been good today, but your heart was somewhere out of the room altogether. Just make sure you don't do something we have to spend all evening unpicking again. What's wrong?"

"Something I ate, maybe. What was in that stew you gave us last night? I haven't been right since this morning. Or the last several mornings, in truth. Not yet a week, though, and only ever for a little while. Most days it's gone again soon enough."

Yeresheth frowned and without thinking looked critically at the food in the kitchen area, then suddenly looked back at Sosanneth again with an odd expression, her needle still part-way through the shawl.

She put her head to one side and opened her mouth to speak, when they heard Halith's voice outside calling to them. Sosanneth got up carefully, putting the garment to one side, and opened the door. Halith came in, looking very weary, and gratefully accepted the seat that Yeresheth indicated. She paused before speaking.

"Lady, I bring news that you will have been expecting for some time."

Yeresheth nodded and straightened herself as she sat there.

"It's about that girl, isn't it? The lowland girl?"

Halith nodded.

"It is, lady." She paused, and then, having weighed up Yeresheth's expression, continued, "Indeed it is. She had her baby last night, a boy. He's a good size. She started in labour last evening, and I have been helping her to deliver him all through the night hours. I have just left there now. There is no name for the boy yet, but they both live and thrive."

Yeresheth looked down. Sosanneth put a hand on her shoulder, and she clasped it with her own in response.

"I don't want to know the name, anyway. Well. Well. Many thanks, lady, for your kindness in telling us so promptly. Better this way than the other. But I see you are very tired yourself now."

"No sleep last night, and little enough the night before. But what of you two?"

Yeresheth made a vague gesture.

"Oh, I am well enough."

She stopped, then suddenly looked up again at Halith with a different expression and squeezed Sosanneth's hand, her voice abruptly stronger.

"But my daughter Sannah feels not so good just now. She says she has been unwell these last few mornings. Food does not seem to suit her so well. Quite sudden. You know how these things can happen."

Halith glanced briefly, curiously, at Sosanneth, and then held Yeresheth's gaze for a very long moment. There was a silence, full of yet-unspoken possibilities, as the two older women looked at one other.

"Ah. I see. Well, you're the best one to help her. For sure the sickness will pass soon enough, a few weeks at most."

"You wouldn't know what might have caused this?"

"I have heard nothing that I can say to help, lady."

A few minutes later, Halith had gone. Yeresheth picked up the shawl again and finished a few more stitches. Sosanneth looked along her edge to see if any more tidying was needed. She smiled with satisfaction at the result, nodded to herself, and then tucked the needle into her sleeve.

"Mother, I think we're done with this. All we need now is someone going up the ridge to Giybon. Maybe Damari could take it for us?"

She looked one last time, nodded approvingly, folded the shawl and leaned over to put it to one side, before straightening up and grimacing at a little wave of nausea that felt like a wave filling her up. She leant back in the seat and closed her eyes for a short time until it passed again. Opening them, she realised her mother was looking quizzically at her.

"You never did tell me what was in that food last night, mother."

Yeresheth shook her head.

"We had exactly the same, you and I. You had a bit more bread, I had a bit more of the leek and herb mixture, that's all. Do you remember, you said you couldn't face the thought of any more of it?"

"Well, it was true enough."

She paused to think.

"Oh yes, Gazala wasn't feeling so good last week. I thought she'd been out too long in the sun chasing after their goats, but she insisted that it was a real illness. Maybe it was and now I've got it."

Yeresheth shook her head, slowly.

"No, daughter, I don't think this is an illness you got from any of the girls in the village. I think it's something else altogether. I wonder who else you've been with?"

Sosanneth went very still and put her hand to her stomach.

"I don't know what you mean."

Yeresheth pulled a face, got up, and poured each of them some mint tea.

"I think perhaps you do. Tell me, Sannah, when did you first start to feel unwell? Tell me how it all started."

She handed one of the little mugs of tea to her daughter, and their conversation went on well into the evening.

Chet

BUL YEAR 18 – MATAN YEAR 19

BLESSED OF THE GODS shall be his land
with the wealth of the dew-filled skies,
with the wealth of the produce of the sun,
with the wealth of the fields and their fullness.

YERESHETH, LOOKING OUT OF HER WINDOW, watched Damariel pass Nerith's house and call out to his aunt, who was collecting the swollen rose hips from the heavily hanging branches. He opened the door of her own house then, ducking under the last few clinging mimosa flowers and coming in to where Sosanneth was sitting with her in the first room. Half-finished pieces of woven cloth were scattered around them where they had both been sitting, but neither was working.

They had been deep in conversation, but stopped as he entered. Yeresheth came over to embrace him: Sosanneth stayed sitting rather heavily where she was on a wooden chair. He set down the wrapping with the dried fruit and beans he had brought beside the other food pots, went over, and kissed her. Her cheeks felt fuller than he had expected, and there was a slightly stretched air about her.

Yeresheth put some water on to boil and crushed mint into a pot. The three settled again and talked for a while. Damariel spoke with enthusiasm about shared life with Qetirah, about places he had gone to with Saniyahu recently, about things he had learned, how Qetirah was making great strides in her own burgeoning ministry, about responsibilities that the seer and his wife was entrusting to them as a couple, about life at the priest's house. Yeresheth drew out from him news of Halith, and then as the water boiled, she looked over at Sosanneth.

"You pour for me, dear."

Sosanneth looked rebellious for a moment, but as the older woman looked calmly at her she got up quite slowly, with a little sigh, leaning a little on the chair as she bent down to pour water on the leaves. The smell of freshly crushed mint quickly filled the little room. Yeresheth watched Damariel looking, suddenly surprised, at his sister as she squatted down, stirring the pot.

He had become aware of a new roundness to her body, a sense of fullness around her that he had never encountered before. He looked, startled, across at his mother, who returned his look with an unfathomable one of her own. Sosanneth collected the three beakers, poured the tea for each of them, and settled back in her chair with relief. Damariel, still speechless, stared at her, and she lifted her head defiantly, holding the beaker in one hand as she smoothed her smock over her womb.

"Sosanneth! You're not? Surely? Are you?"

He paused, hesitant as to how he could go on.

"Pregnant? Yes, I am. What of it?"

He looked around him and into the parts of the other rooms that he could see. Nothing looked different than what he remembered. He paused again, at a loss how to proceed and ending up sounding clumsy, formal.

"Has my mother welcomed a man of yours into the house that I should be greeting?"

Yeresheth kept silent, and after a short pause Sosanneth spoke again.

"No, nobody new in the house. Just us two. Three, soon. Aren't you happy for me? It's not just you and Ketty that can bring children into the family."

"Sannah, sister, I am most happy for you. But how will you manage? Who is he, this man? Which family? Shall I talk to them? Is it a matter of family honour?"

She laughed, her hand still resting on her belly.

"Nobody to talk to, Damari, nobody to make issue with. A thing happened a while ago, that's all. Nobody's fault, nobody to make demands of. My choice, my delight, our mother's happiness."

"I don't understand."

"Damari, my child will be born in Matan of next year. He'll be a boy, I'm sure of it, and when he is born he will be placed on our mother's knees. She will give him his name when the time comes. We know a name already. My child, her child."

Damariel swallowed, memories of death and blood, of two bodies lying in the early summer heat filling his head. Yeresheth was looking into her beaker, the sudden lines on her face drawing out the scars of that day. Sosanneth was speaking again.

"He will be our mother's child, Damari, in every way that matters. Be happy for her, be happy for me as I carry her child for her."

"I am happy, Sannah, for you both, but does your father know?"

"Him! I'm never telling him. That man killed my brothers, killed her sons, and I'm not giving him any satisfaction. Look, Damari, your loyalty should be to our mother, not him. I'm going to give her a son again, a gift out of my own body, and I don't need him to tell me what he thinks. Anyway, he's never once come here since he took up with that other girl, that little rabbit from the lowlands. Bad enough that he's just got his own little brat out from between her legs. He doesn't care what we all think, just wants her for himself, and what she gives him too. Little slut. He doesn't care. She's the same, strutting round with her new baby like she's always lived here. She'll be wanting it to go to the beck with the real village children next. Damariel, don't you know what that means to us? To our family?"

Damariel shook his head at her and touched his finger to his lips, gesturing to where Yeresheth sat with tears on her cheeks. Sosanneth went over to her and wrapped her arms around her mother.

The two clutched at each other for a few seconds, until Yeresheth nodded, wiped her cheeks with the edge of her kef, and looked up again.

"Sannah, I did that too. Not just him, me too. That first evening, a year ago last summer. . . "

She stopped and caught her breath before continuing.

"That night, she wanted my help and I turned my back on her. I could have stopped him taking her away. I tucked her into his bed myself."

She put a finger on Sosanneth's lips as she started to say something else, and turned directly to Damariel.

"My dear son, it is alright. Really it is. I've talked with Sannah about this for this last month and she will manage. We will manage. The weaving she and I have been doing all these months has put us in credit with the village. People will look after us until we can both be at the loom again."

"You've known for a month? How can this be?"

Damariel shook his head, thinking back, trying to work out if he could have known. Yeresheth laughed at him.

"I have had a little more experience than you in this. Don't think badly of yourself."

She sighed.

"Sannah, do something with the bread and that stew. Damari, come out with me and get some eggs."

The two went outside, leaving Sosanneth bending over the cooking fire and the remains of the previous night's dinner.

"Who is he? Tell me who he is, mother. I want to know."

"I don't know. Sannah hasn't told me, and I haven't insisted. I might guess, and I might be wrong. If she wanted me to know she would tell me herself."

"Mother, she's too young for this."

"She'll be in her fifteenth year when the child comes."

They were among a small gathering of hens, murmuring quietly and foraging. Yeresheth sighed but did not answer.

"What about the family? What about her name? What will they think of her? Of you? You can't keep her in the house forever. Someone will see."

"Damari, look now, my sister, your aunt Nerith over the way there, she knows already. She and I have talked of it. Most of the women I know well have a good idea what has happened, even if I have never talked about it openly with them. It's not a thing women hide well from each other." He looked at her, taken aback and still grappling with his lack of insight.

"Mother, do you approve of what she's done? How can you?"

Yeresheth waved aside one of the hens and collected an egg.

"Find me two more, son."

She sat on a low wall and watched as he cast about for the eggs. He found them and brought them over to her, one in each hand. She looked at them very distantly and pushed some loose strands of hair back under her kef before continuing. He realised that her unguarded face was more lined than he remembered, and her hair more touched with grey.

"Damari, I think I care more about my lineage than my reputation now. Am I going to find a man now who will give me more children of my own?" She gestured slightly down her body. "I can't bring back my own boys, and Sannah is giving me something else, someone else. That's important to me, just now."

"I can give you children too! Qetirah and I will have children."

She sighed and met his look.

"I'm sure you will, Damari. You are precious to me, you are my firstborn and opened my womb. You are very dear to me, and Qetirah is like another daughter. But Sannah truly is my daughter, who has come out of my own body, and she carries my bloodline inside her. Just now I need to know that that will carry on."

He sat beside her, looking across at the distant ridge and keeping the eggs in a fold of his smock. She looked down at them and smiled sadly.

"You can't carry all three, Damari. Trust me with one of them."

He found himself abruptly with tears in his eyes and running down his cheeks. He tried twice to say something. She waited patiently until he gathered himself.

"Mother, what about her own future? Who will want her after this?"

"Do you really think she'll have trouble finding the man she wants when the time comes? Look at her, Damari. Another few weeks and all the town will know how it is for her. There'll be a week of gossip and a month of speculation, but long before next Matan comes, most people will give her nothing but respect for what she is doing. As for the others, let them eat locusts in the desert. You can be sure most of the mothers in the village will be looking very hard at this little child as he grows up. Whose son's features can I see there? But Damari, look, you know the young men better than I – how many are really going to turn away from her now they know she can share her bed with a man and carry his child? And next time it will be hers in every way. I've told her this, I won't let her offer me another."

Sosanneth called from inside the house, telling them to bring the eggs, that the rest of the meal was ready and would wait no longer. Damariel leaned against his mother and she kissed the top of his head, then laughed as he put out a hand to steady himself.

"Don't drop them, now."

Inside, Yeresheth broke the eggs into the hot stew and stirred it. Free of his burden, Damariel gathered his sister into his arms and held her for a long time, feeling her breathing quietly against him, wondering how long it would be before her body swelled enough to feel very different when he hugged her. They separated as Yeresheth spooned the mixture onto large rounds of bread, and they ate together.

Time passed. Winter had followed autumn, and then after a struggle had given way to spring. Yeresheth put a pan of water over the fire to start bringing it to the boil, pulled out a bundle of peas and started to shell them. Sosanneth was very pregnant now, with only a few weeks until her term, but as the weather had stayed cool she was still comfortable moving around. She watched her mother busy with the food for a while from a stool in the corner where she was finishing a piece of needlework. She suddenly put it to one side.

"Mother, I think I shall visit Kalita. I heard yesterday she's carrying a second baby from Yusuf. I think I'd like him to see me before I come to term. Both of them, I mean. I want to see them while I can still move. And it's only a few weeks now."

"Go on, Sannah, this will be a while yet. No rush."

Sosanneth looked out of the door, picked up a shawl from the sleeping room and draped it over her shoulders before heading out into the late spring breezy sunshine. Yeresheth heard her voice calling out to Nerith as she passed by her house, then less distinctly to other houses as she moved further away. She started cutting up some onions when there was a knock at the door. She looked up, puzzled. Who would knock rather than call?

She put the onions and knife aside, wiped her hands, went to the door and opened it. It was the lowland girl, standing a pace or two back from the door, both hands wrapped protectively round her baby, who was asleep and being carried in a doubled-over sling of cloth in front of her. She looked very nervous and hesitant. Her eyes were cast down at the ground between them.

"My lady, might we speak? Can I come into your house?"

Beyond her, Yeresheth saw Nerith standing at her own door, a question on her face, clearly ready to intervene if need be. Her voice was very cold.

"Is there anything to say to each other? Perhaps we can stay here at the door."

The younger girl looked up and down the path between the houses, glanced back at Nerith, and shifted a little on her feet. The baby stirred in the sling and made little noises.

Yeresheth sighed and waved to her sister.

"It's all right, Nerith."

Then she continued more quietly.

"Oh, come in, silly to stand here in the wind after all."

She held the door back so the girl could come in, then left it half-open and came back into the room. Her visitor was standing, still hesitant, in the middle of the room, looking this way and that.

"Well, sit down somewhere. There's a stool. Wait a minute."

She found a blanket, folded it a few times and set it down on the floor. “Here, your baby can stretch out on that.” She paused. “Look, I don’t know what to call you.”

The visitor unwrapped the sling, cradling the still sleeping baby as she settled him on the blanket. Yeresheth noticed absently that it was a boy. His arms stretched up above his head as he adjusted to the new position, and he made some sucking movements with his lips. Without meaning to, Yeresheth smiled down at him.

“My name used to be Aliyna, lady. You might have heard me called Amat by some of the others, though.”

“Is that his name for you?”

Aliyna nodded. Both women were looking at the baby and not at each other. He was becoming restive, limbs moving sporadically about and head casting from side to side.

“I’ll not be using that, then. Just like him to rub in your face every day that you were captured. Aliyna, then. You’re not my serving-girl, Amat won’t do.” They fell silent briefly, watching the baby fidget more loudly. “He’s hungry, isn’t he. Feed him if you want while we talk. What do you call him?”

Aliyna picked him up again, loosened her sash and brought him up to her breast. The little questing mouth searched briefly before finding nourishment. He started sucking contentedly, one hand reaching out to her body. His dark eyes opened and fixed on her face with a blissful expression, and both women laughed.

“Marir.”

“Hah. Your choice or his?”

“His. Shomal’s, I mean.”

“I won’t have that man named in this house. But yes, he would want it to be his choice. Did he not allow you to name your own baby?”

“Lady, I know that is your custom, but not ours down near the coast. I would expect the father to name the child.”

“So, your son’s going to be a little strong man, then?”

Aliyna shrugged, concentrating on Marir.

"He thinks so, lady."

The two were silent, and the room seemed loud with suckling noises.

"Well, now, look, since I have asked you into my house, I think you could call me Yeresheth. You don't need to call me lady. You only just missed Sosanneth, she left just before you got here. Her time is nearly due, the baby will come before the next new moon. I need to be getting used to babies again. She could do with seeing a newborn before her own comes."

"I wanted to miss her." Aliyna paused. "I don't think she will want to see me. I didn't want to cause her grief just now. I think, I hear, I mean people say that she blames me for, well, for all that happened here."

There was another silence. Marir detached himself from her breast and waved his free hand urgently, making little complaint noises again. Aliyna swapped him to the other side and he quietened again. The women were still looking only at Marir, not each other.

"Yes, I think she does."

"And you, lady? Do you think that?"

Yeresheth was silent. She adjusted her kef and sat back a little on her stool. She pulled the pan of peas away from the fire. Marir's suckling was becoming slower, more drawn out, and he was starting to look round at other things from time to time.

"I don't know what to think, Aliyna. It's nearly two years now since that day. I lost my two boys. You came. That man we won't name left. Damari moved in with the seer. Now you have this little Marir and my own little baby Sannah is almost due with her own child. But Damari and Qetirah have been together over a year and her womb hasn't opened. Did you do all that? All by yourself? How can I think that you did all of that just by coming up here?"

She shook her head, suddenly overwhelmed by how her life had changed. The lines deepened on her face, and the scars of that day showed more bleakly than usual. She saw a drop of water fall onto Marir's wrapping, then a second and third, and realised that Aliyna was crying, her shoulders moving a little but without sound. Marir pulled away from her breast and looked up, his hand trying to reach her face. Aliyna rested him across her knees, closed and tied her tunic again, and then placed him gently down on his back on the blanket. They watched him wave his arms and look around in an unfocused manner.

Yeresheth reached for a spare length of ribbon and dangled it just within reach of his arms. He paused, staring at the red strip above him, and tried without success to grab it several times. She reached down and tucked it between his fingers, and he pulled on it once, twice before letting go again. His large eyes looked beyond the cloth and looked into her face for a long moment. She knelt down beside him, touched his hand, let him tug at her little finger, then stroked his cheek so that his eager mouth turned towards her hand and tried to suck at it.

For the first time she looked up directly at Aliyna, who was using the end of her kef to dry her tears. Aliyna dropped her eyes to the ground out of habit, and then slowly looked back again at Yeresheth. A little, incoherent noise came from her.

"Look, Aliyna, so much has happened. For a long while I hated you for it, thought it was all your doing, you see."

She held up her hand to stop the other woman's reply.

"No, Aliyna, I need to say this. Let me say it. That was two years ago. I thought it was all the same, but no. Things have changed, and seeing you today, seeing little Marir here today, well, that's it, isn't it? You and I both lost on that day, but perhaps we can make something new."

She fell silent again and looked down at Marir, who was moving more jerkily and making noises of discomfort.

"Aliyna, I think he needs some help."

"He does." She looked around uncertainly into the corners of the room and then back at Yeresheth.

"There, over there just inside the next room."

There was a pause while the baby's needs were met, and then Aliyna brought him back in, happier and brighter, to lie on the blanket again. The two women sat on the floor facing each other either side of him.

"Look, Aliyna, I know what I lost that day. But I've never asked what you lost?"

Aliyna looked away for a moment and swallowed before answering. Her voice had become quite ragged.

"I had been married, down there, married three years."

She saw Yeresheth's face moving in sympathy, and hurried on with her words.

"One of your boys killed him, you know, when they were fighting, before our neighbour heard the shouting, burst in, fought back against them. I don't know which one, there were weapons and blood and things everywhere, and oh, I was screaming, terrified, no idea what was happening in all the world. My neighbour did what he could, he couldn't help, he was pushed back when all your other men came in and saw what had happened, and then they pulled at me and took me away. There he was just lying there dead, nothing I could do. And I never got to see him buried."

Yeresheth looked very grim, very old, and there was another silence in the house.

"I'd had a child with him, with Labayu, but I'd lost her the winter before; she caught ill and never recovered. I lived in a house near to his family, and his parents were always dear to me. I had my house, enough chickens and goats to never be in want, a bit of land for growing food, cousins and friends to help me when I needed it. Now I live in a barren little shed among a few olive trees, and I've lived without kin for two years. I even have to tie my kef differently. I can't tell you how humiliating it was at first, not to be allowed to wear my kef the way my mother had taught me. None of the women will come and see me. Not even now that Marir is here. I thought he might make a difference for me. But no, he hasn't, not yet. The only person who shows kindness is your Damariel, the times he comes to see his father. I thought maybe if you and I could speak, if we could come to an understanding, maybe the other women will change too. If they see you change, I mean. Yeresheth, lady, I am very lonely."

There was another pause. Marir was grasping them, one in each hand, making little gurgling noises and looking from one to the other and back again. Yeresheth's face was still very drawn. When she did speak it was at a tangent.

"Where were your parents?"

"In the next village, where they have always lived. I have no idea what they think happened to me."

"You weren't in your mother's house?"

Aliyna shook her head.

"That is not our custom. I left there when I married Labayu, we lived in the house beside his family."

"How ever do your women bear it? Look, Sannah will give birth soon, and I could never bear to be somewhere else. Even if she had a man to live with her now. How ever could I let someone else be with her in labour?"

Aliyna frowned at Marir, and suddenly laughed.

"Yeresheth, when I left my parents' house it wasn't like that. I was glad to go and make my own home, couldn't imagine my mother being there on top of me."

She laughed again, and Yeresheth joined her before speaking again.

"You know, nobody has ever told me, not once, what happened that day with my boys. Not in all this time. I think Damari knows, I'm sure that Danil told him when he was drunk one night on autumn wine, but he's never told me. Doesn't want to shame me or something. Stupid."

She paused for a long, silent moment before looking back at Aliyna. "You know, he's not actually his father."

Aliyna looked blank for a moment, her forehead wrinkled with puzzlement under her kef. Suddenly she understood.

"Oh, Damariel, you mean. No, I didn't know. Neither of them has ever told me."

"That man couldn't give me children at first, his seed was barren. So I lay with the seer, not this one, the one before, Iqnu was his name. He finished his life here in shame, but this was truly a good thing he once did. At the summer feast in the month of Dabah, it was, oh, lots of years ago now, I suppose about twenty years ago it must be. Damari is a child of the gods out of my womb. Nothing to do with that other man. But after Damari came Baruk and Bashur. You know about them. They were his. And my youngest, Sannah, my little girl who will soon have her own child."

She smiled down at Marir, who was trying to nuzzle her hand and push her fingers into his mouth. "You can't be hungry again, not yet. If you were I wouldn't be so much use to you." She looked up again at Aliyna, the smile lasting a little longer. "So you see that Damari is mine but not his."

Aliyna nodded and tried to sit Marir up against her knees, but having little success she supported him with hands either side of his body.

She looked at the pot of cooked peas, quite cool now.

"Look, I've stopped you cooking. Can I help?"

Yeresheth shook her head, and then suddenly spoke.

"Aliyna, does he treat you well? Is he cruel to you?"

Aliyna looked out of the half-open door.

"How can I speak of that, lady, with you of all people?"

"I know how he can be. Who better? Aliyna, two years ago I could have helped you, I could have kept you here with Sannah, but on that night I just threw you at him. It suited me to do that. It was hardly the best day for me to consider your feelings. But I know how he can be, and I think that maybe I should have spared you that. At the time you were just something I could use to get him out of my house, and I was distraught about my children."

They both looked down at Marir, then back at each other.

"I don't want to talk about those first months, those first nights. But things are better now, and I have my own baby. I think maybe the gods have turned to me again."

Yeresheth looked down again at Marir and stroked his hair, still rather wispy.

"He'll have dark wavy hair before he reaches his fifth year, you know, just like my two boys had. Ah me, how will it be for me to see him as he grows up? Him and Sannah's baby both."

She wrapped the ribbon round Marir's middle and tucked the loose ends behind his back as he lay, looking up at her and waving his arms.

"There, that's for the birth present I never gave you. Not much, and late, but perhaps it's a new start for us both."

Aliyna took her hands and held them tightly. She was crying a little again, and Yeresheth tried to remember if she had been so tearful when she was younger. Maybe it was a lowland thing.

"Yeresheth, dear lady, thank you for this, this gift, this time together as well, I mean, all of it. Look, I would like to come again another time if you will have me. I know you won't want to come down to the field, I wouldn't in your place, not even once, but can I come back up here? I so want to be with people, with women, and Marir will need friends too as he gets older. I don't want my past to be a shadow on his future path. And Sosanneth, she and I should have so much to share. I do want it put right, and perhaps you will help me?"

Yeresheth held her hands a moment longer, thinking.

"Aliyna, come back in two days, just after noon. I will talk to Sannah."

Aliyna nodded, tightened and tied the ribbon like a sash around Marir and slipped out of the door with him in the sling in front of her. Yeresheth sighed and started chopping onions to put in with the peas. Some time later Sosanneth came back in the door and sat heavily back on the stool with a breathless sigh.

"That hill is getting too steep for me, mother. What will I be like in another week? Too big even to waddle over the way to my aunt, maybe."

She looked in surprise at the unfinished soup.

"Mother, what have you been doing all the time while I've been with Kalita?"

Glancing around, she sat upright and said suddenly, "Someone has been here, haven't they? Who is it, mother? Who are you seeing now? Waited until I had gone out, did you? Who was it, then?"

Yeresheth shook her head at her suggestive tone.

"Nothing like that, O devoted daughter."

She paused and added a few herb leaves to the soup. "There, finished now, eat this and don't run after thoughts like that so quickly. Now, just be patient while we eat and I think."

There was a little pause while the two women started the soup. Sosanneth waited for an answer, and eventually Yeresheth put her spoon down in the bowl among the last vegetables and looked at her.

"It was Aliyna, the lowland girl. Came up here with her baby, Marir, he's called, to see me. You as well, if you'd been around."

"You let that little slut into our house? How could you do that? Anyway, she's called Amat, isn't she, not Aliyna? I suppose she wants to wriggle her way into your affections now, just like she did. . . " She broke off abruptly, seeing the expression on her mother's face. "Well, I'm not sorry, someone has to keep saying these things."

"Look, Sannah, who should we be angry with in all this? Suppose you'd be taken in a raid, may the gods forbid, and forced into bed with someone from, I don't know, someone from Yano'am or Pehela. One of those rough northern places away over the River. Would I want the women up there to hate you because of what you'd had to do? If you were carrying the baby of some foreign stranger instead of one of us, wouldn't I want my child's child to find friends, brothers and sisters? You chose who you lay with to conceive your child, whose bed you shared last autumn, but what if you'd had no choice?"

Sosanneth sat, silent and sullen, her free hand wrapped protectively across her belly, her soup cooling.

"I still don't see why she has to come here. She already squirmed her way into that man's bed. I bet she enjoyed every moment. Now she wants you."

When she replied, Yeresheth's voice had sharpened considerably.

"You don't know what you're talking about, daughter. That man didn't always know how to be gentle. What do you know about it? Don't you tell me how it might have been for her."

Sosanneth looked away and then concentrated on her soup. There was an awkward silence for a while until she spoke again, rebellious now rather than righteous.

"Well, she chose him. She went off with him."

"No, Sannah, it wasn't like that."

The two exchanged looks again.

"What do you mean? I was there, too, you know. He asked her and she went off."

Yeresheth shook her head fiercely, a loop of hair slipping out of her kef as she put her almost-empty bowl down. She carefully tucked it back in place.

"Sannah, that day I was furious with that man that we won't name. We'd spoken rough words to each other about Baruk and Bashur. I thought he was just going to beat me then and there and have done with it, but you were beside me and then Damari came back in. I've never been so relieved to have the two of you there with me."

She closed her eyes.

"Just then I'd have done anything to get him out of my house, and the simplest way was to use Aliyna, put her in his way to soak up all his ire. Knowing that he would just take her into his bed. She wanted my help that day and I refused. Simple as that. Some would say that little Marir was my fault, not his."

In the distance they could hear voices of children coming back from the stream. After a while Yeresheth continued.

"Anyway, I've invited her back again two days from now. She wants to be with women. She wants to mend things between us, all of us. Her, you and me, her baby and yours who is coming soon. I think we could all manage that much."

Two days later, at the same hour of the day, Aliyna came again. Yeresheth and Sosanneth had not settled the matter on that first day, nor in the time between, but Yeresheth had persevered with her daughter's opinion in both direct and more subtle ways.

Aliyna knocked again at the door, as though uncertain of the reception. Marir was awake this time, turning his head this way and that to try to see out of the sling. Yeresheth spread out the blanket on the floor again and Aliyna put him down on it as Sosanneth watched them from one corner of the room. He was wearing the red ribbon Yeresheth had given to them. There was an awkward silence, broken by Aliyna as she turned to Sosanneth.

"Lady Sosanneth, I want to wish you every blessing for your child. I also want things to be different between us, and I'm sorry for any wrong I have done you."

She stopped, hands gripped at her sides, waiting to see what would happen. Yeresheth also looked at her daughter and waited.

"Oh, all right. I accept. Actually, I don't know what wrong you might have done me, and my own mother has been trying to tell me that for two days. Please, come in, sit down, be at peace here in my mother's house."

There was a sense of relief like a sigh in the room, and the three women sat down, Marir in between looking one way and another. Sosanneth looked down at him, reached out her hand to touch his fingers. He grabbed at her hand and missed. Aliyna opened the bag she carried over her shoulder and took out some raisins saved over from last year, gave them to Yeresheth.

"How old is he now?"

"About half a year, Sosanneth. He was born in the autumn near the end of Etanim."

Sosanneth teased his fingers a little longer, an odd expression on her face. As she leaned forward a little he suddenly caught sight of her face and turned his head towards her and gazed directly at her. She reached out to touch him, then drew her hand back hesitantly.

"It's all right, Sosanneth, you can hold him. He likes to be picked up."

She reached forward, one hand firmly either side of his body, but then stopped again, uncertain. Both older women started forward to help her. Aliyna laughed a little.

"No, Yeresheth, you show her. She's your daughter."

They got Marir comfortable on Sosanneth's lap, cradled into the angle of her arm.

"Sosanneth, look, down where I come from we say that if a pregnant woman gets a boy baby to suckle her, then she'll have a boy as well."

Sosanneth looked down at him and touched his face, then moved her hand onto the curve of her womb.

"Isn't my boy already formed inside me? How can this make any difference?"

"Sannah, an aunt of mine told me the same thing. What harm can it do?"

Sosanneth shook her head, but loosened her smock and held Marir against her. Yeresheth stroked his cheek with her finger, and he opened his mouth, turned his head, found Sosanneth's breast and started suckling. She looked down, to see his eyes wide open and fixed on her. She gazed back, open-mouthed herself at his contentment. He pulled away after a short time, and she swapped him to the other side. Unsuccessful again, this time he made a complaining noise and looked up at Sosanneth with an accusing air. Sosanneth handed him back to Aliyna to feed.

"Look, Aliyna, you'd better have him back before he realises he's been cheated. Do you think there's truth in that story?

I'm sure I'm having a boy anyway. I am going to have a boy, you know. I've always known that."

Aliyna shrugged, her attention still half on the baby.

"And may he be a blessing both to you and to your mother. What will you call him? Yeresheth tells me that here it is the mother's right to choose the name."

"But you know, I am going to put him on my mother's knees when he is born, so he will be called her son. We've talked about the name, we know what he'll be called already, but she will be the one to give the name to him. He will be Labunasi, and when he grows up he will be prince over all the others."

Yeresheth waved a hand at her.

"I'm not doing any more for your child than any mother's mother would. Certainly not feeding him, he'd be as frustrated and hungry as Marir would be with you right now. I shall sit here in my house like a queen and receive all the praise when people come and see this little prince, but you can do all the work."

Marir waved his hands and looked about at the others as they all laughed. There was a voice at the door and Nerith came in. Yeresheth stood up and they hugged each other.

"No, Sannah, I'll come to you. And who is your guest?"

Sosanneth leaned her head against her aunt as she stood beside her. Aliyna was still trying to arrange herself and Marir, with little success as he kept squirming around to see what was happening.

"This is Aliyna, aunt Nerith. We have become friends now, and this is her baby Marir, and I held him, mother showed me how to hold him right so I'll know how to do it right when my boy is born."

Nerith nodded, then sat down beside Aliyna. Marir was starting to settle down again, and Aliyna looked cautiously at Nerith.

"Well, I can't stay just now. Aliyna, look, if these two should be out one day when you're passing, then I just live across the way. I'd be pleased if you would call to see me sometime."

Aliyna nodded. She started to say something but her voice failed her. Nerith stood up, leaned over and kissed her on both cheeks, then left. Aliyna sat, silent, one hand pressed against her mouth, tears in her eyes, holding still for a long moment as she felt the circumstances of her life change around her.

Three weeks later, Aliyna was working outside her house in the early morning, beating out rush mats over the wall while Marir lay near her on a piece of cloth. Shomal was up one of the olive trees working on some older branches with a pruning hook. She looked up, hearing a voice nearby, and saw Damariel running down the incline, calling to them. A great surge of mingled anticipation and anxiety flooded through her as she stood up straight and dropped the mat she was holding.

Damariel arrived, caught his breath, and then spoke, all in a rush.

"Aliyna, Sannah has had her baby, a boy, mother named him Labunasi just as they agreed, he's big but they're both well. Last night, it was just a short time ago he came out, she's been in labour most of the night. She's fine, he's fine."

Shomal was climbing out of the tree. Aliyna picked Marir up, sat on the wall and took Damariel's hand, unable to speak for a few moments. Finally she found a voice.

"Oh, bless both of them. How wonderful, just what she wanted." She looked over her shoulder quickly and then continued in a lower voice. "Damariel, what about your mother Yeresheth? What did Sosanneth do when the baby was born."

He nodded.

"Sannah asked Nerith to put him on our mother's knees for her and then mother blessed him and named him. I haven't seen her so happy in years. Then they washed him and cut the cord and put him back on Sannah."

He raised his voice a little as Shomal approached. "Qetirah was there too, along with Nerith and Yeresheth and me. Father, blessings to you today, for your daughter is now a mother herself. You have a grandson, Labunasi by name."

Shomal nodded, a great smile across his features. He put his arm round Damariel's shoulders.

"How was it, lad? A boy? Good. Is he well? And Sannah?"

Damariel told them again, missing out the part about Yeresheth receiving the child, putting stress on the safe passage of both mother and baby.

"But look now, I must be getting back up there soon again. They'll be wanting me to do the birth blessing and offer something up at the stones. I am sorry to leave you so soon but I wanted to tell you myself before you heard from someone else."

Shomal held onto his arm, as though unwilling to let him go. His face filled up with the realisation of loss. He started to speak several times before succeeding.

"Damariel, look, son, you know I would be there with Sannah, with my own daughter, if I could. You do know that? You know that, don't you? But they won't want me, won't let me near there. My own grandson."

He looked down at Marir, placid in Aliyna's arms, then looked away across the endless ridges and valleys. He shook his head and made an inarticulate noise. Aliyna put her hand on his arm, very gently.

"Shomal, let me go up and see them. They'll let me do that, and I can tell you all about your grandson when I get back. You take Marir, just leave the trees for a while and play with him. I'll be back as soon as I can."

He pursed his lips, looking profoundly upset, then without speaking bent over to kiss her on the forehead. Damariel stood astonished, for he had never before seen him show any sign of affection to her. She passed Marir over to him, stepped across to the other side of the wall and set off with Damariel to Yeresheth's house.

When they got there, they could hear Sosanneth and Qetirah in the adjoining room. Yeresheth and Nerith were talking quietly in the main room, recounting old baby stories from the town each to the other. Yeresheth stood up as Damariel came in with Aliyna, and hugged them both.

"I'm so proud of my Sannah today. Less time than I took with you, Damari!"

"Mother, mother, we're here, Aliyna's here to see Sannah if she can manage that."

"As it's you two, of course. Nerith and I are keeping everyone else at the door. Nobody gets past us, they just get to hear that all is well. You tell them all, when you make the sacrifice up at the stones, tell all of them that she's fine, the boy is fine, and they can all see in forty days. Until then, she's here under my roof and not seeing anyone. Nobody. Family's different, of course you can come when you like. You too, Aliyna. But the others have to keep out. Now go on in, both of you, while she's still awake."

They went in to the room, gloomy with drapes drawn across the window. Sosanneth was lying in her bed, eyes half shut, her hair raggedly pushed away from her face and untidy without a kef. She looked pale and tired, worn out. Labunasi was beside her, slightly misshapen and very red. Qetirah was sitting beside the bed, holding her hand, so that Labunasi was between the two women. She smiled happily and held out her spare hand to Damariel to join her.

Aliyna squatted down on the floor by Sosanneth, put her arms very carefully around her and kissed her on both cheeks. Sosanneth opened her eyes painfully and moved her legs a little on the bed.

"Aliyna, I'm so tired now. Oh, I hurt. You didn't tell me about that. But do you see him, my little boy?"

Aliyna nodded.

"He's magnificent, Sosanneth, your prince of lions. But you, are you all right? How are you? I am so happy for both of you. Bless you both, health and long life to you now."

"Just now I need to sleep. Health and a long sleep. Everything hurts just now. Qetirah, you've no idea. But look, my little prince is sleeping already. Aliyna, I'm glad you're here today to see us. Come again soon."

Aliyna hugged her again, little tears in her eyes as she kissed her one last time and then stood up. Yeresheth was at the door behind them, glancing from one to another but looking mainly at Labunasi, asleep beside his mother. Damariel let go of Qetirah's hand and stood up. Sosanneth was unaware of them going, was almost asleep.

"Aliyna, I'll go back down the hill with you. Then I need to go and make the thank offering up at the stones."

Nerith spoke from her chair, where she was pressing pieces of bread dough into rounds. "I can take her down if you like."

Damariel paused, thinking about it. Yeresheth was looking pointedly at him.

"That's kind, aunt, but no need. There's no rush."

They passed down through the little tracks between the houses. Almost everyone had heard about the baby, and their way was slow, stopping often to explain how mother and baby were both well and resting. Past the last house, where the ground opened out, Aliyna suddenly stopped, put her hand out to stop Damariel as well. Shomal's house was still hidden by two olive trees.

"The birth blessing, Damariel?"

He nodded. "I say one for every birth, I've done it the last year or so, with Ketty too, one of the first things Saniyahu entrusted to us. Said I needed to start understanding birth. Of course he or Halith would say it if I wasn't around. Mostly it's simple thanks. Sometimes one or other has died, and the blessing comes a lot harder. And there's a thank offering I make at the stones, just something small."

He stopped himself from babbling, looked at her, and suddenly understood.

"Oh, yes. Of course. Yes, Aliyna, I did say a blessing for you and Marir, back last autumn, as soon as I heard from Halith you'd passed through labour. Saniyahu and I spoke it out together. Whatever has come between Shomal and my mother, you and yours are in our care. He and Halith will leave me here as seer with Qetirah soon enough, later this year I think, but this responsibility is mine already. You are under the banner of my prayers and offerings just as much as anyone."

He paused a moment, shook his head, and looked back up the hill.

"To think, now I shall be saying it for my own sister."

She sighed, closed her eyes briefly, squeezed his hand, then ran on past the olive trees to find Marir and Shomal. She looked back once to see that Damariel was still waiting there behind the first trees to see what would happen. On the wall with Shomal, she took her son back and settled him in the angle of her left arm.

Shomal stood up and started to walk towards the tree he had been pruning earlier, but she took his arm and stopped him. Instead, they sat together on the little dry-stone wall and she told him about Sosanneth and the new child, gesturing with her free hand as she spoke. Shomal said little, but absorbed the news intently, and when she had finished he nodded once, twice, then wiped his sleeve across his eyes. As he was looking away across the wooded ridges she glanced back towards Damariel, who waved and started back up the hill towards the high place, leaving them still sitting there.

Teth

MEPAGH YEAR 19 – NISAN YEAR 20

HEAR, O YOU GODS, my outcry,
be attentive to my prayer –
from the land's extremity I cry out with faint heart,
lead me on to the Rock high above.

THE LATE SUMMER WAS STARTING to break up into sudden flurries of wind. The festival of new wine was not far away. Saniyahu and Halith were about to leave. Adonibaal, the old seer at Jarrar's town, had died after a long illness, and they were to take up office there. Already through the summer they had spent increasing amounts of time with him, receiving from him all they needed to know of the people in that community.

He had begun to serve as seer for the town long before Damariel and Qetirah were born, and had outlived his wife and one of his children by several years. He would be missed and mourned. Damariel did not envy his tutors their task up at Woodlands, and said as much to Saniyahu one day when the four of them were eating in the doorway to the house. Halith laughed.

"He thinks it'll be easy here just because we've only stayed four years or so."

Saniyahu was silent for a while, pushing vegetables round his plate with a piece of torn-off bread.

"Look, both of you, you're young to take this on. We've talked with the other seers and all are agreed: there is no choice. Since Iqnu so abruptly left this life – and you know all about that – we are short of hands. Adonibaal should have been able to sit at ease in the shade of his own vine before now, but there was nobody to take the fourth place. You two are furthest along in your apprenticeship, and all of us are agreed. It must be you two. You have done enough, you have learned enough from us to serve here in Kephrath. At least, we all think so."

Qetirah, sitting beside him, put her hand on his shoulder.

"We'll work hard here, sir. You don't have to worry."

"Of course you will. But who knows what is to come? Ill chance might fall on any of us, and none of the other seers have anyone far enough along their apprenticeship if the worst should happen. Qetirah, I have, we both have every trust in you both, but the burden for leaving you here, tomorrow, is a thing we feel very heavily. I wish we had had longer, even just one year longer."

Halith nodded, her expression very serious.

"Look, Ketty, it's been hard enough for me to earn the trust of the older women. How much more then for you, who they remember being born yesterday? I wish you weren't serving in your own home town, but we have no other choice. You must work with them, win them over to you."

Qetirah looked at her.

"What about the men who speak like a father to me?"

"Oh, the men are easy enough."

This time Saniyahu laughed.

"Damari, we will only be a short walk up the track. Any time either of you need assistance you can come up to us. Or send a lad with a message and we will come down to you. But look, there is a great deal we need to do today, before the sun sets and we all enjoy the parting feast. First, these are the people Halith and I have needed to visit recently."

The next few hours were a blur as Saniyahu and Halith spoke about all the various people needing pastoral care. In most cases Damariel or Qetirah knew about the situation anyway, but there were some surprises. After every name they paused and prayed, heads bowed and hands uplifted into the winds of heaven. Then they spoke through every house in the village, top to bottom, whether they knew of a pressing need or not. Eventually that was finished, and they worked their way round their own house, agreeing which things would stay and which would go.

To Damariel's delight, almost all of the musical instruments were staying, as part of the village's own inheritance. Halith was taking the double pipe away with her, but not the round bodied lyre that was Damariel's own favourite. They came out into the late afternoon sunshine, ducking under the generous bunches of grapes draped from the vine around the door.

With a sudden fond memory, Damariel opened the door of the little room that had been his first home here. The vine branch that used just to reach towards it now crowned the top of the door frame. In it was a little pile of things Saniyahu was taking with him, and the room looked small, cramped. He had outgrown it. Qetirah leaned against his shoulder to look in, and he put his arm around her happily. After tonight, they would have a whole house to themselves: indeed, a whole village.

The feast that evening, held on and among the stones of the high place, was a mixture of celebration and sorrow. Saniyahu and Halith, as guests of honour, sat in the centre of the circle and lacked nothing they wanted. Different men and women around the circle got up and spoke one thing or another about them, reciting their deeds on behalf of the village so they would not be forgotten. Damariel noticed Aliyna at one time sitting discreetly at the back of the circle with Marir, saw Nerith go over and sit beside her for a while before she slipped away again, back down towards the olive field. Shomal was nowhere in sight.

Finally it was over. Everyone moved to form a circle. Saniyahu and Halith went around the circle, person after person, family after family standing together, naming every one and blessing them each in turn. It took a long time. Finally the circle was complete, and they returned to their place at the centre.

"Damariel and Qetirah, join us at the centre of the circle."

They held hands as they crossed over to stand there, feeling rather intimidated by the situation. Saniyahu and Halith looked around the group and spoke in turn.

"Danil son of Mahiram, do you accept Damariel son of Yeresheth and Kinreth's daughter Qetirah on behalf of the fighting men of Kephrath?"

Danil stood up at his place in the circle.

"Honoured lord, I do."

"Shelomith-Rahmay, do you accept Damariel son of Yeresheth and Kinreth's daughter Qetirah on behalf of the mothers of Kephrath?"

"Honoured lord, I do."

And so it went round the group, each part of the community being asked in turn, each standing to formally accept the couple and then sitting again. Damariel could see Yeresheth off to his left, Labunasi on her lap, Sosanneth beside her, gripped by the occasion, happiness and pride playing across her face. Eventually all was done. There was a little pause. Damariel and Qetirah untied their kefs and handed them to Saniyahu and Halith, who held them up in everyone's sight and then placed them on one of the stones.

"Today Damariel son of Yeresheth and Kinreth's daughter Qetirah are no longer apprenticed. Today they become your seers and priests. Today they take a place among the seers of the four towns. We accept them as such. We who have been your seers and priests now pass on to them a sign of their office."

They stepped behind Damariel and Qetirah and tied new kefs on each: plain white with three red threads running in and out of the weave around the crown of their heads. Qetirah looked very solemn as Halith embraced her. Saniyahu gestured with his hand, and the whole group rose to their feet.

"People of Kephrath, we have accepted Damariel son of Yeresheth and Kinreth's daughter Qetirah to be seers and priests in our place. You have heard the voices of those who speak for you accept them. Now you must speak as the whole assembly of this place. Are there any who do not accept these two?"

They looked around the circle in the slowly fading light. Nobody spoke. They waited. A great silence settled on the high place and among the people. The pause stretched out, and still nobody broke the silence. Damariel swallowed and shifted his feet as he waited.

"Are there any who do accept these two?"

A great shout of affirmation went up from the gathered voices. Qetirah put her hand to her mouth and gazed around at the cheering people. Labunasi gave a great twitch of his body at the sudden noise and then settled again as Yeresheth smoothed his hair with her hand. Saniyahu turned to the young couple and looked very serious.

"Last of all, do you two accept this choice? Will you serve these people, standing in the places between the earth and the heavens where they ask you to? Will you take your place as seers and priests of the four towns?"

Damariel and Qetirah, still holding hands, looked at one another, then back at Saniyahu and answered together.

"We will."

Saniyahu nodded, then stepped back. There was another moment of silence, then he and Halith began singing the great hymn to the lord of all the gods, and the whole assembly joined in for the responses.

"Turn your face and remember us"
"You are lord over all of the land"
"Stretch out your hand in blessing to us"
"You are lord over all of the land"

Then it was done, and with scarcely a pause for breath the solemnity was over. People, one after another, came forward to offer their respects, blessing, friendship. Finding a little gap, Damariel went over to his family and embraced them, trying to gather all of them into his arms at once.

Sosanneth touched the new kef he was wearing and was about to speak, but someone else came up from the side and caught his attention. He looked at Sosanneth questioningly, but she shook her head.

"Another day, Damari. Labunasi needs his home and his bed anyway. Another day, another day, my brother. It can wait."

As Damariel turned to accept the praise of the newcomer, he saw Shomal at last, at the back of the crowd, keeping out of sight. He raised one hand in recognition and then slipped away again, as Aliyna had done earlier.

Early the next morning Saniyahu and Halith loaded two donkeys with the most urgent of their belongings and set off, up along the ridge to Jarrar's town. The four of them had stayed up late into the night talking, and had finally fallen asleep all together in the great room, one after another. They had woken together soon after dawn, and there seemed nothing more to say just then. Damariel and Qetirah watched them go, away around the great rock that had been their own meeting place long ago, so long ago, and then out of sight into the low scrubby trees. They looked at each other, and then Qetirah closed the door. The house was theirs.

In the early golden light one morning late the following spring, Kothar eased the saddlebag straps across one of the donkeys as the last package was pushed inside and tied off beside the town gate. Over the last few years he had become progressively more flamboyant in his attire, a habit cultivated quite independently of his parents, and somewhat to their disappointment. Along with that, he was still loud in his loves and hates, frankly spoken with the men of the community and flirtatious with their women, and watched jealously by his wife Shaharti while she suckled their first child.

He was waiting for Damariel to come down from his house, hoping that they could get away before the day started to become hot, and pulled again at the harness. Two of the other men were tying down the bundle on the other donkey, talking to each other just too quietly for him to hear. He heard footsteps on the cindered path and turned to see his friend walking at some speed towards him.

"I'm sorry, Kothar, got held up with explaining things twice over to the lad who's taking a message up to the seer at Meyim for me."

From behind him, Kothar heard one of the men say something about sticks that wouldn't catch light and birds that wouldn't cook, and the other chuckle loudly, coarsely, in reply. Damariel paused briefly and flushed a little, then walked the last few steps to the donkeys and fiddled randomly with a harness. Kothar turned and stared at the two, who looked at each other, pulled a strap tight and then went off together. Kothar checked the harness himself one last time, tapped the nearer of the two donkeys with his stick, and the two set off along the track away from the village.

They were heading south-west towards the thicker lowland woods, considerably south of the little communities they sometimes raided. Damariel set both the direction and the pace, aiming well to the west of Shalem and intending to pick up the main track down to Bayth Shamsh. Kothar was content for a while to walk in silence, picking up a fir cone every now and again to shy away at larger trees near the path. He was well aware that Damariel was internally seething at the half-heard comments, and whistled as he two picked their way along the goat paths down the first ridge and up the second.

Every so often the words of the song would come back to him and he would work them in to his whistling. It was a long, repetitious story about two kings and the endless series of increasingly martial messages despatched between them, and he started changing the order of verses. Damariel suddenly became aware that the kings had just exchanged lavish gifts rather than threats. He looked up at the larger man over the first donkey's ears.

"Kothar, you could at least get the verses in the right order."

Kothar tossed another cone across the nodding ears of the animal.

"You've emerged from your sulk, then?"

"I was not sulking. But what those two said was just, well, crude. Meant me to hear it, too. You know they did."

Kothar tipped his hand one way and the other, his eyes on the path ahead where it dipped through young bracken.

"Damari, take no notice of them. Men will make fun at your expense. Worry if they don't! Nobody ever made fun of old Iqnu, ever, and nobody cared much if he lived or died, either. Except for Isheth, I suppose. Of course, you got on with him as well, truth to tell. Most folk just didn't care, though. Just give it more time. How come you and he spent so much time together?"

Damariel laughed briefly.

"He was the one that started teaching me, you know. Songs, poems, journey lists and all that. You could say it's because of him I'm where I am now."

"But he was a close-fisted character at the best of times. Never cared much for Ketty and me in spite of everything. Why suddenly take an interest in you?"

"Oh, he kept saying he was going to do something for you both. And the younger ones. But then, he said a lot of things and not so many of them ever happened. Oh, well, it doesn't matter to say it now, I suppose. I've never told anyone else. I found him coming out of Isheth's house way back, long before anyone else knew about it, when I was coming back from the tomb of our ancestors one night. It was one time when Ethan was away with his flocks. He, Iqnu I mean, well, you could say he traded the teaching for me not remembering very well what I saw."

Kothar stopped for a moment in surprise.

"You did that? Kept that squirreled away well, didn't you?"

He shrugged.

"No point gossiping about it, and I did promise him. It all came out in the end, anyway, without me saying a word. But you're changing the subject. Do you know what those two were saying?"

Kothar met the other's look with a shrewd, brief glance. Damariel swallowed and looked out across the wooded ridges before carrying on.

"Kothar, how many say that? How many? Are we the joke of the whole town?"

"Look, Damariel, take no notice. These men like you. They like Ketty too, for that matter, and wouldn't mind being in your position now and again. Give it more time. I don't know – make some sacrifices, or get one of the other priests in to pray. You're the religious one, you tell me. Or have another woman to bear your little ones. Easy enough."

"Easy enough for you to say."

Kothar laughed. He had married Ayala's daughter Shaharti and moved into her house not long after Damariel and Qetirah's wedding, and it had taken hardly any time for her already ample form to grow more rounded with their first child.

Kothar laughed again, a pleased, self-satisfied laugh.

"Don't tell anyone else, but my Shaharti missed her bleeding this month. Maybe we'll be asking you and Ketty round to give her a womb-blessing again. Likely enough I shall be envious of your peace and quiet up on the hill there. When we have another I'll be looking for a place to get some sleep."

Damariel frowned at him.

"Kothar, I can't have the whole village talking like this about us. I'm the seer. How can she and I have respect from the others if my seed won't take in her?"

The two walked in silence with the pack beasts for a while, until the track levelled out along a long valley side.

"Look, Damari, do you make each other happy?"

Kothar kept looking ahead, his face serious, well aware that the other was glancing sideways to see if he was having fun at his friend's expense.

"Well, of course we do. Don't you two?"

"Ah yes, Shaharti's a sweet one to share a house with, even if one little one is always trying to get in between and another might be inside her right now. But we weren't talking about us, we were talking about you. You're happy with Ketty?"

"More than anything."

"So give it time. These no-good characters you say are laughing at you – they like you, they trust you. Look at these panniers." He tapped the saddlebags on the donkey between them, which twitched its ears in response.

"You let it out that you're off down to Shamsh to trade a few of your holy bits and pieces – an amulet here, some needlework there, whatever – and half the town trust you with their own bits of tat they want traded. These beasts here are carrying little baskets, shawls, sandals, metalwork, I don't know what else. They trust you to do a fair trade with it and bring them back the right deal."

"Maybe they just want to avoid the tithes. Maybe they trust you more to keep an eye on me. Maybe they just want me to do their trade without the chief knowing."

He broke off, cut off the taller man's reply with a wave of his hand before it could come to anything.

"I know. You don't have to say it. But look, I'm supposed to bring the life of the gods into our town, and I can't even sow my seed in Ketty to start our own life. What father will bring his daughter for blessing, what husband his barren wife, when half the time they joke like that at our expense? You of all people – you, me and Ketty – we all know what it is to be one of the children of the god."

"And how exactly does your adopted father like to be reminded of that? Let's ask Shomal what his opinion is, shall we? Damari, if you want a child that badly then go up to one of the women at the big shrines, Sychem maybe, or all the way up to Hatsor even. Or take a second wife. That pretty little Nikkallia would move in to one of your rooms tomorrow. Have you seen the way she looks at you? She'd jump at the chance of living with the seer. Ambitious as anything, she is. And she gets on alright with Ketty, too, so you'd not be spending nights on your own up on the corner of the roof too often."

"I don't want two wives, Kothar. Zakarabi up at Jarrar's town has two, and that's all anyone knows about him, like there's nothing else to say about the man. I don't even know what skill he has. Nobody does. He has two wives, that's all there is to know. It certainly hasn't earned him any respect."

"Well, swap then. Put Ketty away and take someone else. There'd be no shortage of offers of a home for Ketty, that's my guess. You know the way she dances at the feasts. Not as if she'd be homeless."

Watching his friend sidelong, Kothar, abruptly anxious that, as so often, he had run along too far with his words, was relieved to see his friend had taken it as an attempt at humour. Damariel shook his head and sighed.

"And you first among them, I suppose? Kothar, you're not helping. I don't want any of the things you say. I don't want some other woman moving in. I don't want to trade my Ketty for someone else like she was, I don't know, just like one of these empty little baskets here. I just want her womb to open. She wants it too. I see the way she looks at Sannah's little one now he's starting to toddle around. Even Aliyna's child."

"The valley girl? Can't get used to that name. Didn't she used to be called Amat?"

Damariel shook his head.

"Shomal wanted to call her that, keep her in her place, remind her she was a slave and all that. It was him gave her that name in the first place. But she's a match for him. She's gone back to her given name now, Aliyna."

Kothar laughed and slapped the donkey.

"Maybe he's thinking that taking her instead of Yeresheth wasn't such a good idea."

He laughed again, saw Damariel's angry look. "Of course, she's your mother, he treated her badly. But Damari, you've got to laugh how things turned out for Shomal? I bet he thought he was in for an easy life just the way he wanted."

"Look, Kothar, the point is that there's all these children running round Ketty, and none of them ours. Two of them will be yours soon enough. You don't see the hunger in her eyes, the disappointment. I don't want her resenting me about it. She will, you know, before long. What will I do then?"

The little track joined onto a wider path, with the marks of men and donkeys clear in the softer places. Here and there, stones had been moved to fill in holes and ruts. Kothar, lost in a pleasant daydream about Shaharti, walked on steadily, and suddenly realised that Damariel was no longer beside the donkey. He turned and waited, seeing that he had stopped after a few paces to fix the branching-off point in his mind for the return journey.

They carried on in silence as the path curved up a ridge. At the crest, there was a side path on the uphill side. A short distance away they could see a little cluster of houses, with two standing pillars forming the town gate. A faint noise of children and livestock drifted down towards them, along with the heavy repetition of an axe in wood. Kothar paused, but Damariel continued walking.

"That's not where we're going?"

"No, not at all. Look now, you know that. We need to clear these woods yet. You've been to Shamsh before, surely? You've been with me before."

"Yes, but that place looked very companionable, like they'd look after two weary travellers pretty well. Shamsh is a mean sort of place."

"Hardly weary travellers, are we? Early morning when we left, and barely noon now."

"Ah, but they don't know that. Maybe we've been on the road a whole month or more. Heading south from wherever it is our ancestors lived before moving to the four towns. You'll know the name. Got any mouldy bread with you? Look, I'll make up the story and you sing it to them for a meal and a night's lodging. We heard the fame of their hospitality far away in the northern hills and have travelled forty days and forty nights to see for ourselves. When we left we had a train of fifty donkeys barely able to walk with all the supplies. Then. . . "

"Look, Kothar, come on. We're not stopping there, not if we're going to trade today and get home tomorrow."

Kothar sighed and followed the two donkeys along the path, away from the sounds of hospitality. He was well aware that, before too long, they would leave the shade of the trees and be out in the open, and that once they did that, Shamsh was only a short distance away. The track wound down the other side of the ridge, and then at the bottom they forded a little stream. They stopped to let the donkeys drink and sat in the shade for a while.

"Now, Kothar, I shall need the rest of the afternoon at the market, what with all this gear to trade. I want to talk to one of the traders about some incense too, but he won't be there until tomorrow. What do you want to do?"

Kothar shrugged.

"I've never thought much of Shamsh. Not much to do there. You do your haggling and I'll find somewhere to wait in the shade. I wish you'd take me up to Sychem or Yano'am one day. Everyone says they're worth seeing. I'd find plenty to get up to there, no doubt about it. Down here there's not much to do. Where will we stay?"

"I'll talk to one of the seers, Malkisamar. He'll put us up, I've done the same for him once or twice when he was going out across the River on a pilgrimage somewhere into the hills. He's pleasant enough, lives with his wife and a young child, his brother and sister too, looks after a little shrine instead of a high place like we have. But have you never been north from Kephrath?"

"Never once north of the four towns, nor east out to the Valley and beyond. All these other places are only names I've heard from other people. I've only ever been west, or south down to Shamsh where you insist on going. How come this Malkisamar doesn't look after the high place at Shamsh? I thought you knew important people in all these towns."

"Kothar, you've seen Shamsh before. They have a proper temple and two shrines besides, and a Mitsriy holy place as well for all of their people passing through. With a Mitsriy priest and all, at least there used to be. I don't know if they still do all the Mitsriy rites there. You might say that Malkisamar is more important than me, but he's only one seer in a big town. He'll take us in though, don't think you'll be getting me to find somewhere else."

"Whatever you say. But remind me why you like coming down here so much? It's so dull. Unless there are Mitsriy priestesses at that holy place. Everyone says they're worth seeing, and I've never had the chance to make an opinion."

"Well, we get good prices down here, and the Mitsriy garrison makes sure the market's fair for all of us. Just don't get into trouble, least of all with any of the Mitsriy. We're here to trade, not go looking for entertainment, and I want them to let us in here again on another day."

"Damari, you're so serious. Just promise you'll take me north some day."

"Alright, I will. Maybe Bayth Shean. You'd like that. More lively for you. I know someone we can stay with there as well."

They stood up, persuaded the donkeys to move on, and before much of the afternoon had passed they were out of the trees, turning off the main track, and crossing the open ground between the fields of Bayth Shamsh towards the town itself. Once they passed inside the town gate, Damariel explained where the seer's house was and then branched off towards the market.

Kothar, confronting the prospect of the rest of the afternoon on his own, set off to look around the town, stopping first at an inn where the beer and wine could be negotiated to a reasonable value. The wine looked good, the beer thin and pale, for all that the innkeeper claimed it was brewed according to Mitsriy traditions, so he sat in a corner with a small juglet of the wine and watched the passing trade.

The tradition for wearing a kef here seemed to leave much less of the face showing, with a fold coming over the wearer's mouth, and the lower edge tucked inside upper garments instead of flowing over. He didn't feel it was an improvement, and kept looking about to see if he could see other people dressed in the hill country style.

After a while he left again, following directions towards the Mitsriy holy place. It was quite small, with a few undistinguished guards in some shade near the entrance. Behind a low wall covered with the Mitsriy picture writing, and some fabric screens moving gently in the erratic breeze, he could see figures moving, but it all looked very sedate, very ordinary. Once he saw a middle-aged man with shaved head crossing the main courtyard into a side chamber, but nothing else. No priestesses for him to form an opinion.

He made his way back to the market, a small and densely packed group of stalls near the town centre. They varied from large and well-guarded displays of cloth and jewellery, through to single old men and women sitting with a basket of vegetables in front of them. He found an area with bread and baked treats and flattered the young girl looking after them into a very advantageous deal, then wandered round the area looking at this and that, listening to the market chatter and occasionally joining in.

Once he saw Damariel and the donkeys at some distance down between some stalls, but made no effort to join him. Eventually he went back to the inn and settled into his corner again with another juglet of wine, sipping at it in between occasional mouthfuls of bread.

He remained there in a pleasant doze for some time, half aware of the ebb and flow of conversation around him. There were tales of raids on the other side of the River, news of whole tribes migrating south down the coastal roads. In the midst of the noise of conversation, a large man wearing a light cloak of foreign design, and no kef, squeezed onto the bench beside him. As Kothar turned to him, he lifted a hand in greeting and indicated the bench.

"With your permission, sir?"

Kothar nodded.

"Sit here with pleasure, sir, nobody else has a claim on it."

"Ah, you're from the highlands?"

"I am indeed. Where else would you find a kef like this?"

They joined in laughing at the old joke together. "And you?"

"I trade up and down the coastal road mostly, don't often come inland. My father was from Damaseq, but I haven't been there in years. Nobody would recognise me there any more. Call me Qarniyam."

"And I am Kothar. I've been hearing these people here all talking about the coastal road. People coming south on it? Whole tribes on the move? Are the Mitsriy in trouble? What can you tell me about all that?"

Qarniyam shook his head.

"All talk, that is. Well, there's always something going on, but I don't see much travelling on the coast that's different from always. The Mitsriy are building more guard posts up and down the coast, more troops everywhere from their own wadis past Gedjet and on up north, way north of here along the Sea Road. They won't be letting go of the coastal way. Up in your hills, now that's different."

"Meaning what?"

The other man called for a juglet of wine and shared it between them.

"Look, Kothar, how long since you saw a Mitsriy soldier up your way?"

"I don't know." Kothar shook his head. "I was a boy, I suppose. A group of soldiers and one of their scribes came through, counted us all, I think, took some bits and pieces and then went on again. They were alright. No trouble. I think that our chief up at Giybon had a visit more recently, but they didn't make the journey down to us. He sorts out whatever is due to them."

"Nothing since you were a boy? That's what I mean. It's the same all over your highlands. One or two bigger towns still get visited to collect some taxes, but they've let the rest of you go your own way. Just now you're more effort than you're worth."

Kothar laughed.

"And may it long continue! They don't give us anything. Why should we pay them? I dare say the chief of the four towns pays them a sweetener so they look the other way. None of my business. Just so long as you're not collecting."

The other man joined in with the laughter.

"No, not I. I'd avoid the taxes just as much as you if I didn't have to go talk to their guards every month. What with that and the little favours you have to give to the right people. But look, if they're not looking after you, who will? Some day soon, someone else will cast an eye at the highlands, send their own army up there."

"For what? We're not worth the effort. You said it yourself. Look, you should talk to my friend Damariel, he'll know better than me, but from what he says there's less people up there from generation to generation. All over, I mean, not just us. Four or five generations ago there were, I don't know, twice as many people. You come to my town sometime and I'll show you a dozen houses that are empty. Maybe more like two dozen. Ask Damari, he'll know better."

The other man looked doubtful, but changed the subject, and after another little while left the corner seat and went off again into the town. Kothar waited a time, then set off himself and headed back to the market. He made a complete circuit of the stalls that were left this late in the day, picking and choosing a few things here and there, and since Damariel was no longer anywhere to be seen, headed back to the seer's house.

The two donkeys were settled in the little courtyard by the house, packs and harness already removed. Inside, Damariel was deep in earnest conversation with the seer Malkisamar in a side room, so Kothar contented himself with talking to the other members of the family and doing some odd bits of work in exchange for their food and lodging. He tried unsuccessfully to persuade the young boy, Malkisamar's son, to try tying his kef in the upland manner. The lad found the whole idea of wearing it another way to be funny rather than intriguing, and he gave up before long.

When Damariel at last emerged, he showed Kothar the lean-to beside the main house where they were staying. The saddlebags were there, and from their considerably reduced size, and the satisfied air Damariel carried, he presumed that the trading had gone well. The evening was considerably too quiet and sober for Kothar's taste, and Malkisamar and the whole family settled for the night not long after sunset. Damariel seemed tired and not inclined to talk, so Kothar abandoned any idea of excitement and slept early.

The next day was even hotter, and the two were glad to get back into the protection of the low trees as the homeward path started to climb. Kothar looked back and caught a last glimpse of Shamsh as they rounded a hillside into the dappled shade.

In the morning Damariel had met with the incense trader, and the short time he had intended to spend with him had drawn out to most of the morning. They had left considerably later than they had intended, and Kothar was relieved to be finally away from the town and on the road.

The sun was nearly overhead now and was very hot, even under the flickering leaves. As they crossed a small stream Kothar stopped short, took off his kef, soaked it in the water and then retied it. Cool water streamed down his head and body as he stood upright again. He watched Damariel looking quickly, anxiously, this way and that along the trail.

"Ah, you think your dad's about to come round the corner and catch us both without a kef? Well, he's not here and you're all grown up now anyway. Anyway, my dad would never have made a fuss."

Damariel denied it, but they both knew it was true, and looking slightly furtive he followed his friend's lead. The water poured around his head and soaked into his clothes. They pushed on a little further to cross a steeper ridge before stopping to eat some bread and olives that Kothar had obtained from the market girl during the course of the morning.

After a little while he put the remaining piece of bread down, hunted in his pack and pulled out a little clay tablet. It was quite thick, and covered with little wedge marks.

"Look what I got for you back at the market there."

Damariel put his own bread down and studied the markings on the tablet.

"Well, thank you indeed, Kothar, this is a fine old piece."

He turned it over and glanced at the reverse side, before looking along one edge and pointing to a little cluster of marks.

"See, this is Ilimilku's work."

Kothar shrugged.

"Is that good? The lad I got it from didn't think much of it, threw it in with some other bits as a favour."

"Well, shows what he knew. Ilimilku was great in his time. Maybe when our grandfathers were alive. No, older than that, I think. I'm not sure. Been dead a long while now, anyway. He lived way up the coast, a long stretch north of here. Of course nobody writes this stuff any more, this wedge and clay work is all finished, unless you're counting grain in one of the big cities. And who wants to do that?"

He laughed, and Kothar joined him.

"Thanks for getting it though, it is interesting. I've only seen one piece of his work before, when I was up in the Gina valley once with Saniyahu. Ilimilku, he served one of their big city priests. They say that up north there are whole rooms full of what he wrote down, all on clay tablets like this."

"So what does this one say?"

Damariel turned it over again and traced his finger along the topmost row of wedge shapes on the slightly rounded front of the tablet.

"I can't read all of it here, it would take a while, I'd need to think about it a bit. Old writing, we don't use it any more now. Nobody does, not even up north where Ilimilku came from, they write more like us now. But this is part of Gishgimu's story, after his friend Enkidu has died and he is getting weary of city life. It goes on. . ." he paused and turned the table over once more. "Well, it's the first part of his journey towards the sunrise to find out how to live forever."

Kothar nodded and ate his bread in silence for a while before suddenly laughing and tapping Damariel on the arm.

"Tell you what else was going around back there."

"What's that, then?"

"All the travellers from out east were on about it. A new joke, Damari. All of them knew it, all the traders from out there. Right. What's long and straight, dangles below a man's belt, and goes in and out of little holes?"

Damariel snorted and waved his hand.

"I don't know, Kothar, but I'm sure you'll tell me before the day wears out."

"A key. Get it, Damari? A key! You weren't expecting that, were you? Come on, be honest! Nobody up home will know that one yet, and you must swear to me you'll let me tell it. I want it to be my little present for them."

"I'm sure it'll get you more credit than me. Come on, let's move on before you remember anything else from Shamsh."

But instead of getting up he stayed sitting on the grass bank, evidently lost somewhere in his own thoughts. Kothar stood and waited for him, quite content to be patient.

"Look, Kothar, what if it's me?"

"How do you mean?"

"What we were talking about yesterday. Ketty and me. Well, it takes both of us. You know that well enough. What if Ketty isn't getting pregnant because of me?"

Kothar glanced once at him and then looked away.

"I don't know, Damari, I can't say about that. Not my place. But look, Yeresheth had three more babies after you came along. She's got a sister, hasn't she? What's her name: Nerith, that's right. She's had children. Shomal had a brother, even if he did die of the sickness before you and I were born. Your Sosanneth gave birth nearly a year ago. So your family line looks good. And Ketty's got a sister too, little Laylah, isn't it? But what do I know? Not my talent, is it, to know about that."

"I was talking to Malkisamar last night. Not about this, I mean, not directly, I wouldn't talk to someone outside the four towns about it. But he said some things about someone he knows that set me wondering."

"Damari, look, go and make some more sacrifices, or get the seers to pray for you both one night. You do a thing, don't you, where you stay up all day and all night to fast and pray for something? Or a few days even. Whatever this Malkisamar said, you shouldn't trust that more than your own friends, your own people, the other seers. What does this foreigner know about it anyway? Who's he to know? Look, you lived with Saniyahu and Halith for a long time, they're like family to you. Talk to them, find out what they think."

Damariel stayed sitting, away somewhere in his thoughts, and after a long pause spoke again. Kothar was still standing, holding on to the ropes of the two donkeys, but sat down again at the serious tone in his friend's voice. The quiet noise of the stream in the little valley behind them murmured in the background.

"Kothar, what if we can't ever have children? What if it's a blight on us both? Maybe we should never have got married, both being children of the god and all. Maybe we just did wrong and this is a punishment. All the prayers in the world won't help us then, if we kept at it for a full forty days."

"Oh, come on, Damari, you're just being gloomy. You've been good for us. Better for Kephrath than Iqnu ever was, and closer to us than Saniyahu. Think of all you've done for us, any of us. How can you possibly talk about punishment? That's just stupid. Who would punish you?"

Damariel shook his head and looked away into the vegetation lining the road.

"I don't know, Kothar. What else could explain it? It's like you say, my family line is strong, hers is strong too, but as for us, nothing ever catches. How can I hope to make my seed take life inside her womb if the gods themselves don't mean to allow it? Kothar, look, maybe we weren't supposed to marry. But I can't bear the thought of that. All very well going down to Shamsh, trading tit and tat for silver with the traders, keeping us in touch with what's going on in the lowlands, all very well going up to Hatsor or wherever on pilgrimage, all very well calling out the prayers for the dying, or speaking the womb blessing over the unborn, but what I want is for Ketty and I to make life happen between us. If ever I needed to hear some sort of word from the other side about this, it's now. But I never hear anything about it. Nothing."

There was a little pause between the two of them. Kothar picked up a stone and threw it as hard as he could in among the trees.

"Look, here's a thought. What if someone has cursed you? Find a priest or someone and lift the curse. Call in a real Mitsriy priest for good measure if you can, they say they know all the gods and how to do the spells and magic as well. Saniyahu would help you, and the others. He would. They all would, soon as asking. They'll know who to ask. Talk to him."

"I don't know. That makes no sense either. It all makes no sense. Why can't we just have a child?"

"Look, Damari, if this is all because of those two characters when we left yesterday, leave it to me. I'll make sure they leave you be. They'll be sorry they spoke out of turn so we could hear it."

Damariel's voice became suddenly very sharp.

"No, not at all, Kothar. No. You must not do that, ever. How could I ever hold my head up in Kephrath if I got you to go and fight my battles with every man that wants to make jokes about me? I'd be finished, Kothar, nobody there would ever trust me again. Don't do it. Swear that you won't."

"All right, alright, I won't. But you've got to do something about this. You're just talking yourself into a pit at the moment. Think about it. It's not all easy going, having little ones in your home. You wouldn't be able to do all your holy stuff like you do now. Ketty wouldn't be able to dance quite the same. You might think yourself lucky. You might be glad not to have any."

"Oh, come on, Kothar. You wouldn't trade your son for anything. This is all mist in a hot wind, what you're coming out with now. Try and cheer me, by all means, but not like that."

He shook his head and stood up, as though trying to shake his dark mood away.

"Look, Kothar, tell me about something else. What were you doing while I was in the market? What was everyone talking about?"

They walked on at a slow donkey pace. Kothar told him about the talk in the inn, about migrant groups heading south and extra Mitsriy guards along the roads, about Qarniyam's prognostications about the hill country. As he had expected, Damariel agreed with his ideas about their security.

"Kothar, that's why we have the chieftain, that's why we give him our work duty and our tithes every year. He's there for when we need to defend against something more than just a little raid up from the lowland villages."

"Don't tell me about work duty. That's where I have to be, straight after the new moon for ten days. I'll be helping to put up some building he wants done in Giybon, and fixing the tracks north and south if there's time. At least, that's what the lad they sent down to us told me. He'd better be worth it if we do get a big raid. Who here in Kephrath wants to build something we're never going to use? What about you? What do you give him?"

Damariel shook his head.

"I don't have to labour, none of the seers do. But he'll be sent his portion of the trading we've been doing. Well, most of it, anyway. I might overlook a few pieces here and there. His father counted that as half the fair portion from the whole town, and so far Mahur-Baal seems to be doing the same. There's a story that a few generations back, when the chiefs were at Jarrar's town, they wanted to increase the portion. Well, there was a fight, and ever since Giybon has been the chief's town. A different family, and so far they've been prudent about what they take. But just so he feels good about Kephrath, I found him a little Mitsriy scarab with the name of one of their old kings on it. I'll send that up as an extra with the portion."

"Can I see it?"

They paused, and Damariel rummaged through his pack before pulling out a piece of green stone in the shape of a scarab beetle. Mitsriy picture writing was on the base, and Kothar held it up to the light to see it better.

"What does it say? Whose name is it?"

Damariel shrugged.

"Since it's you I'm telling and we're not up home, I will say I don't know for sure. I can't make out all those little signs. But look, this one here, you see that a lot in their king names. I reckon it's the name of one of their gods. And look, this is a bird of prey, a hawk or something, so perhaps it's a god who takes bird form. I think they have several of them. But when I pass this little piece on to Mahur-Baal I shall be telling him it is a scarab of their great conqueror king who passed this way going up north to fight his enemies. He'll like that, he'll think it makes him a conqueror too."

They both laughed.

"Can't you give him something that will get me out of the labour duty?"

"Come on, Kothar, last time you were chosen you spent most of the time sitting in the sun drinking with the men of Meyim. I don't recall it being especially taxing of your skill and strength."

"That's not the point, Damari. A man wants his time to be his own. What business of mine is this place he wants put up? I'll never use this building of his, I don't expect any of us will from Kephrath. For all I know, I might never get to use the road north either. Not unless you take me that way like you promised yesterday. Who wants to work like that?"

"I'll promise again, if it makes you happy to spend the time up there."

They walked on for a while back along the path, branching off up and right, past the town Kothar had wanted to stay at the previous day. After a lengthy silence, Damariel spoke again.

"Kothar, he's not bad, you know. At least, I don't think he is. I hear that other towns have much worse chiefs than Mahur-Baal. You know, making demands, taking all the time and never giving anything back."

"This man has never given me anything."

"Maybe not, but he does give things away. Ketty's father now, Caleb, he did some piece of metal work for him, a dagger I think. The chief was that pleased with it that the next month he gave Caleb a gold belt buckle from down south. Nice work, not like ours at all, but nice. That was a gift, he didn't have any obligation to do that."

Kothar was unswayed.

"I've never seen Caleb wearing any gold buckle."

"Oh, he never wears it. Says it's too special a thing to wear. It's pegged up on their wall, just where you can see it when you go through the doorway. I think he got some ideas from it, did one or two pieces of his own copying some of the designs. Go round to Kinreth's house sometime, it'll be about the first thing he shows you. You won't even need to drop a hint. All I'm saying is that the chief could be a lot worse. Who wants a chief that comes down to your house all the time? Better he stays up there and just sends runners."

"Have you ever met him?"

"Twice, no, three times now. The first time when Saniyahu took me up there, early on when I needed to be formally accepted by the other seers as apprentice. He was at the house of the Giybon seer asking some question or other, I forget what. I think he wanted some kind of blessing for a raid, maybe a prophecy. I don't remember. Then once down at Kephrath when he came down for a feast. I don't know where you were that day, out on a hunt I suppose. Saniyahu and Halith kept him busy, and pretty much kept me out of the way while he was there. He gave some presents out then to a few people. Then I was there when he was anointed chief after his father died. He seems all right. Bit older than us, a few years older maybe. I'm sure there are worse chiefs than him. Oh yes, and

I saw him another time years ago with his father, when we were still children, before ever he was chief."

They fell silent as the ground became steeper. The sun was starting to set as they arrived back at Kephrath. Kothar was aware that Damariel had become increasingly restless as they had neared home. Shortly before the last rise to come up to the first houses he stopped and turned to Kothar.

"Kothar, you won't say anything about this, will you? What we've talked about?"

Kothar shook his head and waited.

"Only, it's not just what those two men might say, or even the village. I don't know what Ketty would think if she knew we'd been talking about this. I don't think she'd be happy about it, even talking to you. I mean, you're like a brother to both of us, we both know that, but I don't know what she'd think, even so. So please, not even to Shaharti? Will you do that for us?"

Kothar shrugged.

"Of course, Damari, you just have to say the word. But my guess is that Ketty's already talking about it with some of the women. Oh, she'll choose who she talks to, she's not a gossip, but someone, for sure. Maybe your own mother?"

"I don't know."

They stood there a few moments, then Damariel started trudging up the hill. Before long some of the children caught sight of them and ran down shouting to meet them, and then all of a sudden they were among houses and people, all asking about the journey with eager voices. Kothar left Damariel unpacking the donkeys at the high place with one hand and hugging Qetirah with the other, answering questions all the while about the trading down at Bayth Shamsh, and moved away down the hill towards his own house. He was already thinking how to tell people the new joke.

Yad

MEPAGH YEAR 20

LORD OF ALL, show me your way
and lead me to the direct path
to answer those who laugh.
Do not hand me over to the desire of my enemies.

SOSANNETH CARRIED LABUNASI up the hill on one hip, a mixed bag of woven goods draped over her other shoulder. Damariel had promised to take them on up to Giybon the next day: they were the first batch of items for Mahur-Baal to trade on their behalf in the autumn, and there would be several more loads over the next few months.

Labunasi was a couple of months over a year old now, and kept wanting to squirm round in her hold as they passed enticing sights and sounds. He kept a little sing-song chatter going with her as they moved, with occasional fragments of words seeming to emerge from the tune.

She reached the high place and went towards the wooden door of the seer's house, but it opened at a rush from inside before she could reach it. Qetirah came out, looking cross and frustrated. She stopped as she saw Sosanneth.

"Sannah! Were you coming to see us? I was just leaving."

"It can wait if you're busy. Just some bits and pieces to go up the ridge."

Qetirah reached out a hand tentatively towards Labunasi and shook her head.

"Oh no, Damari's staying there, it's only me going. You go on in and see him, nobody else is around at the moment."

She turned to go, stopped, and came back again.

"Sannah, could I take Labunasi with me? I'm only going to see mother and Laylah for a little while, and they'd like that. Would that be alright?"

Sosanneth handed him over.

"Here, take him. He won't need anything for a while, but he'll chatter like that so you won't hear yourself think. I'll be here or else back at mother's house. If he gets upset just put him down and let him toddle around. Kinreth will know what to do."

Qetirah looked very serious as she took him and settled him comfortably on her own hip. He reached out and touched her face and gurgled melodiously to her, and she started to sing one of the children's songs as she moved away. Sosanneth shook her head and pushed open the door. Damariel was facing away from the door arranging something on one of the tables, and started speaking as he heard the door close.

"Look, we can't change it. It's the dance that must be done at the autumn feast."

"Damari, it's me."

He turned round in surprise, then looked embarrassed as he came over and hugged her.

"Sannah, I'm sorry, I wasn't expecting you. I thought, well, never mind what I thought. Oh, you've brought some bits for up the way. That's splendid, I'll take them tomorrow. Would you like anything to eat? Where's Labunasi? How's our mother?"

She looked across at the kitchen area and considered.

"Some of that mint tea would be just right. He was with me all the way, but he's just set off quite cheerfully with Ketty now. Mother's fine, sends her love and prayers."

Damariel poured each of them some tea, shaking his head.

"Well, we could use some of them."

She closed the door and sat down near him.

"Oh?"

He was silent for a while. She sat sipping her tea, letting the silence draw out between them so that the distant noise of hens, goats, and children at the stream whispered into the room. Somewhere in the distance two men were laughing.

"Of course, if you don't want to talk about it?"

"Oh, Sannah, it's not that, not with you. I just don't know where to start. It was, well, it seems that it was so easy for you. You've got Labunasi, had him just when you wanted, a boy and all, a boy for us all to love, give mother a future. But with us?"

He trailed off again, and while she waited she poured them both some more tea.

"Well, Sannah, look at us. No children, nothing at all, not even a false hope, and we've been married now over two years." He shrugged, then laughed with her as they both remembered a conversation long ago.

"Not to mention before then. Which I wasn't going to do back then when I thought you were so much younger than me, before little Labunasi came along."

Sosanneth nodded, remembering the wistful look Qetirah had as she reached out to carry Labunasi. She started to say something, but Damariel was looking down again into the brimming beaker of tea and did not notice.

"And don't tell me it's not all easy and we should be glad of the time together. I heard all that from Kothar a while back when we went down to Shamsh. I didn't believe a word of it from him, and I won't from you. And don't tell me how young we are still either, how there's lots of time. I get plenty of that, too."

"I wasn't going to say that. Any of that. But why bring this up today?"

"Oh. Well, it's the autumn feast soon, you know, the feast of new wine."

He looked at her and saw the blank look on her face.

"Well, last year Halith did the dance of Taliy like she has done all the years they were here. You know, blessing the town and the people with fruit of the vine and the field, fruit of the breast and the womb. This year Ketty has to do it, now that we're responsible here. She's not finding it very easy. Well, neither one of us is finding it very easy. In truth, we're finding it extremely difficult. I mean, how can we start to think about this?"

Sosanneth nodded slowly.

"That's why she was so eager to take Labunasi when she left for her mother's house?"

"Oh, yes. Any chance she gets. Why not? I can't seem to help out. But it won't help her in a few days when she gets up to dance at the feast."

"But, Damari, does it really matter? You two do so much here. It's not like anyone minds. I certainly don't mind."

"Sannah, sister, it's putting so much onto you. Our whole family rests on you. I can't help you out. But I want to."

She straightened and put the beaker down and spoke very carefully.

"Damari, of course the family rests on me. In time, I shall be the mother of the family, and generations to come will know me as a mother of the house. You know that, and I know that. Our own mother trusts me with that."

"I know, I know. Look, Sannah, I didn't mean anything against you. But there's more to the village than just our family. More people to think thoughts, and not all good thoughts at that."

She shrugged.

"Well, I know some of the women make light of it, and I dare say some of the men might too."

She grimaced as he nodded.

"But they'd all stand with you night and day if you asked them to."

"I know that, Sannah. That almost makes it worse. Sannah, look, Ketty and I are not just one more family in a house. We stand between this world and the other. Saniyahu and Halith trusted us to do that. All the seers did. Everything we do shapes how the worlds touch each other." He twisted his hands to and fro, the fingers twining around each other.

"Even old Iqnu taught me that."

She smiled wryly.

"Pity he didn't take more notice himself of what he taught you."

"Well, yes. But I didn't want to talk about him. What does it mean that we can't have children, we who are supposed to be like parents to the whole town? Will Ketty's dance even do anything at all? Maybe the gods will just take no notice, laugh at it even. It's not just song and dance for entertainment and delight, not just fun, it has to work. It's supposed to work. Really work. Next year's harvest might well depend on it. How can we dance something like that? What if who we are blights the whole town, the crops and the newborn?"

"Brother, you mustn't say such things. Don't say them."

He shook his head.

"Can't stop thinking them, Sannah, even if I don't say them. And at least I can say them to you. Better said than unsaid."

They sat together in silence for a while. Eventually Sosanneth spoke.

"Look, Damari, I have to get back down to mother soon. But how can I leave you here like this?"

"I'll be fine, Sannah. I can't stay here anyway, I have to go and pray with Issi."

She looked up abruptly and caught his eyes.

"Why? Is he ill? What's wrong? I hadn't heard."

"In truth, nothing that two days fasting wouldn't cure by itself. But I somehow have to make the idea of fasting palatable to him, and that may not such an easy thing to do. My prayers will help him with that at least. Anyway, it's easier to pray for other people. I'll go part-way down the ridge with you if you can wait a few minutes."

She nodded, and he gathered together a few things from the next room, discarding his regular seer's kef and putting on a more impressive-looking one as he did so. She smiled at the transformation, got up, and straightened the knot for him. He caught her hand as she released the ends of the kef.

"Look, Sannah, you will be there at the feast, won't you?"

"Of course, Damari. You don't need to ask."

"Well, I know, but it's our first time on our own and I need to know you'll be there for us. Call it foolish if you like, but I have to ask."

She stood looking at him for a moment, then touched her lips with one hand and put her other over her heart.

"I will be there, Damari. I'll bring Labunasi and he can distract you with his endless chatter as well. And I dare say our mother will be there, but she must swear for herself. I really can't imagine her not being there. We're your family, Damari. Of course we'll be there. All of us."

He looked at her, obviously moved. He put his hand on her shoulder, not trusting himself to speak. She carried on.

"You know that we'd do this for you, Damari. Our family will stand together in this, just like you stood with me when I was carrying Labunasi. You don't need to ask."

He picked up a small bag.

"Yes, of course you're right."

"Of course I am. We're all together in this, all of us. You know perfectly well that we all stand together in this, we all trust each other to stand alongside."

He pulled a face, looked down, and then looked back up at her.

"Not all of us, Sannah."

"Well, no doubt our brothers will make a point of looking in from the other side. I'm sure they'll be having a good laugh, if they can spare the time away from whatever it is the dead get up to."

"I didn't mean them. Come on, Sannah, don't lecture me about all standing together and being trustful when there's one family member you won't acknowledge in any way, word or deed. And you won't show him what he has a right to see. You know what I'm talking about."

There was a long silence. Little village noises came and went around them.

"Look Sannah, I know it's difficult, but you cannot keep Labunasi away from Shomal forever. It's not right for either of them."

"Is this my brother speaking, or the town seer?"

"Does it matter? Good words won't turn bad if someone else speaks them. And you've made good friends with Aliyna, you and mother both. Is it so much more?"

She was silent for a little longer.

"I don't know, Damari. Ask me again in a while. Oh, why did you have to talk about that? I thought we were talking about the autumn feast."

He put an arm round her as they left the house and set off down the hill. "Well, maybe I was, Sannah. What's the autumn feast about, after all, if it isn't about sowing new seeds in faith that they'll grow right? That kind of seed I can still sow. Wish me favour with Issi, now."

A few evenings later, Sosanneth was sitting beside Aliyna at the festival of the new wine, leaning together against one of the great standing stones. Day and night were equal, and a cooler edge had come into the evening wind rising up from the coast. Yeresheth was some way off to her right, sitting in between Nerith and Adonilanu.

Since they had arrived other village families had come up the hill, and were sitting and standing around the stone circle. Marir was wandering a few yards from his mother, picking up leaves from the ground and then dropping them again as something else caught his eye. Labunasi sat on Sosanneth's lap, watching him. She leaned over to touch Aliyna's shoulder.

"So do you think he'll come?"

Aliyna glanced around and shook her head.

"I tried to persuade him after we talked. But he won't come, won't talk about it, nothing, just says it would upset people."

"This is Damari's first autumn festival since Saniyahu and Halith left. Surely he should be here. He needs him here. He's very anxious."

"I know. But there it is."

She held out her hand to take some leaves from Marir, looked round the ring of stones, and nodded her head towards Yeresheth.

"He's always frightened of what she'll think. And you too."

"But Aliyna, how is that for you? You've been with him, what, nearly three years now. Here we are, you and I, we've done something together now."

Aliyna shrugged and took another leaf from her son.

"Better than it was once. I'm making it better."

Sosanneth grimaced and looked at Yeresheth again, then hugged Labunasi tightly against her. Aliyna had not noticed, but was obviously lost in a memory. Concerned that it was a painful one, Sosanneth nudged her.

"What is it, Aliyna?"

"Oh, I was just thinking back to the first time I stood up to him for what needed doing. Nothing for me directly, I didn't dare. But he'd been saying all week that he would fix a loose part of the roof, and he'd never got around to it. So I just told him one night that I was not going to start cooking until he'd done it. That Marir would fall because of it. He just stood there and looked at me, taken all aback, then he turned around and went off to fix it. Not too bad a job, either. Then he came down again and said it was all done and did I want to look at it."

"What did you say?"

"I told him his word would be good enough for me, and I started to cook the meal then. He just stood there for a while, then suddenly started coming over towards me over by the hearth. I was really frightened, I can't tell you, and I kept my face down in the cooking bits, but he just asked if there was anything else I knew that needed fixing badly. So I said two or three things, nothing big, and off he went and did them while I cooked. So you see I am making it better."

All the families had arrived now, and in a loose circle the community watched Damariel pour a ritual jar of the year's new wine over the altar stone, a dark splash of blood red puddling on the top and running in little trickles down the side, back into the earth in little cascades. The other world would taste the new wine before this world. Qetirah was singing at his side, her arms over her head with the white ribbons catching the breeze and chasing to and fro in the gusts like long leaves.

There was a pause. Alloni, who was going blind but still cultivated more vines than anyone else in Kephrath, was led forward by his grand-daughter with another, much larger jug of wine and gave it to Qetirah. She drank a little and passed it to Damariel, who also sipped it. They looked at each other, nodded and handed it back to Alloni, who gave it to be passed around the circle from person to person.

In turn, as it reached them, everyone drank a token amount. Damariel and Qetirah had begun calling out in turn the prayer giving thanks for the fruit harvest, and blessing the crops to be planted for the coming year, and in between each line of prayer the whole community replied in affirmation.

The jug reached Sosanneth, who took a sip, then dipped her finger in it and let Labunasi taste a little for himself. As the wine passed on around the circle Damariel finished, and a few people here and there called out their own prayers and blessings.

Sosanneth listened to Caleb, off to her left, then a few others, and then suddenly, unexpectedly, heard Aliyna beside her speaking out, calling for the blessing of spring rain on the crops. Her lowland accent was fainter than it had been, but could still be heard.

Sosanneth glanced up in surprise, and abruptly realised that Shomal was watching Damariel from beside one of the houses. Looking round, she saw that Yeresheth and Nerith were facing half away from him, could not possibly have seen him where he was standing. He was half in the shadow of the house.

She looked back at him. He turned his head, as though to go, and saw that she was watching him. He stopped, stood very still, and then lifted an awkward hand in greeting.

She was about to look away from him, out of habit, her gaze already sliding off to one side, but she made herself keep his eyes for several long heartbeats. She placed her hands either side of Labunasi and raised him up a little from her lap, nodding to Shomal. He swallowed, his hand to his mouth, and stayed very still as she settled his grandson on her lap again. It was their first exchange since the day her brothers had died.

The voices of the community prayers had stopped. Damariel looked around the circle to see if anyone else wanted to speak out. There was silence. He took up the lyre from beside the altar stone and sat on it, tweaking the tuning of one or two notes, shifting them up and down again before stilling them all with one hand. There was a pause as he held his hand flat against the run of strings. Then he looked up at Qetirah, who had stripped off her kef and left it lying in a pale pool on one of the stones, her dark hair falling around her shoulders.

They held each other's eyes for a very long moment, and Sosanneth felt that her heart had stopped.

Then she clapped twice, three times, and began the dance of Taliy in the dawn of the world, the rippling lyre music following her feet as she brought up the dew from the parched and dusty ground, giving birth to all the good things of the land as she did so.

Little tears squeezed out of Sosanneth as she watched Qetirah dance, her eyes far away in the distant womb of the world.

"When she that is dew rose in mist from the land
and the green and the growing leaf leapt up for joy,
When the rain first fell and the rivers began
and the flower and the fruit-tree came springing to life."

When she had done, and winter and summer, seedtime and harvest had begun their cycle in the world again, then the autumn feast began, with food and the new wine in abundance. Aliyna clapped her hands in pleasure and Marir giggled and clapped in reply.

Sosanneth dried her eyes as Aliyna began speaking to her.

"Sannah, are you going to sit with your mother or with me tonight?"

She broke off abruptly, seeing the last of Sosanneth's tears.

"Sannah, what is it?"

"Nothing, Aliyna, nothing. I'll sit with you for sure, but save a place for me. Oh, if I could only have paid that price instead of Ketty just then. She is so much braver than I. Look now, I'll be back soon. I have to do something for Labunasi first."

She set off down the hill, carrying Labunasi for quickness even though he protested a little at first. She walked down past Yeresheth's house, all the way down along the track, down all the way to the olive patch.

The door of the little house was open. She looked cautiously inside. Shomal was sitting against the side wall, his knees up with his head resting on them, hands making little clutching movements at his side. She watched him, lips pursed, not sure what to do, when Labunasi squirmed in her arms and made a sudden noise.

Shomal looked up, startled, and saw his daughter and her son outside the doorway. He got to his feet and wiped his cheeks, glancing at her, at him, and then looking back again down at the ground. She took a deep breath.

"This is Labunasi. I thought you might like to see him. Well, I thought you should now. And Damari said so too. Actually he was very blunt about it."

"Sosanneth, I hadn't expected to see you."

He looked briefly around the untidy corners of the little room, the coloured drape tied back across the far end, the spare stool nearby.

"Will you come in?"

She shook her head and put Labunasi on the ground. He held on to the doorpost and then took a few steps into the room. He stopped and held both hands out.

Without thinking, Shomal reached out and took the boy, lifting him up and looking into his face. For a second his own expression was quite open.

"He'll have wavy hair, I think. Like your brothers."

She nodded. He moved Labunasi round onto his hip and stroked his head with his free hand. Labunasi gurgled and said something, a long stream of infant words that none of them understood. There was a long pause in which Labunasi touched Shomal's beard and cheeks.

"Labunasi and I are going back up to the high place now, there's food and drink and all sorts. Everyone's there."

He put Labunasi back on the ground and he toddled back to where Sosanneth stood, still outside the door.

"I can't go, Sosanneth. I'd spoil it. It wouldn't be right. Well, look, you know there's some there wouldn't want me, I'd spoil it."

She picked her son up.

"I don't think that's true. Aliyna is up there already with Marir, I was sitting with them. It's the new wine festival. Everyone is there. Look, you saw them all when you came up just now."

She hesitated, a long gap in which the wind from the low-lands sighed around the house. She started to turn away and then, with an effort, turned back again.

"Look, I really think that you should come back. Look now, it's Damari's first time doing this with Ketty since they were left here to look after us all last year. He's feeling awkward about it. Come along for him, at least. They're finding tonight very hard, he and Ketty both."

"Sannah, I can't. What would, what would your mother say? I can't spoil it for her."

"Look, go there for Aliyna if not for Damari. She needs you there too. She and I are friends now. And she and mother as well."

He looked away into the little shadowed corners of the silent house, said nothing, shook his head once. The breeze outside fell quiet again. She turned and went back up the hill to noise and laughter, to the sound of singing. It had been something, at least, and she was not sure how she felt about it.

The months went past. Village life proceeded: the crops grew, the blossom started to emerge as the days lengthened, and new children were born. Sosanneth was going back to

Yeresheth's house after dropping another batch of woven goods with Damariel to take up the hill to Giybon. He and Qetirah were still childless, and Sosanneth had left Labunasi with Yeresheth to ease any awkwardness.

Counting back in time with her steps, she realised that before long it would be three years since their wedding. There was still no change, but at least, so far as she could tell they were both satisfied that calamity had not come on the village after the dance of Taliy at the autumn festival.

She drifted away into her own preoccupations and did not notice Aliyna coming towards her up the hill until they were very close.

"Aliyna! I was far away over the ridge somewhere else, I really have no idea where I was." She looked around to check she had not wandered absent-mindedly past the house, and was relieved to find that she had not. "What are you doing up here? Who are they for?"

She had realised that Aliyna was carrying a little bunch of flowers, little early iris stems in a bunch. Aliyna looked a little embarrassed.

"Well, Sannah, I was going up to the high place to ask Damariel if I could have somewhere to put them to remember my child from before. I know she doesn't rest in the land here, but I thought maybe he would be willing. Do you think so?"

Sosanneth looked at her silently, then touched her shoulder briefly in companionship.

"I'm sure he would do that for you. But where did you get the flowers?"

"I traded the flower roots for some olive oil. They come from near the coast somewhere, though I'm not exactly sure where. I can imagine they grew near my old home, though. Close enough. I planted them outside my door. If I'm going to be a woman here in Kephrath then I must have my own growing things by the door to my house, yes?"

"Yes, indeed. But I had no idea you were looking to do this."

"It's nearly four years I've been here now. You know," she paused, and then laughed quite genuinely, "that means I've been with Shomal longer than I was married to my Labayu down there. About time I made a place for myself, I think."

They parted, and Sosanneth walked down to her house. She stopped just outside the door, listening to Yeresheth talking to Labunasi about food. Her son was answering here and there. Aliyna's words about making a place for herself still sounded in her ears. She stopped with her hand on the door frame and made a decision, feeling a little sigh of relief leave her body as she did so.

Labunasi said something in a very serious tone that she could not catch, and Yeresheth laughed as she answered him, and clapped her hands. Sosanneth pushed the door open and picked Labunasi up as he ran over to her. He had obviously been eating some bread, and she brushed a few little crumbs away from around his mouth. Yeresheth had been preparing some food, but giving it one last stir she got up and the three embraced just inside the door.

"Did Damari take the clothes, Sannah?"

"Oh yes, he's going up to Giybon in two or three days time. He said he could find a lad to go up if it was urgent, but I said there was no rush."

Yeresheth nodded and went back to the pan of vegetables. Sosanneth looked at her fondly.

"Look, mother, I met Aliyna outside, did you know she's started growing irises to be her house plant?"

"No, I didn't. Good choice. When did she start doing that?"

"Oh, I don't know exactly. Recently, I think."

Sosanneth sat down and let Labunasi clamber onto her lap and tug at the edge of her kef. She distracted him with another morsel of bread. The decision she had made pushed at her from inside. She yielded to it.

"Mother, can I ask you something?"

Yeresheth put a flat plate over the vegetables, straightened, and nodded.

"There, that can look after itself for a while. Of course, Sannah. What is it?"

Sosanneth felt abruptly shy. She fell silent, and Yeresheth watched her patiently.

"Well, mother."

She stopped, straightened her kef where Labunasi had dislodged it, and took a deep breath.

"Look, mother, how would it be if there was someone I wanted living here in this house with the three of us?"

Yeresheth put her hand to her mouth, her eyes wide. Sosanneth could not tell if she was excited or taken aback, pleased or disappointed.

"I mean, I do want Damari to marry us, soon, this summer even, as soon as it can all be arranged. And if you agree. But talking to Aliyna, I just want things to move along now. I feel I'm just wasting time, Labunasi's and yours as well as mine. And he wouldn't just be a help to me, he would be a support to you to, he could help us both in all kinds of ways. I think it would be better for all of us if things happened sooner rather than later."

She stopped. Yeresheth was still gazing at her, speechless.

"Mother, please say something."

Yeresheth visibly gathered her thoughts together.

"Well, who is he, then?"

"Qeren. You know, Taliya and Ethan's son. Ethan the wood-worker. Qeren's been learning how to work with wood from Ethan a long time now. He's quite good. Well, I think he is. You know Qeren."

"Yes, Sannah, of course I know him."

She paused, and looked from Sosanneth down at Labunasi, as though studying him carefully all over again. Sosanneth, realising what her mother was thinking, found herself blushing with embarrassment and looked down at the floor.

"Well, daughter, you have chosen Qeren. And yes, it would be a blessing to this household, to you and me both as well as our Labunasi."

She paused again, as though picking words carefully, and as Sosanneth looked up again she caught her eye and spoke very directly.

"I am not asking anything that you don't want to answer. But I am asking if Qeren will be a good father to Labunasi. I want to be certain of that."

Sosanneth nodded, not trusting herself to speak. Yeresheth continued.

"I'm quite sure he knows about Labunasi, and that you are already a mother. But when you have other children, with him, will he treat them all as though they were his own, knowing they may not all look like siblings? I know what that can be like. But it's not easy for a man among other men, and you must tell me, if you can, do you think he will he care what the other men might say to him in jest?"

Sosanneth swallowed and kept her mother's look with determination, though she was acutely aware she was still blushing, that her pulse was racing, and that her hands were sweating more than the temperature of the day warranted.

"I have talked with him. He says he will care for Labunasi like his own son, train him in all that he should, and place him side by side with any children we have of our own." She paused, swallowed hard, and continued. "But I think when we do have children, they may not look quite like Labunasi. But that won't matter to either of us."

Yeresheth nodded, looked again at Labunasi as if turning alternatives over in her mind, and then nodded at Sosanneth.

"Supposing I give my blessing to this, what do we have to give his family? I know Taliya well, and we are in good standing with them. But do they know what the two of you desire? Is Taliya in agreement? What does she think of Labunasi?"

Sosanneth sat back a little and thought before answering.

"They know we desire each other. Qeren says he has talked it over with them but has not spoken of a time, not until we were all ready. They praise you often, and they will accept from our hands what we can bring. I think she likes Labunasi:

she has certainly seen him often and accepts him as my son. And yours."

"Then we shall go now and see them."

"Now? What about the food you had cooked?"

"Food can wait. This, I think, cannot. Not now you have reached this point."

Sosanneth suddenly felt flustered. The world had begun to move faster than she had expected. Yeresheth was already on her feet, covering the little fire in the hearth, pushing the pan of hot food to one side, gathering up Labunasi into her arms. She stood up, hesitant.

"Mother, should we do this?"

Yeresheth looked at her quizzically.

"Do you want to?"

Sosanneth stood in silence while her blood pulsed in her ears. There was a little pause, and then she adjusted her kef more properly on her hair.

"Yes. I think I do. Yes, for sure. But should we talk to Damari first?"

Yeresheth shook her head.

"No. What has this to do with him? I am mother of this house and you are my daughter. It is for us to choose. Not him. He can bless our choice, and I am sure that when he hears about it then he will. But the choice is ours, yours and mine. You can tell him later, but not now. This is our time."

Some time later they were back in the house. Taliya and Ethan had been agreeable, even pleased with the prospect. Qeren had been quietly supportive of Sosanneth, watching her with evident pleasure and satisfaction. He had been somewhat in awe of Yeresheth, happily playful with Labunasi.

The practicalities had been discussed discreetly, the exchange of items between the households agreed without rancour, and when it was done, Yeresheth had embraced Qeren as a new son coming into her house. As they had turned to go, Qeren had suddenly spoken up.

"Lady, when might I move in to your house?"

Yeresheth had turned to him, catching a smile on Ethan's face as she did so.

"Qeren, give me one more evening with my daughter and, if your own family wishes it, move tomorrow. I do not think any of us particularly want to wait until after a ceremony. By tomorrow we will have a place ready for you."

Now they were back in the house. Yeresheth quickened the fire again and pulled the pan back onto the heat. She glanced around the rooms.

"I think you three should have that room and I will move into this one. We can move the cloth and the clothes to the side. Plenty of room for me."

Sosanneth watched her mother assessing the size of the rooms.

"Mother, are you sure about this? Just say the word and I will wait longer. Qeren will wait if need be."

Yeresheth smiled a little.

"I don't think he wants to wait any longer, Sannah. I don't think Labunasi should wait much longer either. And yes, I am sure about this. This is a good thing. Now, before the food is ready, there is a thing we must do."

She stood up and became quite formal.

"Sosanneth, daughter. As mother of this house I say Qeren will be welcome to live here among us, to live as a husband to you, to live as a son to me, to live as a father to Labunasi. May your union be blessed with many more children. May my household, which in time shall be your household, become fruitful and grow many times over as he unites with you, and joins with us. May your breast and your womb enjoy the blessings of Shadday and Rahmay, and may you bring joy to your whole family, those who are here and those have passed across to the other side. Now come here and kneel down."

Sosanneth knelt at her mother's feet, her arm round Labunasi who was clinging to her side. Yeresheth pushed back Sosanneth's kef so she was kneeling bare headed, rested her hands on the crown of her head, and blessed her. Then she bent and kissed the top of Sosanneth's head, knelt down with the others, and the three held each other in a long embrace until Labunasi started to squirm impatiently and move about in their grip.

Yeresheth smiled fondly at him and made sure he did not go to close to the heat of the fire and the pan.

"Sannah, I don't think your other children will look like Labunasi, will they?"

Sosanneth slowly shook her head but kept silent.

"I wonder, are you ever going to tell me?"

Sosanneth followed her mother's gaze, watching her grandson pulling at the bread again. In that moment she felt very close to confiding in her mother.

"I don't know. Do you mind?"

Yeresheth sat back and thought for a few moments, then turned and started to spoon out some of the food.

"Well, I know his mother, and that suffices. But in all truth, I dare say that for the rest of my life I shall be looking at the young men of the village, wondering whose hair and eyes, whose manner of speech and movement he carries. But all that can wait."

The food was ready, and Yeresheth started spooning it into bowls for them.

All of a sudden Sosanneth burst out.

"Qeren wasn't ready to give me what I wanted. You know, it wasn't as though I could wait on and on. There was a time when this had to be done. I had to give birth to Labunasi in Matan. Had to give him to you in Matan. You know that. You know what that means counting back months. If he'd been willing it would have been him, but he was too young, too shy just then. I couldn't wait. Couldn't wait for him."

Yeresheth handed her a bowl with two spoons, one smaller than the other.

"So it was someone else. Who was it, then, I wonder?"

Sosanneth shook her head fiercely.

"Don't ask. You told me you wouldn't."

"I'm not asking, I'm thinking aloud. Someone older, more confident of themselves. A friend of Qeren's, perhaps."

She looked at Sosanneth, who was sitting quite rigid, frozen to her seat. Labunasi started taking little spoons of the food. Yeresheth sighed again.

"Sannah, I don't need to know, not until you're ready. Not ever, perhaps. But I do need to know something from you now, this evening. I must be sure, and Qeren, and your own sweet son Labunasi too, that one of Qeren's friends is not going to make idle boasts on a night when the winter wine flows that will cause any of us, all of us, bitterness and grief."

Sosanneth made herself relax with an enormous effort.

"Mother, I can't tell you just now. But I can tell you that the man won't be boasting about it around the fire. He has too much to lose under the roof where he lives. He gave me what I needed back then. He wasn't averse to the arrangement, either, not at all. Any more than I was. But we each made an oath to the other that names would go no further. He won't ever boast to Qeren, and I won't ever speak to belittle either of them to people that are close to us all."

Yeresheth nodded slowly, clearly thinking her way around the houses in the village and contemplating possibilities in her mind.

"Then we shall talk no more about that."

Sosanneth started on her own part of the food, helping Labunasi from time to time.

"Sannah, it will be good to have a man in the house again. Good for you, for sure, and for Labunasi too. But good for me as well, I think. Will he be happy, living here with us all, do you suppose?"

"Yes, I am sure he will."

Sosanneth paused a few moments while she took the spoon from Labunasi's hand. He was losing interest in the food. She then paused quite a while longer, looking speculatively at her mother as though working out how to say something. Eventually she spoke again.

"But look, mother, no reason Qeren should be the only man here. There's space in that room for you to share it with someone too. No reason you should be the only one sleeping alone."

Yeresheth stared at her for a moment and then laughed aloud.

"Have you been talking in the evenings with our Nerith? What moonshine you two do dream up for me. Can you see anyone taking up with me?"

"Well, yes, I can. And no, I haven't been talking with my aunt about it. But I do look out for who's watching you at the feasts and up by the stones when there's a dance that the men and women can share with one another, and the sun has set over the hills and the light is lower. I have just as good eyes as you do. I'm just using them a bit more than you are at the moment."

Yeresheth put her hands to her mouth and looked much younger all of a sudden, then shook her head again and started clearing up the remains of the meal.

"You might wait a long time for someone to go all soft over me. Look, Sannah, I am most happy Qeren is coming in here with you, with us here, but things don't work out the same for all of us. Now, are you going to help me move things?"

"Yes I am. But I could tell you a name to you as we do that, if you want?"

Her mother laughed again, and Labunasi, looking up at the sound, clapped his hands and laughed too.

"Get along with you. Tell me a name, indeed. Look, we can move the spare bits of cloth first. Anyway, for sure there's no more children to come out of this body of mine now."

"You move the cloth, I'll move all these threads and needles so Labunasi doesn't catch them. But come on, mother? It's not about more children. You have a house and a lineage through Labunasi and my others that will come along. Qeren will give me a daughter in time so the house will continue. You have a future, and your household will thrive. It's not about more children from your body, but about companionship for you both in the days and nights. We'll all be together over in that room there, and you'll be on your own again here. There's no need."

Yeresheth looked down at the little pile of weaving kit on the floor at her feet. There was a long pause.

"Don't tease, Sannah. I don't know how I can even bear it to think of it. Some nights even now I don't think I can bear it, even while you and Labunasi are still there alongside me. What am I to do?"

There was another silence. She took a deep breath.

"When we've done these little bits, there's the main trestles to move across. How are you and I going to do that? Do we need to find someone to help us? And look, if Qeren can work with wood, can he make us something neater than these great things? They're so heavy. Anyway, I'll wager you haven't even one name to tell me."

"We'll get help. We need to tell Damari and Ketty about Qeren, we haven't done that yet. They may be able to get some of the lads to help us. I must tell Aliyna too. But we'll not talk to her just yet, let me run up to the high place and talk to Damari. Look, you keep Labunasi here and move some of the smaller things. You can think about Tobiaz while you're doing that."

Yeresheth nodded and called Labunasi over to her, then suddenly realised what Sosanneth had said and stopped short, looking across at her. Sosanneth waved to them both and ran out of the door.

Kaph

PEGERIM YEAR 21

SHEATHE THE SWORD at your thighs, you Hero –
virile and potent –
O potentate, prosper and ride –
with loyal words and right conduct towards others –
but doing dreadful deeds with your right hand.

DAMARIEL WAS GETTING READY for the midwinter festival. There was a cold wind today, but the sun was bright and the rains had been gentle so far. Qetirah was down at her mother's house but was due back soon. It was only a couple of weeks since they had heard that Sosanneth was pregnant again, this time by Qeren for certain, and Qetirah had not taken the news well. He seemed to have spent more time apart from her than with her.

Realising that his thoughts were drifting away out of the room, he sighed and compelled himself to concentrate, The festival was to be held tomorrow night, the longest night of the year, and this year, in an unusual move, chief Mahur-Baal, victorious over his enemies and glorious in battle, was to join in the celebration at Kephrath.

He was expected to make the short journey in the early afternoon tomorrow, and would stay on after the festival, at least until the next day, as guest of the town. It was all part of the give-and-take of the way the four towns worked, although Damariel had a feeling that Mahur-Baal was steadily becoming more of a taker than a giver.

Danil's wife Rivkah was hosting the chief, who was coming without his wife Asherith, or indeed any of his retinue except the fighting-man Yaraq who served as his bodyguard. Rivkah had been bustling up and down to the high place all day to ask this and that, both proud and anxious at the same time.

Damariel finished sharpening the knife he would use to sacrifice a deer – the blood for the dead, the meat for the living – and set it aside in a black cloth. Another thing all done and made ready. He thought about the next task he would do. Properly speaking, he and Qetirah should be running through the main dance of the festival; of course they already knew what it had to be, but he wanted to be sure they reminded each other of the music he would play and the steps she would trace out.

He sighed. He wasn't sure exactly when she would be back, and it was already mid-afternoon. It would start to grow dark soon, so he went outside and looked around the stones. Some leaves had collected themselves in a hollow where two stones butted up against each other, and he spent a few minutes tidying the place up. Still no Qetirah.

He walked down to Danil's house, meeting Rivkah on the way asking, again, if he was sure that only the two men were coming. She had planned to put the chief on his own in the main sleeping room, his bodyguard in the other downstairs room, and herself and Danil up in the roof area. Her sister was going to care for their children overnight. Did Damariel think this would be acceptable? He did, just as he had done on several previous occasions, but he listened with attentiveness to her as they walked together back down to her house.

When they arrived he saw that they had tied back the branches of her honeysuckle tree to make a neat frame for the doorway. It was some way from flowering yet, but the year's new growth was fresh against the walls of the house. He complimented her on the appearance as they approached.

Inside, he talked with Danil about plans for the feast. Danil had been organising the hunting of two deer. Yes, he had the plans to roast them up at the high place for the feast well in hand. Yes, he was aware that one of them had to be alive. Yes, Kothar knew this as well. Yes, they had plenty of fuel for the fires. Damariel suddenly, acutely, realised he had asked all this before, and that Danil was answering him just as he had answered Rivkah. He nodded gravely as though he had not known all the answers anyway, and made a solemn exit before long to go back up the hill.

As it was getting gloomy, Qetirah returned. She had stayed longer at Kinreth's because Laylah had wanted to talk. Then Kalita had come in to the house carrying her new baby, and she had needed to stay. Did Damariel remember that she had had her first baby a little while before Sosanneth, and her second soon after ? Well, this was her third, and she looked thin but happy. Damariel sighed inwardly. It seemed the whole world around Qetirah was full of pregnancy and babies, and she was living a vicarious motherhood by involving herself with the other women.

Eventually he steered the conversation around to the dance tomorrow. They settled down to practicing the words and music, the ritual and dance. As usual they found each other again better in the actions than the exploratory words, and Damariel felt his earlier sense of gloom being displaced by higher levels of optimism. Perhaps it was, after all, only a matter of time.

As the first stars of the early night started to brighten, Danil, Kothar and two or three of the other men brought up to the high place the dead deer and the live one. Bundles of brushwood and some larger pieces had been accumulating through the day.

Damariel took one more look outside just before sleep, walking around the high place, taking station by each of the stones in turn and praying beside them, and attending to the tombs in the bluff of the ridge.

He stopped especially to pray by the little cairn he and Aliyna had made together, to commemorate the far-off body of her lost child. From time to time, when the seasons permitted, she decorated the little stones with some iris stems, but just now there were none.

He realised that it was more than half a year since she had asked him if it would be permitted, and he had shown her a suitable piece of ground sheltered under an overhanging jut of rock. The next time he had visited the hut in the olive grove had been a surprise. Not only was there a small but flourishing clump of iris flowers nodding beside the door to denote it as her household, but she had transformed the interior of the house as well.

The dwelling-place had shifted from being a hut in his olive patch to a household in which she was the mother of the domain. Something had changed. She spoke to Shomal no longer as a humiliated captive, but as an equal. In turn, he replied to her with consideration instead of command, and seemed to

Damariel's eyes to have worked his way through to a genuine marital relationship with her.

She had found a way to wear her kef so that, although it was still tied in the highland manner, it reached further down her back in a way reminiscent of the lowland style. It was a creative solution to the problem of identity she had faced, the potential loss of her own heritage, and a very effective one.

She had rearranged the interior of the house, to erode the original distinction between her domain and his, and had even inspired Shomal to add a storage area onto the side using the stones that had lain in a ragged heap for several years. It was a different world altogether.

Still reminiscing as he moved across to the large stone on the northern side of the circle, he revisited the memory of when Sosanneth and Qeren had married, soon after midsummer. The two of them had stood beside this very rock as they made their vows and left adolescence behind, this time as a community enactment rather than a private act.

Shomal had even come to most of that, even if he did remain out of the way at the back of the crowd while Aliyna and Marir watched from the front. He had not stayed for the whole ceremony, but it had been something. Yeresheth had studiously ignored his presence the whole time, but instead had made a point of talking extensively to one or two of the other men.

That was also the first day when he had seen her set aside the married woman's kef she had clung on to all that time, returning to the plain white of a single woman. It had been a moment of public transformation for her just as much as for her daughter. Since then she had worn the white kef as part of her regular clothing. Damariel had no idea what she had done with the married one, and had never quite plucked up courage to ask her.

He sat on the stone for a few minutes, lost in the memory of that day and trying to remember who Yeresheth had spent time with. Surely there had been some that she had spent longer with than others. Finally he gave up the attempt to remember, got up and went back inside. Qetirah was already nearly asleep, and he kissed her half-awake forehead before settling down himself.

The next day they both woke and rose early, before the sun had crested the ridge to the east. The day passed in a blur of activity, arranging and coordinating all that had to be done for the festival.

Mahur-Baal and Yaraq had arrived at the expected time, and after formally greeting them Damariel had handed them over to Danil and Rivkah to attend to their needs. He had been slightly concerned that Mahur-Baal would want to spend the time with him, but as things turned out he showed much more interest in being with Danil than with the village seer. The men who joined in the raids and some of the older boys of the village took turns in and out of Rivkah's house, leaving Damariel and Qetirah free to get everything ready.

At last it was time. The village gathered in their families around the high place, the fires were lit, and the festival began. The live deer was brought across. Damariel went up to it, sacrificial knife in hand, and then, as was the custom, turned to Mahur-Baal to offer him the privilege of making the kill. This was an unknown: a guest might accept or might refuse, and there was no knowing which choice would be made on a particular day. Mahur-Baal accepted and, in the sight of the whole town, took the knife from Damariel. He walked around the trembling deer three times, as though selecting his moment with care, and then in a single swift movement made the kill.

Damariel, watching him, admired the precision of the act, while at the same time being slightly repelled by the evident pleasure he took in its execution. Mahur-Baal stood over the dead, twitching body for a few seconds, cleaned the knife, gave it back to Damariel, and took his seat again. Three of the other men took the deer away in order to prepare it for the feast.

The ceremonial part of the festival came first. Damariel recited parts of the great cycle of songs for all to hear. There were prayers for the year that was dying, and for those who had gone across to be with the dead in the year. There were prayers for the year that was coming to birth, and for those who would be born in it. There was singing for the whole assembly. Lastly, the blood of the deer was brought over to Damariel and Qetirah, who mixed it with oil and poured it between them onto the fire by the largest stone.

The serious part over, the food followed. That continued while the sun's light in the sky-dome above faded, and the great stars unfolded in the heavens. To Damariel's great relief, Mahur-Baal seemed genuinely to enjoy every aspect of the event, and received with patience the various little gifts brought to him from time to time by the younger children. With the food gone, the children were whisked away each to their homes. Alloni's son brought out two skins of last year's wine, and shared them around the circle. Then there was dancing, great circles of men and women dancing in the firelight and the starlight. It was going well.

Finally, as the night wore on to its centre, Qetirah got up to dance the death of the old and the birth of the new. The moon was full, bright with potency, poised above the uplands. There was a hush around the circle as she moved to the centre, stripped off her kef and outer wrap, and began to dance in her tunic. The early parts of the dance were in silence, with long languorous movements, but after a while Damariel started to play the round bellied lyre to accompany her as she quickened. He smiled as he watched her move, and smiled, too, as he remembered that this was the very first piece Halith had taught him on this instrument. That seemed an age ago now, and he knew he was a very much better player now than in those early days, but the memory filled him with warmth and pleasure.

Qetirah's dancing became increasingly enlivened with the passing of the old year, and the imminent arrival of the new, and his own playing kept pace with the quick circling of her hands and feet. Pidray, daughter of mist, had been courted and was now joining in marriage to the new year. As the vow was spoken came, she cast aside her tunic, and danced in a gauzy slip like a veil around her body. The full moon shone like silver on the slip and on her body. Every eye was on her as she moved towards the climax of the dance, and as she finished and stood, poised in her final pose, there was a great shout of approval and delight from around the circle.

Damariel looked at her with pride, and then suddenly realised that Mahur-Baal, who had been sitting beside him, was also gazing at her. The chief leaned over to him.

"There's a pretty thing, now, surely?"

Damariel did not know how to answer, and covered his confusion by packing away the lyre. Qetirah, flushed with the energy of her dancing and obviously very aroused, left her kef and outer garments where they lay and came over to them. Mahur-Baal stood up and made a little bow to her.

"A fine show. I am pleased to have seen it. Great satisfaction."

Qetirah smiled happily still breathing hard, and then, taking Damariel completely by surprise, put her arms round the chief and kissed him on both cheeks. He smiled at her, the action making his face look slightly more cruel, and kissed her twice in return before releasing her.

Kinreth called to her from across the circle, and Qetirah ran happily over to her mother, charged with female vigour and power. Kinreth had picked up the discarded tunic and wrapped it over her shoulders as they talked. Mahur-Baal was still following her with his eyes, until Damariel suggested they sit down again. The chief was silent for a few minutes, lost in some distant place of thought. He suddenly turned to Damariel.

"She's still not a mother, is she? No children to you?"

Damariel shook his head, confused and feeling belittled by the comment. The chief nodded thoughtfully and turned and spoke briefly to Yaraq, who was sitting on his other side. Yaraq shrugged and then nodded.

After a while the festival broke up, with people drifting away in small groups to go back to their own houses. The chill air of midwinter was starting to settle as a thin mist in the hollows of the land nearby. Mahur-Baal and Yaraq went off with Danil and a group of Danil's friends. Damariel and Qetirah were last to leave the high place, and Damariel slipped an arm around Qetirah as they walked across to the largest of the fires, still radiating heat into the winter air.

The town was slipping back into night again, with only occasional noises of laughter sounding through the still air. They stood in the heat of the fire, enjoying the moment. The full moon was still well above the horizon, bright in the hill country sky.

"Ketty, that was a most wonderful piece of dancing. You were beautiful."

She laughed happily and opened her arms up in a great, expansive gesture in the heat and light of the flames. "I know. I felt really alive tonight. Everything was good about it. You know how it is, sometimes, when the veil between the worlds gets very thin. It was like that, I felt both worlds watching me, the people here and the people on the other side, all the gods too. I felt their pleasure in me. You've felt that, haven't you?"

Damariel nodded.

"Yes indeed, Ketty. It's a wonderful thing to be that close to the crossing place. A fearful thing too, being out in the little open space between the worlds. I was sure that's what was happening to you."

He paused, then grinned mischievously and carried on.

"That wasn't the only veil that was thin."

She laughed again and caught the material of her slip between her fingers.

"Another year I might not bother with the slip. It wouldn't matter to anyone for that dance. Anyway, you know the songs.

Why should I care what anyone thinks about it anyway? I'm not doing it to please them. Anath danced naked before all the gods, and Hurriy went in like that to bargain for her brother's life. I could do that in the two great festival dances, summer and winter. Summer especially, although it's just right for Pidray's wedding, when the whole land is lying bare of leaves and is waiting for the flowers of spring. Halith said that one of the women seers used to do that up at Jarrar's town when she was just an apprentice."

Damariel nodded, pulling a name back from memory.

"Iliuri, she was called. She was married to Adonibaal. She died some time ago of a winter sickness. And Iqnu use to say that the seer he was apprenticed to, Dawidiya he was called, he did that. He used to say that the gods had given him his skin and nothing else, and he'd never heard of a baby coming out of his mother's womb already clothed, so why should he do any different when he was serving them?"

"Well, maybe I should do that here. I would another time if I felt even half as close to the land of the gods as I did tonight. It would be for them. I wouldn't care about people here, the dance is not all about them anyway."

Damariel found another, much more recent memory, and felt a slight nudge of anxiety pushing at him.

"The chief said a strange thing."

"Oh?"

"He suddenly asked if you were a mother. Well, no, actually it was more like he was being critical."

Qetirah straightened up.

"Critical? Of who? Me? You? Both of us? The town?"

"I don't know, Ketty. It was just a strange moment."

Qetirah paused, her arms still open to the fire.

"Well, Damari, everyone sees it. The whole town. Everyone. It's not something we can hide. I live with it every single day. It just never changes."

"Maybe it will soon."

She shrugged, looking away from him into the flames.

"Ketty, look, it can change any time. You said you felt the gods' favour over you while you were dancing. Maybe things are changing for us. Maybe tonight. I think tonight could be something life-changing for both of us. Look, where you're going now you can practice not needing that slip."

They looked at each other and laughed.

"Come on, Ketty, let's leave this fire and go inside to bed."

He put his arm around her again and they started to walk towards the house, the open tunic her mother had draped around her flapping in a light breeze.

"He said something else odd. I don't know, it was like a plan he was making."

Qetirah began to say something, but at that moment Yaraq appeared along the path, followed by Danil a few paces behind. Yaraq came up to them.

"Seer, lady, I bring greetings from the great chief Mahur-Baal, victorious over his enemies and glorious in battle. Lady, the chief requires that you go down to him now and provide some dancing for his private pleasure. He wants the opportunity to become more familiar with you. You should come with me now, down to this man's house where the chief is waiting."

Damariel looked at Danil, who shook his head uncertainly, looking profoundly embarrassed. Yaraq was quite blatantly studying Qetirah, who paused and carefully tied her tunic closed with her sash. She looked across at where her kef was lying, and took a step towards him, her head on one side.

"Why this honour?"

"He was pleased to see you dance before, and wants to see more of you. There is room to spare at the house of our host, ample room for you and him. He said to tell you that if you would give him this particular gift, there is another gift he would be pleased to give you. One which, he thinks, you have been craving but have not received. Not in this place, and not, perhaps, with the seer who stands beside you."

Damariel took a step forward, and Yaraq looked at him in an appraising way, as though sizing up a potential threat.

"He said also to say to you, seer, to remember what it is that your wife lacks, and that he might be able to fulfil. At this time when the priest seems to be without power, perhaps the chief will be able to supply the need. But lady, with you he was wholeheartedly delighted and wishes to do you greater honour. But after all, he is your chief, and in the four towns his command is not to be considered and weighed but obeyed. He says to ask you what better gift he could give you than the thing you most desire, and most lack."

Damariel stood rooted to the spot, mouth open, trying to understand what was happening. But Qetirah left her kef where it lay on the nearby rock and took another step towards him.

"Would my lord be wanting me to dance for a short time or a long time?"

"I think, lady, that it will be a long dance, until the morning. Seer, there is no need to remain awake waiting for her."

Damariel took another step forward.

"Qetirah, no, don't go."

Yaraq moved slightly into a relaxed, competent posture, a little smile crossing his face. He was entirely focused on Damariel for the time being. Damariel forced himself to stop moving, knowing himself outmatched by the fighting man.

Danil opened his mouth as though to say something but stayed silent, staying in his place a little away from the rest of the group. He avoided Damariel's eyes when he tried to catch them and secure his help. Qetirah turned her head to look at him, then turned back and spoke to Yaraq.

"Sir, give me a moment."

Yaraq glanced at her but kept his focus on Damariel.

"A moment, lady, but the chief is not to be kept idle."

Qetirah pulled Damariel over to one side.

"Look, Damari, don't make trouble about this. It's all right. I'll go with this man and dance to satisfy our chief's wishes. I will dance for him, and I am sure there will be a place in Danil's house I can rest after the dancing is over."

"Ketty, it's not your dancing he wants. Anyone can see that. Just don't go. We can sort something out."

She looked at him very seriously, but with a remote air about her.

"I don't think we can, Damari. This man Yaraq is not going to accept no for an answer from either of us. Nor is the chief. He didn't send this man to hear us reject him. But come on, look, we know we can't sort out the bigger matter by ourselves. Look at it now. What if you can't ever give me children? I can't live with that. Not on and on with nothing changing."

"But Ketty, look, you said yourself things are changing. Maybe even tonight for us, but soon. Don't go with him."

She took a step back and held herself very erect.

"You lay that time with another woman to see if the seed of the gods would catch in her womb. I don't see this is any different." "It's not the same."

"Why not?"

"That was done properly, with all the rites. With everyone consenting. With all the people knowing that everything was being done right. In accordance with all the traditions. He's just taking what he wants. It's not the same at all. He can't just take from the priesthood, not even if he is the chief. It has never been done like that."

She swallowed and shook her head.

"I don't think there's any choice about this, Damari. Look, you said that tonight might be life-changing for us. Maybe that was a word of truth and prophecy, just not what you expected. Maybe this is how it has to be. And if it is a gift he won't be taking anything against the customs."

Before he could reply she turned to Yaraq again.

"Sir, I am my chief's maid-servant. I will go with you to him now and do all that he wishes. Everything. Take me to him now."

"Ketty, don't do this."

Yaraq positioned himself between Qetirah and Damariel, took her arm and started to lead her away down the hill. His head was half-turned towards Damariel still, so that he could be aware of any threatening move. In fact, Damariel was frozen to the spot, unable to move this way or that. Danil stood irresolute for a few moments and then turned to follow the other two. Damariel caught his arm, finally compelled him to recognise the situation.

"Danil, what are you doing? This is Rivkah's house he's using. Your house. This isn't right."

Danil shook his head and pulled himself away.

"He's the chief. I have to do what he says. It's just the way things are. Don't blame me, you said he should stay with us."

The three of them went down the track. Qetirah did not turn round. They turned the corner by Sara and Abiram's house and disappeared from view. Damariel was left standing alone. It was very cold. He went over to his house, their house, and opened the door to go in, but stopped on the threshold. How could he possibly go to their room and stay when Qetirah was dancing for the chief, when she would be taken by him for his pleasure? He closed the door again and ran along the track on the ridge towards Giybon for a while, trying to make himself exhausted. He ran and walked like that for half the night, all around the area, up onto the ridge back and then down into some of the little valleys that ran with water when the rains came. They were dry now, and cold.

Finally, when the sky was starting to become a little paler in the east, he walked back, picked up Qetirah's kef where it still lay amongst the cold stones of the high place and went back into the empty house. He sat in the main room, leaning against a wall, facing the door, her kef across his lap. In the end he dozed fitfully, but woke every so often as the light in the room gradually grew. The time passed extremely slowly.

Morning came, and the sounds of the town awakening gathered and swelled outside his walls. Finally the door opened and Qetirah came in. She closed the door behind her and walked past him to the sleeping room without saying a word. He got up after a few long breaths and followed her. She was lying in the bed under a light covering with her eyes closed. She had clearly tossed her unfolded slip and tunic into a corner, careless of how they fell, and had one arm stretched out across the blanket, the other tucked under her head. He sat beside the bed, not sure whether to touch her arm or not. As he hesitated, she opened her eyes.

"Ketty, is everything alright?"

She shrugged, avoided his eyes, and finally nodded.

"Did you dance?"

She nodded again.

"Then afterwards, did he, I mean, did you? What happened?"

He stopped. Her eyes had closed again as she withdrew inwardly from his questioning. He reached out and touched her arm, but she pulled it away from him and tucked it under the blanket. He waited a short time.

"Well?"

She stared at him in frustration.

"Of course he did. Or we did, if you want to say it. What do you think he wanted me for? You knew that even before I went down there. But I don't want to talk about it. It happened, it's over, and he's going up the track in a short time."

Damariel sat back and closed his own eyes.

"I'm not going to bid him farewell, if that's what you want. Danil can do that well enough on his own."

She shrugged.

"As you wish."

There was a silence in the room. It stretched out longer than he wanted.

"Look, Ketty, can I get you anything? Some water?"

She shook her head.

"Rivkah gave me some water and mint tea earlier before I came up the hill. She wanted to be kind to me."

"I'm glad someone was."

"Oh, Damari, stop it. He did what he felt a chief ought to do. I don't think he was disappointed in the hospitality of the town. I don't think he was displeased with me at all. Quite the opposite. Quite satisfied. He offered me gifts before I left him but I turned them all down. He laughed and said that he had already given me the gift I most wanted, and that I would know it before long. He said to tell you that you should be grateful to him for helping you out where you needed it, and that he would reward both of us as he saw fit soon. At the end of the month if I don't bleed as normal. We have to wait until then. Then we'll know one way or the other. That's all. Two weeks to wait. Maybe three at the outside."

Damariel shook his head as though not believing what he was hearing.

"How can you just speak like that? This should have been our night. You danced, we were both close to the gods, very close. Everything was fine until he just stole what he fancied. Then to talk about giving you gifts as though you were a prize animal in the flock of one of his villagers. And giving some sort of gift to me as well, like I was being paid for the inconvenience. Like you were some shrine girl up at Hatsor or somewhere. This was supposed to be a night for us, where things would change for us. For both of us."

"Look, Damari, I need to sleep now. Just need to sleep. We can talk about gifts and changes another time. Just now I feel all churned up inside, like my insides were turning into butter or cheese. I can't talk about this now. Two weeks, Damari, that's all. Then we'll know."

He reached over and tried to caress her forehead, but she shook her head and turned away from him.

"Just don't touch me right now, Damari. I've had too much of that all night. Just let me rest now."

Damariel got up and started towards the door. She had turned on her side to face away from him, and her voice was slightly muffled by the blanket.

"We're not to lie together until those two weeks are done, either."

He turned back towards her.

"What?"

"That's what he said. He wants there to be no doubt whose child it is. So we mustn't lie together until we know one way or the other. I asked what if there was no child and he just laughed, said that in that case he would have no more interest in me. But until then we have to keep apart."

He stood silent, grappling with the situation. She turned her head towards him briefly.

"It's only two weeks, Damari."

He shook his head and turned away to leave the room.

"It's not two weeks, Ketty. It's my whole life."

She said something he could not hear.

"What was that?"

"I said if you need a woman so badly, go and see Nikkallia. She'll oblige, I'm sure."

"I don't want Nikkallia. And I don't want this."

She shrugged and pulled the blanket over her head.

The two weeks passed slowly. Damariel and Qetirah tried hard during the days to rework their life together in a normal routine. But then at night, she went into their sleeping-room and he, angry and resentful, went up to the room on the roof. He slept very little during that time, sometimes going out onto the roof and looking across the ridges in the slowly waning moonlight, and sometimes going across to the high place and the tombs behind it. He became very familiar with the little night noises that surrounded the village. Over the fortnight he became increasingly fatigued and irritable.

The night sky darkened as the time went by. The moon rose ever later in the night, and the stars grew in strength to rule more of the sky.

Qetirah did not bleed after those two weeks. She waited one more week in case she was simply late, but her monthly flow had still not come by the end of that time either.

Damariel was devastated, and spent a whole day working up at the stones, cleaning and arranging odd pieces of equipment that needed no effort, moving them here and there to pass the time. Finally in the evening he came in to Qetirah, who was preparing food for them both.

"Look, Ketty, how are we going to manage this?"

She stopped and sat down. He could see absolutely no alteration in her face or body yet, but was acutely aware that somewhere inside her something had changed.

"I need you to be a father to this child. No matter whose seed quickened in me. Mahur-Baal is never going to be husband to me or father to this child, he just wants to know that another baby in the hill country is his. To add to his collection. So I need you to do that for me. For both of us. Can you do that?"

He took several steps towards her and nodded.

"Yes, I think so. But I need you to be a wife to me as well."

She nodded in turn. They came together and embraced, a little hesitantly at first as though out of practice.

"Damari, now we know for sure then you don't have to be upstairs. Share my bed again and be with me, night and day."

He held her against him, not trusting himself to speak. For a time it seemed that everything could be most well again.

The next day a boy came down from Giybon with a donkey loaded on both sides. He brought the donkey to the high place, handed it over to Damariel, and ran off again.

In the panniers was a small bag of silver, some wine and unusual foods, a glazed pottery vessel, and a small gold brooch wrapped in some soft cloth with Qetirah's name inked on the side. Damariel recognised without difficulty the slightly spidery writing of Eli, the seer at Giybon.

The brooch was very fine workmanship, traded from outside the four towns somewhere. Damariel silently gave it to

Qetirah. She tried it on her tunic. It looked delicate, beautiful. Damariel hated it.

"How did he know about this?"

"I sent Galmet up the track yesterday."

"I didn't know?"

"No reason you should. He asked me to tell him when I was sure one way or the other, so I did."

He gave the food and drink to others in the village, passed the silver along to the widows, and to those whose crops had not thrived last year, and kept nothing of it in the house. The pot somehow got broken one day. Qetirah wore the brooch for a few days until they argued fiercely over it one evening, and after that she hid it somewhere in the rooms. Once or twice he looked for it in a desultory fashion but could not find where she had hidden it.

Then one evening she had gone down to her mother's house and he had another search. He was not sure what he would have done with it if he had been successful, and was quite relieved that her skills at hiding were better than his at seeking. He was sitting at the writing frame copying out letters from a very old clay tablet, which was starting to crumble towards unreadability. It was a fascinating piece of writing, but so badly worn that he had repeatedly set it aside rather than tackle the arduous task of copying. Now it seemed a useful way to fill the time.

Lost in the close work, he did not notice the passage of time until she opened the door. Looking up, he realised then that the time had become very late. He stretched, abruptly feeling stiff and cramped, and then realised she was looking quite anxious. He pulled himself back into the room, into the relationship with her.

"What is it, Ketty? You've been gone longer than I expected? It's late. I don't know where the time has gone."

He gestured vaguely towards the writing frame, but neither of them looked at it. When she spoke her voice was odd, forced.

"I was at mother's for a while. Then down to your mother's, talking both to her and Sosanneth. Then a few others, even Aliyna. I wanted their advice."

"Oh?"

"I just don't know if what I'm feeling is what's supposed to happen. It's sort of sharp in here sometimes."

She held her hand against the side of her body, between her ribs and her hips.

"What did they say?"

"Well, nothing really. Every woman feels it a bit different, they say. None of them had felt quite the same as me, but they didn't seem worried."

"So that's all right then?"

She made a little helpless gesture.

"I don't know, Damari. They think it is, but I don't know. I'm a bit afraid of it, it's like I'm completely on my own."

"I don't think I can help much."

He paused, then looked down and carried on.

"I mean, I couldn't help at the outset, and I don't see what I can do about this just now either. Ketty, I'm not a healer, none of us is really here at Kephrath. Not since Qerith, anyway. I think she might have taught Shelomith a few things. But if you think about it, none of the seers has a real talent for that just now."

"I know. I just need you to help me in it."

He looked up at her again, mixed feelings chasing through his heart and mind.

"You know I'm here. Here with you, not just here one night and then gone again to abandon you like this. I'm not like him."

"Damari, please don't talk about that again. You said you wouldn't."

"All right. I won't. Well, I'll try not to. But I'm not like that. I'm not like him. You know I'm here."

"You're here in the house. But you're not always here with me. Not always here with this child. Look, Damari, I need you to want this child. Can't you just pretend it's a waif we found in the woods and took home to care for? Or some baby whose mother died in the birthing and needed other parents? Or that I was some woman a seer lay with at a festival and was now with child. Or think about how it might have been for your own mother. Or Sannah."

He paused for a long time, thinking about her words, thinking back to his own childhood with Shomal, reluctantly seeing some justice in the comparisons she was making.

"It doesn't come easy, Ketty."

He was silent again, and she waited for him to carry on.

"Look, Ketty, I can try, but I don't know if I'll be able to. But for you, I can try."

"I need you to try, Damari, both for me and for the baby."

He nodded, seeing the great need in her face, but feeling both wounded and inadequate for the task. He had grave doubts about his ability to find the strength she needed of him.

Lamd

NISAN YEAR 22

YOUR SWEETLY SCENTED limbs,
all gone
your milk and honey body in the moonlight
gone
the clinging shroud that gave your last embrace
all gone.

IT WAS FOUR WEEKS since Qetirah had known for sure that she was pregnant. It was Hiyaru, and the weather was cold and wet. She was not long-tempered. Damariel was by turns sullen, solicitous, angry and avoidant.

He was, he felt, failing to find the compassion she needed. He spent a great deal of the time out of the house, visiting one person or another. When he was home he said very little, but busied himself with any of the little tasks that occupied a seer's time.

The first two weeks had been especially difficult, but after that they each made greater efforts to bridge the riven gap. They were sometimes successful, and one or two golden evenings illuminated a dark time. But success was quite rare, and failure rather more common.

At the end of one especially difficult evening, Damariel suggested that he would go up to one of the pilgrimage sites to offer some sacrifices. Qetirah, who had felt ill and unsupported all day, had just shrugged and been noncommittal. The next morning he had woken earlier than her, and lay there filling in details in his mind.

He would not go all the way to the holy mountain Tsaphon, but rather to the big temple at Hatsor. Saniyahu had taken him there on one of his first serious trips away from the four towns, so it would be very fitting. He could stretch the trip out for nearly three weeks, what with the journey time there and back, and a decent time at the shrine itself.

He lay there, counting weeks to himself and thinking back to what Kothar had told him about how long this period of the pregnancy would last. Three weeks – more than two, anyway – should be about right, he thought.

There would be time for Qetirah to feel better, time for himself to stay away from the constant reminder of the chief and the festival night, time for both of them to miss each other and want each other's company again. It all sounded just right as he thought it over, and full of enthusiasm he nudged the still-sleeping Qetirah to wake her up.

She jumped, startled, a little anxious cry coming out of her as she clutched her hand over her belly. He glanced down the line of her body to convince himself she did not look very different yet, and shook her gently to wake her up properly. She groaned and put one arm over her eyes, then looked around, confused, at the still-grey light of the spring morning.

"Whyever did you wake me up? I've slept so badly. What's so urgent?"

"Ketty, look, I've been thinking about what you said last night. You're right, I'll go up to Hatsor on pilgrimage, make some sacrifices for the both of us. It's what we're missing, I'm sure. It's just what we both need."

She groaned again and turned away from him.

"What I need is sleep. Whyever did you wake me up to tell me that? You don't think about me at all."

"It was your idea. I thought you'd want to know I was going to go with your idea."

"It was your idea. I'm sure it was your idea."

"Well, you thought it was a good one. Didn't you?"

A grimace crossed her face, and she rushed out of the room into the kitchen area. He heard a noise of retching and followed her. She was bent with her head over a large pot, holding her hair away with one hand so it trailed down her naked back. He poured some water into a little jug and offered it to her, but she waved her free hand, retching again, and knocked it onto the floor. Water splashed them both.

He picked the jug up, silently wiped it clean, filled it again, and this time held onto it until she reached out for it. She stayed there another few moments before going back into the bed and pulling a cover back over her. She drank the water slowly and eventually looked at him. "Hatsor."

"Yes, that's right. The big temple up there. On the hill. You remember, we were going to go there together in the summer, but I could go for both of us."

She pulled a face.

"Damari, get me something to eat, will you?"

He went back into the kitchen and looked around at the various containers.

"What would you like? There's some dates in honey here, Nikkallia brought them up here yesterday, if you remember."

"I couldn't eat anything sweet, Damari, not if all the gods had come along together to bring it to me. And nothing from that woman anyway, she'll have brought them up here for you, not me. Give me something dry and plain. Some of yesterday's bread, maybe."

He brought it back to her on a plate and she ate one or two mouthfuls, closing her eyes as she did so.

"Well, how long did you think you'd be gone?"

"Oh, not long, Ketty, a week or two. It's not so far. Why don't you come too?"

She shook her head, eyes still shut, and pushed the plate away.

"How will I manage? I've not felt this bad before."

He paused, considering options.

"I could ask my mother if she would come and sleep with you up here. Or Kinreth might, maybe."

"I don't want your mother or mine around here when I feel like this. I want you to be here, not someone else."

He paused a moment, and then rushed on.

"Should have thought of that before."

Her eyes opened and she looked at him, her expression that of the lioness.

"What does that mean?"

"Well, you haven't been very easy these last few days, you know. Doesn't feel like you want me around either. Ever since you found out about, well, I suppose ever since you lay with Mahur-Baal. You've been very difficult, you know."

"I thought this was about making a pilgrimage and a sacrifice, not about an easy life for you. You try feeling like this."

"It is about the sacrifice, really it is. That's my job, you know. It can't stop just because you don't feel so well."

She closed her eyes again and pulled a face.

"This is my job too. He's the chief. I'm the seer's wife who has no children. Anyway, you've lain with barren women to bring the seed of the gods to life in their womb. It's just it hasn't worked for you."

He was silent for a long moment, then started to pull on his clothes with quick, jerky movements.

"I'm sorry you feel that way, Ketty."

"Oh, Damari, I feel terrible just now. You go on your pilgrimage, sort out how you feel about all this and then come back. But right now, please just get me some more water, another jug. And I can't face any more of this bread. Sorry."

He took the bread back and filled the little jug with water again. By the time he got back to her bedside he had calmed down a little.

"I do think I need to do this pilgrimage, Ketty. I mean, actually we both need it. I think we both need to think about what we've sacrificed, but just now you can't do the journey. Let me do it for both of us."

She nodded and leaned back against the wall.

"You do that. Tell me all about it. Just stay away from the shrine women. Promise me that. You've always said they're just for the ordinary people, not the seers. Promise me you'll keep to that. Now. Especially now. And not someone from up at Hatsor anyway. If anything happens I'd rather you found someone from down south. Not one of those northern girls."

He finished tying his kef. She looked at it, shook her head, and leaned forward to adjust it slightly. He kissed her forehead, cautiously, and then very carefully kissed her lightly on the lips.

"Nothing's going to happen to me, Ketty. I'll be back soon. It'll seem no time at all to you. But so's you know for sure, then yes, I swear it. I won't go with a northern girl while I'm away. I swear it."

By the time he had prepared what he needed, left messages for people, told his family and Kothar of his plans, and sent a boy up the track to Woodlands to let Saniyahu and Halith know what was happening, it was noon. He ate a brief lunch with Qetirah, a cautious but more settled affair than first light had been.

Then he was away, up on a diagonal path to the crest of the ridge near Giybon first, making sure he did not come in sight of the town. He turned north along the great ridgeway track. The air was fresh and the flowers abundant, and he felt himself relaxing step by step as he walked northward.

Towards sunset on the fifth day he arrived at Hatsor. He had deliberately set himself a very leisurely pace, stretching out the regular times of prayer during the day and stopping to camp earlier than he needed to. He had loved the northward road since first walking it with Saniyahu, and felt that just to be treading it again was a healing thing.

His first couple of days had wound along the ridge past Sychem and Dothan. Then he had dropped down in a loop into the eastern end of the broad valley that ran from Kishon at one end to the River at the other. He crossed over the road in the hollow of the valley that angled back again to Bayth Shean, watching a squad of Mitsriy soldiers passing by as he ate some bread and olives.

Turning away from the marshy region at the southern end of the Sea of Kinreth he climbed over a long ridge, smiling to himself at the coincidence of names with Qetirah's mother. He scrambled down to the lake shore at the foot of a sheer scarp standing up like a knife blade, skirting some distance away from a busy town growing up near the water's edge. The last stage of the trip was an easy stroll along the valley floor, with swampy reeds and pools off to his right and gentler ground to either side.

He arrived at the town gate as the sun was low on the horizon on his right, and persuaded the town guards without difficulty to let him through to see the high priest up at the temple. He had visited him a few times with Saniyahu, and the man greeted him warmly.

It was a big establishment, with several lesser priests and priestesses living in a cluster of buildings close to the shrine itself. The temple area overlooked a large part of the surrounding town below, and the houses seemed, to his village eyes, to squat in an ungainly cluttered heap.

He was shown to a small room and a bedroll, and left to his own devices. There were several other bedrolls placed around the walls, neatly tied up, and it was clear that the room was able to house several transients like himself, but there was no sign yet of anyone he might be sharing with. He left his pack on the indicated bedroll and went to carry out chores for a few hours before going back to the room to sleep.

He was woken before dawn by a young apprentice, who took him silently to the shrine for morning prayers, and with that, his time at the temple truly began. He had at first intended to remain there just over a week, participating in the daily cycle of worship from before dawn until sunset, helping with the daily round of household tasks, spending time as directed by the high priest with supplicants and petitioners from the town and the surrounding land.

He was assigned to an old priest for his personal prayer and direction needs, and found himself speaking at considerable length to the old man about his home situation. The two men prayed for hours together, fasted for a day, and sacrificed a pair of doves at the full moon.

One night he found himself sharing his room with a young couple from across the River. They were a few years older than he and Qetirah, and the three remained awake for hours talking about their lives as seers, the joys and frustrations of working in a small community before, one after another, drifting into sleep. He felt an acute pang that Qetirah was not with him, not able to share in the time together.

The next day they moved on again, on their way up to Tsaphon, and he found the room almost unbearably empty afterwards. The sudden lack of young company, and the abrupt silence after the pleasant experience of sharing a room again, was painful in a way he had not expected. He almost left for home that morning, but the high priest asked him to remain another three or four days. He wavered in two minds all afternoon, but in the end stayed. The simple repetitive lifestyle was alluring.

Finally, on the twelfth day after first arriving in Hatsor, he decided it was time to leave for home. It would, he worked out, be almost exactly three weeks by the time he arrived back in Kephrath, and that seemed long enough for Qetirah to be on a more even temper from day to day. He had also promised to be back for the new moon ceremony, and if he missed that then his people might start to become anxious. He talked the decision over with the high priest, and with the old man who had become his confidant, and it seemed good to all of them.

He packed up his few belongings into the little pack, took a last look around the temple buildings, and set off southwards again. The two weeks had not made much difference to the temperature or the flowers, but the wind was kinder now, and in the mornings when a little rain fell, it felt gentle on his face. Before leaving the city he had traded some silver for a small brooch for Qetirah. Silver for silver. She could wear something of his rather than the gold one the chief had sent. As he walked he turned it over and over in his pocket as the path rose and fell.

It was early evening on the last day of the third week. It had rained a little at midday, but soon cleared, and now the sun was setting in an empty sky off in the distance far away to his right. He had branched away from the ridge, heading across at an angle towards Kephrath. The path was well away from the main track up to Giybon and the other two towns, and he was not expecting to meet anyone. The brooch was in his pocket. He would give it to her a little after he got in, once they had passed the excitement and delight of meeting again.

As he crested the last ridge but one he saw one of the village boys on the far side of the valley, at about his level, sitting near some goats, a single crow on a branch quite near him. He stopped to make sure he had recognised the boy, then called out and waved.

The boy looked around this way and that at the call, then saw him. He half raised an arm in response, then abruptly turned and ran back towards the village without calling in reply, out of sight, looking back just once as he ran.

The crow flew off. Damariel followed the little path down into the narrow valley, up the other side, and in the gathering twilight emerged by the tomb of his ancestors, close to the high place and his home.

He quickened his pace, calling out as he crossed the open space between the stones.

"Qetirah, Qetirah".

There was no answer from the house. Nobody else was nearby.

"Qetirah, Qetirah?"

He wondered if she had gone down to Kinreth's house to stay. There was a single lamp burning just out of sight around the near corner.

"Qetirah? Qetirah?"

He could see shadows flickering to and fro as the wind stirred the flame. There was still no answer from the house. He rounded the corner towards the front door quickly, almost at a run.

"Qetirah?"

Kothar was sitting on one of the stools in the doorway, the drape flapping loosely behind him. He sighed with relief.

"Kothar, whatever are you doing here? Do you need something? Look, Kothar, where's Ketty? I'll just go down to Kinreth's house for a few minutes if she's not here, but I'll be back if you need me for something."

He half turned to go, then realised that Kothar had said nothing, had risen to his feet quite hesitantly and taken a step towards him.

"Kothar? What is it? Are you alright? Shaharti? The little ones? Why are you here?"

"Damariel, I think you should come inside."

He looked down the hill in the direction of Kinreth's house, lost in the gloom.

"Right now? Of course, if it's urgent, I'll do it straight away. But can it wait until I've just seen Kinreth and Ketty? I can come down to Shaharti's house straight away after that. I'll be almost there anyway. I just want to see Ketty first."

He saw Kothar swallow in the lamp-light, saw the muscles in his throat and face tighten. A sudden coldness gripped his heart. He shivered, and felt all the organs in his body clench together. He took a step towards Kothar.

"Kothar, what's wrong? Where's Ketty? Where is she? What's happened?"

"Damariel, come inside. You must come inside. Please."

Damariel let Kothar take his arm, let himself be led in to the first room of his own house. It was quiet inside, and very tidy. Nothing had been prepared in the kitchen area for some time. It had been cleaned up and left uncharacteristically neat. His skin was cold and clammy, and his innards crawled with anxiety. He looked around again, opened his mouth to speak and closed it without a word. Kothar had let go of him and was standing near him, watching him.

"Where is Ketty? Kothar, she's not here, is she? Look, tell me, where is she? Is she down at Kinreth's? Or your house? Not up at Giybon, surely? Tell me that."

Kothar shook his head, slowly, looking directly at him, with a very odd expression on his face. He felt his hands trembling with unfocused dread.

"Damari, take off the pack and sit down."

"Kothar, by all the gods, tell me where she is. I can't bear this. Look, just tell me, tell me now, is she ill?"

Kothar shook his head again, bit his lip, and closed his eyes before replying.

"Worse than that, Damari. I'm so sorry."

Damariel felt icy blood pound in his head and leaned back against the doorframe. He shook his head.

"No, no, don't say things like that. Just tell me where she is. Is she alright?"

Kothar took a step towards him and gripped his shoulders.

"Damariel, listen. She's not alright, not at all. She's not with me, nor Kinreth, nor your mother, nor Saniyahu. Nobody. Not at Giybon. She's...".

He stopped as Damariel put a hand over his lips to stop him. He was shaking his head again and again.

"Kothar, what are you saying? This can't be. No, surely not. Where is she?"

Kothar closed his eyes briefly, gripped Damariel's hand to take it away from his mouth, and looked directly into his eyes.

"Where is she? Damariel, she's in the tomb of her ancestors. She's not with us any more, brother. She's gone across to the other side. Damariel, forgive me, and may all the gods forgive me for saying it, but, Damariel, she is dead."

He gripped Damariel's arms as he staggered away from the doorway. The chill in Damariel's body had spread out, and he felt a cold pain in his heart, in his throat. He was still shaking his head.

"Look, Damariel, I'd cut my own heart out if it would help, but nothing will help. I wasn't there when she died, but I saw her afterwards."

He was silent for a moment, holding Damariel upright, gripping his hands where they were shaking. He eased the pack from Damariel's back and half-lowered him onto a stool. Damariel bent double, his head pressed against his knees. There was a loud roaring noise in his hears that made it hard to hear as Kothar started talking again.

"Look Damari, she was coming up from her mother's house, back up here to the high place. Sara was nearest but she didn't see it either, just heard her fall over, cry out, and then she rushed over to her. She told me. She said. . . "

He swallowed again and stopped. Damariel shivered again and looked up at him, gripped his hands.

"Tell me, Kothar."

Kothar took a long breath and looked across the room, before turning back to him,

"She said she was all blood running down her legs. She was pale, turned white as anything. It was all over in a few minutes, Sara stayed with her but there was no time for any of us to do anything. Kinreth came too late, your mother, Sosanneth, all too late. All of us too late. I don't know what any of us could have done anyway. It was all just too quick. She hardly said anything, just kept holding her hand over her womb and shaking her head. She was asking for you."

Damariel groaned with anguish, a deep groan from his own belly.

"What did Sara say to her?"

Kothar shook his head.

"Said you were coming back to her, you were nearly home, just a little way down the track, something like that. None of us knew, but she had to say something, give Ketty something that might keep her here on this side."

Damari knocked the stool over as he stood up abruptly and ranged around the room from end to end. He suddenly turned on Kothar and shouted.

"Why didn't you wait for me?"

Kothar was silent for a few moments, facing towards him.

"Why did you put her down into the earth, Kothar? With the others. I didn't see her as she went across to the other side. Now I'll never see her. Not in this life."

Kothar stepped close to him and looked very directly at him.

"Look, Damari, this was four days ago. We didn't know when you were back, and we couldn't just keep her body out. Not right, not fair on anyone, least of all Ketty herself. Saniyahu and Halith came down that same day as soon as they heard, laid her in Kinreth's family tomb the next morning. Even if we'd known where you were we could not have waited four days. You know how it is."

Damariel nodded, and, at a whisper, replied, "Yes, I know."

There was a long silence.

"I'm so sorry, Damari."

Damariel nodded, setting the stool on its feet again and sitting on it. He leaned back against the wall, pulled his kef off and tore it in half. Then he took the collars of his tunic and ripped that in half down from neck to waist. A single tear ran down one cheek, and he wiped it absently with one half of the kef.

"I wasn't here, Kothar. Why did I go away?"

Kothar pulled up another stool and sat opposite him.

"Look, Damari, we all know you have to do these journeys. Nobody blames you. I've listened to what people have said. They don't blame you."

"I blame me. I didn't really have to go, not this time. I should have been here. Or I could have come back sooner."

"Damari, it was too quick. Nobody could do anything. Sara said she was just gone in a few minutes, all that blood coming out of her. You couldn't have saved her if you'd been here with her every moment."

"That's not the point. She died without me. Now we're both alone, me on this side and her on the other. I should have been here to hold her, talk to her, pray, I don't know, be with her at least. But I shouldn't have been on the road back from Hatsor, wandering along like an idle man."

He was silent for a little pause, and then the harsh edge was back in his voice.

"Four days ago, you said? Just four days? Oh, oh, if only I'd known. I could have come earlier. What was I doing?"

"None of us knew. How could we? The older women were talking, Shelomith said there was another woman died the same way years back. Long ago, before you and I were ever thought of. She was pregnant and died the same way, blood out of her with no warning, and at about the same time along. I don't remember the woman's name, but there was no warning that time either."

"Are you saying she died because of the baby?"

Kothar held both hands up.

"I'm not saying one way or another. But this other woman was pregnant, and they both died the same way. At about the same time through. Look, talk to Shelomith, she might help. She'd remember it. She could tell you directly so I won't get the story wrong in the telling. You must talk to Sara too, she was with Ketty right at the end. What do I know?"

"Then it's his fault, curse him."

Kothar shook his head and reached out his hand, a little uncertainly.

"What are you talking about, Damari? The baby died too. And we don't know if it was a boy or girl. Hardly formed yet, I should think."

Damariel stood up again and paced around the room. The icy chill in his veins had moved into his thoughts, and a cold rage was pushing its way through his head and his heart.

"No, not the baby, Kothar, don't be ridiculous. Not the baby. I mean Mahur-Baal, curse his name and his family. He took her for his pleasure, you remember, back at the winter festival, and his filthy seed caught in her. Now she's dead. It's because of him. He killed her just as much as if he'd thrust his dagger in her. Like the deer he killed. He killed her."

Kothar looked up to where he was pacing.

"Damari, what are you saying? Be careful about this."

"What's there to be careful about? It's plain as anything."

"Look, Damari, take your time over this. Sit down again. Look, you must talk to people here, Sara, Shelomith, Saniyahu and Halith, all your people here. Yeresheth and Sosanneth. Kinreth and Caleb. All of them. Talk to them all. Take your time before you do anything. There's no blame in this, it's a thing that happened, that's all. Your heart's cut open because of it, but the people out there have had their own hearts cut open too. They all loved Ketty, all of them, not the same way you did of course, but they loved her too. Take your time and sort things out here first. Don't just go rushing off and accusing like that. It's just not wise. Trust me. You need to take your time about all this."

Damariel walked over to the door and looked out into the evening darkness. Here and there he could see little lights among the houses. He looked at his hand, trembling slightly where it rested on the doorframe. He clenched it tightly, then relaxed it again and turned back to Kothar.

"Alright. That can wait. But I swear to you, Kothar, this won't just be forgotten."

Kothar stood and joined him at the door, put an arm around his shoulders. Damariel suddenly stiffened.

"Kothar, when they put her in the ground, please tell me that they didn't put that filthy brooch in with her?"

Kothar shook his head.

"No, I don't think so. I think Sara still has it. Ketty was wearing it that day. Saniyahu said that you should have it and decide what to do with it."

"Good, good. This will not be forgotten."

"Alright, Damari, alright, nobody's going to forget about it. Now, look, Damari, Shaharti knows I might be late back. I can stay up here if you'd rather not be on your own tonight. You've always said you wanted to lose me in this maze. I'll pick a room and see if I can get back to the kitchen here in the morning."

Damariel gripped his arm in reply, but shook his head.

"Thank you Kothar, but no. And bless you for being here when I got back, for being the one to tell me all this. I don't know how else I would have. . . "

He stopped, his mouth twisted with unspoken passion, his hands clenched again into tight, empty, fists. Kothar waited for a few moments, then looked away from him out into the village.

"I wouldn't have let anyone else be here for you."

"I know. I know. Bless you again. But as for tonight, no, I don't want you here. I won't be in here myself anyway, I'll spend the night outside, you know, outside where she's been placed. Up there."

They both looked across the shadowy stones of the high place to where the higher ground stood up against the stars. The great stones across the cave mouths could not be clearly seen from the door, but the nearest one or two loomed pale against the darker rock of the bank behind. Damariel felt Kothar shiver a little under his arm, but for him it was a familiar place, a liminal space between the worlds, and it held no especial fears.

"If you're sure?" He waited until Damariel nodded.

"Well, then. That's it. You know where we live if there's anything you need. Anything. I'll be back first thing in the morning, first light, and I'll bring some food with me for you, bread and whatever there is. Shaharti will put something together for us. But, look, even if it's the middle of the night, you come on down if you want. We'll hear you."

The two men embraced again, clung to each other for a long heartbeat, and then Kothar set off down the track to Shaharti's house and the almond tree around the door. Damariel, left on his own, sat in the porch under his vine for a long time, looking across the stones of the high place, before gathering the torn halves of his kef and walking the slow path to the tomb of Kinreth's family. Sitting in front of her resting place he took the knife he used for sacrifices and cut two long gashes down his arms and another across his chest.

He stayed by the great stone that sealed up the tomb most of the night, lying full-length with his face down on the flat stony space in front of it. The night went very slowly, and the chill in his heart swallowed up the chill from the cold, damp ground below as the blood from his arms soaked into the soil. It seemed a fair exchange.

At one point, when the stars had wheeled above him for some hours, he found himself so racked with uncontrollable shivers that his own life seemed to be clinging only by a thread to the world on this side. For a little while it seemed best just to give in to the desire to let himself slip across the boundary. It was only a little step: how well he knew that. Ketty would be waiting just the other side. It was not far to go.

He wondered, in the slow, heavy way his icy thoughts allowed, if she would be angry about the extra time in Hatsor. He knew how she would look just the other side of the stone in front of him, her body arranged for death, a few bits of this and that beside her. He could not think of her as decaying, worm-eaten or rotting, but rather with an other-worldly perfection illuminating her limbs.

He was profoundly relieved that the little golden brooch was not in there, polluting her body and her memory. The thought of its intricate beauty remaining changeless over the years to come while her own mortal frame crumbled and corrupted was unbearable. But then his inner sight caught a vision of her lying on the ground, just a short journey down the hill from their house, ashen pale as the blood ran from her betrayed womb and he knew that there was still a matter of vengeance, of retribution left unfinished.

Suddenly afraid of the lassitude of his body, he tried to get up. He was very stiff, and his legs would not support him. He pushed himself to a kneeling position and rested his forehead on the cold stone. He whispered into the silent vault behind it, to the body he could imagine still there, arranged neatly for the passage between the worlds.

"Wait longer for me, Ketty. Wait a while longer until I've made amends."

He pushed himself, awkwardly, to his feet and staggered a little as his own blood started to move around his body again. After a few minutes he felt able to leave the supporting rock wall behind, and set off, clumsily, across the hollow centre of the high place.

At first he had no real idea where he was going: he only knew he had to move about to return to some semblance of life, to keep himself on this side of the world, and so he crossed over to their house. His house now. His alone. He paused at the lintel, not really wanting to go back inside, and then, suddenly moved by a memory of one of Saniyahu's early lessons, set off to walk all around the perimeter of the village.

The light was fitful, and he found himself stumbling across rocks and into thorns as he made his way all around the edge. The exertion, and the discipline of bringing to mind every family as he passed by houses, steadied him, brought him back more completely into the world he knew.

Here and there the domestic animals stirred as he passed by, but the dogs all knew his scent and his movement, and there was no great outcry. He named the families as he passed their houses, the parents and the children, the newly born and the recently dead, the individual trials and delights of each house and family.

He knew them all, and the weight of responsibility for them rooted him firmly again. While he was carrying this duty, Yeresheth's house, Aliyna's house, Kinreth's house, were no more to him than the others. All were under his care.

Finally he was back up at the high place, looking across at her tomb again. He sat on the flat rock where, long ago, he had sat beside the Mitsriy scribe and watched him write how long his name might become in that land, far away to the south. Indeed, his name needed to get long enough to finish the task of finding a just recompense for Ketty.

He sat there for a very long time, cold still but no longer at risk of just slipping across the boundary line, trying to think how revenge might be accomplished. Kothar was right. It was not the time, not yet, and he must bide his time, let himself cool down and plan something. Just now he could not see how it might happen.

Eventually morning came. Little noises of village life began around him, but, true to his word, Kothar was the first to come up to him. He was heading for the house but, seeing Damariel sitting on the stone, angled directly towards him. He sat beside him and pulled some bread, cold meat, and olives from the bag he carried. As he sat down he looked quizzically at Damariel.

"Had a fight with thorns and thistles in the night?"

Damariel touched his face, felt the little scratches over it where he had, indeed, had the worse of the encounter, and grimaced. Kothar shook his head and placed some bread in his hand.

"Look, you're cold as a desert stone at night. Did you stay out all night?"

Damariel nodded, looking down at the bread as though unsure what to do with it, turning it over in his hands. Kothar took his kef off and wrapped it around Damariel as a scarf, as though he was ill.

"Come on, eat this. If you won't eat I'm under orders to take you back to Shaharti."

Damariel obediently took a mouthful of the bread, then pulled the rest apart to put some of the meat in it. He ate some olives. None of it tasted of much, but Kothar seemed more satisfied. Down the hill, a door opened and Abiram, Sara's husband, emerged with some tools. Seeing Damariel at the high place he turned, ducked under the branches of the pistachio tree curling over the door, and went back inside. A few minutes later he and Sara both came out and came up the hill towards him. Kothar looked at him quietly.

"Do you want me here or not?"

"I don't know. Yes. Yes, I think so. Just for a while. But this will go on all day, won't it? Just go whenever you think it best."

Sara came up to him, tears already in her eyes, and squatted down at his feet. She gripped his legs and looked up at his face.

"Honoured one, I am so sorry. There was nothing I could do for her. I held her in my arms so she had someone's touch as she crossed over, but that was all I could do."

Damariel took her hands and held them a moment.

"Sara, please get up. It should be me there on the ground, not you. You did everything any of us could do, abundantly blessed her in that terrible hour. Her crossing would have been made easier because of you. I am so grateful to you."

Abiram stood near, watching Damariel sombrely. Damariel remembered how they had lost their first child during the birth, how they had listened without expression as he had spoken blessing and committal all in one. He felt a sudden terrible kinship with them. How would it be, he wondered, when he met Yeresheth this morning? He nodded to Abiram and then turned back to Sara.

"Look, Sara, sit here a while. Tell me everything you remember."

She told him. The story was not very different from how Kothar had spoken yesterday, but from her lips it had an immediacy that wounded him. Part-way through her story she opened her hand, which had been closed like the tomb itself all that time, and gave him the golden brooch. She had been wearing it. Now here it was, in his hand.

The day went on very slowly. He heard the same account from different mouths many times, until it became something like a song he had learned. Meeting Yeresheth and Sosanneth was very hard, and the heavy shroud he wore over his heart almost softened into a veil at that point. Yeresheth sat with him in silence for a long time while others came and went. Her wordless presence felt as solid as the rock behind the ancestors' tombs. Sosanneth was filling out with her pregnancy, and stayed only a little while before going back down the hill again with Qeren.

Kinreth was distraught, and not trying to disguise her fierce anger and betrayal. She had lost her daughter twice, once in marriage to a seer and now once again. She and Caleb were both scarred down their arms with mourning gashes, but that was almost the only part of the agony he could share with them. That meeting was extremely painful.

Kothar went off at some point, came and went from time to time, people came and went all morning. Even Shomal came briefly up to the high place with Aliyna and spoke some words. Around noon Saniyahu and Halith came down. Kothar had sent one of the boys running up the track. They sat with him on the stone, and then, as the number of people still to see him dwindled to a trickle and then halted, took him back inside his house.

They talked with him most directly then, more so than the village had done, even than Kothar had done. They would come down every two or three days. They would conduct the observances. They would perform the new moon ceremony this time, but would he be ready for next time? If there were marriages or, unexpectedly, deaths to be attended, they would stand in his place. They would all see how it worked out. It was too early to see what would happen.

Damariel listened to it all, accepted their word. He would be ready to work again soon, he knew that. He told them so. People died in the village, and their wives or husbands or parents or children continued to work. So would he. They left late in the afternoon. They would be back the next day. He looked around. It seemed a very large house now, very empty, full of empty rooms.

He went out again to the largest of the stones at the high place and took out the little golden brooch. It was, truly, quite exquisite, a loving piece of work by some unknown craftsman.

He turned it over a few times, admiring the delicacy of the workmanship. In other hands, from another giver, in another life it would be a magnificent thing to treasure.

He laid it on the flat rock beside him, took up another stone and systematically pounded it into a featureless heap.

Then he took it back into the house and hid it in a secret place. It could wait for another, more opportune day. The silver brooch he pinned to one of Qetirah's kefs, and left it folded neatly on a stool beside their bed.

Mem

DABAH YEAR 22

I TURN MY FACE to the doorway – O sweetness –
See! My brother will come for me.

My eyes are on the way,
my ears are straining
for the footfall of he who might forget.

YERESHETH WOKE QUITE EARLY, even though it had been the midsummer festival the previous night. Quietly in the next room she heard Sosanneth talking with Labunasi as they busied themselves preparing some food, and realised what had prompted her wakefulness. She sat up, pulling a blanket behind her so she could lean against the cold stones of the outside wall with comfort, and took stock of her situation.

Tobiaz was still asleep beside her, and she looked down at him thoughtfully for a long time, unsure how to sort through her feelings about his presence there. It was the first time she had invited him to share her bed, indeed the first time that she had seriously contemplated lying with anyone since the day that her sons had died. Last night's festival had been exciting, the summer air and the music had had an intoxicating quality, and after a considerable time dancing up around the stones of the high place she had found herself bringing him back to her house.

Now it was morning and here they were. After a while she sighed to herself, got up, wrapped the blanket around herself without bothering with her kef, and went from her room out into the kitchen area. As she suspected, Sosanneth, showing her pregnancy very considerably now with only a couple of months to go, had nearly finished putting together some food; three plates of bread with a little honey to take into the other room for them all.

"Hello, mother. You must have been a lot later than us coming back from the festival last night. I didn't hear you come in."

Yeresheth nodded, poured two beakers of tea, picked out two plates, and started to pull off two portions of the sweetened bread. She did not feel ready yet to talk with her daughter about the time she had come back down to the house, and certainly not ready to talk about coming back here with Tobiaz. Sosanneth chattered a little with Labunasi, persuading him to carry a plate across to the door of the room they shared now with Qeren, when she suddenly noticed the double portions of food her mother was preparing. She stopped still for a moment.

"You must be hungry this morning, mother. Isn't that twice over what you have normally?"

Yeresheth nodded without speaking, and did not respond to her daughter's quizzical look. She took the double helping of food back into her room and pulled the drape across the opening again behind her, putting the two plates and the two beakers down in pairs, one either side of the bedroll. Tobiaz was just starting to stir as she slipped back under the blanket beside him.

A little later she came out into the kitchen area again, this time fully dressed for the day. Qeren was there, just getting ready to go outside. He stopped as she came into the room and looked at her.

"A bright morning to you, mother."

"And a day of peace."

He finished putting some sandals on, looked at her again, apparently wondering whether to say something else, but as she offered no further comment he continued getting ready, not very sure of his ground with her yet. Before she had finished sorting out the empty plates to her satisfaction he was gone. Sosanneth and Labunasi came out into the main area at the same time as Tobiaz emerged. There was a little pause in the room which suddenly seemed very full.

"A bright morning to you, Tobiaz. Will you stay longer?"

"Sosanneth, Labunasi, peace to you both. But I must be going now."

He took a step towards Yeresheth, then stopped as she glanced pointedly at her daughter. Sosanneth took Labunasi's hand, led him back into the other room for a short time saying something about fetching a plate they had left. Tobiaz grinned, came over and kissed her carefully, and then kept his mouth very close to her so he would not be overheard as he spoke.

"Yeresheth, may you remember this summer festival with as much happiness as I will."

Taking a little step back then, he touched her cheek where it curved out from behind her kef, then said in a rather louder voice.

"Yeresheth, I must go now to work on the terracing along the ridge, but perhaps we will see each other again before long. I hope so."

Then he was gone through the door, closing it quietly behind him as he went out into the morning sunshine. She stood watching the closed door for a while, her hands gripped together, not quite trusting herself to say anything or to move.

His departure had left a little silence which filled the house for a short time, until Labunasi trotted back over to her and handed her one of the little juglets. She knelt down to take it from him, then looked up again to see Sosanneth watching her from the door. She found herself, much to her amusement as well as embarrassment, blushing slightly under her gaze as she stood up again.

"Well, Sannah, what are you going to say?"

Sosanneth laughed and came over to hug her mother.

"Why should I say anything?"

"You're not upset? Surprised?"

"Only that it has taken you a year to bring him here."

They sat together at the table. Yeresheth felt herself to be flustered still, in contrast to her daughter who was still calm with the serenity of mid-pregnancy. While she had been caught up in the exhilaration of the festival last night, and afterwards in her room, she had not contemplated sitting here at the table the following morning.

Seeing Sosanneth put down the beaker in her hand and rub her womb, responding to some inward movement of the child she carried, she found her own hand pressing below her ribs. Was she simply a reflection of her daughter just now? Sosanneth looked at her across the table and smiled. Yeresheth shook her head.

"This is all too much for me, Sannah. You may say it is a year, but now it feels like running at breakneck pace down a steep hill. I don't know I can do this."

Sosanneth took her hand and held it firmly.

"Don't pull back from this, mother."

Yeresheth shook her head.

"I don't know, Sannah. I don't know what to make of all this. Maybe it's too sudden. I need to talk with someone, I don't know, someone I'm not going to meet every day in the street after we've talked about all this."

She paused for a while, thinking.

"Maybe Halith. That might be good."

Sosanneth nodded. "We need some of that woven stuff from Woodlands that Shelsheth makes, with the red dye. You could collect some of that and see Halith at the same time."

"I can't go on my own up there. I know it's not far, and I'm sure it's safe enough along the track just that short way, but I want someone with me."

Sosanneth laughed.

"I know a man who will go up the track with you and make sure you get there safely."

Yeresheth stared at her.

"I can't do that, Sannah. I'm going there to talk about him. How can you suggest such a thing? What would he say if he found out? And anyway, people will see us go off together. What would they be thinking?"

She shrugged.

"Probably half a day too late to be worrying about that. And do you really think it will be a surprise to anyone? As for being with him, I think a morning's walk along the ridgeway track might be just what you need to see another side of each other. He'll have friends up there for while you're busy, and you don't have to say why you're seeing Halith. After all, she was seer here with Saniyahu at the time everything happened to our family. He'll just think you're going to talk to her about that. Something that you can't tell Damari."

She closed her eyes a moment, thinking about it. What Sosanneth said did make sense, after all. She looked up again, glancing with a sudden softness into her sleeping room then back to her daughter.

"All right. All right, yes, I will. And I'll see Damari now and make sure they're not away on a pilgrim trip or something like that. Then I'll go up there today or tomorrow, whichever suits Tobiaz better. And look, Sannah, I'm not going to say anything to Damari about this, and I don't want you talking about it either. Not to him or to anyone. Not yet."

A little while later she was outside the great house beside the stones. She called out, then waited for an answer in case he was busy, but then his voice came in reply from inside. She pushed the door open. He was sitting turned half away from her, looking out of one of the windows. Qetirah's kef was across his lap, with a silver brooch she had not seen before pinned through it.

As she came in he got up with a slightly distracted look, carefully hung the kef in its place beside the musical instruments, and offered her a stool. Looking around, she saw that only the table of instruments had been kept immaculately neat. The kitchen, and the other parts of the house that she could see had a slightly unkempt look as though they had been neglected. He poured her some water and they sat together.

"Damari, I need to see Halith soon, today if that were possible. Do you know if they are at Woodlands or away somewhere?"

"So far as I know they are there. There's no reason for them to be away. Why? Is it something I can help with?"

She felt herself starting to become embarrassed again, and took a deep breath.

"No, son, but thank you. This is something I need to talk about with Halith. That's why I'm going to Woodlands to see her."

He nodded, accepting the decision.

"Surely you will not go on your own up there, though? I mean, it's not as if it was dangerous, and it's hardly any distance, but it would be better to go with someone. Look, I have to go in a couple of days anyway. If it can wait, I will go up there with you. But that can't be today or tomorrow. They say Mahur-Baal is going to visit there in the next day or so to hear the annual pledge of loyalty. I've managed to avoid him so far, and I don't want to have anything more to do with him than I can help just yet. Sitting here, I think I could show respect to him as chief, but in truth if I was caught by surprise I don't know what I might say. Of course, he'll be down here too in a short while to do the same for us, but that's another challenge for another day."

"Well, I understand that, but I want to go sooner. I promised Sannah I'd bring back some of the dyed cloth that Shelsheth makes, if this batch is as good as the last. We need to get started with it. And I have arranged for a friend to go with me."

To her relief, he accepted the statement without question, without asking who the friend was. In an effort to divert attention away from herself, she leaned forward and caught his eye.

"So why are you going up there?"

"Oh, I've been making sure that I meet with them every week or two. It helps, I'm sure of it. They have been magnificent. I don't think I could have kept going as priest and seer through this without them. And they insist anyway, at least for a while longer. Mostly here but sometimes there. It just depends. This time I need to meet with them to talk about the dance of Taliy at the autumn festival. I know we've only just had summer, but I have to think about the autumn already. My plan is that Halith will come down to do the dance here, but they want me to talk it over with the new apprentice woman they have started training. I think she should dance it there with Saniyahu playing. But that's a bit different from what they were expecting, and they want me to go up to Woodlands so we can all talk about it together, make sure we're all in agreement. It will be all right, I'm sure. She'll understand. I've met her a couple of times already. Rakham-Taliy is her name, but they call her Rakhmit. What irony though, with her named for Taliy's mothering womb."

"That seems odd to me. Why shouldn't Halith dance up there at her home with Saniyahu, and this Rakhmit come down here to dance with us? It makes no sense to swap around like that."

He shook his head with complete finality. It was his turn to look embarrassed.

"I can't do that, mother. I just can't bring this woman down here for the dance of Taliy. You know Ketty has done that dance the last couple of years. This is the first time I shall be here without her for it. It's not like it's any regular dance either. It's all about union and fertility. You know. So I can't just bring her down here for that dance, here into this house, without people thinking all manner of untrue things. It wouldn't be right. No matter if it's Halith comes down, we all know her and Saniyahu, nobody will think anything of the two of us being in the house here. But not some woman that nobody has ever met here in Kephrath. People would talk."

She spoke slowly, putting thoughts delicately into words.

"Do you think anyone really would gossip like that? Or even, would anyone really mind even if there was something in the gossip? I mean, there's no shame in sharing a bed with someone, is there? If you've been on your own a while and are drawn to someone?"

He looked shocked.

"Mother, it is far too soon. How can you say something like that to me? And anyway, it couldn't be with someone from the town. Which family would that be? Whose daughter? And not Nikallia, for all she keeps pressing."

"So you think a time might come when it was not too soon. How long is it right to wait after all? But anyway, she's not from here, you said so yourself."

He glanced across at the kef hanging on the wall, looking away from her.

"I don't want to talk about this. And I can't say anything about when. Or how long it might be. Or indeed ever. But just now, even by the time the autumn feast arrives, I can say it's too soon. And what would Kinreth say if she saw another woman coming in here?"

She took a deep breath, unable to halt the conversation but finding it profoundly hard in ways that he did not seem to realise.

"You are seer and priest to the town. Women and men come in and out of your house every day. Everyone knows that."

"Not like this. I've been very careful about who comes and goes, and at what time, and who is nearby to make sure we're not alone in an improper way. So you see that there is no foothold for gossip at all. But being in here for the dance of Taliy, and with a woman nobody knows, from another town, that's another matter altogether."

She fell silent for a while, thinking to herself that his excuses would wear thin before too long. How could he possibly try to maintain at one and the same time that someone must not be from the town, and also must not be from another town? It made no sense, but today was not a day for her to be saying those things to him. Certainly not today, when she was carefully avoiding talking to him about her own enjoyment of the summer festival and after. She had been silent a little too long, and he glanced up, frowning as though trying to remember something.

"You stayed out dancing here by the stones last night for a long time. Later out here than I can remember you doing for years. You stayed on here well after Sannah left, didn't you?"

"Damari, I have been thinking the last few weeks how well you are telling the stories and speaking to us all at the celebrations every week."

He looked surprised at the change of subject.

"You think so?"

"I do. Last week, when you sang that part of the story of Kirtu and then talked about it, it was full of conviction."

He leaned back, pleased.

"Well, I am trying. But in truth the song of Kirtu is not a difficult one either to sing or to talk about. That part's easy enough. But oh, in other things."

He stopped short, shook his head and looked down at the table again.

"In other things it's not easy at all. I don't mind telling you, mother, but I haven't told anyone else except Saniyahu and Halith. Some days it's especially hard. Even just trying to feel my way between this world and the next. It's like trying to find my way through a thick forest on a dark night."

"But the words you are bringing to us every week sound so vivid. Like what you said about pursuing the things that are truly the gifts of El, the thing that is promised above all else, and not being distracted by other things on the way. How Kirtu had found the bride of his heart when he followed exactly the words of the dream he was sent, and nearly lost her when he strayed to one side or the other. Lots of people thought it might have been spoken just for them."

He shook his head again.

"Some weeks it all flows right, it all joins up. But others it just doesn't. I can't explain very well. But after all." He paused and looked rather shamefaced. "After all, I know how a word like that ought to sound. And I know the situations of just about everyone in the town. Right now I'd have to say that some weeks I'm relying a lot more on what I know from this world, and a lot less on what I might hear from the other."

He looked at her rather defiantly.

"Does that sound shocking? Does that make me a cheat?"

She thought about it. If not shocking, it was at least unsettling. Was she talking to her son just now, or to the town priest and seer? He waited anxiously for her answer.

"I don't think so, Damariel. But I don't know what to make of it. For sure I'm not the right one to ask."

"I've talked about it a lot with Saniyahu and Halith. I felt like a cheat at first. But they said that sometimes you can't really tell if the words are everyday knowledge from this world or special insight from the next. I mean, you can't really pull the two apart, they're so close together. And it's not as if I'm doing any of that for my own benefit or anything. It's all for the good of the town, and I would never make personal gain out of it. But see, a word is a thing that you can pretty much fake if you've ever felt the real thing before. Which I have. Pray for me it doesn't become all fake every time."

He looked troubled by his own words as she held his gaze. He swallowed nervously and carried on.

"It's just a temporary thing, mother. These last few weeks have been very difficult indeed. Harder even than the first few weeks, when everything was so raw. Now it's going back a bit away from me, and it seems like most people in the town have forgotten about it. But I just can't have the town thinking I'm not able to do all this still. They need to be confident in me, so I can get back confidence in myself. It's important that they go on trusting me. That's why I really can't just have some new woman coming down here for the autumn dance. It would be too much for anyone to bear just now."

She nodded slowly, and he relaxed again.

"Would you like more water now? There's plenty here if you would like."

She was still thinking about what he had said.

"Thank you, but no. I must get ready to go. Hopefully this morning even."

They both stood up together.

"Are you sure you don't need me to come along with you? I might be able to change who I'm seeing when."

"No, I don't need that. Tobiaz is happy to come with me."

She regretted the words as soon as she had spoken them.

"Tobiaz? He's still living in Binti-Rahmay's house, isn't he? I remember now, you were dancing with him last night at one time. I saw you together. I must say, the dances men and women can share together are such a great relief; even I can dance with women without anyone making up stories."

Flustered, she snapped back at him.

"He's just a friend who's going with me today up to Woodlands. There's nothing to make of that. Not like anyone would make anything of it. It's not like I'm going to be doing the dance of Taliy with him."

Instead of becoming angry, he looked at her appraisingly, and she suddenly felt that he was seeing her afresh, piecing together clues, as though the other world had decided all of a sudden to pour insight into his heart about the matter. Before he could say anything in reply she rushed on.

"Look, Damari, I'm so sorry, I didn't mean that. I don't know why I said that. It just came out."

"No harm done, mother, nothing to forgive. I hope your journey to Woodlands is successful."

He came over to hug her, and although she felt awkward at first after the words that she had spoken they relaxed into the familiarity of the action. She rested her head against his shoulder a moment, then stepped back and looked at him.

"Damari, take care of yourself. And don't be always looking back at what has been. A time will come to change, you know."

He nodded slowly. "I wonder. Perhaps for some of us sooner than others? I think it's no accident you spoke of this today."

She felt a little shiver run down her spine, and wondered again what little whisper of truth he was hearing inside, knowing for sure that this was an other-worldly insight and not just ordinary conversation. Then the moment passed, and they parted by the front door of his house.

Tobiaz was only too pleased to leave the repair work he was doing on some of the terracing and walk with her to Woodlands, even though he had only been working at it a short time since leaving her house. He took the opportunity to take some jars of wine and vinegar with him to trade for tools at the other town, and they set off along the track with a borrowed donkey carrying the jars.

After curving around the bluff where the tombs of the ancestors were, the track looped around a valley end up to the next ridge. There it forked, with one path going off to Giybon and the other to Woodlands. After that the way was mostly level, with little rises and falls as they continued along the main ridge that ran north and south like a backbone.

Yeresheth had only been away from Kephrath a handful of times, and never to Jarrar's town, and she drank in every undulation of the ground, every stand of trees and meadow of flowers. The summer heat was starting to dry up the land, but the colours were still startling to either side. Tobiaz knew the way rather better, from making trips to trade or swap goods every few months. He did not have any of Damariel's detailed knowledge of what places lay in which direction, or how to navigate long distances through the land by means of waymarks, but he had a fair memory for the names of the nearby hills and valleys they passed by close to the track.

It was an easy walk, and a pleasant one, and she felt her soul expanding in the roomy swing of the land. But every so often she would look sideways at the man walking beside her, and wonder if it was still possible for her to share her path with another. She found herself inwardly rehearsing Damariel's own claim that it was too soon, that the situation ought not to be rushed. But then, as she listened to his voice explaining where the track turned off to Shalem, and his excitement at seeing an eagle hunting over the ridge ahead of them, she found herself wondering how it could possibly be too soon for her, after all the wide waste of time since her sons had died.

Surely her heart was fickle, and blew winds that were both dry and moist across the landscape of her soul. Fortunately, Tobiaz seemed oblivious of the way her thoughts about him flitted this way and that in the breeze. Before long they came to the town gate of Woodlands, with the letters making up Jarrar's name cut into the stone arch above them.

They separated then, he to meet friends and find out who would trade what he had in exchange for tools, and she to negotiate for cloth first and then talk with Halith. They arranged to meet back at the town gate just after noon. In fact the discussion about the fabric took hardly any time, and very soon she found herself outside the door of the house beside the high place. It was about the same size as Damariel's, she thought, but it was hard to tell as it was quite irregular in shape. At some stage an extra room had been added on to one side, giving it a lopsided appearance. Perhaps in another few years the town would see its way to adding something similar on to the other side to restore the balance.

She hesitated outside the door, listening to Saniyahu and Halith talking inside, remembering back to when their voices had been heard like that in Kephrath. As she stood there, a voice came from behind her.

"Lady, can I help you in some way?"

She turned to see a young woman standing there, about the same age that Baruk would have been if he had lived. She was quite short, with a narrow face and large dark eyes. She was also wearing the kef of an apprentice. Rakham-Taliy, she presumed. She was quite pretty, and had a confident air. She wondered briefly if Damariel's reluctance to have her come down for the autumn dance was in fact because he found her attractive, and was anxious about the possible consequences of them being together. With a swift appraising glance, she decided that was probably true, but that they probably would never form a lasting match. Something did not quite fit, would not work.

"I think you are Rakhmit?"

"I am, lady, but I do not have the honour of knowing you."

At that moment Halith opened the door, having heard the voices outside. She embraced Yeresheth with obvious pleasure at the reunion.

"Yeresheth! How good to see you. And unexpected, but all the better for that. Like finding a fountain when you are thirsty in the hills. And I see you have met our new apprentice."

They went inside and talked idly for a while, until Saniyahu and Rakham-Taliy took a hint and found tasks that needed their attention elsewhere, leaving Halith alone with her. She talked with her about Damariel for a while, about her anxiety for him. Then, feeling more liberty than she had expected, she told Halith about the summer festival and Tobiaz. Sitting in a different town, with Halith who had already shared so much of her difficulty, it seemed possible.

In the early afternoon she walked back down to the town gate, to see Tobiaz already sitting there in the shade of one of the pillars. The donkey had some tools strapped to its sides and back, but none of the jars they had brought down. He was facing away from her, working away at something in front of him, and did not notice her approach until she was very close.

He had been carving away at a little piece of bone, she noticed, creating a little animal shape that was scarcely formed beyond the rough outline of body and head. It was too early to tell what it might become. He put it into one of the panniers and stood to take from her the bundles of cloth and secure them on the donkey.

They set off back again along the track towards home. Just over half way they stopped to share some food Tobiaz had gained at some stage at Woodlands, and she realised that she was very hungry. They sat on a flat rock overlooking a wide valley. The land dropped steeply away from them for a short time, and then flattened out to curve gently away into the distance. They could see most of the track ahead of them in glimpses through the low trees along the ridge, until it dipped out of sight around a rocky outcrop. One or two of the outlying Kephrath houses were just in view, and higher up to their right they could see two of the village boys out with some goats.

"Thank you for coming with me today."

"My pleasure." He laughed. "Both to be spending the time with you and to be getting out of the terracing for a few hours. And I needed those tools. So a good outcome for me all round. And for you?"

"Oh yes. Halith was most helpful. And I picked up the cloth. And it has been good to get away from the town, even just for a morning. It all looks different from out here."

"What did you talk about?"

He stopped, seeing a wary expression come over her face.

"No, forgive me. Were you able to get all the material you needed?"

"Nothing to forgive. Yes, the woven stuff was all that Sannah and I had hoped. That took no time really. Then Halith and I talked about Damari for a while."

She took an uncertain breath, put her kef straight, and looked all around at the sweep of the land before turning back to face him.

"Then we talked about you and I. You see, I could not speak with Damari about it, not even Sannah, and I was looking for a person to confide in. Halith spent so much time with me after what happened to Baruk and Bashur, and everything after that. She knows me better than anyone."

He nodded, not very surprised. There was a little silence. After a while he prompted her.

"And?"

"Oh yes. Well, I talked about how things were for me. I mean that my heart seems to me like these hills and valleys we are looking at. It climbs up high here and it sinks very low there, and I never know whether the path goes up or down around the next turn. I think I know the landscape inside me even less well than I know the ways to the four towns."

He nodded again, looking at the swell and dip of the terrain around them, but said nothing.

"I don't even know what I shall do, when I think that by now most of the town will know we have been together, we lay together. Do I mind that? Will they approve or not? What will they say to me? At least, the women will be talking about it."

He laughed.

"Oh, the men too. Two men talked to me first thing this morning as I started on that terrace. One asked whether I was going to be wearing some new clothes all of a sudden, and the other if I was going to start taking lessons in weaving."

He laughed again, turning to her, but she found it difficult to join in the humour.

"Did they mean harm in it? What did you say to them?"

"Those two? Harm? Oh no. They're all right. It was just some fun. But I told them I'd rather be having some new clothes than an empty room, and I would happily take any number of lessons in weaving soon as anything. But I also said that the new clothes might wait a while since I was in no mood to chivvy the seamstress into a rush and a hurry that she wasn't sure of."

"Tobiaz, you said no such thing."

"Well, not exactly. I expect it sounded to them more like I was suggesting they keep their own terrace wall straight instead of trying to find the odd stones in mine. But if I had said it the other way I'd have meant every word."

She looked away again, wondering if she would find herself in one of the dips in the path after all. He leaned back a little on the rock.

"Look, Yeresheth, let me tell you something. Two years ago and more, Binti-Rahmay died of a winter fever. She saw that her daughter was going to be happy with Uzziel but she never got to see them married. So I watched all that ceremony up at the stones for her, and I welcomed him into her house just as though she were still there. Of course, properly speaking Gazala counted as mother of the house even then, but she's very young for that, so I help out where I can. Then hardly any time after that, only a little over half a year, see, he dies in that rockslide. Kunor has already left to live with Binti Samit in her mother's house."

He hesitated for a moment to steady himself.

"So there we are, Gazala and I, each on our own in a room where we were expecting four at least. No children born to my Gazala from him either, nothing except for one false hope early on. That was a very low point in the path, if you like, and I think both of us have been toddling along the miry bottom of that low place most of the time since. Gazala swore at first she would never go with another man, but I told her that those were the words of a foolish woman, and the best way that both our hearts might find some healing, and the household endure, was to make another choice."

He stopped, gauging her reaction.

"Hasn't she been seeing Yosheb this last little while? That's what I hear, anyway."

"Well, indeed she has. She started bringing him back to the house a little while ago, and if both heavens and earth smile on it then I think she'll invite him to live there before long, and maybe even get your lad to marry them up at the stones. That would make me very satisfied, especially if her womb truly opens up for him and there are children born. But at the same time for me that would be something of an ending. I'd go back to being like a fifth leg on a donkey."

She smiled at the phrase, looking out at the hills and the sky.

"So you don't mind these others teasing you about lessons in weaving."

"I'd learn everything there was to know about weaving if it would help."

"Do you think I'm a fifth leg on a donkey in my house?"

He pursed his lips and shook his head.

"You are mother of the house. It's different. At least, it seems so to me."

"I don't know. Sannah is well able to care for the house on her own. She doesn't need me to be holding her hand."

"She needs you to be holding a baby sometimes. Two now, nearly. I reckon she still looks to you as mother."

"I know."

They were silent for a while as the quick clouds chased each other across the summer sky. Eventually he started speaking again.

"So I want to say that I understand a little about your loss, and although I'll very happily come along for weaving lessons whenever I'm invited, I really can wait for new clothes if the seamstress doesn't want to be rushed into anything."

She leaned into him and felt his arm, very cautiously, wrap around her shoulders. She sighed, feeling once again an internal anxiety well up and push aside her initial contentment. Shomal had seemed kind at first too, and only later showed another face. Was Tobiaz just the same? Would his caress after all turn out to be just more aggression?

She wanted to think he was different, but it was like meeting someone at a crossroads or at the door of a house. There was hesitancy, uncertainty as to which way the encounter might turn. She felt his hand against her shoulder, rubbing gently at the tension which had gripped the muscles all the way up her arm, and she sighed again.

"Look, Tobiaz, it's not just about haste for me. There are other things that I don't want to talk about. One day soon, perhaps, but not now. Do you mind if the new clothes wait a while, and the weaving lessons are just from time to time? I am so sorry, but my heart is very delicate just now."

She did not look up, not quite sure what his expression might be, but she felt him nod his head. She relaxed a little. Again there was a little silence between them, and after a while he chuckled and squeezed her arm again.

"Just so long as I don't have to wait for another summer festival."

They unloaded the cloth first at her house, then Tobiaz went away with the tools to return the donkey to Danil. She and Sosanneth spent the remainder of the afternoon working together while Labunasi was down at the stream, laying out the fabric, and planning how best to use it.

Much later on, Damariel came to the house to make sure she had gone and come back again safely, and did not need him to go with her another day. She showed him the pieces of red material spread out all over the floor of her room and spoke about a successful trip. She omitted any mention of the conversation with Halith or the journeys either way, and was aware of Sosanneth watching her curiously.

"And also I met the new apprentice, Rakham-Taliy. She seems pleasant enough. Her family is from Meyim, but she wanted to be apprenticed at a different town."

"That's true. Also the couple at Meyim are quite young, and not long in the vocation. They were not happy about taking the responsibility on their shoulders just now. So she's at Woodlands. I think everyone's happy with the arrangement."

"So after meeting her, I think that maybe after all we said that she could come down here to dance for the autumn festival, Damari. I really don't think that would be difficult at all for anyone."

He looked at her very distantly.

"I told you, mother. We're going to arrange for Halith to come down here. It's almost settled now, I just need to talk with them all. I think it's a better plan all round."

Sosanneth was looking from one to the other, trying to sort out the undercurrents in the conversation.

"Isn't she good enough to come and dance here, Damari?"

He stopped and thought about how to answer.

"It's not so much a matter of being good enough. It's to do with what is best. All round, I mean, here and there, and for everyone concerned. Everyone."

He glared at Yeresheth as he finished. She shrugged.

"I'm just saying that you need to think about other possibilities, Not just the ones that come to mind first."

He stood up.

"Well, whatever gets decided for then, just now at any rate I have to go and get myself ready for the next part of Kirtu. That won't get sorted out by sitting around a table talking."

Yeresheth stood and went to the door with him.

"I will come up to the high place with you. I need to make devotion at the tombs of the ancestors, and I shall walk with you there."

He waited while she got some seeds and a little oil in a jar, then the two of them threaded their way among the houses of Kephrath.

"Mother, you must let me make my own choice about the autumn festival. It's not just about what you think might work for me. There are two whole towns to think about, both in this world and the other. It's not about you looking out for a partner for me."

"Actually now I have met her, I don't think you two would be a good match for each other. That's why I think it doesn't matter if she comes here to dance. Everyone will see it straight away, just like I did. And it would make so much more sense for Halith to dance there in her own town. Tell me, how would the people of Meyim feel that their own seer was going somewhere else to do that? Think about that while you're deciding what's best for both towns."

He stopped to look at her. They were standing in the middle of the track where it broadened out to merge with the open area at the top of the town.

Before he could say anything she went on, gesturing first to his house and then at the stones and the rocky bluff behind them.

"But I am keeping you from your preparation, and I need to go up there."

"If you don't mind I will come with you. Kirtu can wait a little longer."

They went up to the flat stone above the cave where their family lay. They spoke through the prayers together, pouring the barley grain and oil down the fissure in the rock. She wondered, watching the little puddle shrink as it dripped down into the darkness below, if her heart was more like the oil that trickled away, or the crack in the rock that remained long after the offering had gone. Then they climbed down again and stood beside the door of his home. She put her hand on his arm.

"Damari, I have to tell you this before we part tonight. You know Tobiaz, who went with me today to Woodlands. Well, that was no accidental choice. You said that I had danced with him at the festival last night. That was true, But then afterwards I took him back with me to my house. I think I will do that again. Perhaps it will grow into something. I think it might. But it's still early. For both of us, but mainly for me, I think."

He watched her, waiting to see what else she would say.

"Now, I am very happy about that. But I am also very anxious about it. You know a little of what happened between me and the man who lives with Aliyna. I am very fearful that this now will turn into the same thing all over again. That things will just repeat themselves. I don't think I could bear that. So half the day I have wanted to be with him again tonight, and half the day I have wanted to never cross his path again in case it all turns bad."

She took a deep breath and placed her hand over his mouth as he started to speak.

"I could not tell you any of this earlier. But I do want to say now that I know you saw something with true sight this morning. I know you did, and I felt through my whole body that something true was welling up inside you to do with me. I want to thank you for not saying then all that you felt. And now I am trusting my heart into your hands so that you can care for it. Not to ask you what I should do, for that is my burden, but to know that you are holding me along with the rest of us mindfully in prayer. The living and the dead."

He looked deeply moved and with an effort gathered himself to speak.

"Thank you for that, thank you."

They looked at one another for a time beside the stones of the high place, under the vine that crowned the doorway of the house. Then, since enough had been said, they turned, and each went alone back to their own house.

Nun

ETANIM – MERAP YEAR 22

THE GODS PITCHED a tent for the sun –
and he is a bridegroom seeking his chamber,
a hunter pursuing his prey –
the whole of the sky is his journey
and nothing can hide from his heat.

KOTHAR WAS WAITING FOR DAMARIEL some way up from the high place, at the start of the trackway going north. He was half-sitting, half-leaning on one of the larger rocks beside the path, absently rubbing his right arm which was still recovering from the teeth of a particularly ill-favoured wildcat that had strayed into one of his traps a few weeks ago. He laughed a little to himself. What with that latest wound, and the long scar across his shoulders he had acquired just before last midwinter, he was becoming more visibly wounded than any of Danil's raiders.

This time they were headed north towards Bayth Shean to trade, and for Damariel at least, to spend some time in prayer in the little temple there. As on their southern trip the better part of two years ago, they had two donkeys laden with all kinds of goods. Kothar had only half an idea of his own plans once there, but was extremely satisfied to be heading on the long-promised northward journey. As Damariel was still not in sight, he pushed himself more fully onto the rock and leaned back against a convenient tree behind it.

From this vantage point he could see most of the houses spread along the northern side of the ridge, including his own where Shaharti was still in mourning for the miscarriage of their third child. Kinreth's house was also not yet in the light, with the great shadow of the ridge to the east of the village sprawled across it. The morning sun had already reached Shomal's olive patch.

He watched one of the village boys lead out some goats away from the houses into the wide sunlight, and then finally heard Damariel's voice from amongst the stones of the high place, in conversation with Issi. He turned to watch as Damariel appeared and then came along the track, carrying some small pieces of pottery and with a bag looped over one shoulder.

"Ah, he talked you into taking some more bits, did he?"

Damariel grinned ruefully.

"I'm afraid so."

He shrugged his shoulder to indicate the bag.

"And Shelomith persuaded me to take some of her latest embroidery work."

His smile faded quite rapidly as they found places to stow the extra items. To Kothar's eye, his friend had settled into a colder, more detached demeanour than in the spring; in many ways it was not an improvement. They set off northward, where the trackway had been levelled and smoothed as part of the village's annual duty to the chief. After they had walked for a while and were quite out of sight of Kephrath, Damariel suddenly spoke.

"How's Shaharti? I was meaning to come down to see you both yesterday, but had to stay longer with Pirigalla and Putiheba. Their boy had a fever and I had to stay until we were sure it was easing back."

"She's fine. Grieving still, but fine."

"Well, I will be there of an evening soon, once we're back from this trip. In what I suppose you might call an official capacity, not just as a friend. But look, just for now I'll say to you not to rush into anything. Give Shaharti some time. They say a year, you know. Don't rush anything."

Kothar nodded and glanced briefly at Damariel, and they walked along in silence for a while. As they turned another corner, the quality of the road declined to merely a well worn track amongst the low trees and scrub, winding here and there to avoid larger outcrops of rock. They were now beyond the area the village considered it its responsibility to maintain, and were in the common wilderness land. Damariel laughed shortly and gave a rare smile.

"Well, we're finally going north like you've always wanted. All those months of nagging."

Kothar grinned back.

"Years, more like. Yes, I'm finally going to see the north."

"Only some of it. There's a lot more beyond Shean."

"It's a start. Tell me which way we'll be going. Where is Bayth Shean from here anyway? I want to make the most of this trip if it's going to be this long between journeys. And Shaharti wanted to be told about everything."

Damariel glanced across at the route of peaks along the higher ridge to their right, then over his shoulder at the sun.

"Well, getting there will take us just a little longer than when we went down to Shamsh. Coming back will be slower, though, as it's right down in the Valley and something of a steep climb back up. If we were heading further north we'd stay on this track a long while, past Sychem indeed, until it winds down into the Kishon valley. That runs east to west from the Valley itself right out to the Sea. But we don't need that. Anyway, I don't want to go on that track."

"Why not?"

Damariel shook his head and glanced briefly at his friend.

"That was the way I took back in Nisan, up to Hatsor, when I came back to find - well, you know what I found."

"So there's another way."

Damariel shook his head again, but to clear it of shadows and memories rather than to disagree.

"Oh yes. Soon we branch off to the right, at a large boulder shaped like a grindstone just after a large clump of mixed pine and broom trees, and go in amongst those fells over there, in the lower ground between those two crags you can see. There's a smaller track right along the crest, a bit less even than this one. Should be all right for us, though. We follow that for the rest of today, camp out tonight, then in the morning drop down into the Valley to Shean. It's a shorter road even if it is rougher, and it's nothing these beasts won't manage. Anyway, I'm just not going along the main drag any further than I have to."

They plodded along at what Kothar thought a pedantically slow pace. It was therefore considerably longer than he expected before they branched away from the main path, although the track itself was unmistakable from Damariel's description. This smaller route would have been quite easy for the two of them on foot, but was much more difficult with fully-laden donkeys picking an uncertain way amongst shale and slabs of loose stone.

The path was, in fact, very poor. Kothar suspected that Damariel had never actually been this way with beasts before, and that several times he was on the verge of retreating to the main ridgeway route. It was at best a route for foot-travellers. However, they persevered doggedly along the little path than took them in slow loops roughly parallel to the Valley, sometimes far from the rim and sometimes close enough that the steep banks fell away at their right hand.

They made their camp under the lee of a craggy outcrop with a good part of the daylight remaining. Damariel had said that the path turned down only a short distance away, and that this was the most sheltered place until they reached the Valley floor. He was happier staying up in the hill country, and did not want to camp down there below, so they stopped. They tethered the donkeys loosely beside a clump of juniper, fed and unloaded them, and settled themselves against the angle of the crag, looking westward away from the Valley.

Somewhat to Kothar's surprise, for he had imagined nobody had walked this way for years, it was clearly a place that had been frequented by other travellers. The ground had been cleared and smoothed in a broad arc in front of the rock face, and a low wall of nearby stones had been built up as a rough shelter from westerly breezes. For their part, the two men added a few more stones to the top and filled in some of the bigger gaps with pebbles and moss. The solid rock behind them gave shelter from the wind blowing out of the wilderness eastward.

They talked as they ate, scattered puffs of conversation that were easy enough, but made no pattern and reached no conclusion. Kothar, sensitive to Damariel's moods through years of friendship, kept away from specifics that might be too painful, and dwelt instead in safe generalities.

In the morning, Kothar woke, rose early, and then scrambled up the steep bank behind their sleeping place, made his way to the top of the craggy flat-topped summit and sat at its highest point watching the sunrise. Beyond the Valley shadowed below him, beyond the fringes of the sown land and the grazing, from behind the distant wilderness ridges, the sun leaped up like a hunter for the chase, or a lover for his desire.

He sat watching it for a while as it grew too bright to look at, and with increasing heat started to dispel the wreaths of mist on the hollow places of the land. Sighing a little as the mystery of dawn was swallowed up in full day, he started looking left and right along the ridge for the animal trails, and the little places he would be setting traps if he lived nearby.

Behind and below him he heard waking noises from Damariel, who stirred, looked vaguely about and then after a short time came up the steep bank to join him. He was clearly still part asleep and Kothar sat in silence for a while with him. Eventually Damariel rubbed his eyes and stretched.

"What came over you, Kothar? Couldn't you sleep?"

"I slept very well, thank you. But I would never miss seeing this."

He gestured out across the deep expanse of the Valley to the far away ridges, which by now were starting to lose their sharp morning edges in heat-haze. The sun was well above the hills. Damariel blinked and rubbed his eyes again.

"I suppose so. But you've seen days start before."

"Oh yes, but hardly ever like this. This is magnificent. Back home we don't get the sun until it's well up. What it must be to live facing east."

He sighed again and stretched, satisfied with the sunrise. Damariel smiled and held out a small vessel of water.

"Pour for me please, Kothar, and say the morning prayer with me while it still is morning."

Kothar nodded and poured some of the water over both of Damariel's outstretched hands. Damariel shook off the excess, turned to face north, and they both spoke the first lines of the prayer. Damariel carried on well past the part that Kothar could share in, so he sat back, listening still to the ritual words but with half of his attention on the expansive lands around.

From some distance to the north came the sound of a mountain lioness exultant over her prey. While Damariel completed the prayers he looked intently but in vain for her up and down the rock faces, then joined in the final blessing and poured another splash of water over the seer's hands. He leaned back against a convenient rock and watched Damariel pull himself back into this world. Damariel looked at him and nodded.

"Thank you."

He shook his head. "Nothing owed. My pleasure."

He gestured up the Valley.

"If you were praying to Qedeshet, then she was hunting up there just now."

Damariel looked at him, puzzled, then nodded in understanding as the distant lion sounded again. He pulled a face.

"El and Athirat for the most part. But yes, I named her along with the others. I dare say she would be too busy to listen to my prayers anyway. I haven't exactly felt alive with the life of the other world these last months. Maybe she thought it was a better day to be along mountain ridges rather than listen to some priest from a little hill country town."

"Do you think the goddess hunts like that?"

Damariel shrugged.

"Well, maybe. No, not really. More likely she has little lioness servants who she sends out to do that kind of thing. I expect she has greater things to occupy herself with."

Kothar said nothing, but shaded his eyes and looked out into the empty space above the Valley where a bird of prey was circling in vast sweeps high up. He gestured towards it.

"I dreamed I was a bird last night, with the ground so far below me I could hardly see it. Just empty air all around."

Damariel glanced at him. "Oh yes? And?"

Kothar shook his head absently, still watching the bird.

"Nothing much I remember now. Just the air holding me up. I could see my house, tiny below like you'd see it from a ridge, only smaller. And it wasn't my house at all, not any more, someone else lived there. But I knew it had been mine. What about you?"

Damariel shook his head, abruptly, finally, looked away, and did not answer. Kothar waited for a while for him to continue, then pulled a face and pointed to the juniper bush behind him.

"So what do you think trees dream about, then?"

Damariel laughed at that and stood up.

"I'm sorry, Kothar. Poor company for you. Maybe these trees dream of walking all the way up the Valley to Bayth Shean. Let's eat quickly and do their dreaming for them. We'll be there before half the day is gone."

Indeed, it was shortly before noon that they came into the town. They went in past a detachment of guards at the city gate, headed by a Mitsriy officer and scribe who jotted down their names and home town, and glanced in a token manner into the donkey panniers before passing them through. Damariel answered all the questions with a confident familiarity while Kothar sat in the shade and waited for him to finish. It was all quite casual.

Once inside the gate and the buildings clustered beside it, he saw that the community was built around a main street running slightly to their left and slowly climbing. Smaller streets branched off left and right into little mazes of homes. The town was perched on a low rise close to the River, a little larger than Bayth Shamsh and on the whole arranged in a more orderly way.

There was an obvious Mitsriy central area with a low barracks for soldiers, a taller and more impressive building for the official overseeing the area, and a decent size temple. For all that, it was clearly a Kinahny town with only a thin Mitsriy veneer. Kothar's eyes were all about him as they went through the streets, and he kept up a running commentary.

"Look, Damari, that's hardly a kef at all she's wearing. More like a ribbon my little Yasmit won't be dressed in once she's past being down at the stream. All just out here on the streets too."

It was true. Most of the men wore their kefs over their shoulders, almost like a shawl, not covering their heads at all, and the women wore theirs well back, or folded and doubled over. Women's hair was everywhere Kothar looked, and the kefs themselves were in a bewildering variety of colours and patterns. If there was a link between a kef and the wearer's status, it was too complex for him to guess.

Damariel listened good-naturedly for a while, but finally, as they worked through the streets towards the market area, he stopped and turned to Kothar.

"Look, Kothar, the way you're carrying on everyone will know we're strangers. Bad enough we dress like highlanders. If you talk like this we'll never get good prices for these things. They'll think we're just ignorant hill farmers and peasants out of the beyond. You might as well ask them to rob us blind. Look now, go and explore the town and let me do the dealing at the market. Just don't. . . "

Kothar interrupted, laughing. "Just don't get into trouble?"

Damariel nodded and tried, rather unsuccessfully, to join in the humour.

"That's right. Go round the town, look around, look at women's kefs if you want, but don't arouse anyone's anger or jealousy. Sit down somewhere where they'll listen and tell them all about your fight with a wildcat."

"The way I tell it, it was a lion. Face to face, and me armed with nothing but a weaver's rod."

"Fine. A lion, then. I'll be a while doing this, and I'll see you, well, let me think, I'll see you at the inn we passed just now looking south towards the gate. Give me until late afternoon."

They parted and Kothar began a circuit of the town, ending with plenty of time at the inn Damariel had indicated.

Near the start of his search, his half-formed ideas had come to birth, and before long he had found exactly what he had been expecting and looking for.

Rather later, Damariel appeared. Kothar watched through the window as he tethered the two donkeys outside. They looked satisfyingly unladen, and Damariel looked pleased as he came in with just a single pack, spotted Kothar after a quick glance around the room, and came to sit on the trestle beside him. He nodded as Kothar poured him a large measure of beer from the jug in front of him, and leaned back against the wall. He looked weary as well as successful, and Kothar rested his hand on his friend's arm by way of support.

"All done, then?"

"Yes indeed. All done, and at prices nobody can complain about back home. Even those few last bits Issi gave us to bring."

"Good. In that case I have a proposition for you. It'll help you relax and take your mind off your troubles. Now, don't argue, just listen. I know you were going to have us stay with this priest friend of yours."

"Yes, Abiel he's called, up on the other side of town, just north of the temple area up the hill from here. I've stayed with him before. I think you'll like him, though you'll likely say he's not very energetic."

"I have a better plan. Just by the temple there's a house with two women. We'll stay there and have some better company tonight."

Damariel looked at him.

"Shrine girls?"

Kothar shrugged.

"Nice religious girls."

"I won't."

Kothar grimaced and leaned back.

"Look, Damari, it does no harm. They're connected with the temple, it's clean, they're quite obliging. It's away from home so nobody's father or brother can take offence, and you need to find your feet again somehow. Nobody from Kephrath to wonder who you're with. But I knew you'd argue."

"I won't."

Damariel suddenly stood up and left the inn. Kothar finished the last draft of beer, nodded to the inn keeper, and then followed him outside to where he stood by the donkeys, fists clenched, facing south.

"Look Damari, what is it? What's the problem?"

"I can't. Not with one of those."

"Whyever not? Nothing shameful in it."

Damariel was silent, his face twisting with passion for a long space. Slowly his hands unclenched again.

"No, there's not. I didn't say there was. But that's not it. Look, Kothar, it's something I promised Ketty. She made me swear. It's almost the last thing we ever talked about before I left for Hatsor that day. She made me promise that I wouldn't go with a northern girl while I was up at Hatsor."

"Come on, Damari, that was when she thought you'd be together again in just a few days. You can't let some hasty words control your whole life."

"I can, Kothar. I promised her most solemnly. Swore it faithfully to her. She never released me from it. And she won't ever now, not from the other side. Don't try to make me break my word like this. Whatever would she think of me if I did that, looking back at me now? I kept my word then and I'll keep it now."

"Alright, all right, I won't say it again. Now come back inside again and eat something. You're weak as a spring reed just now anyway."

Damariel let Kothar take him back inside, and sat at the trestle while Kothar negotiated a plate of food for them. It sat on the table between them as each alternately picked at this or that. After a long silence Damariel looked directly at Kothar and continued.

"Look, Kothar, no reason you shouldn't go up there. Spend the night there and tell them all about your fight with the mountain lion. Throw in a bear as well if you like for good measure. But if I came along it would be like a dry fountain or a spring day without flowers. I'd be breaking an oath and dishonouring Ketty, body and soul."

Kothar thought for a while and opened his mouth several times to reply before finally speaking.

"Damari, look, you are the village seer and I have no right to instruct you. But you are also my friend, and you are a brother to me since we are both children of the god. So I am going to speak to you out of those bonds between us. Look, Damari, you must take another woman to be with you."

He sensed Damariel recoiling, withdrawing from him, and once again took his arm.

"Look, I don't mean a shrine girl just for the night, not if you think that would break some promise you made. Especially if it was to Ketty. I can understand that. But for the sake of the village you need a companion for your days and nights. You need a woman to be your companion. The whole village needs you to have someone at your side. You can't just carry on like this for ever."

He paused. Damariel had been looking at him in surprise, but when he stopped he turned half away and looked again out of the window.

"So who do you suggest, Kothar? Ketty's little sister Laylah? How will that sit with Kinreth and Caleb? To lose another daughter from their house? Kinreth would never allow it. Nor should she for the sake of her lineage. Or Nikkallia, who only wants anyone if it means advantage for her? She won't even set foot inside a house unless it's a step upwards. Or maybe my own sister Sannah? Who can I possibly go with, Kothar, that won't offend this family or that? Especially Kinreth and Caleb. They've been wounded enough by all this. How will they look on any of the village women if I take her instead of their daughter?"

"I can't answer that, Damari. None of it. But we need you to have a companion - not just to have some satisfaction at night, but so we know you are alongside us in our clans and families. So you know what it is to have all those pains and pleasures. To understand what it is to live with another person, night and day. The joy and the hardship of it."

"Is this just your notion, Kothar, or do others say this?"

"Well, they might not be saying it yet, or even thinking it in so many words. But look, Damari, it's what everyone will be saying before too many more seasons turn around us all. Before another year, to be sure. Right now it's just a feeling unspoken. But look now, you can turn my words around and argue all you like, but you know I'm right about this."

Damariel grimaced, and then looked profoundly troubled.

"Enough of this for tonight, Kothar. I can't hear any more about this tonight. And I don't think it's time yet. I can wait. Everyone can wait. They'll have to wait."

He put up a hand to forestall Kothar's reply.

"Look, for tonight I am going to stay with the priest, like we arranged."

He pulled a face.

"Call it keeping another promise, if you like. You go and lie up at the shrine girls' house. Lie with both of them at once for all I care and make up for me not being there. Not my business. I'll see you at the city gate just before mid-morning tomorrow."

He stood up suddenly, not giving Kothar space to speak further, and left him sitting with the remains of the food. He untied the donkeys and set off up the road.

Now Kothar was back in the village, back in his workshop again. About a week had passed since their return. Damariel had been aloof and largely silent for the first part of the journey, but slowly loosened as they turned away from the Valley floor and climbed up again to the ridgeway track. He asked nothing about the rest of Kothar's stay in the town, and offered nothing about his own time. Kothar simply assumed he had spent the time with the priest Abiel, and in prayer up at either the temple or the high place.

They had met as planned, and set off south again homeward. The first part of the journey had been awkward, difficult. Finally, in the sunlit track winding along the Valley rim Damariel had relaxed and begun to return to his normal self. Kothar had scrupulously avoided mention of village life, but drew him out with questions about the tracks that branched left and right, or landmarks they saw in the distance.

Now, back in Kephrath, Kothar was working away in the long back room of the house, where the window caught the afternoon sunshine and he could still see clearly to mend old snares and make new ones. Shaharti was on aunt-duty at the stream and not due back for some time yet, and he whistled aimlessly to himself as he worked. He was taking the edge off a wooden lath with a rough file when suddenly his dog barked twice. A shadow fell across the window light. He looked up, to see Saniyahu leaning on the outside watching him. Kothar straightened his back and, belatedly, pushed his kef into some kind of order.

"Seer, it is joy to see you. Health and long life to you."

"And to you and yours. Your family are well?"

"Indeed yes. And yours? Halith is with you?"

The former seer shook his head.

"She is visiting others. We were both with Damari, but now here I am with you."

Kothar nodded in some surprise, then gestured over his shoulder at the door.

"You are welcome in Shaharti's house, of course, but she is not here to greet you."

"No matter."

There was a pause as Saniyahu came around to the door and then came in, touching the lintel over his head in blessing as he did so. Kothar glanced towards the kitchen area, but Saniyahu shook his head.

"No, Kothar, thank you. I have been well fed at Damariel's house."

"You must take some water, to be sure. Shaharti would not forgive me if you came inside and I gave you nothing. Please accept it."

The other took the beaker of water that Kothar drew for him from the large vessel sunk into the floor, then gestured into the workshop room.

"I always liked the western view. Might we go back in there?"

Kothar cleared a stray coiled rope and some small nets from a stool and leaned back against the table. Saniyahu went first, though, to the window and looked out again over the wooded ridges before turning back into the room. He walked up and down beside the table, seemingly acutely interested in the tools of Kothar's trade spread out there. Kothar watched him with a growing sense of mystification. Uncertain how to respond, he picked up some blades from one end of the table and put them in a box.

"You'd have to watch out for these, lord. Very sharp, like a razor. Shaharti insists they are put well away before the children come home."

Saniyahu nodded absently and put the water down in a spare part of the table. He moved over to the stool Kothar had cleared, and suddenly looked directly at Kothar as though having made a decision.

"Kothar. I am here to talk about Damari, to talk to you as his friend. You are as a brother to him."

Kothar sat down on another stool and paused before replying.

"Lord, are you speaking as someone who has been seer of my home town? Who has been my priest? Or as something else?"

Saniyahu sighed and pursed his lips.

"To you, I am speaking as a friend of Damari, and as a man who I have known well before we moved away. But to

Damari, I spoke as another seer, and as one who has indeed some authority over him. I have come from a difficult visit."

Kothar scratched his head and spoke cautiously.

"You know that he and I went up to Bayth Shean? To trade, and to visit the temple area. Some parts of the town more than others."

Saniyahu nodded.

"Yes, I have heard all about that."

He fell silent, but under the pressure of Kothar's quizzical look continued after a pause.

"I have told him of a decision the seers have come to as a group. Not just me, but all of us. I told him that we would not permit him to continue to minister indefinitely, young man as he is, if he remains single."

Kothar broke in excitedly.

"Just what I said to him while we were up at Shean. I told him it wasn't good for him or for any of us. He didn't like it, not at all, didn't warm to the idea the way I explained it. I think the words came out all wrong somehow. How did he take it from you?"

"Well, you gave him a suggestion as a friend and a brother. I gave him an instruction from his elders. He was not very receptive to my words any more than yours. But the difference is that he is free to take or leave your advice. I did not leave him free to take or leave my instructions."

Kothar looked at him, astonished and becoming angry.

"You're taking away his seer's vocation from him? Lord, that's all he has right now, he doesn't have anything else. You know what happened to him back in the spring, with Ketty and all. You can't do that. It would be cruel beyond measure. And think of all he's done for all of us."

Saniyahu nodded.

"I know that. I know all of that. But I cannot, we all cannot, only think of Damari's feelings. We have the well-being of the whole community to bear, the living and the dead. He cannot just carry on forever single. You know something of the task of the seer and of his partner, and you can see the problem. I, who know very much more of it, tell you it must not be attempted. Not just that it cannot be done well, but worse than that. It would, in the end, ruin both him and those he wants to serve. Come on, Kothar, think how long it will be before men resent his position. He cannot and he must not try to just carry on."

Kothar was not appeased.

"This isn't just the chief's doing, is it, getting rid of him one way when he couldn't by another? You seers still haven't brought that up with him. Damari says what he did back at that feast was wrong. Why aren't you saying it too?"

Saniyahu grimaced.

"We have said it. We don't know how to say it better. Chief Mahur-Baal has admitted fault in the matter. He has made sacrifice at the great high place on the hill outside Giybon. He says he has sent gifts of recompense to Damari."

"And you trust him in that? Do you know what Damari did with those gifts? Every last one of them went to the widows and the orphans. He wanted nothing of that man to pass his own lips or be in his own hands."

Saniyahu nodded, took the beaker again from the table, moved it from hand to hand.

"I have not said that I trust that his heart is clean when he gives the offering. But I am saying that we cannot do more than we have just now. His position is very secure, and he has done enough in public with us that we cannot do more."

He put the beaker down again firmly and caught Kothar's eyes quite sternly. All of a sudden he was seer of one of the towns again.

"But that is a separate matter. Suppose Ketty had died for another reason. Any reason at all. Suppose she died in pregnancy while she was carrying Damari's own child, or had simply fallen ill with a winter fever or something. Anything. It would make no difference at all. However Ketty had died, by whatever means, Damari cannot remain as village seer and also remain single. Not at his age. Even for me it would be difficult. An older man, or an older woman, can continue to minister single. Not someone of his age. It must not happen."

Kothar swallowed and disengaged his gaze from the seer with an effort. He shook his head.

"He won't like that."

"No. He did not. But nevertheless it is the way of things."

"So that's it? He is no longer seer? You came to take him away from us? Lord, if that is what has happened, I should be with him."

Saniyahu smiled a little and shook his head.

"We are not quite so abrupt, Kothar. No. I came to tell him that he cannot continue without end in this way. I gave him a time limit, a target to aim towards, if you will. I told him that nobody would expect him to find a wife before the seasons had turned around us once. Of course, some men would not wait so long, nor some women either, but a year is a fair span of time. That brings us to next spring. But I told him too, that he must not get to the great summer festival after that without having a new partner to stand and sing beside him. He has until next midsummer, Kothar. Look, that is one of the festivals where the men and women dance together and not in their own circles. How can he minister at that, year after year, without having his own companion beside him?"

Kothar pursed his lips, accepting the justice of the situation. It was, after all, not so different from what he himself had said while they were up at Bayth Shean. He frowned and looked back at Saniyahu.

"You know he says he made some sort of promise to Ketty before they parted, about who he might go with?" Saniyahu nodded. "Can't you get him to change his mind about that? He kept giving me reasons why he couldn't go with anyone."

Saniyahu stood again and looked out of the window.

"If indeed he took the vow in the way he says, I will never in any way urge him to set it aside. Neither should you. He must not let his words fall to the ground. Too much hangs on them.

But I agree, it is hard to think who he should be with. And I also agree that it should not be anyone from Kephrath. We rarely encourage a seer to minister in their own town. Damari and Ketty were an exception that seemed good to us."

"But he hardly knows anyone from the other towns. And I don't know, the way things are just now, which town the people here would be happy with. Whose daughter she would be. Whose family."

"I know. I have no easy answer for that. Damari asked me many times, as though it should be my choice, but I will not make it for him. Nor must you. He must choose for himself, or else choose to stand aside. Though in truth, I do not know who else could minister here. And I do not want to lose him."

Kothar nodded and stood up.

"By your leave, seer, I would like to go to be with him."

Saniyahu also stood. The two men embraced and left the house together, but as Kothar turned up towards the high place the seer turned away at an angle and threaded his way between the houses, talking briefly to different people at their doors as he went and soon disappearing from view. Reaching the top of the village, he found that Damariel's door was open. Kothar glanced in before seeing him stretched out full-length on the ground beside the great stone across the mouth of the cave where Qetirah lay.

He went over to him and sat without speaking on a nearby stone until Damariel rose to a kneeling position and looked at him. He was looking distraught, and his hair was full of the dust of the land in front of the cave mouth, scuffed by generations of mourning feet. The two men looked at each other, then Damariel stood up, a little unsteadily, and led the way over to the seer's house.

Kothar ladled out a beaker of water for each of them. He noticed absently it was nearly empty, and thought briefly who he could ask to bring a fresh supply up the ridge. Damariel sat untidily on one of the stools, little trails of dust scattered around him.

"Do you know what I have just been told?"

Kothar nodded.

"Ah".

There was a pause.

"Saniyahu came to see you, then?"

He nodded again. Damariel grimaced and shook his head slightly.

"He said to me that death was a shepherd who had never yet lost any sheep. That my Ketty was someone he had called home early because she was greatly favoured. That the place she was living now was more blissful than here, and in higher company, and that we would be reunited one day. As if any of that helps."

He stopped, looking blankly across the room to where one of Qetirah's kefs still hung from a hook beside a door. As Kothar started to speak he held up his hand and carried on.

"Do you know, the worst of it is that I've said exactly the same things to people here. Here in this very room. Like Abiram and Sara only a year or two back, when they lost their first baby before the birthing and he came out dead. He was just a little scrap to look at, but he'd been alive before. She'd felt him move and all. What must they have thought of me? I thought it was the right thing to say. What a fine priest I make for Kephrath, hey?"

The two were silent for a long time, with the sounds of village life quiet in the background. Damariel finished the water, poured some more for each of them, and then looked directly at Kothar, his voice suddenly more determined.

"So, Kothar, what am I going to do? What do you think? I can't just give up the priesthood. I won't, not ever. In spite of everything, it is the right thing to do."

Kothar leaned back against the wall.

"Then you must find someone else to live here and be your partner. Your companion, if you like. Someone to sing with you and lead the service."

Damariel laughed in a slightly strained manner.

"It's all right, Kothar, you can say that she must be my wife. I do know that, even if I can't see how that can be just now. Everyone says it. You, Saniyahu, Halith. I dare say my own mother would say the same if I asked her. And I can't make myself different from the rest of the village. Tobiaz lost Binti-Rahmay, Alloni was married twice before ever he moved in with Anniyt. Gazala lost Uzziel in that rock fall, and they'd been together less than a year. And so on. Every family in Kephrath has a story something like that. Who am I to be any different?"

"Did Saniyahu and Halith suggest anyone?"

"Of course not. They're not here to tell me what to do. At least, not about that. And I don't want one of your shrine girl suggestions again. Not in this house, not in that room over there. Bad enough to think about when we're in another place. This has to be someone that the community can take in and welcome as though she was a daughter or a sister, as well as a singer and a spiritual leader. Not just some fly-by-night."

Kothar thought about the words for a while.

"So you're not thinking about anyone from here?"

"I'm not thinking about anyone from anywhere just yet. It's too soon, too soon. And they've given me a few months to find the right person. But here, right now, I would say it would be nobody from Kephrath. I told you this up at Shean – how could I do that without causing even deeper wounds to my people here?"

"Who then? And where from?"

"Oh I don't know, Kothar. Don't ask me that just yet. I can't bear it. But I won't break the oath I swore to Ketty. Never."

He stood up suddenly and prowled around the room, like a hungry lion speculating on the best approach to some prey.

"I'll tell you what else, Kothar. This won't be forgotten. I'll find some way to have Ketty rest easy, some way to get justice against him."

Kothar looked blank.

"Who?"

"The chief, of course. Mahur-Baal, the one who says he is glorious in battles and victorious over his enemies. Curse him. It's all because of him. And Saniyahu says there's nothing to be done, he's made himself secure against anything we can do. But I will find a way."

"You're the one that's always telling me to be careful. Don't rush this, Damariel, don't do something foolish. We all need you here, not driven away from the town. Or worse."

"Oh, I can be patient now. I've learned that lesson out on the ground in front of where Ketty lies. But it's just being patient, Kothar, I'm not forgetting about it."

"Nobody is asking you to forget, Damari. Just don't rush up to Giybon and tell him what you're thinking. Anyway, however are you going to do anything? You're not going to challenge him for the chiefdom, are you? You would never want it if you were able to get it from him. And anyway, do you think Danil would take your side if it came to a fight? Seriously?"

Damariel sat down again and shook his head disconsolately.

"No, Kothar, I don't think that. Right now I just don't know. It doesn't look easy, does it? But I will find a way. You're right, of course, I need to find some sort of allies that will take my part in this. Just now I have no idea who they might be."

Kothar nodded, satisfied for now with the answer.

"All right, so long as I know you'll bide your time on this. Ketty was like a sister to me as well, and if you are right about this then her blood will not rest in the ground until justice is done. So I am with you in this, Damari, but just for now let it be me that says we must be careful. There are some in the town that might see advantage in making sure these words of yours get repeated where you don't want just now."

"Yes. Yes, of course. Kothar, look it has to wait for the time being anyway. I have no plan. And I must look to my calling as seer first. That has to come first. And that means that to satisfy the other seers I must find another wife. Somewhere. But not today, Kothar, and not for a few months yet. I won't rush into this. Even Saniyahu won't make me rush."

He looked at Kothar with some defiance, and then sighed profoundly.

"Well, if I'm still to be seer and priest then I must earn my keep, to be sure. Kothar, I must go down to Shelomith's house with some herbs for her. Saniyahu brought them down the hill with him, but I told him I would deliver them to her and help her with the preparation and the prayers."

He picked up a small bag that, as he moved it, smelled quite strongly of garlic and mint. Rummaging through the kitchen area he found a small container of oil and some seeds that Kothar did not recognise.

They left and walked together until Damariel stopped at Shelomith's house and called out. Kothar turned towards him and nodded, before carrying on along the ridge as Shelomith's daughter Kalita pulled the door open and welcomed the seer inside.

Samk

MATAN YEAR 23

MOST SPLENDID OF TIMES, you are going with me,
I am going to open the snare:
this is beauty – the journeying out to the netting
for this one, the one that I love.

DAMARIEL WENT THROUGH Gedjet town gate, along with a whole crowd of strangers using the coast road. So far he had not seen anyone he recognised, which had surprised him at first and then been a source of relief. Of his own people, only Kothar, Yeresheth, Saniyahu and Halith knew where he was and why he had gone; he had not even told Sosanneth, though he suspected she had guessed something close to the truth of the matter.

To the rest of the town he was simply on another religious journey, to a shrine perhaps, off somewhere for a few days and promising to be back well before the next new moon celebration. A few had looked dubious at that, their minds going back to the time just over a year ago when Qetirah had died.

He had set off west from his home at first, down the sloping roads to Yabneh where he had accepted the hospitality of an old friend, the town scribe Gilem. Gilem had confirmed what he had heard from a trader up in Meyim, and what he most needed to know: here down at Gedjet was a Mitsriy chantress, Sheded-em-duat-iset, wanting a vocation in the region. Here, perhaps, was the wife everyone said he must have.

He had set off again early the next morning, cut across to the Sea Road and followed it south. The road gradually converged with the sea itself, bright sun dancing on the distant waves through the scrub and low trees bordering the roads.

Once through the gates he asked for directions and passed through the street market in no special hurry. It was clearly a Mitsriy town: most men and women wore no kef, but walked bare-headed through the streets, and all around him the soft sing-song of the Mitsriy language mingled with the more guttural Kinahny. Where kefs were worn they ran the full gamut of styles and designs. Most of the houses lacked bushes and trees kept by their women, though from time to time, turning a little corner, a sudden shock of colour across the white walls brought relief.

Once he passed a mimosa tree and touched its bark in recollection of his mother's house. He made his way to a large building only a short distance from the governor's residence: it was the home of the senior Mitsriy priest. Taking a deep breath, he approached the door warden and announced himself and his business there.

The warden, disinclined to move, sent a young boy off at a run, then left Damariel on his own in the shade of the wall while he waited, looking idly at the dense lines of picture glyphs around the doorposts and lintel. He smiled a little, remembering once again the Mitsriy scribe from his childhood, tallying the town's resources. After a pause the boy came back, spoke briefly to the door ward and then conducted Damariel into the interior. They crossed another courtyard, and turning to one side walked down a colonnade past several doors opening into domestic areas.

The central house was of two stories, three in places where single rooms were built onto the flat roof, but the boy gestured down the side to where a table and stools were set under the shade of a large olive tree. Grapevines were trained along the wall beside it. There were two people at the table already: an older man seated, and a woman of about his own age, presumably Sheded-em-duat-iset, standing by him. The boy called out as they approached, and the two turned towards Damariel.

Senenptah Sa-Meryma'at was older than he had expected, but had very clear eyes. He wore no kef on his shaved head, and remained seated as Damariel came up to the table. Damariel was uncertain how to greet the man and his daughter, but the older man gestured to a stool beside him. Two servants brought beer and some dates to the table. Damariel waited in silence. The old man looked him over carefully and then poured beer for all three. When he spoke, he pronounced the common Kinahny language clearly enough, but with a strong southern accent.

"So you are Damariel of the hill country. This is my daughter Sheded-em-duat-iset, and I understand that you want her to come with you to your town? It would be more proper to have sent word in advance, but we have made allowance and are prepared to hear you. You may begin by telling us who you are and from where you have come."

"Yes, lord and honoured sir, and please accept my thanks for all your gracious generosity. My town is called Kephrath: it is three or four days journey from here into the hills, near the road running north from Shalem to Sychem and Bayth Shean. I am the son of Yeresheth, a child of the god, and I was made ready for the service of town seer first by Iqnu, and latterly by Saniyahu and Halith, serving now at Jarrar's town. I passed the final stage of my apprenticeship well over two years ago, and was accepted into office by the other seers of the four towns, and by the people of my own town. Now as El shows mercy on us all, highland and lowland, I am here because I have heard that your daughter seeks vocation."

He stopped, feeling suddenly rather pompous. Surely this man, this old Mitsriy priest, had served his own gods more than twice as long as Damariel's whole lifespan. Surely he was clearly a man of considerable religious experience, and would not consider very highly a village minister.

He looked round again at the courtyard with its little offset rooms opening on each side, out from the shaded cloister to the midday sun hot in the open space in the centre, the white marble, the door lintels thick and colourful with the Mitsriy picture-writing, the servants attending discretely away in the background, Senenptah's fine linen tunic and delicate golden chain of office, and he felt suddenly rough and common.

"In my own land you would address me as father, but here you must call me as you see fit, and as your customs permit."

There was a laugh in the other's eyes.

"Quite suitable, if you are thinking that you might soon be calling my Duat your sister. Do you think you'll be a good brother to her?"

Damariel was aware of missing something in the words, and looked at the woman, who laughed and handed him one of the dates.

"Duat, daughter, if you go with him, teach him our songs while you learn about Kirtu and Hurriy, about Taliy, Rahmay, and the rest. I know these songs even if I have little cause to sing them in my own house, but if you go you must sing them as though they were yours. Tell me", and he turned again and looked directly, disconcertingly, at Damariel, "Tell me, Damariel, what would this daughter of the great river do up in your hills?"

Damariel looked across at Sheded-em-duat-iset standing beside her father, bright in the white linen of her smock.

"Well, father, she would be my companion and would sing the songs and dance the dances with me. She would live in the house by our high place and share in the rituals with me. She would take her place amongst the seers of the four towns and their wives, who set the spiritual direction for all my people. She would comfort and inspire the women by her words and ways, and be honoured by them. She would be loved and desired by the men, followed by the children. She would be the mistress not just of our house but of the community. So few have seen a Mitsriy woman, and all that she is will be their image of your land."

"Ah, but my beloved land is neither loved nor feared as she once was. City rulers along the coastlands refuse us justice, and extort taxes for timber that once they felt was an honour to see put to holy use in our temples. We have more need of bowmen and less of scribes today. Perhaps this rare southern woman will be mocked and despised rather than honoured or desired? Can you pledge me her safety?"

Damariel paused to take another sip of beer before meeting the older man's eyes. He felt acutely aware of the scars of his mourning for Qetirah across his arms.

"No, father, I cannot. Where is safe for any of us? Kephrath has not been a safe place for me or my family."

"Tell me. I had heard that your custom was that your seers were married. Your apprenticeship is long over, and yet here you are, looking for a companion."

"I have been married. My wife died last spring, about a year ago now."

He stopped, swallowed hard, gripped the edge of the table.

"She was carrying a child, but something went wrong. She died of it. Father, I was not there with her, I came back from a pilgrim journey to the north to find her already in her tomb, gathered to her ancestors. We had, I have, no children."

Senenptah was silent for a while, watching while Damariel gripped first of all his lower arms where he had cut himself, then the edge of the table. After a little pause he steadied himself. Eventually he looked up again, his cheeks and his heart cold and rigid, gripped by shame and anger.

"No children, and her so recently dead. Will you not take more time to grieve? I know something of this in my own life, and a year is barely enough."

Damariel shook his head, and the older man watched him for a while before speaking.

"So are you looking just to replace your former wife? You require a wife, don't you, to carry out your duties? And Gedjet is a long way from your home."

The older man spoke in a matter of fact way, but to Damariel the words sounded haughty. He sat straighter and looked directly back at the priest, about to retort with some anger. Senenptah's expression was hard to read, and seeing that, Damariel stopped before he spoke. After a little pause the Mitsriy spoke again.

"Well, at least you have some coolness of temperament. So, why do you look for a foreign woman? Is there nobody in your town you can turn to for, shall we say, companionship? Will your people accept this alien?"

"There is nobody I would choose. Not in my town, not anyone of those with whom I grew up, not without causing still more grief and division. But my people will accept my choice, when I make it. Your people have walked in our land for generations, yet so few of us have seen a Mitsriy woman. Your daughter, Sheded-em-duat-iset, will be welcomed in to

Kephrath as though she was, well, as though she was an exotic southern princess."

The woman laughed. Senenptah shook his head and smiled at her.

"In times past this exotic princess would not have been permitted to leave her household and join your town in the hill country. In those days your plea would have gone unanswered, whatever your reasons. But my people are less sure of their foothold in this rough province now."

He turned to his daughter.

"So, my exotic southern princess daughter, what do you have to say? Do you want to go up into this wild hill country and live like a modern-day Sanehet among its people? Become a little sycamore yourself? Perhaps come back to the River one day with your little tribes-children behind you?"

"Well, father, he lived well enough in his wanderings. Perhaps I might do that. I don't know yet. But if I start to crave stone mansions, I will simply come back down from the hills and see you here. How long can it take? Just three or four days, we have heard. It is nothing."

"No, child. It would be a very long journey. I will return to the Beloved Land in just a few short weeks, whatever happens for you in this matter. The high priest who is my master has asked me to return and tend one of the great temples, all the way up-river in Waset. He has had a dream in the holy place, and if the god confirms the dream during the great festival later this year I shall move there. If you scramble down from the hills, I shall not be here. If you go with Damariel, or indeed if you make any other choice to remain in this province, we may never meet again."

Damariel stood up in consternation. Sheded-em-duat-iset stared at her father, clearly surprised at the news. They both spoke at once in protest, but he waved their objections aside.

"What could I possibly want more than to be back in the Beloved Land in my final years? Why ever would I want to stay here in Gedjet, pleasant though this house has been for us? Gedjet is not the Beloved Land, and I have no wish to go to my last mooring out here. This is not home, has never been home, simply a tent on a desert journey by a wadi. I will go home again to settle myself, and I will not stay out here in the provinces any longer. Perhaps I shall provide a ferry-boat on the River so that the poor will remember my name with gratitude. This is not a chance I shall turn aside: perhaps it is the only such chance I shall get. I tell you, daughter, when I read this word from the high priest I felt such an excitement in me that reminds me of times of delight with your mother who lives in bliss on the other shore. But, Duat, Waset may not be the place for you, or at least, not yet. You must choose for yourself."

"Blessed father, you speak as if you were almost dead. The gods may grant a great span of life. May you live for millions of years and see thousands of generations of your lineage."

Senenptah waved his hand at her, laughed again, and lifted his empty beer jug to the servant for it to be filled again.

"All my life has been down the River, child. An exciting youth amongst the rapids and perils of the upper streams, streaming past new sights every day. A long stretch in the date palms and scented reeds of Iunet and Abdju, sharing a boat with Tutuia-Meriteset, your mother precious of memory to both of us. Ah, we felt that we were resting on the boat together, that the river would go on forever. But in truth those peaceful, still waters were carrying us downstream all the while at such a great rate, past Min-Nefer and On. All that time, all those turns and eddies in the river, and me thinking only of the view alongside, never seeing the changes. My sweet sister, companion of my youth, plucked from the boat. All that time when I thought I had a view that would never change, and it was sweeping me always along with it at its own pace."

He sighed, shook his head.

"And now, all too soon, the river is slowing down. The stream that was so fast, so vigorous, is spreading into a thousand little pools and islands, settling down towards stillness. And one day all there will be is the endless horizon of the sea. My child, I want to see that horizon from my homeland, not some alien place we have occupied."

He looked east and a little south, gesturing slightly.

"I want to pass through the sea of reeds on this side of my homeland: I want to pass them in this body again before I go to them in the land of light. Duat, I want to live out those millions of years of your blessing beyond the marsh and the sea, not here, and I want to be walking in that blessed light with my sweet Tutuia, tasting the good things of that deathless land together. I have lived a good life as priest out here, but it is time for me to look towards the western horizon. How could I want to face the sunset anywhere but in the Beloved Land?"

There was a silence. Sheded-em-duat-iset and Damariel looked at each other and then down at the table. Senenptah smiled and called to one of the servants, who brought a tray of little raisin pastries and another jug of beer to the table. Senenptah himself offered the food to the others.

The breeze from the sea ruffled the long drapes nearby that kept the sun from the inner rooms, sighed softly around the marble pillars. From the distance the sounds of the market place drifted in flutters and eddies around them. The pause stretched longer. Eventually Senenptah spoke again.

"Let me ask you both a question. Damariel, tell me again, why is it you want a Mitsriy woman to be with you up there in the hill country? And daughter, if you do not come back with me to Waset, where else would you go?"

Damariel's head was still down, avoiding the others' eyes as the young woman spoke.

"Father, you know that the envoy from Djedenen sent word this afternoon. He will choose today between me and another chantress which of us will go with him and sing. Two roads are still open for me if I am going to sing out here among the Asiatics. Who knows which I might prefer? What Damariel offers is not – forgive me, sir, for saying this – a place in a royal court, but perhaps it may suffice if the other door closes. I don't want to leave myself without choice."

Senenptah nodded.

"I know what the messenger said. But who knows yet what the evening sun will bring? And you, Damariel?"

Damariel had had a little time to compose his thoughts, so took a breath and began.

"Honoured sir, my community needs a marriage of the spirit which can call life into the songs and the sacrifices. When they see us, when we call upon our gods in the rites and the rituals, they must hear both conviction and excellence. They must see something of such beauty that belief follows, just like the eyelids of the dawn open wide to reveal the life-giving eye of the sun. I cannot do that alone. Just as my people are partnered with the land that nurtures and nourishes us, so must I be partnered with a woman. The reputation of Mitsriy singers is known to us, known to everyone, even up in the hill country, and I am here today to ask this one, you, Sheded-em-duat-iset, if you will come and live with me in Kephrath to do this. That is why I am here."

There was a little pause. Sheded-em-duat-iset looked at him curiously, her head to one side, as though surprised at his eloquence. He saw himself again as a rough, ungainly provincial. In the silence, Senenptah spoke again.

"And if my daughter bore your children, my grandchildren, up there in the hill country, to what race will they belong? Customs vary up there in the hills, I hear."

"We count descent through the mother, sir. They would be your daughter's children before they would be mine."

"Would you raise them to know the gods of their mother's household? To worship them correctly? We do not call out to our gods in rites and rituals as though they were unaware of us: like a caring mother they are close to us every moment, and we speak to them knowing they are with us already. We kiss the ground at their feet, we do not cry out as though they were ignorant of us. Would these children speak my tongue or yours? Would they learn how we Mitsriy know the world, or just your Kinahny stories?"

Damariel sat back, taking another drink of beer while he thought. A servant hovered nearby with a full jug, but Damariel did not notice.

"Sir, I would take every step to honour your wishes. I mean, Sheded-em-duat-iset would teach them your traditions so long as they learnt those of my people too. I suppose, well, of course I could learn your tongue from her and use it in our house."

He stopped, uncertain. Senenptah nodded slowly when it was clear that Damariel had finished. There was a longer silence. A servant woman, about Yeresheth's age, approached from one side and Sheded-em-duat-iset moved to listen to her out of earshot of the men. They both watched her and waited until she came back. The servant stayed off to one side, tidying some leaves as she waited.

"The girl wants to know if our guest is staying for a meal, or overnight? The household seeks time to prepare."

Damariel looked at Senenptah hesitantly.

"Damariel son of Yeresheth, as you have heard, we are even now waiting on news from the envoy from Djedenen. Unless you have prior plans, I would be honoured if you consider this house as your house for a time. You are welcome to eat. The girl here will show you a room. Stay until the morning and bless this house."

He glanced up and waved a hand towards the woman, who bobbed with respect and took a step or two closer to Damariel.

"In any case, my daughter and I have to consider our choice, and it would be vulgar to burden you with talk that is personal to us. Please excuse us, refresh yourself, and make yourself comfortable."

The three stood. Damariel, once again in doubt about the etiquette, bowed to both of them, his hands over his heart. Senenptah nodded with a little smile, and then taking his daughter's arm went off along the columned path. Sheded-em-duat-iset made no response as she left. Damariel, looking a little blank, and feeling very depressed about his prospects, turned hesitantly to the woman.

"Lady, I am in your hands, I think. Where should I go?"

She set off back along the colonnade, passing the grapevine on the left and taking him to an entrance set into the wall. A white linen drape flapped idly in a little gust, and she held it aside for him, letting him go through first and then slipping past him to take him along a hall. He realised then that she was not Mitsriy, but as Kinahny as he was. She wore no kef, though, and had her greying hair bunched behind her shoulders in a plain copper ring. She stopped by a wooden door on one side of the hall, opened it without going in and bobbed again, her eyes towards the floor, still saying nothing. Damariel paused before entering and turned to her.

"Thank you."

She kept her eyes down as she replied.

"An honour, sir, to serve you. You will be brought refreshment soon. It will be arranged for you."

She had a definite accent, which Damariel recognised after a moment's pause.

"You're from the Valley, aren't you?"

This time she glanced up at him and then down again. "My family lives there, near Bayth Shean but on the east side. I have served my master here for many years."

Damariel stepped inside and then stopped, holding the door open, still looking at her.

"Your master, what do you think he will do? Is he?"

He hesitated, seeing the careful noncommittal look on her features. "I mean, will his daughter?" He shook his head suddenly. "It's nothing. Thank you."

She bobbed again, meeting his eyes briefly before turning and walking silently away down the corridor, past the cloth barrier and out of sight. Damariel sighed and closed the door, looking around inside. He had expected a single room but realised at once that there were two, one after the other.

Near where he stood were some stools and a low table, with some beakers, a clay vase and some flowers. Beside the vase was an alabaster lamp half-filled with oil, and against one wall was a pale wooden chest, inlaid with some darker wood he did not recognise, making a scene of marshes where birds flew up to escape the hunt. A man stood in the prow of a boat with a spear, while a woman dressed in a tight swathe of cloth that showed every curve of her body sat in the stern and watched him. Little inlaid lines of the picture-writing floated around the edges of the scene.

On the opposite wall, a window, with a linen drape tied back on one side, opened to the courtyard where some household servants were tending a vegetable plot. In the distance, at an angle off to his left, he could see the sea. He put his satchel on the chest and glanced in to the other room: as he had expected, there was a bedroll on the floor. There was also a large clay vessel half-full of water, so he took the opportunity to clean face, hands and feet.

Back in the first room, he took out a clay tablet and waxed wooden writing frame from his satchel and went back to copying the poem that Gilem had loaned him, transferring it from clay to wax. The afternoon was warm, but little breaths of wind drifted through the window and stirred the linen, bringing the distant noises of Gedjet with it. Closer at hand, from time to time he heard the sound of activity in the house, footsteps up and down the corridors, Mitsriy voices, clatter of pots, laughter from outside. Nobody came to his room for some time, but he hardly noticed in the satisfaction of his work.

Hearing a discreet knock, he opened the door. The woman who had escorted him to the room, the woman whose family came from the Valley, was back again, with another younger woman and two men. The men were carrying refreshments, food and drink on two trays, while the woman had a large bag under her arm. The men waited until he stepped back from the door and then brought the trays in and arranged them on the table.

The woman with the bag came in and stood in a corner of the room. She was Mitsriy, he noticed, but dressed as a servant in a simple cream smock down to her knees, with a plain linen sash and a copper ring binding her hair back like the older woman. Like the others, she wore no kef. Her skin was a little darker than Senenptah and his daughter. The three others left the room without a word, closing the door quietly and carefully.

"Is this food for me? All of it?"

She nodded. "For you, lord, yes. All of it."

He sat back on the stool, moving the clay tablet and writing board off to one side.

"Well, I can't drink all this. Will you join me?"

She shook her head but said nothing.

"Who are you, anyway? Why are you here?"

"Lord, I can give you songs, or I can give you dances, all for the entertainment of your heart. Would that be good for you?"

"Yes, that would be good for me. Very good, in fact. A song, one of your songs, please. What am I to call you, though? My name is Damariel, and I am no lord: they call me seer at home. You might call me a priest, I suppose. But I sing, too."

She nodded uncertainly and started taking things out of the bag, a sistrum, a stringed instrument like a small harp, some wooden blocks.

"I am called Nepheret-er-sefet-Tefnut, sir, but the mistress says you do not know our names. Please just say Nepheret. What song shall I give you?"

Damariel shrugged and poured himself a beaker of beer.

"I don't know your songs, and I don't expect you know mine. Don't expect you've ever seen the hill country. Whatever you sing will be new to me."

He looked up at her and realised from her expression that she was not catching his meaning. Her grasp of Kinahny was fair, but not good enough for the speed of his conversation. He sighed and started again, slower.

"Look, where do you come from? Sing me a song of your own people, of your own land."

She brightened a little and picked up the sistrum as she replied. She was starting to look at him a little more than at first, though still carefully avoided eye contact.

"From Pa-Yam, sir, the town of Shedyet. Up the River from Min-Nefer. I will sing for you a song of the women. Sir, but look, you will not know the words?"

Damariel laughed.

"No matter, Nepheret. See, perhaps I learn them from you."

He realised, too late, that he had started to make his short simple sentences sound more like hers, and worried briefly she would be offended. Without comment she stepped away from the wall, stood in what was obviously a formal posture holding the sistrum above her head, and after a pause for breath started to sing. It was a short piece, with tinkling ripples of the sistrum echoing in the sibilant phrasing of her voice.

As they had expected, Damariel was completely unable to understand the words, but he found himself drawn in to the rhythms and the patterns of sound. Her singing voice was lower than he had guessed from her speech. She stopped, looking at him for approval. He nodded and clapped her as he would at home. She laughed briefly and then stopped, looking towards the door.

"Tell me, Nepheret, what was that song?"

"Sir, well, each year the young men and the young women, they stand each side of the waterway. We sing that to them, the women to the men. It says the water is too large for them and how none dare cross it. Then in another song they sing back how it is only a step, and they do not fear the water beast, the", she paused, frowning, "the mesech we call him, very fierce, they have no water beasts like he is anywhere else in the whole world, only at home in the Beloved Land.

But anyway, when they sing, they say to them he is only a little fish. They say they will cross anyway. And then there are other songs, and then we all go to the market and drink some beer. Was your heart pleased by it, sir?"

"Yes it was. Will you sing me another? Your home, Pa-Yam, does it have hills and mountains?"

He gestured with his hands. She shook her head.

"Oh no sir, it is flat. We have all marshes all around, with rich fields where the River gives us richness each year. There are birds everywhere, and every one of our kings, may they live in prosperity and health, every one of them comes from his great house to hunt the birds."

Damariel nodded and pointed at the wooden chest against the opposite wall.

"Like that picture? That man hunts for his wife?"

She went to the chest and touched the writing.

"Not wife yet, sir, but he wants her, and so he shows her what a hunter he is."

"You can read all that?"

She shook her head and went back to the instruments.

"Well no, no, but I know the story, sir. But I can write my name signs, and I know to read the signs for the king, who lives in prosperity and health, and for the old king who went to the horizon to be a god, and some of the names of the other gods. But I cannot read all that story."

"Is your name on that writing?"

She looked again and shook her head.

"Not all together, sir. But look, this one sign, and this together with it, here is Nepheret. He says she is his *nepheret*. But my name would need a woman sign like this one here. And here, this is *nepher*, she calls him *nepher*. That would please him. Look, shall I sing you a bird-catcher's song?"

This time she took up the pair of wooden blocks and kept a steady, complex pattern of rhythm going. The song was full of guttural consonants, with the click and clack of the bird traps running through the words, and the sudden flight of bird cries flitting to and fro in the music. He listened more carefully to the words this time.

"Your name, Nepheret, that was in that song too? Right at the start?"

"Oh almost, yes sir, the very first word. But not quite the same. She says to him, well, *nepheru en senetek*, that is, your most beautiful sister, then later again almost the same, *nepherowy*, when she sings of their travelling together."

Damariel had a sudden, sobering memory of Senenptah joking about brother and sister, out in the sunlit courtyard.

"When you say sister and brother, what do you mean?"

"Oh, well sir, maybe sometimes just family. But in this song, and often, a man and woman will use it of each other when they want to be together."

She held her hands, fingertips lightly touching, and then crinkled her fingers so her palms pressed close against each other. She pointed at the picture on the wooden chest.

"That man there, he wants the woman to be his sister so he shows her that he has skill. Maybe she is not sure, maybe she needs to be convinced, maybe the time in the boat will persuade her. He has desire in his heart for her and wants to persuade her."

He poured some more beer into his own beaker, and then some into a second, frowning as he thought back to the conversation outside earlier in the day. She watched him pour the two drinks without comment.

"Are there other bird-catcher songs?"

"There are eight all together. All to be sung by the sister. Sometimes she is happy, sometimes sad, sometimes jealous of the other women. It ends well, she thinks about her brother as she ties back her hair for festival with him."

She took her own hair, dark like a raven's wing and quite long, out of its copper ring for a moment and held it piled back on top of her head to demonstrate. When he nodded, she carefully rethreaded it through the ring again and smoothed it behind her shoulder.

"Would you like to hear another song, sir?"

"No, wait a moment first. Shall I sing to you?"

She looked doubtful.

"I was to serve your pleasure, sir. And you have not eaten."

"Nepheret, it would help me be at ease here if I could sing too. I am not used to just having someone sing to me without joining them. Now, I cannot speak any of your language, and you cannot speak all of mine. And we do not know each other's songs, but let us take it in turns, you then me, to sing to each other. And look, there's far too much food just for me. Here's a thought. When you sing, I will eat and drink something, and when I sing, you eat and drink."

She thought about it for a moment, and looked again, hesitantly, at the door before nodding.

"But I must sing again first, then you."

Damariel nodded, and bowed with his hands held together as he might after agreeing a transaction with a trader in his own town, before lifting the cloth away from over the food. The first thing that caught his eye were some figs, each wrapped in a thin strip of some meat and stuffed with cheese. He put two onto a plate, picked up his beer, and ate and drank as she sang another song, this time without using any of the instruments.

He found himself listening out for phrases, finding occasional combinations that sounded like words from his own language, hearing the strong patterns of sound that shaped the song.

When she stopped he got up and went to stand where she had been. She moved to stand behind the table, but did not touch anything on it. He sighed, put one of the fig parcels on another plate and pushed it and the second beer towards her.

"How can I sing if you won't sit down?"

She perched slightly awkwardly on the stool, and picked up the food.

"This is a song we sing when the olive harvest is in, when the first wine is just ready, and before we start digging the ground for the vegetables, the beans and so on."

He had thought about trying to use the little harp, as he might have used the lyre up in the hills at Kephrath, but realised he had no idea what the tuning would be and gave up the idea. At home one person would have sung a verse and then everyone join in the refrains, and the song could easily go on for a long time as different people made up another few lines. Some verses were really very poor, some were frankly quite rude, but the song worked well at the harvest festival when the new wine was flowing.

He made do with four of the better-constructed ones, and sang the refrain twice over at the end. She watched him attentively as he sang, eyes bright and head slightly to one side, nibbling slowly at the fig without paying it much attention. When he had finished she stood up again quickly, moving away from the table.

"And my turn again now. More of the bird-catcher?"

"No, wait. Do something that you just say, not with music."

She nodded, thought for a moment, and then started. The piece was longer this time, slow and solemn at the start, quick and eager as the end drew near. Damariel finished a piece of flat bread and hummus, and put a similar size piece onto her plate.

"That was a prayer to the lady Tefnut, sir, the holy goddess name at the end of my name, Nepheret-er-sefet-Tefnut. It is a prayer for her to send moisture on the land, to say sorry first for what we have not done for her, then to delight in what she sends. Here in your country the moisture falls out of the sky, but for my family it rises out of the land at dawn, and at dawn we might sing that song on the feast days."

"In my land, then, we would call her Taliy. Look, this tablet that a friend gave me yesterday is about Taliy. I am copying it to take home. Look, here is her name."

He held up the clay tablet with Gilem's scratched writing on it, and as she walked over, turned the wooden frame round as well and ran his finger along a few of the signs. She looked at both, one after the other.

"Your writing is more even than his, more neatly done. But I think you have not finished? Yours is not so long as his."

"No, but I'm nearly there. I will return it to him on my journey home."

"Can you sing it to me, sir?"

"It's not to be sung, but I can say it to you. There's no music for this. Here, you sit again and eat. My turn to stand."

He stood where she had been and recited the poem. She listened acutely, the fingers on her left hand tapping against the table with the cadence of his voice. When he stopped he came to the table and picked up his beaker of beer. They both drank. He noticed that she was still looking thoughtful and, more surprisingly, was still sitting.

"Sir, look, you make your songs differently."

He looked at her quizzically.

"Of course your words are Kinahny, mine are Mitsriy. That is not what I mean. But when you have two lines together, they are the same length."

She held her hands a short distance apart, fingers pointing up, palms parallel with each other.

"No difference. But listen."

She repeated two lines of the poem to Tefnut and spread her hands, her fingers further apart than her wrists.

"You see, sir, they are long then short, not equal."

He put the beaker down, intrigued.

"But why? Why not the same."

"Oh, sir, but the lines are a heartbeat, there is a long one and a short one that join to make us live. Or they are the red hills either side of the black land, one higher and one lower, that look at each other across the great River. Or they are the two parts of the land, one long and one broad, that join at Min-Nefer. Or they are a man and a woman, they are a different shape and join together in union. Why ever make them the same?"

He pulled the wooden writing board towards him and read out the first two lines of the poem.

"This pair here, this pair, Nepheret, you are right, they are like one another. How might I change it to be like yours?"

She shook her head.

"It is your people's hymn to the Lady Taliy. How can it be changed?"

She suddenly stood up and went back to the wall, picking up the little harp.

"What may I sing for you now, sir?"

Damariel heard footsteps outside the door, and before he could answer, it swung open and Senenptah was there. Nepheret bobbed her head and stood very still. Senenptah ignored her and came over to Damariel.

"Damariel, my honoured guest, you are comfortable? You have eaten well? Has my household cared for you?"

"Most certainly, good father. There was more food than I could ever need, and my heart has been eased by the company. Your home has been my home today, and you are a generous host."

He looked across at Nepheret, but she made no response. Senenptah did not look at her, but moved his hand in a dismissive gesture. She collected her instruments into the bag and slipped out of the door without a word.

"Excellent. You honour my house. But I fear to say that I must bring bad tidings. The envoy from Djedenen sent word that he had chosen my Duat to be his chantress, and she is minded to accept his offer."

Damariel felt a great gloom settle on him. It must have showed in his face, for the older man looked concerned and reached out a hand towards him.

"I am sorry, Damariel, to disappoint you this way. Your journey must seem to be in vain, and the homeward path will seem long and most excessively steep."

Damariel shook his head slowly.

"Sir, I must think of you and your daughter. She has done well to be so chosen. Your family is honoured, and you are kind to think of me in this way."

"You must stay tonight anyway. I would not have it said that I sent a guest out with a heavily burdened heart only a short time before dusk. Continue your journey tomorrow."

As Damariel nodded, he smiled again.

"So that is settled. The meal is ready soon, when I return from the afternoon prayers. You will be told by one of the household. Perhaps tonight will lighten your heart."

In fact Damariel found the evening quite depressing. He was in no mood for company. Senenptah had invited two other men as guests in a generous attempt to cheer him up. One was a Mitsriy military commander, with his wife and daughter. He had travelled widely in the Asiatic provinces as messenger and envoy. He seemed to have met every governor and king in the region, although had never passed through Kephrath. He thought he had heard of Giybon, but Damariel suspected he was merely being polite. The other was the son of a high ranking Gedjet family, who had spent most of his teenage years among the Mitsriy, mostly in the north but a few trips southwards.

There were entertainments – a juggler, some musicians, and a troupe of acrobats with very dark skins from a country called Kush. The maid-servants who waited on the tables were naked except for scraps of jewellery, while the entertainers were simply clad, and only slightly more modest.

The evening, and the company of the other people, should have intrigued Damariel, and would have done on another occasion, but he was aware that he was only following the conversation with half his heart, and contributed less than he might. There was no sign of Sheded-em-duat-iset, and he gathered from things that were said that she had already packed and was to leave during the evening. The spring sun had started to set when the others left and he bid good night to Senenptah, who asked him three times if there was anything else he could provide for his comfort and delight. He refused three times, and in the end was taken back to his own room by the unspeaking woman from the Valley. He slept badly.

The morning was bright, and when Damariel had woken and packed his few things he felt restless to be away. During the night he had reached a decision. He pushed open the door to his rooms and looked up and down the passageway. From further in the house he could hear kitchen sounds, so he went back to the courtyard with the grapevine and sat in the sunshine to finish the last few signs on the copy of Gilem's tablet: he had completed most of it before the meal yesterday evening.

Two gardeners passed him, glanced towards him and then sent the door warden's boy running into the house. A few minutes later the Valley woman, who Damariel had realised served as housekeeper, and who Nepheret had called mistress, came out to him. She waited silently a few paces away until he looked up at her.

"Sir, if it is your pleasure, the master would enjoy sharing a small meal with you before you depart. He is inside the house, this way, when you are ready, sir."

He had in fact finished, so he stood and went with her to a small room through a door, the lintel covered with the little glyphs that he could not understand. It faced south-west, and Damariel caught his breath at the sweep of coastline in the distance, and the desert-coloured horizon. Senenptah turned from the window as the two came in.

"Ah, Damariel. Is it not a magnificent view? I eat my first meal of every day here, looking towards the Beloved Land. Soon now, very soon, I shall go back there and settle up River at Waset. Soon I shall be able to feel the Land beneath my feet again. But this horizon has served me well for a few years."

"Sir, my own house faces the same way, although I cannot see the Sea or the wilderness from it, just ridge upon wooded ridge of the hill country. I love it best at evening when the sun leans across it. With your leave, I shall go back there soon."

"Of course. Again, I regret that you must travel back without success."

Damariel was still rather subdued, and the two sat as food was brought and spread out in front of them.

"I suppose, though, that you are happy with her choice of Djedenen?"

"Ah yes, very much so. It would have been more of a risk, if she had gone with you up into the hill country. Perhaps the gain would have been worth the risk. We shall never know. Out there in Djedenen she will soon be able to influence the court, and I expect her to achieve great things. Her life with you would have been, perhaps, more unusual for a Mitsriy woman. Very stimulating, no doubt, but I think she will become accustomed to life in Djedenen more rapidly."

Damariel nodded absently, not really paying attention to his host's effort to be generous about his rural home. His decision had begun to shape itself into words in his mind. The meal was quite scanty by the standards he had come to expect in Senenptah's house, and before long they were finished. Once he was sure Damariel wanted no more, Senenptah stood up first.

"Damariel, I know that you are not leaving here with the prize you wanted, but perhaps there is another gift I can give you to remember the name of this house with gladness. If there is, then speak without hesitation."

"Sir, I could not accept a gift from you, although the offer is kind and I acknowledge it as the sign of a generous heart. But you could, perhaps, assist me. I need to buy a slave here in Gedjet, and I met a suitable person in your house yesterday. I pray, do me the favour of selling them to me so I can be off without going to the market. It would speed my journey."

Senenptah shrugged. "Man's work or woman's work?"

"Woman's work. I have enough men. It is the Mitsriy woman from Pa-Yam."

The older man frowned and looked puzzled for a moment, then turned to the housekeeper, who was standing against the wall near the door. She came over to him and bent to whisper something in his ear.

"Ah. That girl."

He paused, rubbing his chin with one hand.

"Well, perhaps forty-eight of silver, seeing as you are a guest."

Damariel smiled to himself but kept a serious expression; at last he was on familiar territory, not puzzling his way along line after line of a strange language.

"Sir, she is hardly of that much value to me. Perhaps you mistake the person I have in mind. Twelve is the very most I would consider if I had found her at the market, but in recognition of your kindness and hospitality let us call it fifteen."

A little while later, and the weight of twenty-two shekels of silver lighter, Damariel waited in the hall. The housekeeper, the one who reminded him of Yeresheth, brought Nepheret out, and gave Damariel the wooden docket of ownership. Nepheret was wearing a plain white linen dress and carrying her sistrum and wooden blocks, but had nothing else. Even the copper ring that had bound her hair back was gone. The two women looked at each other in silence for a moment, before the woman from the Valley turned away, stepping back inside the corridors of the house. As Damariel went across the courtyard towards the gate, Senenptah came to meet him.

"Damariel, it has been a pleasure making your acquaintance. May the hill country and your mountain gods treat you well."

Not to be outdone, Damariel, who had been pondering parting words since breakfast, replied in rounded tones.

"And may your own journey back to your homeland bring you joy and contentment in every venture that still awaits you, and may the horizon in your future be bright with the light of the sun."

Senenptah nodded appreciatively, and the two men bowed to each other. Senenptah turned away without looking at the woman. Damariel and Nepheret stepped forward, crossed under the shadow of the gate lintel, passed the sedentary door warden and his boy, and went out into the heat and bustle of the town. He breathed a sigh of relief and looked at Nepheret. She had a cautious look, and glanced back into the courtyard as though expecting to be called back

He took her arm and led her away from the house, down the little hill towards the Gedjet market. There he bought her two smocks and a skirt, another dress, two ribbons for use as belts, a shawl together with a thicker wrap, a creamy-white unmarried woman's kef, and a small bag to hold them all. His supply of silver was somewhat depleted, and some more of it went on bread, olives and fruit. Nepheret was silent, apart from brief and functional answers to practical questions, and he had no idea how to interpret this.

After the market, he led them to the town gate. The soldiers there, knowing she belonged to Senenptah, insisted on checking his ownership docket for her. That done, after a brief conversation with the gate commander they passed through the entrance and turned north onto the stones of the Sea Road. They walked on, mostly in silence, while the groups of people clustered around Gedjet thinned out.

Ayn

Matan Year 23

THE SCENT OF your fragrance, yours alone,
  only this enlivens my heart.
I found you, my gift from the Hidden One
  for all time, here and hereafter.

THE SUN WAS PAST THE ZENITH when they passed the fork on their left down to Iskalon and the sea, and not long after that Damariel led them to the right, away from the main track, behind a ridge into a little thicket of trees near a stream. He gathered some wood and built up a little fire while she broke one of the flat bread loaves into pieces and shared some of the olives between the portions. The flames caught in the dry wood and burnt with hardly a wisp of smoke rising up into the scrubby trees. She waited silently as he arranged some more small branches to his satisfaction, her eyes down to the ground, her hands carefully folded in her lap.

"Well, Nepheret, here we are. We're away from Gedjet. Now for home."

She looked very briefly up at him and then lowered her eyes again.

"Look, sir, where are we going to? What do you need me to do for you?"

He took out the wooden ownership docket.

"See this?"

She nodded.

He tossed it into the fire and watched the flames first tease in ringlets around it, then suddenly grip it in an intense rush of heat. The ink on it paled in the hot air, the name-glyphs burnt in with a hot metal chisel lost their shape in the ash, and the hard wood shrivelled. It was gone. She watched a few last sparks crackle upwards with the thin smoke, an unfathomable expression on her face.

"Nepheret, I am not 'sir' to you any more. I am 'Damariel' to you from now on. You come and go at your own pleasure. I hope very much that you will come with me up to Kephrath, to my town up in the hill country, but when that thing burnt, it left you free to make your own choice."

"But you paid my former master for me with your own silver, and you bought these other things for me in the market, these new clothes, the headscarf, all the rest. You showed me how to tie the headscarf to look like one of your women. I have nothing to repay you. I am in your debt. How can you say that I am free? Sir, did you just buy me to have a woman on your journey?"

He flushed, acutely embarrassed, and looked away. There was a silence, in which she remained staring into the fire. Eventually he got up and picked up some scattered pieces of thicker wood. He tried to speak a couple of times, but did not trust himself enough to carry on. After a long pause she spoke again, her voice forced and rather cold, her eyes still on the curling flames.

"If that was your will, it would have been simpler just to say to the housemistress down in Gedjet. I could have been sent to you. Or maybe a Kinahny girl if you had preferred. They say the master asked you three times if you wanted anything, and that every time you turned him down."

He came over to the fire, tipping the pieces of wood on the ground near it and sitting back down near her.

"Look, Nepheret, I don't want... well, I... I won't... "

She watched him obliquely, her head raised a little but still not looking directly at him. Her eyes, he noticed, were a shade lighter than Qetirah's, contrasting with the darker hue of her skin. The creamy colour for the kef had been a fair choice, he thought abstractly, still struggling for words.

"Look, I see now it must look as though that was all a bride-price for you, but it was shameful for him to send you out in just one piece of cloth. He wouldn't even let you take that harp. He made me very angry in that. I wasn't buying you with that silver, not at all. It was like, oh, I don't know, more like making a thank-offering to the gods."

"But all that was later. When you bought me you knew nothing of that, it was still to come. It had not happened."

He looked away, fiddled with the fire for a few moments.

"Look now, you are not a slave any more, you are just the same now as any other woman of my town."

He broke off again, seeing the wary look still filling her features, and pulled out the wooden writing frame.

"Look, Nepheret, look I'll swear by the gods to treat you well. I know, I'll swear by Tefnut and Taliy. Here, you write the signs for Tefnut and I'll write Taliy's name, and I'll swear an oath on both."

She looked more directly at him, softening visibly, took the bronze nib and scratched out five signs from right to left, the first four in two vertical pairs, and a taller curved shape on its own to the left, pursing her lips at the rough shapes.

"There. But it should be made with a brush. These shapes are not so good."

He took the nib back.

"We can do a better copy up at Kephrath. This is my part."

He scratched out three quick signs. She looked at them and traced the first with her finger, moving her hand quickly away as he placed his over both the names. He bowed his head, closed his eyes, and thought for a moment before speaking.

"These are the words of Damariel, seer of Kephrath, who came down from the hills and is now come up out of Gedjet with this woman Nepheret-er-sefet-Tefnut. Now,

listen, all you gods of the nations,
in the divine assembly take note:
record the words of Damariel,
the oath of the son of Yeresheth.
Taliy, I call to you to hear me,
Tefnut, I kiss the ground at your feet.
Nepheret's freedom was bought for her pleasure,
and for her own delight has she been released.

May I find blessing when I look out for her well-being, body and soul, and may I find a curse if I do anything to her, soul or body, against her will and invitation."

He opened his eyes and looked up at her, seeing a heaviness lift away from her. As his eyes met hers she looked down out of habit, then with an effort looked back up at him again and tried to smile.

"Thank you, thank you, and may all your blessing return to you, Damariel."

She handed him the bread and olives which had sat unheeded all this time.

"You know, I was sure when you took me from Gedjet I was only a second choice. Surely your first choice was to leave with the master's daughter."

He frowned, remembering his time with the chantress.

"Up at Meyim, and at Yabneh, and along the road, they told me about a chantress, daughter of the priest at Gedjet, who was looking for a place out here. Nobody told me about a woman of Pa-Yam who was a servant. I did not know there was a choice to be made. But it was you who understood my singing, not that other woman. She never even asked."

They ate the bread, shared some of the fruit. A cooler breeze sprung up, and the sun brushed the top of the ridge behind them. Nepheret suddenly laughed aloud.

"What do you think, Damariel? I have two warm cloths to choose. Should I wear this or that?"

She laughed again and pulled the shawl and the wrap from her bag, tried both on, and settled with the thinner shawl over her shoulders. "Two different cloths, and different clothes to wear both tomorrow and the next day and the next. Nobody would know me back in Gedjet. But in your town, perhaps everyone has two wraps?"

She looked around. "Which way is Kephrath?"

Damariel glanced to where the sun crowned the ridge, then pointed away uphill at an angle.

"That way, about two days if we took the direct paths up through Gath and Bayth Shamsh. But we will go along the Sea Road first, to my friend Gilem at Yabneh to return his poem, stay one night, then go up into the hills. In the afternoon of the second day from his house we should arrive home. Then you will meet my mother and sister, and her children, my friend Kothar, everyone."

She ate a date slowly, tossing the stone into the fire.

"How will you introduce me to them? I mean, what do you want me to do there? Where will I live? How will I work and earn my bread?"

"Nepheret, I would like you to sing with me. I need someone to sing with me to be seer up there in Kephrath. And I want someone with me who can understand the songs, who will work with me to make new ones and bring old ones to life again. You can do that. When we first started talking about songs I knew you could do that."

"In the kitchens, they talked about what you wanted. Everyone heard what you and the master were saying."

She chuckled, evidently remembering a conversation from the day before.

"What they said was that you wanted not a singer, but a sister. A man whose family came from up the coast said you all had lots of sisters up there, and you kept them just in one room, and the master's daughter would have to fight for her place inside and maybe would have to live on the roof. He said maybe you had ten sisters already but you wouldn't tell her until it was too late to change her mind."

She sobered again, frowning.

"But they also said you used to have a sister and she went to wherever your horizon is, so you had no woman and would go after any woman at all."

Damariel shook his head, trying to sort out truth from rumour in his mind. In the gap she spoke again.

"Is any of that true, Damariel?"

"Some and some. No, hardly any really. I most certainly need a singer to partner me. I also need a wife, a sister as you say, and it would be more fitting if the singer was the sister. It's been done differently before but not so often. But none of the men in Kephrath has more than one wife. Of course there's Zakarabi up at Woodlands."

He realised she was not following him.

"Well, I'll tell you about him some other time. All that about ten sisters and making them live on the roof – that's all just lowland stories, anyway, they say that kind of thing about us down there. Take no notice."

He was silent for a few breaths.

"But yes, I had a wife, a sister as you say, and she has indeed been gathered to her ancestors, to the horizon if you like. That was, oh, over a year ago. I was very, very grieved when she went. It was – oh, Nepheret, it was as though she had been murdered, taken away from me."

He looked away from her, his face hard, cold, unweeping. She sat very still, watching him without speaking until he swallowed and looked back at her.

"If she was murdered, your lord will take up your case. You must get your revenge."

"Nepheret, it was my lord who killed her. The chief Mahur-Baal, victorious over his enemies and glorious in battle."

He realised that a vicious edge had moved into his voice, and saw the look of incredulity on her face.

"Do your people not have laws and customs about this?"

He clenched his hand with memory.

"Yes, of course we do: what he did was wrong, though not quite in the way you think. He took her one night for his pleasure after he saw her dance in the firelight. He's the chief, he has no business meddling with the affairs of the seers. But he did, and his seed took in her, curse him, and it killed her. Before she even reached half way through her term it killed her from inside her womb."

He hesitated briefly.

"I wasn't even there, I was up in Hatsor on a pilgrim journey, came back to find her dead. They said she just collapsed in the street, bleeding from inside. Nobody could help her. By the time I got back she had been in her family tomb for two, three days, they'd got one of the other seers to do the singing and all. So would I take just any woman: no, certainly not, but if the right one was around I'd be courting her."

There was a very long pause. Damariel forced himself to relax and rubbed his hands on his smock as though to clean them. In the end she put some wood on the fire and spoke rather quietly.

"Look, Damariel, when you bought me from the master, were you hoping that I might be your new sister?"

They looked at each other cautiously.

"Nepheret, I took an oath. Just now, you heard me. This is difficult for me. Can we talk about this another time? I don't know how to walk along this path."

He waited for her to nod, once, twice, and then relaxed a little. The sun had now gone completely behind the ridge, and the day breeze had stopped. It was very still, very quiet in their camp, and the trickle of water sang from the pools in the nearby stream. After a while she took out her sistrum and sang back to it as the evening settled around them. He sat listening, but knew none of the words.

They were on the road early the next morning, heading northward again before the sun rose too high. Nepheret had disappeared towards the stream while Damariel was scattering the stones that he had placed around the fire and covering the ashes with earth. She came back wearing the dress he had bought yesterday, looking pleased and content. The road was largely empty as they walked northward, except for a small cloud of dust some miles ahead raised. Each time they crested a ridge they would see it, never getting closer or further away. After several such sightings, Nepheret spoke.

"You know, I just thought that could be the master's daughter with her baggage donkeys and all. The envoy from Djedenen sent some men to guard her and a wagon for the return journey."

"Really?"

"Oh yes, the stable men were all full of the news, how many men, how many donkeys, even a real horse, but I think that was going to be a gift for the master along with some other things. The envoy himself will have visited the master after we left yesterday morning, but I think he will have overtaken us after we stopped."

She looked across at Damariel's surprised expression.

"Well, Damariel, what did you think, that the master's only daughter would just have set off walking up the road with you like I did? That was never going to happen. Where was your bride-price? Did you think she would just walk up to your house? With all her finery and belongings?"

Damariel shook his head.

"They never said anything about that."

"Oh no, of course not, the master would not have spoken that to you. I think, well, in the kitchens they were saying, that he found you quite interesting, quite amusing to talk to. Perhaps he liked you even. But for his daughter he would have standards."

"Oh, so he liked me, did he? They never said any of this to me. I thought it was a simple choice for her. He treated me well, made me feel like an equal. Well, some of the time, anyway. Not always."

She spread out her arms in a gesture that suddenly made her seem very foreign.

"I think maybe the master saw you not so different to me. If the envoy from Djedenen had chosen some other woman, perhaps there would have been another reason why the master would not let his own daughter come with you."

She shook her head.

"To think of her walking up the road like this and sleeping out among the trees."

They reached Yabneh in the early afternoon. The main road continued north, but they turned right at a crossroads towards the small town, away from its small port. They made their way through the narrow streets to Gilem's house, part of the outer ring of houses on the eastern side. As Damariel called out, Gilem's eldest son Kinor opened the door and welcomed the two in.

The house was built in the coastal fashion, with several rooms leading off every side of an open courtyard, entered directly from the street door. Some of the rooms were also joined together by corridors inside the courtyard walls. Gilem and his wife Beliniri were in the open area at the back but were already coming forward to welcome them. Nepheret hung back a little as Damariel embraced the seer and his wife warmly.

"Gilem, Beliniri, this is Nepheret-er-sefet-Tefnut."

Gilem brightened,

"Ah, Beauty like the Fragrance of Tefnut. Be welcome in our house, lady, though I imagine you'll be wanting to head on soon up to that backwater place that Damari calls home."

Nepheret beamed.

"Thank you for your welcome, sir, and bless you for your knowledge of my language. What does your name mean, sir?"

Beliniri spoke before he could reply.

"'Little boy', that's what, and I'm sure you'll find out why before the evening is done. Don't let him fool you, or he'll dazzle you with his vast knowledge of the Mitsriy tongue."

Gilem said something that Damariel did not follow, and Nepheret, shaking her head, replied so he could understand.

"No, sir, only a word or two, so far."

Gilem nodded and switched back to Kinahny again.

"I must have got your name wrong, lady, I heard it was Sheded, chantress, or something."

Damariel opened his mouth to reply, but Nepheret was too quick for him.

"Ah, sir, that would be the master's daughter. She has by now surely passed through on the road up towards Djedenen."

Gilem looked curiously at Damariel. There was a little pause which Beliniri broke.

"But what use are we as hosts? Nepheret, Damari, come in and settle yourself as though this was your own home. Damari, you'll be happy in the same room as before, won't you? Kinor, help the lady with her bag. I'll be cooking down the hall when you're ready. "

She ushered them out of the open courtyard and pulled back a cloth drape on one side to show a small room that looked out toward the rising ground eastward. A low table had a Mitsriy-style oil lamp and wick. A single roll of bedding was bundled against one wall. Nepheret stepped in and glanced around.

"Oh, perfect, lady Beliniri."

"Call me Belith, dear. Everybody does. Just come along down when you're ready."

Nepheret pulled things out of her bag and put them back in again, unrolled the bedding and then went to look out of the window. Damariel was still by the door, not coming in.

"Look, Nepheret, Gilem has other rooms. I can ask him to put me in a different one. I can tell him we have taken a vow of some sort. Well, we have. On the road, earlier."

She turned and looked at him curiously.

"It's all right, Damariel, no need."

"I made a vow, Nepheret."

"And I'm sure you'll keep it. But I'm not going to be in a room on my own, here in a strange house in a town I have never even heard of before. I wouldn't sleep. I haven't slept in a room on my own since, oh, I don't know, not ever."

Then a smell of cooking wafted into the room and her eyes lit up. "Oh, fish!" She slipped past him neatly and started down the corridor. As they approached they heard Gilem.

". . . but I don't think he even knows, Belith. You know what he's like. He wouldn't."

"Not our concern, Gilem. Just let it be."

As Gilem started to reply, Damariel scuffed his sandals loudly on the sandy floor of the corridor and coughed. They went into the kitchen where Beliniri had already cleaned two large fish and was cooking them on a griddle, her face flushed with the heat of the little fire and her kef tossed to one side of the working area.

"Lady Belith, are the fish for us?"

"Got them today from Yabneh-Yam, dear. Fish alright?"

"Oh, I love fish. In Pa-Yam we had fish three times a week, but in the master's house at Gedjet we were never allowed it, it was only for the guests."

Gilem looked pointedly at Beliniri, who waved her hand at him.

"Look, Gilem, take Damari away and talk about that tablet of yours. Just keep out of our way while we sort this out."

The two men went back into the courtyard, half-filled with angled sunlight still, and Damariel got out Gilem's tablet and his own copy cut into the wooden frame. They spent some time checking through it before being satisfied.

"So, Damari, is Nepheret all that you expected?"

"How do you mean? She's very talented, I think. I haven't even told you about the idea she had about this piece."

"Yes, Damari, I'm sure she is, but is she, well, is she really what you were looking for? Who is she exactly? I'm sure I wasn't all that wrong about the name of the chantress. And what does she mean all the time about the master, and not being allowed to do this and that?"

"Gilem, let me tell you about what she said. Look, I was reading this out to her, and she asked why we make the lines the same length."

"But we don't always. You know that. Look here, or here, they're quite different. But that's not what I was talking about."

"Not always, no, not every single line, but as a rule we do. On the whole. But she said, why not a rule with one longer and one shorter, like a heartbeat, or like a man and a woman coming together. That's how they do songs down in Mitsriy, out in the towns like ours I mean, not in the palace or among the lords. Think about it, Gilem. There's a chance here for doing things we've not done before."

"Damari, why ever would you want to copy their style? What's wrong with the way we do it, we've always done it? They're different down there, that's all. But I wasn't asking about her ideas about singing. Stop avoiding the question."

But at that point Beliniri and Nepheret appeared with the food. Beliniri had changed kef to a long blue drape hanging in fringes nearly to her waist, in the formal lowland style.

All through the evening Damariel was aware of Gilem's occasional probing or doubtful looks, the unanswered question still lying like a discarded bone between them, but neither of them brought the matter up again. When the sky had darkened and the town was settling into rest around them, and the evening star had been joined by whole shoals of companions, the conversation wound down.

"So, Damari, will you leave tomorrow?"

"Yes, Belith, as early as we can, I think. I'd like to get some way into the hills before we stop tomorrow night. Many thanks for your hospitality to us."

Beliniri picked up the oil lamp, shading its wick from the sudden movement, and lit the way back into the house. They parted in the corridor, with Gilem still restless and unresolved. As they pulled the curtain across behind them, they heard Gilem's voice across the courtyard in another room talking to Beliniri, but the words were too quiet to make out. If Beliniri was replying, they could not hear her.

Inside the little room it was very dark now, and Damariel listened, sightless, to the rustle of feminine fabric as Nepheret settled herself for the night. Suddenly her voice drifted towards him out of the darkness.

"Damariel, do you think Gilem likes me?"

Damariel sighed.

"I think he does, but he's always been suspicious. He kept wanting to ask me who you were, why your name wasn't right, were you the right person, did I know what I was doing. Of course he had heard the name Sheded-em-duat-iset. I kept just ignoring what he wanted to ask. It's me he thinks might be wrong, not you."

Her hand moved in the darkness, gripped his hand.

"Damariel, I am sorry if I have come between you and your friend."

"Nepheret, that's his problem, not mine. He wouldn't listen to me when I was telling him what you said about songs, what you and I might do together. He wouldn't listen at all. He just wants to keep it all the same. But things have changed since the days of the ancestors. They're changing now, even now. We could do that together, you and I, I'm convinced we could. He wasn't there, he didn't see what happened."

Her hand relaxed again, but he held on to it as he lay awake beside her, listening to her breathing, listening as it became slower and more regular, listening as she fell asleep.

The next morning dawned clear and bright, and Damariel left with Nepheret as soon as they could. Gilem was still clearly unsatisfied, wanting to ask little darting questions of the couple, but he restrained himself and was gracious as a host in bidding them farewell. Once away from Yabneh, Damariel led them north-east, cutting at an angle away from the main road running parallel to the distant sea. For a while, through gaps in the scrub, they could sometimes see the distant water, but before long shoulders of land obscured their view.

They found shade in the hottest part of the day near a stream, and soon after setting out again skirted a little settlement at some distance and then turned uphill. Damariel did not intend to have dealings with people in this area, as it was uncomfortably close to places his people raided from time to time. Indeed, it was not far from Aliyna's original home. He kept well away from the town and stayed some distance from the main track that ran down from Giybon to the sea at Yaffa.

As they walked, he persuaded Nepheret to start to teach him her language, mainly through hearing the words of poems and songs, and the names of family members, words that could be quite alien or suddenly familiar. In the evening they camped against the west side of a craggy rise which rose sheer above them like the side of some ancient beast, watching the sun set in the distance into the haze over the sea.

They arrived at Kephrath late the following afternoon, after a slow but steady rise up into the hill country. Damariel had become increasingly excited as familiar landmarks came into view. They came in sight of the town quite suddenly, cresting a ridge and looking across at the high place. From their left they could hear the shouts of children at the stream. Damariel stopped Nepheret and pointed out his house, the house where Yeresheth and Sosanneth lived and where he had grown up, Kothar's house, Shomal's olives.

Nepheret disappeared into the bushes and came back a few minutes later dressed up in smock and skirt, pushing nervously at the arrangement of her kef. The track dipped down briefly and then up again, past the last line of trees and along past Shomal's field.

Aliyna was outside the cottage shelling beans, waiting for Marir to come back with the other children from the stream. As she saw the couple coming up to the low wall she called back over her shoulder to Shomal, half-way up one of the olive trees, and came to meet them, one hand outstretched to each.

Shomal followed, wiping his hands on his apron, standing back while Aliyna hugged Damariel and kissed Nepheret.

"Shomal, Aliyna, this is Nepheret-er-sefet-Tefnut from Pa-Yam in Mitsriy, who has been living in Gedjet. She has come here to be with us, to sing with me, I hope."

He glanced briefly at Nepheret beside him, but without replying to him, she reached out and took Shomal's hand. He wiped his free hand again on his apron and nodded.

"Shomal, sir, and lady Aliyna, it is my delight to meet you."

"What did you say your name was? Didn't catch it. Nefterefet-tenut? What sort of funny name is that, anyway?"

Aliyna looked at him with old memories in her face.

"It is the name her family gave her, Shomal. We should learn it to honour her."

"Shomal, Aliyna, look, it is a Mitsriy name. In our tongue it would be, let me see, it would be Jasmina-Taliy."

"Well, why didn't you say so at first? Look, if I can't manage the foreign stuff I'll just have to call you Jasmit. How about that?"

The two looked at each other solemnly, and then suddenly laughed together. They stayed talking there for a short time and then Marir came running up the path towards them together with a group of other boys. Damariel and Nepheret continued on into the village and stopped again under Yeresheth's mimosa.

He called out and Sosanneth rushed out to meet him, wrapping her arms round him tightly before seeing Nepheret standing there. She released Damariel again and looked questioningly at him. Behind her, in the doorway, Yeresheth was standing, with Labunasi clinging to her skirt and her granddaughter Sophireth in her arms. Qeren was behind her in the shade.

They all went inside and Nepheret was noisily, confusingly, introduced to each of them at least twice. Her name was repeated several times over, in longer and shorter combinations, experimenting with the Mitsriy and Kinahny variations. In the end Damariel threw up his hands, told them he would be back later when they had quietened down, and led Nepheret up between the last houses to the high place, to the vine, to their house.

There was a little bag of onions and herbs outside the door, and he picked them up as they went inside. It was cool in the big room, and he stood, happy to be back, trying to see the house through Nepheret's eyes as she looked around. Counting back, he realised it was barely a week since he had left the house. Everything was as he had left it, but around him the world had changed once again.

He took Nepheret from room to room, starting with the little outhouse where he had first lived when he moved in to join Saniyahu and Halith. She had laughed to see that, telling him how much smaller it was than the place she had been allotted in Senenptah's house in a big room amongst some other women, and that even the garden labourers had more space than that.

She put the little bag of her possessions in the room with his sleeping roll, draping her spare clothes across the back of a chair. When they got to the room with the other musical instruments, she put her sistrum and wood blocks with them and then picked up the lyre that Damariel used to play while Qetirah danced, that Halith used before him. She plucked some of the strings, experimentally, untunefully, and then put it down again, shaking her head.

"I think your strings are set differently to ours."

"I haven't played for months, Nepheret. They need tuning."

They had finished looking around, and he was in the process of lighting the fire, when Kothar called from outside. Damariel ran to the door to open it for him, and the two hugged each other. Kothar suddenly caught sight of Nepheret, who had stayed back in the doorway of the kitchen, and took a step into the room.

"Well, Damari, who's this you have brought back with you, then? Lady, you must be the chantress the traders told us about. Persuaded you to come up here, did he? If he's glad, I'm glad for the both of you."

He reached back to put an arm over Damariel's shoulders.

"Very glad indeed. More than glad. Lady, we've been without a singer up here far too long. Kept telling him so myself, and eventually he listened. What do they call you, down there? What does Damari call you? I'm Kothar, I'm like a brother to Damari. So, have you come to be our singer? Are you going to marry him, put him out of his misery?"

She gave a little bow.

"Sir, they call me Nepheret-er-sefet-Tefnut, though your people seem to say it better as Jasmina-Taliy. Damariel calls me Nepheret."

She stopped, hesitated, and looked at Damariel. There was a little pause, in which Kothar looked from one to the other.

"Look, Kothar, we've only just got back. Can't that sort of question wait a day or two? What a thing to ask when Nepheret has only just arrived."

"No, Damariel, it's good; your brother has a right to ask."

She straightened her posture and looked directly at Kothar.

"Damariel invited me here and I have chosen to come. He bought my freedom from the master in Gedjet and then gave it to me as a gift, and then he made a vow on the road to make everything well for my heart. I might have gone anywhere I chose, but I wanted to come up to Kephrath. To come here. To sing and dance for you all would give life to me."

She paused again and looked at Damariel.

"For the rest, who can say?"

Kothar nodded slowly, taking in the strain on Damariel's face.

"Well, I'm very glad to see you, to see both of you. Look, I brought a rabbit for you, caught it and three hares at the traps along the ridge earlier and was wondering what to do with them. Rabbit's fine for tonight, the hares'll be ready in a few days. I'd better be away shortly, get back to Shaharti and the little ones. Look, Damari, those hares are outside, just go and pick out the best one for yourself. And the rabbit."

Damariel went out and spent several minutes choosing, though there was hardly any difference between them. Mostly he wanted to immerse himself in the sights and sounds of home. Cooking smoke and smells were starting to arise from house after house, friends called out as they caught sight of him, the sky was a vivid dome of blue over his head.

He felt a great surge of homecoming joy, finally chose one of the hares and pushed the door open again. As he did so, he heard Kothar and Nepheret speaking quietly in the adjoining room, stopping suddenly as they heard him come back in. Kothar crossed to the door.

"Well, Damari, I've persuaded Nepheret to come and see Shaharti soon. You'll show her where we live, now, won't you? Don't worry, I'm going now, back to my own home."

He hugged Damariel again.

"I can't say how glad I am to see you back here again."

He left, closing the door behind him. Later, they sat in one of the smaller rooms as they ate the thick soup they had cooked, together with some flat bread rounds that they had somehow accumulated at Yeresheth's house. The room looked out towards the high place and the higher ridge behind it, and Damariel started to talk about the little community, how it worked, how it managed both good and ill fortune, how the living and the dead existed together alongside each other within the orbit of the high place.

When the sky darkened they moved into the large room, facing westward to catch the last of the light. Nepheret looked again, more thoroughly this time, at the instruments on the long table. Damariel watched her as she tapped the timbrel gently with her fingertips, then more firmly with the heel of her hand, then put it down and picked up the lyre.

"Why didn't he let you take the little harp with you?"

She turned, puzzled for a second.

"Oh, the master. Well, I'm not sure it was mine. He let me use it, nobody else played it, but he found it somewhere in Gedjet, not me. I think it was his."

"Well, now you're here, you can play it anytime you want."

Her fingers strayed across the strings, plucking one and another at random.

"I think I would like to hear you tune it and play it first. I still think the strings are set to different notes."

He shifted position on his stool, shook his head, and looked away from her out of the window.

"Not just yet, Nepheret. I can't – it's still too close."

She put it down gently, carefully, and came over to him.

"Did your sister play it? Your wife I mean, not Sosanneth."

He nodded.

"Qetirah, she was called, yes, Ketty. Yes, she played it sometimes. Mostly I would play it and she would sing. Not just us, of course. Halith played it before us, and Iqnu before her. I don't know who before that, or who made it. Maybe it is a hundred years old. But for me, the strings remind me of her fingers, and if I play it I expect to hear her voice."

"If you play it now, I can sing for you."

He looked up at her, shook his head again.

"Not today, Nepheret."

He stood up and walked about the room to clear his mood.

"Look, Nepheret, I don't know how you came to be in Gedjet. Tell me about that as the sun sets, then maybe we can sing something else, something without the lyre."

"At least you must tune the strings. Do that while I talk."

He nodded, picked up the instrument and started to work his way along the strings, one after another. She sat nearby and folded her hands in her lap.

"Well, Damariel, you know I was a child in Pa-Yam, near the town of Shedyet. When I was counted a woman I was sent from my home with other girls to make a travelling group of women going around the great houses. We called ourselves the Seventeen Hathors. We would go along to a banquet, sing and play and dance for the guests, please them, stay with them, do whatever they wanted, then go on to the next one. Along the way we learned what we needed: how to take care of ourselves, how to make the guests pleased with us and be generous to us, how to be midwives. That was for two years, until everyone I knew had babies, or had been taken into service in this or that household. I did not know what to do, so I talked with a priest. He said that a singer should always work, and I was given over to a nearby house."

Damariel was fascinated, though slightly repelled by what seemed the crude practicality of the idea.

"And did you have babies?"

She spread her arms out wide.

"I had a son. He was taken away after I weaned him. I like to think he has become a scribe, or an overseer, and is not just another labourer. I used to dream that he would come to the house as an important man and buy my freedom. Many of my friends who had become pregnant found husbands. I did not. But since I was now in service, I went from one place to another, until the housemistress of my old master took me away and moved me to Gedjet. I had been there, what, two years and half a year until you came. And now look, here I am beside such huge hills and valleys. Pa-Yam is a beautiful fragrance in my heart, with the reed beds and the birds, but it is flat like a great plain. When the inundation comes the water spreads ever so far across it. I know that upriver they have taller hills, both sides of the River, but not like this place. Who would have thought I should be living here?"

Damariel smiled a little.

"Perhaps one day you will come with me to the north, to Hermon and Tsaphon, and these ridges will look like little places to you."

She nodded absently and looked out of the window at the darkening sky, the great shadows already covering the valleys. Getting up, she lit the wick in the little oil lamp and pulled the cloth drape across the window. Crossing to the table, she ran her hand lightly across each of the different instruments in turn.

"Well, Damariel, if you won't play the lyre tonight, what shall we do? Will you start teaching me your songs?"

So they started on some of the songs, none yet from the great cycle that was sung on the main feast and fast days, but shorter ones that might be sung any time. They sat opposite each other on stools and went through one and then another, male and female voices working together, sometimes in unison and sometimes separate, each complementing the other.

"Now Hiwwi was a good king
took Ishkarra as his wife.
They protected the widow
and provided for the waif."

Eventually Damariel called a halt, stood up, and stretched.

"That was excellent, Nepheret, quick work, but enough for today, I think."

"Look, Damariel, I need to move about. Will you play something while I dance?"

He picked up the long thin ribbons that Halith used to dance with, caught by a sudden memory of his first few days in this house, Halith dancing in this very room.

"Halith used these. They were like wings as she danced."

She ran them through her hands, looking a bit doubtful, then slipped her kef off, shook her dark hair to loosen it, tied one of the white ribbons into it and put the other one back on the table. Damariel moved to pick up the timbrel, but she handed him the wood blocks instead. He took one in each hand, as she had done down in Gedjet, and began a steady beat. She shook her head.

"No, a bit faster than that."

He quickened the pace until she nodded, then kept the pulse going while he thought about how to introduce little rhythmic ornaments here and there. She started dancing, a fast, sinuous movement that took in all the corners of the room, the pale ribbon tossing in her dark hair as she moved, the shadows from the leaping flame of the oil lamp curving around her against walls and ceiling. From time to time she would cry out with a high, wordless birdcry as she moved.

Damariel watched, his breath taken away by the dance, barely able to keep the beat going.

After a while she stopped, breathing hard. She untied the ribbon from her hair and put it back on the table.

"Oh, Damariel, I think I am going to be happy here. But I'm tired now."

Then she picked up the oil lamp and led him away towards the sleeping room. As he followed her, the little dancing flame of the lamp shone out around the halo of her hair.

She blew out the flame as she went in past the door curtain, and, suddenly blind, he heard her move about the room: the lamp going down onto the little table, the rustling of material from her smock, her sigh in the darkness. He slipped carefully into his side of the bedding.

"Nepheret, tomorrow I have work to do here all day. I must tend the caves of the ancestors, pour oil and wine at the high place, see people, talk or pray with them, find out if there is word from the other seers. What will you do?"

He heard her turn onto her side.

"You must do your work. I will visit Shaharti like your brother Kothar wanted. And I promised Sosanneth I would see her. You will work, and we will be together later."

"Will you be alright?"

"Oh, Damariel, of course I will."

She reached out, took his hand as she had done in Yabneh.

"Your town is like Shedyet, more up paths and down paths but you live together the same way. My heart shall be very happy. I like it here."

He lay there, hearing her voice very close, feeling the touch of her hand against his, and after a while spoke again.

"Nepheret, I'm finding this difficult."

She made no reply, but left her hand holding his as he lay there in the darkness, waiting.

When Damariel woke in the morning, she was already out of bed. He heard her singing in the kitchen area, trying to work through one of the songs they had sung together. He smiled as she got a line wrong, stopped, got it wrong again, stopped again. There was a pause, then she started a poem in her own language.

He lay there listening to the foreign words, listening to the patterns of sound, listening to the pulse like a heartbeat running through the poetry. When he joined her there were two little plates with bread set for them. They ate and drank, then he took her down to Shaharti's house and left her there to go back up to the high place and do his work.

It was early evening when he got back to his house. There was a smell of cooking as he called out and opened the door, and when he went in he saw that she had prepared food and drink for them both. She brought in two bowls of the rabbit stew, covered with a crust of bread and herbs cooked in egg. There was also a larger bowl of curdled milk and honey with figs sliced up in it. He stopped, surprised. She was wearing a new ribbon belt with the smock: the colour matched both the smock and her skin tone slightly better than the old one had.

"How did you do all this? You must have worked all day."

"Well, you see, I stayed with Shaharti for a while, then she and I walked out to show me where the good herbs grow. Then your mother the lady Yeresheth gave me some eggs after we had talked for a while, and her sister Nerith gave me the milk. Your sister Sannah and I swapped belts."

She paused, placing the stew in front of each of them, then looked up at him.

"Also, the lady Kinreth who was the mother of Qetirah gave me the honey to go with the fig pudding."

"You went to see Kinreth?"

"Yes I did. And her husband Caleb was there as well. I spent a long time talking with them. Look, he gave me this."

She untied her kef, draped it over her chair, and showed him a little bronze hairpin she was using to hold her hair back. Damariel recognised Caleb's workmanship. He ate the stew for a while, silent, feeling several different emotions run through him. She watched his face. Eventually he spoke.

"Why did you go to see them?"

"Well, you see, I realised talking to the lady Yeresheth that I had to. Look, Damariel, put yourself in their house. Maybe they heard you brought me here yesterday, or maybe they would have got to hear today. For sure by the end of one week. How would they feel if I did not go to see them? I know Qetirah was your wife, but she was also their daughter. I wanted to know that things were plain between us."

He shook his head, carried on eating.

"How could you do that? Things between you could have been bad, could have been made worse. How could you know what they would say? I have hardly been to see them myself."

"I know."

Her voice was quite soft, quite gentle in reply, and after a startled look into her eyes he turned half away and looked out of the window. There was another silence until he had finished the stew.

"That was very good. But look, Nepheret, I wasn't expecting this. Never thought."

He shook his head, wiped the bowl clean with a last piece of bread and then pushed it away.

"Well, what did they say? How were they?"

"They were well and send their blessing to you. We talked a long time. I think it was good for them. It was important for me. Look, try this pudding, it is one we used to make back in Pa-Yam. Near as I could make it, anyway."

He took up the bowl absently, tried it cautiously and then with enthusiasm. She relaxed as he ate it. They finished eating as the last of the sun went, and then she lit the oil lamp and closed the drape.

"Damariel, I want you to do something for me."

He looked curiously at her, watching the light from the flame jump uncertainly across her features until it settled to a steady glow, warm across the darker tones of her skin.

"Just name it."

She got up and crossed to the table of musical instruments.

"I want you to play this lyre for me tonight."

He swallowed, his throat abruptly dry. He shook his head as she held it out towards him.

"I haven't played it in so long. I won't remember the tunes."

"How long?"

"About a year."

She crossed over to him, put the instrument into his lap. Automatically his hands curled around it, touched the curved sounding bowl, caressed the strings and traced his fingers along them from the base to the cross-piece, but he shook his head again.

"Nepheret, please don't ask me."

She sat on a stool facing him.

"Damariel, I am asking you. I think it's important."

There was silence for a while, then Damariel shrugged.

"Well, I won't be any good, you know, it won't sound right. You won't like it. I don't know any of your music."

Nepheret said nothing and just waited. He shifted the position of the lyre on his lap, moved his hands on the body either side of the strings, plucked one or two of them experimentally and changed the tuning imperceptibly. She still waited. He opened his mouth as if to speak, then closed it again and looked down at his hands. He started to play a few notes, little practice runs and chords.

He stopped again, flexed his fingers, repositioned them on the strings, took a deep breath, and started, finally, to play. He plucked out a few measures of one piece, then another, unsure what to choose, and then settled on the first piece he had learned all through from Halith.

It was a simple piece, telling the story of the courtship and wedding of Pidray, daughter of mist, made up of several long blocks joined by shorter bridges. He settled into it, relaxing into the familiar lilt of the notes, enjoying the piece, when all at once the memory of Qetirah dancing to this tune under the stars at the high place in midwinter came crushing down on him. His hands froze, rigid on the strings, hands that had unexpectedly betrayed his heart, and as the submerged vision came welling up like the mist through the valleys of memory, drifting up from the fissures in his soul, a great cry of anguish came out of him.

Great sobs shook his body and year-old tears ran down his cheeks. He felt the lyre being taken from him, and he pressed his now-free hands against his eyes, weeping in misery. Then Nepheret's arms were round him, holding his head against her breast as he wept, and he reached out and held on to her like a drowning man as his cooped-up misery, blocked like a dammed-up river in the spring, finally found a channel of release.

A long time passed, and eventually he became aware of his surroundings again, aware his head was cradled against her body. Feeling awkward, he started to pull back, but she kept hold of him and settled him against her again. He found himself listening to her pulse running like poetry in her heartbeat, to the little wordless sounds of comfort she made as she smoothed his head against her, felt the tears again running out of him, gentler this time now that the first turbulence of passion had passed.

Eventually he looked into her face and took a long, deep, slightly trembling breath. She picked up the oil lamp in one hand and took a step towards the door. He sat there, still on the stool, rooted to the spot, still unmoving. She reached out, took his right hand in hers, and waited.

"Nepheret, I'm finding this very difficult. I took that vow."

"I know, Damari. But let me choose the way of my well-being, body and soul, and may this be blessing to us both."

She led him through the house to the room with the bedroll. She set the little oil lamp on its table again, but left it burning this time instead of putting it out. The little flame danced in the shadowy room, pushing back the great darkness.

Peh

DABAH – MERAP YEAR 23

O LIFT ME UP to the heights of the land,
to eat of the fruits of the hills,
to suckle honey from the harsh crags,
and oil from the flinted rock.

SOSANNETH WALKED with her mother back down towards their home from the high place, each with one of the children. Sophireth was nearly asleep in a sling across her chest, and Labunasi, active and eager, kept running ahead to the next turn in the track and then running back to walk beside Yeresheth for a few paces. Qeren had stayed up at the stones to help tidy the area, and would be down in a while.

They had all been up there to witness and enjoy the marriage of Gazala to Yosheb. It had been a rather poignant ceremony, with the shadow of Uzziel's death never far from the background even through all the affirmation and dancing. Yosheb could not help but be aware of a pressure to prove he was not going to repeat the pattern by dying young.

The kef that Gazala had put away during the ceremony was not the plain kef of adolescence, but the mourning kef she had worn for months after Uzziel had died. She had set that aside on the day she had asked Yosheb to join her in the family home, but after a great deal of family debate she had decided to wear it one last time today.

So now the mourning kef had been torn in half, top to bottom, and buried in a tight bundle with the one Yosheb had worn as a boy. The choice had stirred up a considerable amount of discussion amongst the townspeople, but in the end it was generally felt to be a good gesture, if slightly defiant.

Tobiaz had stood beside his daughter as she married again. After several months of sharing the house together, the event was hardly unexpected, but because of the previous calamity, conversations at the stream and in houses had circled round whether Gazala would have the courage to enact a wedding at the stones a second time.

They arrived home.

Sosanneth settled Sophireth to sleep a little longer, and Labunasi ran off to the stream with several other boys. The two women sat at the table.

"Did you think she would go through with it, mother?"

She nodded.

"Oh yes. Damari has been helping them to decide how best to stand up to face all that has happened before. I think they ended up with something just right. And Tobiaz has been favouring it these many months. I suppose he'll be back here soon with Qeren. It can't take all that long to clear up."

"And here tonight?"

"I don't know. Maybe he'll go back to his home. Gazala's house, I mean."

"Mother, you cannot make him go back to sleep on his own at her house on her wedding night. That would be entirely heartless. Anyway, it's about time he began to think of this house as his home."

She made an inarticulate sound. Sosanneth stayed silent waiting for a more coherent reply. In the pause, Sophireth became restless in the next room, and Sosanneth brought her in to join them.

"So, Sannah, you have it all worked out."

"Not everything. But enough to tell you what everyone else says about it. I'm sure you know that anyway."

"I don't know. Maybe I need more time."

"Maybe you just need to make a decision. Gazala did."

At that point the sound of Tobiaz and Qeren laughing together came from outside, and soon after they were coming in through the door. Both men had been sampling the wedding wine, but were merry rather than drunk. The two women looked at each other, then Sosanneth got up, handed Sophireth to Tobiaz and hugged Qeren. Tobiaz bounced the now fully-awake Sophireth gently up and down. She beamed happily at him and reached out a hand to touch his face.

"I swear she grows every day, Sannah. Every day. And where is Labunasi?"

"Down at the stream. You'll see him when he gets back later."

She pushed a pan onto the embers of the kitchen fire and prodded them into a more active flame again.

"I mean, you will be staying, Tobiaz?"

He looked at her, then at Yeresheth, and passed Sophireth over to Qeren.

"I don't know, Sannah. Maybe."

Qeren laughed again, rather immoderately.

"You cannot possibly go back to Gazala's house just now. Not the right time at all for going there. They won't want to be entertaining you just now."

"Just what I said to mother a short time ago."

Yeresheth sighed.

"Tobiaz, please stay. If only to protect me from these two children here and their schemes."

"I can do that."

He and Qeren struck up mock fighting positions against each other and then laughed again. After his considerable anxiety beforehand, and the liberality of the wedding celebrations, his release of tension was quite evident. But then he turned to Yeresheth, his face very drawn.

"Yeresheth, I wish I was able to give them years and years. But I cannot know that for sure. I would like to give them a few days. Could I stay here until the end of the week?"

She looked at him, then at Qeren, still holding his exaggerated battle pose and grinning, and nodded without saying anything at first. Then after a little pause, seeing Sosanneth watching her intently, she continued.

"Please stay. It would be good for Gazala. And I should like that too."

Much later that evening, Sosanneth lay beside Qeren in their room. The half moon had just passed from visibility at the edge of the window frame. Labunasi and Sophireth were already asleep, one either side of them. She tucked herself against him and arranged his arm around her so that she could speak very quietly to him without being overheard from the next room or disturbing the children.

"Qeren, you must get mother to ask Tobiaz to stay here properly. All the time, I mean, not just days here and there."

"If you can't persuade her, what makes you think I can?"

"Because I think she won't ask him in case you get offended."

"That's foolish talk. She knows that he and I are good friends. I like him. She knows that; you both know that. There's more going on inside her than that, Sannah, it's not just my opinion that's holding her back."

"Maybe so. But I still think you need to talk with her. She needs to hear it from another man that she trusts, and Damari won't say anything to her about this, in case it sounds like he's giving advice."

He nodded in the nearly dark room, then after a short silence spoke again.

"Look Sannah, the chief has called me up to Giybon next week. Not just me, of course. Me and nine others. Some sort of building he wants done. Danil came over and told me after you had left the high place today."

"But we only sent a working group up there last month. It's less than a year since you were last there yourself. How are we supposed to do the work around here if he keeps taking everyone away?"

He shook his head.

"I don't know. But as well as that, you know my cousin Naomah over at Meyim, well she said he had just sent word to them that the half-yearly giving must increase again when it falls due in the autumn. I expect that will happen here too."

She sighed.

"I don't know how he expects all this to happen. We can't go on giving more and more up the hill with fewer hands to do the work. It can't go on like this. Surely he must know."

At the end of the week Tobiaz had, rather reluctantly, gone back to Gazala's house again. The next day after the weekly celebration, Damariel came down with Nepheret to eat with them. It was clear as they spoke that Nepheret's Kinahny had improved rapidly with continual use. Although she still tied her kef wrongly sometimes, she was starting to integrate more thoroughly with the women of the village. With her Mitsriy face and hair, she would never look like a native of Kephrath, but from all that Sosanneth had heard, she was working very hard to be accepted alongside those who had been born there.

There was no house in the town that she had not visited, and the lack of prior history with different families and factions was a positive advantage to her. Damariel was telling them, with evident pride and relief, that the other seers had just yesterday formally accepted his choice of her.

"And of course although by way of the formal seer training there's a lot she needs to do to catch up, in other ways she has a better grasp of the essentials than I do."

She laughed.

"Well, look, I can often tell what is moving in the hearts of people gathered together. I learned that first as a young woman at Shedyet in Pa-Yam. There was a priest who taught me about that all that time ago. Then as well the house mistress at Gedjet valued it in me, and would get me to serve bread and beer to guests and then tell her something of their desires and intentions. And now, see, I find that the seers here in the four towns have need of it too."

Yeresheth, beside her, put her hand on Nepheret's arm.

"For sure there are some days we all need that. There are some days I wish I had known what was coming towards me. Damariel tells me you are learning to sing our songs for the festivals?"

Nepheret nodded, but instead of replying to the question, turned on her chair to look at her directly and held her hand.

"You must be made very happy in your heart that your daughter has brought Qeren to live here."

"I am, Nepheret. First she gave birth to Labunasi, then just three years ago we talked about Qeren, and he came to live here. And then little Sophireth. Looking back, neither of us can see why she waited so long before asking him."

"So all your family are cautious about a change like that?"

Yeresheth stopped to think about that. Sosanneth laughed.

"Do you think my Damari is cautious?"

"Well, yes, I do think so. He would not be rushed into a thing he was not sure of, even though others wanted him to move swiftly. I think he is sure now. And I like it that you all need to be certain about a step before you take it."

The two women looked at one another, then Yeresheth nodded slowly.

"I sometimes think I am becoming more sure of myself. About the choices that I would like to make for myself now. But then, you see, part of me is still so very full of anxiety. Very fearful. Tell me, Nepheret, do you think a woman should wait until she is quite certain where to tread, or should she step out in hope, before the ground in front of her is clear?"

"In the Beloved Land we speak of how the judges at the gates of the other world weigh the heart in a balance scale. But I think here in this world the heart is a balance that weighs each moment as we come to it. Then all of a sudden something tips the balance over from one side to the other and we find ourselves on a different path entirely. Look at me. There was I in Gedjet as a slave in the master's house, and now I live here with you all."

Yeresheth fell silent. Sosanneth poured some more mint tea for them all, and passed the juglet to Damariel last.

"My Qeren has been called up to Giybon for a work party again, from tomorrow for a few days. How often is this going to happen, Damari? The chief won't be calling men up there to work so often as we come up to the autumn work, will he?"

Damariel pulled a face.

"The work parties are his sole decision, Sannah. The seers have never had a say in that. Nor should have, I think. That should be the chief's decision according to whatever needs he sees. Now, I had heard from other people about next week, but I never know the names of who is called until they tell me."

"But it's so soon after the last time."

"It is. Too soon, I think, but that's not mine to pass judgement."

"My cousin at Meyim has said that the half-yearly gift request will increase as well."

"Now that is a thing that we have protested about. The giving has always varied a little year on year, sometimes more and sometimes less. In one year, you remember, the spring gift was overlooked entirely because the winter had been so hard. But now each time in the last two years the request has been for more. Some families are already stretched too thin to meet the amount."

"Who is that, Damari?"

He shook his head.

"I must not say. But on their behalf, with the wellbeing of people of the four towns at stake, we have raised a voice."

"But no change?"

"But no change. Just a few days ago Saniyahu and Halith, as eldest of us, went to the chief to talk it over. He listened to them for a while but would not change the total he was looking for. The only concession he would make at all was that one town's shortfall could be made up by another's overflow, so long as the combined amount remained the same."

After a while Qeren spoke again.

"Damariel, is this just a thing of a few seasons? Perhaps he has in mind some particular deed. Maybe he needs us to give more just now for that, and he will ease off when it is done."

"Perhaps, Qeren. Who can say? But I have seen no sign that he knows how to let go of something that he has once grasped. I am not invited to share in his counsel, and in truth I would not willingly go if he invited me to. I cannot comfortably be in his presence without our past casting a shadow over us. A few times now I have not been able to avoid meeting him, but it is a great effort, and not at all pleasant. I would rather he did not think of me just now. Indeed, I have even tried not to let him become aware that Nepheret is now here with me. He never comes down here these days anyway, so that task is easier. Now, I am quite sure that he has heard of her by now, but it suits both him and me to act as though nothing has changed."

"But that cannot go on forever?"

Damariel looked at Nepheret, who was still holding Yeresheth's hand. She shook her head.

"No, it cannot. There will come a time when he will see me for sure, but Damari thinks it best that I live here for a while and become known and valuable here in Kephrath. And perhaps we shall share a wedding up at your high place before that day. If that would be acceptable to you, lady, and to your own people here."

Yeresheth looked at her contentedly and thought a moment before replying. Around the table, they all waited for her response.

"Well, Nepheret, as seer, Damari lives in his own house. It is not for me to say who should come and go there. But if he were still in my house, and since you have no mother's home of your own in Kephrath, I say to you that you would be welcome to come in under my roof like a daughter, and become like a sister to Sannah. Though our customs mean that she would be mother of the house on the day that I go to be with my ancestors, not you. If you wish it, come here and kneel and I shall bless your life here and your joining with Damari. That should be worth more than the approval or otherwise of a chief."

Nepheret got up from her chair, knelt in front of Yeresheth, pushed back her kef, and bowed her head. Just as she had with Sosanneth three years before, Yeresheth invoked blessing on the union, and prayed that the fruitfulness of Shadday and Rahmay would fill her.

Sosanneth, the memory of receiving her own blessing very clear in her mind, held Qeren's hand as she listened to the words. Surely that blessing had indeed filled her body both with and for her children. Then it was done, and the room relaxed, each holding the sacred silence for a few heartbeats.

Nepheret stayed kneeling, bent her head down to rest on Yeresheth's legs for a moment, then took her hands and held them between her own.

"Then let the lady Tefnut, who you call Taliy, who hears every true word spoken both in the red land and the black, and even to the very ends of all the lands, hear this. She who walks alongside us day after day, let her write on her heart this word of mine to be a true daughter to you, lady, a true member of your family, and a true companion to your son Damariel. And with her lioness face may she turn upon me and devour my heart if ever I break this word. So shall it be, come what may."

A week later, Sosanneth was taking some woven stuff up to the high place in the afternoon. As usual, Damariel was going to arrange for it to be traded as he saw fit when an opportunity arose. She was nearly at his open door when she heard voices coming down the track towards the town gate. It was Qeren, Kothar, and the others who had been up at Giybon for the work party. She put the bundle down beside the doorway and ran over to Qeren. He looked weary, and very pleased to be back in Kephrath.

"Well, how was it?"

Qeren shrugged.

"Too much to do in one week, in truth. But we did finish it. Some kind of store building he wanted right next to his own house up there. Nothing very difficult really, but the patch of land had to be cleared out and levelled first, then the building to be put up. Another party last week had collected together stones and wood for the beams and all that. Someone else is going to put in the doors and such like inside. We did our bit, that's all. All done, and I'm very glad to be home now."

Kothar, beside him, nodded.

"Time was when the work parties were a bit of fun. Bit of a break. I mean, you got things done but there was time to be with the other people too. Not any more. It's just work from first light to dusk, and that Yaraq and his men hanging around to make sure you don't let up. Makes you resent it. I've never liked it, you know that, but it's worse now than ever before. I hope it's a long time before I get called up there to work again. Now there's all sorts to catch up with down here as well."

Damariel, coming out of his house, had heard most of what Kothar had said. He looked briefly around at the other men to check on their well-being, received nods and shrugs from them. The group started to disperse towards their own homes.

"Look, Damari, how often is this going to happen?"

"I don't know, Kothar. I said it to Sannah last week, the seers have no say in how often work parties are called on. It's the sole decision of the chief. Always has been, for that matter, although most of them have not exercised the right nearly as often as Mahur-Baal is doing just now."

"So there's nothing you can do?"

"Not really, no. Not unless the well-being of the townspeople is seriously threatened by all this. And in all conscience I cannot say that yet."

"And why is it always Giybon that gets to benefit? It used to be spread around a bit, something here, something there, each town in turn. Not any more. Always Giybon that gets the place built, or the track cleared, or whatever. Is he chief of four towns or just one? Does he know what anyone needs except himself?"

Damariel glanced around.

"Kothar, maybe that's not such a wise thing to be saying."

Kothar shrugged.

"Someone needs to be saying it."

"Well, at least come inside the house and tell us all in there instead of out here where the whole land can hear your great voice."

They went inside and sat around the table. Sosanneth had wanted to get back down the track towards home, but Qeren had followed the others into the seer's house and she did not want to go off without him now that he was back.

As they went in, Damariel picked up the bundle of clothing she had brought, nodded as he saw what was in it, and carefully placed it beside the musical instruments. Nepheret was nowhere in sight, and Damariel saw her look here and there.

"No, Sannah, she's down with Tagi and Dadua just now. Not sure when she'll be back, but she'll be a while yet."

Then he turned to Kothar.

"Look, brother, you have not been so outspoken about this before? Isn't it usually you telling me to be careful about what I say?"

"Indeed it is. But this is going too far. It used to be that we would appoint a chief to look after things outside the four towns. Not interfere with what went on inside. We all knew he would need something from us to do that, and we all gave. I know we didn't exactly give cheerfully or willingly every time, but we could all see what he did with the gifts. There seemed to be some purpose to it. But now it's like I said outside, it's all just for him. When was the last time anything got done here? Or Meyim, or Woodlands? It's all just for Giybon. We should tell them we've had enough of it."

Qeren nodded.

"He's right, Damariel. I listened to men from the other towns when the work parties crossed over at the start and end of the week. And it is like that all the time now, you know. As one lot goes, the next lot comes in to take their place. No gaps in between. But anyway, all of them said the same thing, it's always just Giybon where things are done. But Kothar, it's not for the town. I don't think the people of Giybon see any benefit from it themselves. I talked to one or two, quietly like, to one side. They weren't keen to say anything in case someone was listening, but it seems they never get any benefit out of the work either. It's all just for the chief. His plans. Just him, not his town; they never see any good from it."

They fell silent for a while. Damariel got up and walked to the window that looked in the direction of Giybon. The town itself, of course, could not be seen because of distance and the rising ground holding the tombs of the ancestors, but they all knew what he was looking towards. Eventually he turned round to face them again.

"I wish I knew what to do about it. You all know that if there was an easy answer I would have taken it before. I have no love of him, and all these latest changes have simply confirmed my opinion. He has no love of the towns and no fatherly care for the people. But what is there to do? You told me this months ago, Kothar, just after we got back from Shean. He's got the strength of men and weapons to insist on his own way just now. And there's some from our own town that don't mind what he is doing at all. So far as they are concerned, it helps them. You all know who I'm talking about here. It's like we said before; we need allies from somewhere who will take our part in all this."

"So who are these allies, then? Where are they going to come from?"

"I wish I knew. That is the point I always circle around to every time I turn these things over to myself. I sit here sometimes and think my way up and down the land, the different towns and tribes, and I can't think of anyone who would have a real interest in helping us in this against the chief. Either they're too far away, or they have no reason to favour us over them. Or he's already cultivated good relations with the chief there, or the king as may be. This wealth he's been gathering in, it doesn't just go on new barns and sheds now. A good part of it goes in gifts and goodwill offerings to nearby leaders. Why would they turn against him? That would be like the donkey that kicked his own stall to pieces."

"Somebody new, then? Somebody who wants to move in to the hill country who has no relations with him?"

"Maybe. But who? I know of no group like that, wandering just across the River or down in the Nagb, just waiting to come here. Do you?"

There was a little silence. None of them knew. After a while Damariel continued, this time with an air of conclusion.

"It all sounds very gloomy just now. Maybe Qeren is right and this is just a passing whim on his part. But I don't really believe that, and I cannot ask you to either."

They stood up to go, but Qeren remained sitting. He was obviously lost in thought somewhere. Damariel looked at him fondly, touched him on the shoulder.

"Are you alright, Qeren?"

"Oh yes. And my apologies to you all. We should be leaving, and here am I holding you back. But I was just wondering. If you find your group of eager helpers somewhere, how do we know that the cure is not worse than the sickness? What if they end up taking more than he does now? At least we know him, what he's like. It could be like the man who invited the locust and his family into his home, all because they spoke friendly words to him."

He got up, finally, and went over to Sosanneth.

"Well, Sannah, let's be going. Take me back to your house and tell me how the children have been."

The next time Sosanneth was up at the high place, she saw Aliyna kneeling on the ground over near the little cairn that she and Damariel had made. There was a second small heap of stones beside it now; Aliyna had miscarried not long before. Sosanneth went over and waited silently while Aliyna finished her prayer and poured some oil from a little flask over both cairns. Then she got up, a little awkwardly, and saw Sosanneth standing beside her.

"Is it three months already, Aliyna?"

"Three months today, indeed."

They walked together towards the great house, but Aliyna went straight past the door on her way down towards the olive patch. She turned back when she realised that Sosanneth had stopped.

"Sorry, Aliyna, I thought that you might be stopping here."

"No need, Sannah. I have done all I need to today. No need to disturb him. But you go in if you like. I'm going back on down."

Sosanneth shook her head.

"Nothing important. I was impatient to see what Damariel had been able to do with the last lot we gave him, but it's too early really. He'll not thank me for chasing after him so soon. I'll come with you instead."

They walked together through the top half of the town, then Aliyna turned off towards the northern side of the ridge in a gap between the houses. Sosanneth followed her, curious. Her friend led them through to where a large rock made a gap between two of the terraces and they sat down there. Ahead of them, a little to their left, there was a dip in the wooded ridges. Through the dip, hazy with distance, they could see the far-away lowland plain. Aliyna looked a little shame-faced as Sosanneth, seeing the view, nodded in realisation.

"My little secret place, Sannah. Not so secret really, of course, I often see Tamguta and Abiram working away on either side. They don't mind me here. Once I'd found this place, I made a point of coming here once a month or so just to look. Today is an especially clear view. Some days you can't see anything really and I just imagine it."

"Do you still miss it down there? I'm sure Damariel could take you down that way on a journey one day if you wanted. Not as if you're a prisoner here. Not any more, not for a very long time now. You'd just have to ask."

Aliyna looked for a long time at the haze in the distance.

"Better that I don't, I think, Sannah. Do I miss it? Well, some days when I sit here I long for it so much I ache inside. Other days I love it so much here I would never leave. But either way, there's no going back. What would I do if I went back to my old village? Perhaps the house I lived in is pulled down, or perhaps someone else is living in it. Which is worse? Perhaps my parents are alive and perhaps dead. Better that I don't try, I think. Though I would like to show them Marir.

If there was a way to meet them by accident, on a trackway somewhere, I think I could bear that. But not the thought of going back there, walking through the town gate along to the house. Better by far that I only look at it like this."

They sat together for a while.

"You know, Sannah, I think now that I will never bring a baby to birth again. Don't ever say that to Shomal. He would feel dishonoured if people were saying he could no longer father a child. He needs to keep that bit of pride now. But in all truth, I think his seed will never come to be properly grown in my womb. And I don't know that I can bear to miscarry again. Better for us both that I make sure he lies with me on the wrong days for the seed to quicken. Then he can tell himself the fault is in me."

Sosanneth put her arm around Aliyna, who did not respond but kept looking out towards the lowlands. She did not know what to say at first, and was struggling with a very fierce inner conflict between supporting the other woman in her sorrow and the idea of maintaining Shomal's pride.

"But you must not give up hope, Aliyna. Something may change. So much has already changed for you."

Aliyna looked at her then, briefly.

"Do you think I am greedy, Sannah? I have lost two children now, one each in the lowlands and up here. But I have Marir. I have a household of my own, with a mother's dignity and even my iris plants outside the door to show it. I have a place in this town where I arrived as a captive. Should all that not be enough for me?"

She paused and shook her head.

"But I think I should have liked a daughter to run alongside Marir. Maybe that can never be, after all. I don't know. Just now I cannot even feel grief about it all."

Sosanneth did not know what to say, and stared out across the wooded ridges of the land as though an answer might be written in the sun and the clouds as they chased each other across the midsummer sky. Aliyna glanced at her again.

"There, now I have brought you low as well. That was not my intention when we came out here. Forgive me."

Sosanneth shook her head.

"Nothing to forgive, Aliyna. I don't really know how to understand your sorrow, but I can sit here and listen to it. You have seen so much more of the land than I. I have hardly set foot outside Kephrath and can't imagine what your home town was like, all that long way away."

"Well, not so very different. A little smaller. Much more built on level ground. We do not need terraces like this to hold in the land and its goodness. The fields just stretch out however we want around the houses. Otherwise, much the same. There is a big road a short distance towards the sea, and every day so many people go along it, north and south, traders, soldiers, Kinahny and Mitsriy, northerners, everyone you can imagine really. Sometimes when we were younger we would go and hide near it to get out of the village work and just watch the travellers, guessing where their homes were and where they were going."

"Damariel has talked about that road. When he brought Nepheret here they went along it to his friend at Yabneh."

Aliyna nodded.

"Their journey went close to my town."

"Then here in Kephrath we have the big trackway going along the ridge, and Damariel has told me that over the River there is an even bigger one."

"The Sea Road is bigger than the ridgeway track here, and more people use it. I don't know about the other one."

Sosanneth suddenly laughed, relieved that Aliyna's mood was lightening again. She felt more on solid ground.

"You know, I was thinking that although we have here no great track running up to our gate, yet still people have come to be with us here. First you from the lowlands and now Nepheret from among the Mitsriy. Do you think that happens in other places too? Or are we so very special that you come to join us?"

"Perhaps. Who can say? These are places I have never seen. You could ask Kothar if you didn't want to bother Damariel about that. He has been to other towns. Once, early on when I was talking with your brother, after Marir was born and I was starting to find a place among you all, he said that he thought it was a good thing for Kephrath that new people came in. He was worried, all the seers were worried, that the people here were dwindling. He thought that foreigners coming in from outside would be a good thing to bring new vigour to the town. At the time I thought he was just trying to be kind to me. But perhaps that is a true thing."

"Perhaps. I have never heard him say such a thing before. But I am very glad that you have been brought here. And Nepheret too."

"Well, I think that Kephrath has become a good place for me, on the whole. After a difficult start. And for Nepheret too. She has done well in establishing herself in people's opinion since coming here. And she seems very happy living as the woman seer. What a change for her though."

"He's very happy with her too. You know, none of us knew what he would do after Ketty died like that. I don't think he did either, but he just carried on until something changed for him. But there were times I was very fearful for him. Mother was too, even more so."

"It's an odd thing, Sannah. Down at home we would see Mitsriy men quite often, along the track or even in the town itself. Traders, soldiers, scribes. I suppose every week or two I would see some. But now Nepheret is the first Mitsriy woman I ever met. We had all kinds of stories we would tell about them, you know. That their men would never let them outside into the sun or the rain so as to force their skin to stay pale. Or that they must hide themselves away because they were fearfully ugly. And since we knew they didn't wear the kef that made it even worse. We decided they must be quite shameless as well as fearfully ugly, both at the same time. When Damariel first brought her up to the olive patch that day she came up to Kephrath, there she was all dressed properly, and I could not believe I was seeing a Mitsriy woman. She was not what I was expecting."

Sosanneth laughed again.

"I doubt that Damari finds her fearfully ugly."

"No, surely not. But what I am saying is that it has not been easy to learn to live alongside her. Even when I was a captive here, I knew what to expect of you townspeople. You are not so very different from me, and so in time I was able to find my own place here. You know that. But though you would think I would feel kinship with Nepheret since we have both come from outside, actually it has not been so easy for me. It has been difficult to forget the stories I had been told about Mitsriy women. I don't think she knows anything about that, though. They say that down in Gedjet where she lived, Mitsriy and Kinahny walk together in the streets every day. So maybe she has never heard the tales we told each other. I don't know. I am trying to set all that aside when she and I are together."

"Like you and I had to when we first became friends?"

"Yes, Sannah, that is exactly what I am saying."

She took another long look at the view out into the lowlands, then stood up.

"Well, Sannah, we had better be going home. Shomal has been called up the hill for a work party next week, just like your Qeren was a while ago. He really does not want to go, but what say do any of us have in that? He's as helpless in the face of the chief's demands as any of the rest of us. He gets very anxious when things happen that he can do nothing about. But better anxious than angry, I think."

They walked on together, and then Sosanneth turned off towards her home while Aliyna carried on down towards the olive patch. When she went in, she found Qeren and Yeresheth sitting together at the table. Sophireth was sitting on Yeresheth's lap, and waved her arms vigorously when Sosanneth was close enough for her infant eyes to recognise. Sosanneth scooped her up and hugged her, filled with a sudden wave of protectiveness and relief. Talking with Aliyna about her loss had, she realised, affected her much more deeply than she had thought at the time.

"So, what have you two been planning here?"

They looked at each other. Neither seemed especially keen to start talking, but Sosanneth's concentration was still focused mainly on Sophireth, and she did not notice the exchange of looks. The pause stretched out, until eventually mother and child had arranged each other to their mutual satisfaction.

"Well? I've been with Aliyna. I was going to see Damari but never got around to that. I can ask him tomorrow about the last lot of clothes. It's too soon, really, so there's no rush to do that. You don't mind, do you? I know that's why I went out a while ago but it just wasn't the right time and Aliyna needed me to talk with her more than I needed to ask Damari about the clothes. Do you mind?"

"Sannah, Qeren has been talking with me."

"Oh yes? And? I am sorry about the clothes."

"The clothes don't matter. There will always be more of those. And I'm sure you and Aliyna had a lot to talk about."

"So what is it, then?"

Yeresheth paused again.

"Look, Sannah, there was a time three years ago if you asked if I minded if you brought someone to live here with us. Qeren, of course, and his living here has been a great good for all of us. Well, now I think it is my turn to ask you the same thing."

Sosanneth nodded in understanding, and reached out over the table to hold her mother's hand.

"So who is he? Is it anyone I know?"

Yeresheth pulled a face and then laughed.

"I suppose I deserved that. I think you do know him. I am going over to Gazala's house now, if you think it good, and I am going to ask Tobiaz if he will come in and live here. I know you've said it before, but I wanted to know what was in Qeren's heart about it. Do you think it good?"

"I do. I think it long overdue, but perhaps you would say the same of me about asking Qeren. Maybe Nepheret is right and we are all just very cautious. For my part, I shall be very happy for him to live here with us all. Do you think he will agree? He may want time to think it over."

Yeresheth looked up in surprise, and then saw the provocative grin on her daughter's face. She smiled in response, but then became serious again.

"Look, Sannah, I am still anxious about this. Even now. I cannot bear the thought that maybe it will turn out badly like it did before with that other man. You know me, and you know him. Is this right for us both? And for this household?"

Sosanneth nodded, becoming solemn herself all of a sudden in response, and squeezed her hand.

"I think this is right. I think this is a good time for you both, and for all of us here. I think you should go over there now and talk with him."

Yeresheth stood up, adjusted her kef, looked round at the house as though parting company with it for the last time, and then left.

Tsadeh

Mepagh – Bul Year 24

FOURTEEN FATHERS in these hills begotten,
fourteen fathers: all now overthrown
and shattered lies the covenant of stone.

DAMARIEL AND ELI, the seer from Giybon, were deep in conversation. Eli had arrived quite early having set off walking down the ridge not long after sunrise, after the morning prayers had been said. It had, however, taken him a long time to get round to the point of his visit. Eli's wife Birketh had not come down with him, so at first Nepheret had busied herself around the house to let them speak.

Damariel, however, was becoming increasingly curious and a little frustrated with the conversation, which though pleasant and mildly interesting was largely aimless. He wanted an intervention, and picking a moment when Eli was looking down at the floor, searching for the right word to use to describe a domestic dispute that threatened to involve wider family members, he glanced over at Nepheret and moved his hand in a little gesture. She nodded, came over, sat down close beside Eli, and put one hand on his shoulder. Distracted from his train of thought, he blinked and looked at her.

"Eli, forgive the interruption, but I feel that your heart is troubled about something that you have not yet said."

Eli nodded, sighed, then stood up and moved over to the window. He looked across to where the trail back up to Giybon curved around the edge of the rock bluff which held the tombs of the ancestors. There was a little silent pause.

"Yes indeed, Nepheret. You speak correctly. The problem that troubles me concerns Mahur-Baal and his ambitions."

He paused to sit down again. Damariel leant forward, his expression carefully neutral.

"Can you explain more? Under this roof, at least, if not elsewhere."

They waited a little longer. Finally Eli, clearly reaching some kind of internal resolution, continued.

"Yes. I think I must. You know about the news we received from the Mitsriy governor down at Gedjet concerning the regular patrols of his bowmen through the hill country. That they were stopping, but that in every other way our position was to remain unchanged. Loyalty, tribute and so on. Well, since that news, Mahur-Baal has felt himself at greater liberty to arrange matters as he sees fit, not just in relation to the Mitsriy but in other things as well. For one thing, he has been seeking and renewing alliances with some of the other town chiefs."

Damariel shook his head.

"Nothing very new in that, surely? The chiefs have always held that responsibility in name, though in recent years they have not exercised it regularly."

"Well, Mahur-Baal is pursuing it diligently, like a hungry wildcat stalking prey, and he is going to chiefs with whom we have had no relations since first arriving here from the north. Not all of them show interest, to be sure, but he is trying. And he is not involving the seers in this, which again in all honesty is his right as chief, but is disturbing nonetheless. It is his own play for importance, not a thing attempted in the best interests of the four towns. Or so I think. Saniyahu and Halith as well. But perhaps Kenizzi and Sallarsheh at Meyim see it differently."

He stopped again. Damariel and Nepheret remained silent, aware that there was more that he wished to say. Eli sighed.

"Forgive me, both of you. I am not accustomed to speaking freely of him as we are doing now. Which of itself must tell you something. There is more. He wants to change from being chief and war-leader over us to being king. He has been talking to some of the town leaders in the lowlands that have called themselves king for many years now, and he wants the same for himself here."

Damariel nodded. Nepheret replied, doubtful.

"But what difference will that make? It will not change the size of his roof, or the number of people in the four towns. Why not let him say this of himself if it flatters his vanity?"

"No, Nepheret, it is not just a matter of a title to flatter himself. He will use this to change the manner in which things are done. He will change how the towns share wealth, from us all giving freewill offerings together at springtide and harvest to a demand for tribute by way of taxes month by month. He will change from a call for occasional work parties to carry out specific tasks for the community to having a regular monthly group of men and women to do whatever he pleases to set in front of them. He will station some of his men in each of the other towns to ensure things are done as he directs - trade, covenant, even friendships must be as he decides. He will use the opportunity to greatly increase what he can take."

He paused, and Damariel continued.

"I expect he will have a group of men on permanent military duty, a kind of standing army of his own men, instead of calling for support from the towns to fend off threats as they arise. And these men will need to be kept and fed, since they will not be working the land for most of the year."

Eli nodded.

"Yes, that is his plan. He has seen this done in other towns and feels that he needs to do the same. And he will set up a house for the women he chooses, drawn from households loyal to him, or else from those where he feels a need to impose his authority. His first wife Asherith is in almost every way a prisoner now who cannot leave the house he allotted to her. Since she is Iqnu's daughter, nobody is minded to speak for her now. But one or two of the other households have promised a daughter to live in what he calls this house of women as well."

"How can that be? What will happen to the households if the daughters move out?"

He shrugged.

"I think those families consider that Mahur-Baal's favour is worth more to their lineage than descent through an eldest daughter. They will gamble their future on his family, rather than their own. But there is even more. He intends that the seers are subordinate to him, instead of being a free voice of support or dissent. An unpredictable element in his new way of organising the four towns. He wanted me to draft that in a writing that each of the seers would agree to."

"Did he now?"

"He did indeed. I was vague and temporised, saying that I would need to discuss such a thing with you all before ever writing it out. You know how it is, Damari. Once a thing is written down it is very hard to unwrite it again, and I was not going to do this lightly or on my own. So for now he has accepted my position, with the condition that I raise this with you all before long. But my fear is that he will simply go down to Kenizzi and Sallarsheh and seduce them into writing it."

"That is twice now you have spoken of them? Why them?"

"Well, they are young and eager, and responsible only for the smallest of the four towns. Sallarsheh's family has long-standing ties to that of Mahur-Baal. She is with child and feels a need for security just now. I can easily imagine him offering them advancement in exchange for this. One night, after one of the festivals, in an unguarded moment, he talked to me of how some of the kings he spoke with had a single high priest overseeing everything to do with the spirit, not a group of independent-minded men and women serving as seers. There would be considerable advantage for him to have just one person to deal with instead of eight, especially if it was a person who felt they owed him a debt of gratitude."

There was a long silence in the room. Eventually Eli continued.

"He will not come to you, of course. I think he believes that you are still loyal to him, or else he would have taken measures already. But he would not risk a test of your loyalty over this, and I think he believes firmly that you would not support it. He will not go to Saniyahu and Halith - they are eldest and most experienced among us, and would never yield their authority for this purpose. And they have had a great deal to do with you. I have had to play a waiting game, listening to all that he says but acting on very little of it. But he will become impatient before too much more time has passed. Kenizzi and Sallarsheh are the obvious couple for him to persuade along his path. You know them, Damari. Tell me, how long do you think they would keep in step with the other seers before yielding? The rest of us will be left on a hillside."

Damariel shook his head slowly.

"How long indeed? Who can say? But you are right. Of course you are right. These are difficult times for us."

"More than just difficult, Damari. My fear is that he will do away with the place of the seers in the four towns altogether. Look at it from his house. If he can persuade Kenizzi to be a high priest under his control, what need of seers? We will be left standing outside the town gates. What then? Can you farm, Damari? Look after goats and sheep? Go hunting and trapping? There will be no place for the ministry we have offered all these years."

Nepheret stirred, shook her head.

"Surely the people will not accept that. They know all that the seers do for them. One high priest will not sit with every person in their delight and their distress, visit every woman in childbirth, comfort all who are bereaved. One person cannot do it. In the Beloved Land to be sure we have a high priest who stands in the presence of the great king and has his ear. But he cannot hear the voices of all the people, so there are priests and magicians in every town, men and women who serve both worlds as we do here. Eli, even if Kenizzi is made high priest, your people will still need you and Birketh."

Eli looked grim.

"Nepheret, I am sure your people came to that arrangement over the span of many generations. And your land is a great land so that a man would need weeks to go from one end to the other. But we are just four towns, so close that we say that a hearth fire burning in Meyim might cook bread in Woodlands. Mahur-Baal will forge his plans without regard for any generations to come. Except his own. I am certain that his plans have no place for the seers. If we do not handle this right we may be the last of all those who minister like this. Who knows, perhaps our best plan would be to go down and serve amongst the Mitsriy. Would they take us in?"

"But if we stay here, are you saying that we should submit to this agreement he wants you to write down now? That that is the most prudent way to go?"

"Damari, I am not sure. That way might lead to the same end after all. Like killing a man by starvation instead of a knife - the dying is longer but the end is the just the same after all."

He shook his head.

"We have stood in the gap between life and death for our people all this time. Are we now facing the death of our whole way of life? Of all that we have stood for and represented? Are we strong enough to stay standing in the face of all this? Things are changing rapidly."

"Then you must find allies to stand beside you."

Eli laughed.

"She is not wrong, Damari. But who will stand with us?"

Damariel stood up and prowled around the little room.

"I think that here in Kephrath, perhaps three families in four would want us to carry on serving just as we have done. I suppose the same holds for the other towns. But that still leaves one family in four, and I do not want to cause division like that until there is no other turning to take. In any case, with his new gangs of men at arms not needed to work the land, he may simply intimidate others. Nepheret is right, we need help from outside."

"Who will you go to, Damari?"

"Well, in the first instance, to the seers up at Dothan and Sychem. Then down to Gilem at Yabneh as well."

He paused, sat down and shook his head as though reconsidering. Nepheret nodded.

"Exactly. Why would they help us in an affair that is purely our own here in the four towns? And if they were willing, what could they do? Can you see Gilem coming up here to confront Mahur-Baal's armed men? Have you ever seen him wield anything more than a knife for cutting bread? You must meet this strength with the same kind of strength. What about my own people? Could they be persuaded that he is a threat to their interests here in the hill country?"

Damariel thought for a while.

"I don't see how. Why should he become more of a threat because he calls himself king rather than chief, or if we seers were no longer serving the people?"

But Eli broke in with some excitement.

"No, Damari. I do think that Nepheret may have a lead here. You know that the Mitsriy have not sent their scribes or soldiers up here to collect the dues from us this last year. No, longer than that. They instructed him to send the tribute down to Gedjet with a docket written by me affirming the correctness of the amount. He has done this twice now, autumn and spring. But he has spoken about overlooking this duty next time, this coming month. He said to me he will hold the goods in reserve in case they challenge him, and if they ask, say that the roads were not safe enough to travel down with a valuable donkey train. But in truth he thinks they will overlook the matter - the entire amount due from all four towns together is a little sprinkle compared to the torrents from some of the big coastal regions. He intends to gamble that they will not consider the sum worth the effort, I think. That will give him the resources he needs."

"Eli, that is excellent news. Then we must ensure that the matter comes to their attention. Nepheret can help me write it in the way the overseer of the region will want to read. But we must not carry the tablet down ourselves, none of us. Nor trust it into the wrong hands. Someone of integrity must take it down in secret, while we stay clear and visible to all here."

Eli pulled a face.

"It's a plan, Damari. But it is only a little patch that you are trying to stretch over a very large hole. Perhaps it is the only plan we have, but all it will do is buy us a little bit of time. It will not solve the greater problem."

"Unless they remove him as chief. They have done that before, Eli. The chief up at Pehela was removed when they thought him about to rebel. They might do the same thing here if they felt the risk was too great."

"Pehela is close up by Bayth Shean. That chief was too reckless, too conspicuous. I think Mahur-Baal is more shrewd than he was."

"But maybe a little bit of time is all we need, Eli. In the time we gain I will go up to Dothan and the other places to make our case. With more time we may have more fortune."

"Well, it is more than nothing. And if we do nothing then we may all of us be learning how to plough or harvest after all. Or Nepheret may be teaching all of us the Mitsriy tongue. Do you want me to stay and help with the writing?"

Damariel shook his head.

"No, not at all, Eli. You have done more than enough by speaking to us of this. To do more would be too great a risk. Does he know you have come here today?"

"No. He went up to Shalem yesterday and returns tonight. Or perhaps even tomorrow. I left at daybreak and let it be known I was seeking a vision out in the wilderness."

He laughed.

"Not so very far from the truth. A vision of a highway through the desert is what we need just now, and if those who heard me thought I was meaning only the land beyond the sown ground then the fault is in the ear that hears, not the voice that speaks. But look now. I must leave soon and this needs prayer as well as thought."

The three stayed quiet in the room for a time, with the everyday sounds of Kephrath clear in the background. After a while one or other spoke their prayers aloud, the others assenting and echoing the petitions. Before long, enough had been said, and they fell silent.

"My thanks to you both today. Especially Nepheret for prompting me to speak. If it should be that our way is passing, I shall miss the times of prayer more than the great festivals, I think. I regret that Birketh did not come down here with me, but we thought it too risky for both to be here. I must get back to her now, after a decent pause and a time out in the wilderness to seek this vision."

He left. Damariel and Nepheret talked for some time how best to write the letter to the governor. They settled on the content first, having discarded a great deal that Damariel wanted to say, but which would be of no interest to the overseer. Then Nepheret explained how a Mitsriy letter should be set out, and Damariel wrote it down. To be received, it had to be written in the wedge-and-clay script, not the common Kinahny letters. As Damariel had not used this for some years he wrote some practice signs on some clay before attempting the master copy.

It was challenging work - the clay had to be stiff enough to hold the wedge shapes making up the signs, but not so dry that they could not be impressed in the first place, or worse still that it would damage the reed stylus. Since the flat pillow shape of the clay was drying out with every passing moment, it was a race against time to keep the letters clear and legible while still completing the whole text. He became profoundly grateful that Nepheret had insisted on shortening the content.

Remembering the tablet of Ilimilku that Kothar had once found for him down in Bayth Shamsh, he felt a renewed respect for the scribe who had packed so many beautifully fashioned signs onto the tablet he had used. For his own part, the first three attempts went badly wrong, and the clay had to be softened into a featureless lump and pushed out flat again. There was no such thing as a partial tablet - it was either completed in one attempt or else completely rejected. After the third time, watching the words and sentences soften and vanish in front of him, he shook his head.

"You are sure we cannot use a wax frame? Then we could do it in stages and make sure everything was right. Even wood would be better than this."

Nepheret did not reply, just looked at him patiently and without yielding. He sighed and began all over again as she dictated. The fourth time was deemed acceptable by both of them, and he set the clay to one side to dry thoroughly.

> From the loyal people of Kephrath and the other towns of Giybon to the overseer of this Kinahny region, may you be at peace as you serve the great sun over all the lands, who lives in prosperity and health and at whose feet we fall seven times and seven times. Every day we pray to the great gods and to Amun to keep you strong. Now, see, let our lord the overseer know that the man who our lord the king has entrusted as chief over the four towns of Giybon is being led astray in his heart by wicked men. And he has in mind not to provide the produce from this land when it is the time of giving after the next new moon, even though it is a fair amount decided by our lord the king himself, who lives in prosperity and health. And you will know the truth of this because the giving will be late from his hand, and when one enquires after it he will say that travel on the roads is dangerous.
>
> And another matter. This same chief is even now arming a band of warriors to serve him day by day, not just to call upon in a season of need and threat as has always been done in this your land. Our lord will be diligent to enquire whether this warband shall be used to intimidate and unsettle those many town rulers who remain unswervingly loyal in their hearts to the great king who lives in prosperity and health. As though he was another like the wicked ruler of Pehela who his majesty overthrew in the heat of his just anger.
>
> And another matter. Your loyal people fear the retribution of this chief if he hears of this our letter to you, and our gratitude would be without limit if he does not know why you enquire after this.
>
> So let our lord the overseer decide on these matters as he sees fit in the service of the great sun over all

> the lands, who knows the wickedness of other men's hearts and is not deceived by it, and at whose feet we fall seven times and seven times again.

Damariel got up from the table he had been sitting at all this time, stretched, walked around the room several times, then hugged Nepheret.

"Now that is a most splendid piece of work, I think."

"So who will take it down to Gedjet for us? You cannot go, as we said while Eli was here with us. Far too conspicuous. Shall I go?"

Damariel shook his head and kept his arms around her.

"No. If he would suspect me, he will suspect you too. He would do to you exactly what he would do to me if he thinks news was spread because of either of us. I am not prepared to let that happen. So it cannot be either of us, certainly not while he thinks that we are harmless and obedient. And indeed, it should be someone who comes and goes from the town often enough that one more trip will not be noticed."

She leaned back against his arms and straightened her kef into proper hill country order again.

"Well, you cannot pick Danil or anyone close to him. If he did not understand the reason, he would take it straight to Mahur-Baal. And we simply do not know which of his party of raiders will remain loyal to us."

"It can only be Kothar, I think. He can take a trip along the ridge south towards Bayth Shamsh to hunt and trap and then cut across from there to Gedjet. It took us about two days when you first came up here with me, but we took a long road round by Yabneh to see Gilem. I think Kothar can do the trip in just one day each way if he knows what is to be his target, so if he is away for five or six days nobody will be the wiser about this. I will go and talk to him about the route."

She nodded, but looked at him very seriously.

"You must ask him, Damari, not just tell him which way to go. He needs to know everything about this, the reason why as well as the risks and the cost."

"Yes, of course, I'll go there now and tell him all about it."

He turned to go, but she held on to his shoulders and would not release him.

"I have not finished. Damari, from now on you must live as though anything you say or do in this town could be reported back to Mahur-Baal. By anyone. You have not ever learned to walk like that, but I have lived in houses where this kind of suspicion was the rule of life. Do nothing that is out of the ordinary and cannot be explained as an innocent act. So yes, of course you must see Kothar and explain it all to him. But do not just go and come back again as though that was the only reason for leaving the house. Visit others. See your family. Find out how it is for the long-suffering Tobiaz to actually be living with your mother the lady Yeresheth in her house every day instead of a few nights here and there. See Kalita and Yusuf and pray with them for the health of their eldest child. See Danil and ask if he wants to mark in any way the passing of a year since the death of Mahiram. And others. And in the midst of all that, see Kothar and if he is agreeable give him the tablet to take with him."

Damariel frowned.

"These are my own people, Nepheret."

"Yes, they are. I know that. So do not place them in a position where their loyalty and commitment to you might be tested beyond bearing. Allow them this dignity, so that ruin does not come to them or to you and I. Be sure that the paths you walk in front of them are so undeniably plain and beyond reproach that they remain your people in this very difficult place."

He took a deep breath, closed his eyes for a long moment, then caressed her cheek with one hand.

"I am not used to this, Nepheret."

"I know. But I have lived in households like this, back in the Beloved Land, not the house of the master in Gedjet where we first met. For the time being, walk as though you are already the slave of Mahur-Baal and anyone around you might be his eyes and ears. You do not know who you can trust and who not, so go about your business in the town with great diligence and with great caution. Then come back into this house and we will uphold each other at every sunset and every sunrise."

She kissed him, then pushed him firmly away.

"Now go and see all those people, and come back to me tonight when everything has been arranged."

A week later, Damariel was in one of the back rooms cleaning one of the vessels that held the blood of sacrifice in the autumn festival, when he heard voices in the kitchen area. It was Nepheret welcoming Kothar at the door, asking after his hunting trip and thanking him for the gift of three game birds. He gave the silver vessel a last rub, placed it carefully back in its cloth holder, and went through to see them. He was very anxious.

Kothar had clearly not yet gone back to Shaharti's house to clean himself, but he was brimming with energy and excitement. As Damariel entered he stopped describing the traps he had set along the edge of one of the ridges where the grouse had a run, and turned to him.

"And so I made the trip down to Gedjet following the landmarks you taught me, every one of them. Nobody from up here saw me, I am sure of it. I asked at the city gate where to go, not that they were very keen to tell a hillman like me, and went there. Put that thing of yours in the very hand of the scribe to the governor. Older than us, he was, bald as anything, spoke with a southern accent but he could read your stuff all right. I waited while he read it through three times, then he told me to carry back the message mouth to mouth, nothing committed to clay or wood or anything. He says to tell the writer that the matter is a grave one and that the governor himself would be told. Then they gave me some meat and drink, let me wait a while and off I went again. Camped out in the woods somewhere the other side of Bayth Shamsh, don't ask me where, and then back to the traps. No problems."

Damariel felt a wash of relief go over him and closed his eyes for a moment. The matter was in someone else's hands now, and Kothar had gone there and back again safely. Now it relied on the efficiency of the Mitsriy governance system. Could he rely on them to respond?

Looking up again, he saw that Kothar was hovering near the door, clearly eager to be gone. He thanked him profusely, told him he would be down in another day or so to hear more about the journey, then held the door so Kothar could slip swiftly out and go back down to Shaharti. He sat down then and looked at Nepheret.

"Will your people answer, do you think?"

She sat opposite him, slipped her kef off and draped it across her knees, as she often did while thinking.

"The governor should take action, if he is at all diligent. The trust placed in him requires him to take the writing seriously. Much more so than a report by word of mouth alone. That was why we took the time to write it properly. Now, the master in the house in Gedjet spoke well of him, so I have every hope that he will follow the matter through. Unless there are greater things that chance brings along at the same moment. Then he would weigh the one against the other and make a choice. Who can say what would happen then? But the balance should be in our favour, I think."

"So what do we do now?

"We wait. We carry on with our daily tasks as though nothing had changed."

Etanim had passed by, beginning with the autumn equinox, and given way to the month of Bul. Damariel and Nepheret stood with the other seers at the edge of the great high place up at Giybon. Eli had sent word to call all of them together on receiving word that the Mitsriy governor was sending a detachment of soldiers there, together with the chief scribe of the district. As expected, Mahur-Baal had not sent the tribute at the appointed time.

Exactly three weeks after the day it was due, three Mitsriy scouts, lightly armed and moving swiftly through the terrain, had arrived to enquire the reason. Hearing Mahur-Baal's reply about the hazardous roads they left again without comment. Two weeks after that Eli had received word from a friend at Bayth Shamsh that the soldiers were en route. Today they would arrive, and Eli had persuaded the chief that the most convincing response would be a show of solidarity of all the four towns together. As a result, all eight seers were waiting beside the stones, having spent some time with the chief who was keen to ensure that all their testimonies would agree.

A few representatives from each town were also there, with Mahur-Baal at the front of that group. A number of the residents of Giybon formed a loose ring at a little distance, eager to see what was happening but not at all eager to be too close. The seers had assembled together with the others in the middle of the morning, but it was almost noon when one of the village lads ran back from a vantage point he had picked, where there was a clear view for some distance along the track. They were coming.

The soldiers marched in formation, about fifty all told, fully armed, well organised, and clearly very experienced. A vanguard of half a dozen bowmen was followed by the main body of spearmen, each with a side-arm of sickle-shaped sword. Then came an officer and three scribes, one older and more authoritative than the others. A rearguard of another dozen bowmen completed the squad.

As they arrived, the soldiers peeled off left and right after passing through the town gate of Giybon and dispersed in small groups at intervals around the hilltop, scattered among the nearer houses and alleyways. The officer and chief scribe looked at Mahur-Baal, then at the group of seers, and chose to speak to Saniyahu as the eldest among the group of leaders.

The two more junior scribes waited at a distance, but were already looking here and there around the village as though making a rough and ready assessment of wealth. The officer spoke to Saniyahu.

"I am here concerning the overdue arrival of the allotted tribute from this town and its three daughter towns. To whom am I speaking? What is the reason for the late provision of goods?"

"I am Saniyahu, seer and priest at one of the daughter towns you speak of. The chief Mahur-Baal, victorious over his enemies and glorious in battle, who you see standing there, is the man who assessed the hazards on the roads down to Gedjet. He considered the risk to be excessively great to the goods that properly belong to the great sun over every land, who lives in prosperity and health."

Mahur-Baal nodded. The officer looked at Saniyahu for a long moment, then walked over to stand in front of Mahur-Baal. The chief scribe remained standing beside the group of seers.

"You are the man Mahur-Baal, permitted to serve as chief over these towns by the will of the great king in the Beloved Land, who lives in prosperity and health and is aware of the hidden motives of every man's heart?"

"I am."

"And it was your decision to withhold the goods?"

"The roads, my lord. They have become hazardous to travel upon. If you have wealth in goods with you, that is. See, I did not want the wealth of the king my lord to go astray."

The officer looked at him in silence. Mahur-Baal made as if to speak again, but then clenched his hands and said nothing. The silence stretched out. He collected himself a second time with a visible effort and opened his mouth to speak, but the officer interposed.

"But naturally you have kept the required goods in a safe place."

"I have, my lord."

"Where are they?"

"In the storehouse just there, my lord, just beside my own house so that I could assure myself of their safety night and day."

The officer glanced at the chief scribe, who in turn signalled the two scribes to go to the building indicated. As they started towards it, Mahur-Baal turned to Yaraq and gestured that he should go with them. The officer held up one hand to stop him before he could move.

"My scribes do not require help. They are well able to check the tally of the required goods by themselves."

There was a pause. The officer stood waiting in the sunshine, dappled by little clouds high above them. To break the silence, Mahur-Baal spoke again.

"You know my lord, I am most grateful that my lord the overseer takes so seriously the matter of safety on the roads. We are relieved that he has not neglected us."

The officer frowned.

"Are you suggesting that he might have forgotten his responsibilities?"

"No, no, not at all, my lord. I was not at all suggesting that. How could my lord the overseer ever forget any of his duties? I only meant that his humble servants are always happy to be reminded of his attentiveness to us."

He trailed off in the face of the impassive, slightly amused expression on the officer's face, who made no effort to help the chief. Silence fell, and stretched out as they all stood there in the drifting autumn sunshine.

At last the two scribes came back out into the light again and spoke briefly to the chief scribe in their own language. He listened to their report, then nodded briefly to the officer who had half-turned to watch the exchange, and now looked back at Mahur-Baal.

"Happily the full total of required goods has remained safe so close beside your own house."

Mahur-Baal nodded in relief.

"Then may I extend the hand of hospitality to my lord so that he might enjoy the fruits of our little land?"

"I must not accept, in case others misunderstand the generous gift you offer. But you and I will talk a little in private now so that I may make a full account of all this to my superior. The chief scribe will talk at the same time to your own priests to assure ourselves that all is well. Appoint men under the authority of these two scribes here to bring the full quantity of goods out here beside these stones while we talk. Once everything is out here my own soldiers will assume responsibility."

Mahur-Baal, clearly uncomfortable with the whole situation, looked across at Eli and the others. Under the pressure of the continuing gaze of the officer he spoke briefly to Yaraq to organise workers, then led the officer into his house. Yaraq called half a dozen men to begin moving the sacks and other goods into the ring of the stones, where each item was opened, rechecked and marked off on a leather roll by one or other of the scribes.

The chief scribe collected all eight seers into a tight group just outside the stone circle. He was noticeably more frail than the other Mitsriy, and seemed glad of the chance to be seated on one of the stones. He carefully unpacked his own writing set, with a very pale, thin leather roll, three colours of ink and a beautifully carved reed pen to use with them.

Damariel, watching as Mahur-Baal and the officer went towards the house of the chief, saw Asherith looking out of the window, then opening the door for them as they approached. The officer bowed slightly to her as he came up to the lintel, then said something that Damariel could not possibly hear across the distance. She nodded, drew herself up, and welcomed them in as though into a palace. Glancing around, he saw that Birketh had also seen the exchange with approval.

The chief scribe kept them as a group at first, asking them a series of questions about the tribute and jotting down quick answers on the leather roll. Damariel, acutely aware of Nepheret's warning eyes on him, ensured that his own answers kept within the agreed boundaries.

Yes, the tribute had been gathered up at Giybon before the date it was due. Yes, it was always kept together at Giybon on behalf of them all. No, he had no recent experience of travelling on the roads down to Gedjet. Yes, he had heard that the chief was anxious about the possibility of capture or theft. No, he had not heard that personally from the chief himself, but indirectly through conversations with Eli.

Then the scribe took each couple in turn to one side and asked them about details from their own town. Damariel and Nepheret were last to be taken out of earshot of the others, and when they had gone to one side the scribe turned to Nepheret and spoke at some length in their own language, standing and speaking with her as an equal. Damariel, still not fluent in the Mitsriy tongue, nevertheless caught most of the exchange between them.

The scribe called her a daughter of the great river and invoked a blessing over her life beyond the borders of the Beloved Land, and Nepheret in turn told him of her family, her place of birth, her new home. The scribe switched back to Kinahny, and the subsequent conversation was surprisingly brief, no more than a notional confirmation of what had already been said in the group. After that they were led back to be with the other seers.

The day was fine and becoming warm. Most of the townspeople had drifted away from the stones some time before and had gone back at their usual daily work. The tribute was being watched over in a heap by the stones by about half the soldiers. The other half, still in groups of three of four, were walking around all points of the village, taking note of the layout of houses and paths and the terrain beyond them.

Eventually the officer emerged again from the house into the sunshine with the chief following along behind. Mahur-Baal looked weary, and wore an expression as though he had narrowly escaped great danger. The officer came over to the chief scribe and the two talked in low voices for a while. Apparently satisfied, the officer sized up the pile of tribute and then turned back to Mahur-Baal.

"See, lord, here then is all of the king's produce as agreed."

"Who lives in prosperity and health and is the great sun over all the lands."

"Yes, of course."

The officer waited, and after a little pause Mahur-Baal continued.

"Yes indeed. Of course. The king who lives in prosperity and health and is the great sun over all the lands."

"Excellent. Now, there remains only the matter of the goodwill offering to turn eyes away from the late delivery of these goods."

The chief swallowed, looked bleak, and glanced here and there at the groups of soldiers nearby.

"My lord, I am not familiar with that."

"It has not been necessary to tell you about it before today. In this case, considering your swift cooperation and the fact that the required goods had already been gathered together before I arrived with my men, I shall accept four donkeys to carry the produce, together with a weight of silver equal to this my staff of office, and..."

He paused and looked across at the chief scribe who held up his left hand and sketched a quick sign in the air. "...and let us say three small bags of food to meet the reasonable needs of my men who were not expecting to have to make their way up into your hill country. Or the whole value in silver, the choice is yours. So long as gathering the additional items does not cause us excessive delay. Or additional cost."

The officer smiled pleasantly, but Mahur-Baal shifted nervously before turning to Yaraq again.

The silver was retrieved from his own house and balanced against the weight of the staff, and the extra food was collected from some nearby households together with the donkeys. The soldiers, grinning amongst themselves, started loading the beasts. Just as they were finishing, the officer turned once more to the chief.

"Perhaps you can help with one more small item, just a little thing now. The wife of my commanding officer has always been enthusiastic about the metal work done up here by you Kinahny in the hill country. More delicate, she says, than the coastal craft work. Now, of course I could look elsewhere, but if you had something small I could take back, a pin for a cloak perhaps, or for one of your headscarfs, then, well, I would be very grateful for your assistance, and my men would be grateful not to have to march to another village, and my commanding officer would be grateful too for the opportunity to please his wife. So much gratitude from such a small trinket. I don't suppose you would have such a thing to hand?"

Mahur-Baal, his expression stony, looked around at the villagers nearby and called one of the women over who had a silver clasp in her kef. Looking up at the officer, she unclipped it and placed it into his hand. He gave a little bow.

"Lady, I am deeply grateful. May your family and your lineage be fruitful for tens of thousands of generations and may your name be remembered always in your home and in this place. Chief, I am certain that you would not want the generous heart of this lady to suffer loss. So naturally you will make good the value of the item to her and her family. She has, after all, helped both me and you."

Mahur-Baal nodded. The officer turned to go, then turned back again.

"How could I forget? How careless of me. Do you require any payment for this little clip the lady has given me?"

Mahur-Baal shook his head, his face very grim.

"Of course not, my lord. Consider it a gift from my people to yours."

"Excellent. How happy is my heart that this whole matter has been resolved so peacefully. I am quite certain now that the roads will be less perilous by the time the spring rains come."

"Lord, now that your troops have shown themselves along the trackways again, I am sure that the thieves and vagabonds that blocked the way before will go elsewhere, and journeys will be easy in the spring."

The Mitsriy officer nodded again, and turned to scan around the village and the surrounding land, as though like his men before, he was estimating its defensive capability. Then he called to his men, who arranged themselves into roughly the same formation as before but now with the four donkeys in the middle, and set off down the track.

As the chief scribe passed the group of seers, he looked at Nepheret and inclined his head briefly in acknowledgement before moving on. The group of Mitsriy moved away, and as they disappeared from view around a curve in the path, Mahur-Baal sighed deeply in profound relief and turned to Yaraq.

"That could have gone much worse, you know. The officer reminded me what had been done up at Pehela. But not here, they left me in my rightful place. We got off lightly, Yaraq."

Yaraq said nothing, but looked without expression at the chief and turned away to go back to his house. Mahur-Baal, hardly noticing, walked up and down for a few moments, then took off his kef to wipe the sweat away from his head. He sat on one of the nearby stones and shook his head.

The woman who had given the clasp from her kef was still standing close at hand, uncertain whether to stay or to go. He had not noticed her. The edge of her kef flapped idly in a breath of breeze.

Birketh started to move towards her, but Asherith came across from the door of the chief's house and took her arm. Kissing her on both cheeks, she took the clasp from her own kef and fastened the woman's kef with it. Little flecks of lapis lazuli stood out dark against the silver and the woman touched it gently where it lay against her throat.

Asherith looked at the chief, who was still sitting on the stone with his gaze fixed on the path where the group of Mitsriy had gone. She came over and stood in front of him, so that her shadow broke into his thoughts. He looked up at her.

"My lord the chief, I have made good to Hurriy the gift of jewellery that she made to the Mitsriy officer. I am sure that you would want to honour her like this."

Mahur-Baal stirred, looked at both women, and grimaced slightly when he saw the value of what had been given. He glanced at Birketh who had moved nearby, and then nodded after a short pause.

"Hurriy. Yes, you did well to be close at hand to please that officer with your gift. It was right to honour you for that and make good what you gave away."

He looked again at the costly clip, then back at Asherith, cold and distant.

"Ornaments and jewellery can always be replaced."

He stood and walked over to the seers.

"My thanks to all of you for your support. I am grateful for your loyalty to me and to all of the four towns."

Saniyahu replied on behalf of them all.

"Nothing owed, my chief. I am sure your gratitude will find ways to express itself in time. I think perhaps that the Mitsriy officer found the combined testimony of eight to be more compelling than a single voice, whoever that might belong to. There is advantage in numbers."

Mahur-Baal pulled a face.

"Well, today it was a good thing."

The group started to break up, each heading back to their own home or their own village. Kenizzi and Sallarsheh left first. Damariel and Nepheret talked briefly to Halith, then took their leave of Eli and Birketh and set off together down the track to Kephrath. The little tablet, with its wedge-and-clay message, had not been mentioned from first to last.

Qoph

MERAP – IBALATU YEAR 25

NOW THE BLOOD-RUSH makes my body tremble –
new agreements stretch across the land –
no deceit, no need now to dissemble –
noisy revels pass from hand to hand.

NEPHERET WAS WALKING up the track back towards her home after seeing Kalita and her youngest child, who was just recovering from one of the childhood ailments. Nearing the high place, she saw that several of the villagers were clustered in a little group around two donkeys. There was noise and bustle, and other people were being drawn towards the place even as she was.

Coming closer, she saw that a trader was sitting there in the shadow of the town gate, accompanied by a young boy who might perhaps be his son. Or perhaps not. They both had the clothing and mannerisms of one of the tribes across the Valley, and the trader was finding that the inhabitants of Kephrath were more interested in his news than his wares. Seeing Nepheret approaching and evidently making a quick decision about her based on the look of her kef, he turned to speak with her.

"Lady, I have incense with me that you must try. Out of the east. I have carried it several weeks now and every single village seer and priest I have met has begged me for more. But I have saved a little for you."

She looked at it, came to a quick conclusion that it was not of much interest, and shrugged a little.

"How is your trade here among us?"

The man pulled a face.

"Hardly worth me staying longer. You all keep wanting news, as though news was free to tell. I would remember more, and talk more, if the trade was better."

She nodded, squatted down beside one of the children and sent her off to get some bread and wine from her house, and looked into one the panniers he had opened.

"I have need of some cloth for a skirt, if you have anything suitable?"

He brightened.

"Just the thing, lady."

He rummaged underneath some little figurines of naked pregnant women, amulets with pictures of animals arranged among poorly executed Mitsriy signs, and pots of assorted contents, and pulled out a piece of cloth.

"Here, see this one, lady. Excellent stuff."

"Scarcely long enough."

She saw his mood turning, sensed his imminent departure.

"But perhaps it would do for a friend's child. Yes. I think it is just right for that. I know exactly who it would suit. And look, in that pot, is that kohl, or something close enough that I can use as kohl?"

"Ah, indeed it is, lady. True kohl, real quality. This was going down to Gedjet for the Mitsriy ladies there, but supposing I were to trade some of it here first then there would be no loss. Do you know good kohl when you see it?"

"Extremely well. The lady of a house I served in once was most particular about her eyes, and she trained me well what to look for. In the end she trusted me to buy it all for her."

He looked at her dubiously, clearly trying to estimate the truth of the telling but still not really seeing her behind the fringe of her kef. She looked back at him unblinking.

"Well, in all truth then I have to tell you it is not the best of the season. In fact it has not been a very good year at all. This is what your lady might perhaps have called second grade. But good for all that, you wouldn't want to miss it."

"Then I will think of a price, and these good people will look at your other wares, and while we do that you can please us with all the news you have heard on your long journey."

The girl came back from the house at that point, carefully carrying a little plate with sweetened bread and a small juglet of wine. Damariel had appeared at the door with her, and was watching the scene from under the leaves of the vine. She made a brief sign to him, and he nodded and turned back in. The trader watched him return inside with some regret.

"Would the seer there be interested in the incense? Or some good herbs for fever?"

"If you can interest me, I can interest him. Not, I think, your incense. But you were telling us news from the Valley."

She picked up another pot, delicately unstopped the lid, and sniffed the contents. She nodded and put it to one side. Beside her, one of the village men was looking at a set of metal clasps. Settling back against a rock and nudging the boy with him to spread out the goods from the other panniers over the stone beside them, he started to talk about things that were happening down in the Valley and up in the rugged heights on the other side. It was not very interesting at first, tales of unknown chiefs and war band leaders vying with one another for control of towns and settlements none of them had heard of.

"And then there's another lot, nomads, moved up from the south somewhere. Kept to their own camp for the most part until they got provoked by one of the little princelings up there. Well, they didn't take that lying down. Tricked his raiding band in an ambush, forced their way into his town and killed him, took what they wanted and burned his house over his son's head, then off again. Didn't want to live in the place, but they weren't going to put up with aggravation. After that they all went back into their camp and kept to themselves. Nobody bothers them now."

"The Mitsriy would call them Shasu, I think."

He looked at her again, this time finally seeing past the kef she wore.

"You know, lady, I'm thinking perhaps you'd know a lot about what the Mitsriy would think about this and that."

She smiled and put another jar of herbs to one side.

"Well, as you can see, I live here in the hill country, married to the seer who lives in the house there. You don't know my family, and I don't know yours. But I might know a little of what a Mitsriy person would value."

One or two of the townspeople grinned, enjoying the verbal play between them while they browsed. Rivkah, wearing a sprig from her honeysuckle tree, picked up some ribbons and a little piece of woven brocade, holding it against her neck and looking to Nepheret for her reaction. Nepheret considered, then nodded and put the items beside the little pile of goods collecting to one side. Rivkah ran another piece of cloth through her fingers and shook her head.

"But those towns over there are poor and pitiful, and their leaders are corrupt and weak. Everyone knows that. To think that they would be taken in so easily by some group living in tents."

"Well, lady, I won't say you're wrong. But this lot are very determined, and they're well used to war. And you're right that over the Valley they're not used to defending themselves. But I wonder how you'd do on this side if they ever came up here with an eye for land?"

"My husband leads the raiders from here. He'd know how to look after us."

"I'm sure he would, lady. And I dare say he'd appreciate this little holder for a dagger now. With real Mitsriy spells on it. Think how much better you'd feel if he went fighting, knowing you'd given it to him."

Nepheret watched as Rivkah wavered, obviously feeling slightly cornered. She put her hand on Rivkah's and came to her rescue.

"I don't think there'll be a need for war up here. We won't be causing provocation in their tents, and we don't have much wealth to cause envy. But look now, sir, isn't it true that the people have declined in numbers over the years across the Valley as they have here? And even more, perhaps?"

The man shrugged.

"Perhaps you're right. Who can say?"

There was more haggling, and in the end both the trader and the villagers felt they had achieved a good transaction. Later. long after the trader, his boy, and his donkeys had moved on, Damariel listened with interest to the account of the nomads.

"Is that an answer, Nepheret? A people from over the River?"

"Why would a group of tent people help us? What can we possibly offer them in exchange for their help?"

He thought about it.

"Some land, maybe, for a holy place they can come to for festivals? Or assured access to springs and wells? Or maybe we can goad Mahur-Baal into provoking them like those chiefs you talked about out there."

"So long as they know their quarrel is with the chief and not the people."

The new moon celebration the following month was, to say the least, lively; indeed the most lively that she had yet seen. A little while before, only a week or two after the Mitsriy soldiers had come to collect the overdue goods, Mahur-Baal had sent down a request for more tribute to be collected from each of the towns. It had been presented as a way to share out the burden of the extra tribute claimed. On the whole that had been accepted with only a little grumbling, though some could not see why the sole decision of Mahur-Baal should rebound upon everyone else.

But now there had been a second request. Once again, the chief had sent messengers down seeking gifts from Kephrath and the other towns, and the mood of the townspeople had turned hostile. In response, Damariel had let it be known that after the time of devotion, there would be a time when the whole adult community could come together to talk about it, and decide on a course of action. Well over half of the community had gathered.

Since it was hardly more than a month since the last request, the grumbling had turned to outright resentment. He was asking for another collection nearly half the size of the regular twice yearly offerings, but out of season and so soon after the previous tribute. Many were now asking questions. What was the reason? What extra benefit would flow down to Kephrath? The request, briefly written by Eli on a spare pottery tile, had been sent down by Yaraq and half a dozen other men, leaving little doubt of the chief's ability to back up the request with force.

The real question, the one which had occupied Nepheret and Damariel for much of the week as they talked with each other and with disgruntled villagers, was whether force would in fact be used if a crisis came. Would Mahur-Baal resort to that? Would the men with him, most of whom had friends and relations in each of the towns, obey him if it came down to a confrontation?

Nobody knew, and the uncertainty lay like a heavy mist over the town.

After the celebration, Damariel had opened the whole issue for anyone to offer their opinion. After a slow start, with hesitation and some awkward silences, opinions were offered, in some cases heavily laden with emotion.

Danil and a few others had spoken out in favour of the additional sum, on the grounds that the chief knew the wider picture, and that he provided protection that would be needed if the Mitsriy continued to withdraw from the hills.

Others disagreed, pointing to the swift response that had come two months ago when the tribute was late. Many families had widows and orphans in their care, and were concerned how the winter would be if supplies were taken now.

The debate went on for some time. Nobody except Damariel and Nepheret had read the few extra words that Eli had carefully written onto the edge of the sherd: "now is not the time". But how could they steer the discussion into that direction without offending the needy?

Danil and Yusuf ended up on their feet shouting at one another. At that point Nepheret also stood up in her place and waited, watching them both. First one, then the other noticed her, stopped, and sat down. Her experience in one household and another had given her an aptitude at managing the diverse undercurrents in meetings like this, which most of those born in Kephrath did not have. Now, as on other occasions, it was a useful skill to deploy.

"Friends, we need a middle course. I do not think we can ignore or refuse the chief's request. But we all know there are those among us who cannot meet the request in all its fullness. They do not have enough to give what he asks and support their family. I propose we send up to Giybon one part in three of what is requested, with an undertaking that as soon as possible a second part will follow. One part in three is fair considering that about two months have passed since the autumn gift. And we must make clear that we are unable to meet any more demands this side of the spring gift, and the amount requested then must be no greater than is usual. Damariel and I will spend more time trading with nearby towns to earn wealth from the work of your hands. Perhaps the chief is too busy with his new responsibilities to be conducting this trade as he used to in the days before I lived with you."

She paused, looked around, and sat down again. Different voices around the circle started again.

"But we already gave once over for his loss in challenging the Mitsriy."

"He is our chief. He needs these things so he can protect us. It is his right."

"His father would never have done this. I remember he once overlooked the gift completely when there had been a hard winter."

"Times have changed since those days. We need his men to protect us."

"A chief doesn't have to do things this way. There have been chiefs in the past who did things quite differently. I think we all remember that. My family certainly remembers those days, even if some families have forgotten."

The last speaker was Kalita. There was a little silence when she spoke, and she looked around the circle as though weighing up different people's opinions. It might have been many generations since her family had produced a chief, but few people had any doubt what she was working towards with her words. Yusuf certainly had no doubts, and he was gathering himself to say something to follow after Kalita when Damariel stood to speak instead. Words once spoken were hard to recall again, and he did not want Yusuf compromising his position in the four towns or running afoul of Mahur-Baal's ambitions.

"At this time there is no question about chiefs who might do things differently, and there is no question of the town's loyalty to the chief. We must provide a response before the next new moon, and it must be a cautious one. We must also ensure that the other towns are aware of our choice and that extra burdens do not fall on them as a result. If we follow Nepheret's plan of offering one part in three – and I think it is a good plan – then Meyim and Woodlands must do the same. I will go to Meyim, Nepheret to Woodlands and confirm this with the other seers. What we do not have we cannot give."

"Why should we give him any more than we already have done?"

"He will send his men down to take it anyway. He'll send that Yaraq down. I don't want him round my house or my children. I don't trust him."

"But we can look after ourselves. Danil and his men will take care of us. They'll look after our side in this."

People looked at Danil. He was obviously uncomfortable at the attention he was receiving with this turn of events, and his gaze was fixed on the ground. He did not reply at first, and in the gap Tamguta spoke up.

"I'd certainly take Kephrath's part. My loyalty is here before ever it goes up the hill to Giybon."

A few of the other raiders nodded, but Danil finally spoke, in a voice only just audible around the circle.

"We ought to send the tribute. We cannot send nothing. It is his right as chief to gather it in, you know."

Rivkah, who was next to him, leaned towards him.

"Danil, you know him better than I. Surely he wouldn't send Yaraq and his men to take it by force, would he?"

When Danil refused to answer, refused to look at her, she touched his arm, insistent.

"You would protect us if he came down like that to take things from us, wouldn't you? Danil?"

Danil remained silent, and she recoiled a little away from him, After that, although there was some desultory disagreement it was of a token nature. Nobody felt strongly enough to force the issue further.

"Why does he not make up the extra from his own wealth?"

"It's not his wealth he's spending, but Asherith's."

"You mean Asherith the daughter of Iqnu? Better then that her wealth goes back to the towns. Does she deserve any help from us?"

As the discussion died down, Nepheret kept watching Danil. He was still avoiding people's eyes, and conspicuously not talking with Rivkah. He glanced in little arrow darts around the group when he could do so without making contact with another. Later that night, as she lay beside Damariel in the dark of their room, she told him what she had seen.

"Danil is like a ship foundering in the sea, Damari. He may not survive all the waves as they come at him from this side and that."

He turned to face her.

"He has never been strong in his convictions, and Mahur-Baal gives him strength of purpose that is not in his own nature. I think if it comes down to it that nothing in Kephrath, not even Rivkah, will hold him back from the chief's side. At the moment we cannot afford to force the issue."

A month later, Kothar came back from one of his regular trips along the trap-lines south towards Bayth Shamsh. The crisis that had called for the meeting in Kephrath had come and gone, and the chief had appeared to accept, albeit with an ill grace, the reduced amounts that each of the towns had sent.

Clearly he was also unsure of his ground and was unwilling to force the matter just yet. As usual, Kothar called first at their house on his return.

Nepheret was outside by the standing stones when he arrived, and went over with him to open the door of the house. Damariel was in the middle of making a copy of a tablet that Kenizzi had sent across to him from Meyim recently, but he stopped when he heard Kothar's voice and joined them. Greetings over, Kothar sat on one of the stools in the kitchen area.

"The oddest thing happened on my way back. I was up along the ridge that runs towards Meyim from Bayth Shamsh and I heard voices on the track below. Sounded a bit like yours, Nepheret, or rather like some of the Mitsriy we heard up at Shean that time, but speaking Kinahny. Well, speaking it after a fashion. Half a dozen of them, just setting up camp for the evening. Not in a very good place, though, like they don't know the land. I wouldn't have stopped where they did. So anyway I watched them for a bit and decided they weren't minded to be aggressive, hid my stuff up a ways under an outcrop and then came around to join them along the track so they wouldn't think I was creeping up on them."

Damariel nodded patiently and handed him a juglet of water. "Here, you'll need this before the story is done. I suppose it turned out to be a long lost relative of yours determined to give you treasure."

Kothar laughed.

"Not quite like that, no. But I could make the tale even longer in the telling if you wanted me to."

"Not if you're wanting to get back to Shaharti before the night is gone."

"So it turns out that they're scouts from some group of people that have been camping out across the River. Their main camp seems to be on this side now, somewhere right down in the Valley. I don't remember the name. They'd been sent to find out what was where here on this side, the big towns and such like. I could tell them a bit, here and there, but you know, Damari, I'm not that well up on all those places. You could have told them a lot more than I could."

"They sounded like Mitsriy?"

"Well, Nepheret, yes and no. I mean, they were talking Kinahny like us, near enough, with a few odd words I didn't follow. But then again they sounded like the Mitsriy I heard with Damari up at Shean that time. When he and I went up there before you joined us here in Kephrath. Like they were speaking a mixture of the two tongues together. They call themselves Ibriym."

Damariel and Nepheret exchanged glances.

"Look, Kothar, did they talk at all about what had happened over the River? Do they want to stay here or move on?"

"I couldn't say for sure. They seemed friendly enough to anyone that would help them. Good company of an evening around a fire. Seems they'd had to fight a bit over the Valley on the other side, one or two of the little chiefs gave them trouble. Then there was some sort of dispute at a village on this side and they lost a dozen or so men in a skirmish that nobody wanted."

He paused and gesticulated as though in a fight.

"So their leader, an older man called Yahusharar apparently, called them all back together, took stock, and then set an ambush, made the score even and then some. I don't think they really know what they want - sometimes they square up for a fight, other times they just up camp and move on. If there's a pattern to it all, I couldn't tell it from listening to them. Not sure they could either. I don't think they all agree among themselves. This Yahusharar though, he seems to want to make a home for them up here in the hills somewhere, but hasn't decided where they'll settle yet."

"So where did you leave them?"

"Oh, they'll have moved on from where I met them. But their main camp is only a morning's journey from here. Down in the Valley. Give them another few days and they could be up here so you can see them for yourselves."

Not long after that, Kothar left, having described for them in more detail where the main encampment was pitched in the Valley.

"Nepheret, we have to make sure that we meet these people before the chief does. It has to be the same group of people that the trader talked about a while ago. But now they've crossed over onto our side of the River."

"You're looking at them as possible allies?"

"It can't harm to talk with them. And it sounds like they have more quarrel with town leaders than they do with the people. A visit from the seer of a town might be just what they want. Above all we must not let him ally with them first."

"I think a visit from both seers in the town would be better."

He looked at her, his anxiety very clear to them both.

"I don't know that's a good idea. We don't know how they might react."

"If they react by speaking Mitsriy, what will you do? For sure you have been learning, but we both know you are not fluent. If they sound like my people, perhaps I will understand them better than you."

"What if they despise your people and ran away from them? If you are there, how will that be anything other than a provocation?"

"I think we have to take that chance. The gain we could get because I know how they will think will be considerable. More than the risk, for sure. And you forget, I can tell my story so that I too ran away from a Mitsriy master."

The next day they made their way down from Kephrath into the Valley, carefully bypassing Giybon and Meyim, which lay either side of the direct path there. As they had dropped down the last few steep hillsides they had seen the smoke of campfires and heard the noises of occupation, but had encountered nobody. Now they were on the fringe of the trees overlooking the Ibriym encampment.

It was situated in a large bow of the River, and a recently dug ditch formed an adequate defensive perimeter on the open side. A little to their left a sizeable track, which had clearly seen heavy use in the last few weeks, swept out of the trees and crossed the ditch to disappear in among the patchwork of tents. Some men were stationed as lookouts at the crossing point. Small groups of the Ibriym were coming and going into the trees to hunt game or gather green herbs and dry wood. The whole area, normally a rather empty part of the Valley, was alive with the activity of the newcomers.

The camp itself was roughly square, insofar as the arc of the River and a few encroaching outcrops of rock allowed, and was divided into unequal regions of tents by interior paths. Nepheret supposed that, like islands in the inundation that she remembered from childhood, the tent groups were occupied by different families. The people she could see wore a range of brightly coloured kefs, and for a moment she was reminded of the flower fields that filled the hill country in the spring time.

Damariel touched her arm and pointed across to the large path. They looked at one another, each gauging the other's resolve, then stepped out from among the trees towards the main path and the group of lookouts. They were seen almost at once. One of the men nudged his companions and pointed, then another left the group and disappeared from view among the tents. They crossed over the open space, came up to the ditch and crossed it using the track. The men watched them as they came, making no effort to either greet or challenge them until they were very close. At that point one of them called out to stop and identify themselves. They spoke Kinahny, but with a strong southern accent.

She judged from their conduct that they expected Damariel to speak for both, so she kept silent and studied them while he replied. Her first thought was that they tied their kefs differently. It was an amusing thought really, since it was less than two years since she had ever tied one on herself. But it had become second nature now, except when she was in deep thought or prayer when she still preferred her hair unbound. So now, these people tied their kefs differently, and when they spoke it was with something of the lilt of her own people. Damariel had bowed his head in respect to the one who had addressed them.

"I am Damariel and this is Nepheret. We serve our people as priest and priestess up in the woods about half a day's journey up there."

He pointed back up the ridge behind them.

"My people came down from the north a little while ago, a journey of many months, and now we live here in four towns. The journey was long and hard in our memory, and our food and supplies ran short as we came. Now we are eager to welcome you as newcomers who have also made your way into this land, and offer to share what we now enjoy of its goodness with you."

The men looked at each other.

"You must speak with Yahusharar of this."

"He is your chief?"

"He is our appointed warleader. For now we have no chief, but Yahusharar instructs the family heads, until the time comes for us to settle in a land of our own."

At that point the man who had gone away earlier came back, and there was a brief conference too quietly spoken for Nepheret to catch. Then they were led away into the interior of the camp. There was a central open space for the people to gather, with a separate tent surrounded by decorated curtains, which she assumed was these people's equivalent of the high place at Kephrath. One of the labourers at the house at Gedjet, a metalworker, had once described something similar he had seen out at the copper mines in the desert, where nomadic groups carried out seasonal labour.

Fanning out in quadrants from the central area were tents to live in, storage areas, and roped pens for animals. It looked confusing, but she presumed there was a pattern that was obvious if you lived there. As she walked, listening idly to the voices coming from the tents around her, she caught the rhythms of a song that were the rhythms she had been used to since childhood. Whoever these people were, they sang songs like the people of the village of her youth.

They were led to a particular tent not far from the central area, and a little to the west of it. A stocky man with greying hair and a shrewd, calculating look in his eye came out to meet them and ushered them inside. It was cool and light inside, with internal partitions screening most of the interior from view, so that they seemed to be sitting in just one room of a larger house. At his invitation, they sat on wooden stools.

"They have told me that you two are priests for a people who have come down from the north recently. But that you live in towns near here now. You have heard that we have come and want to welcome us. What else should I know?"

Damariel spoke of Kothar's recent meeting with the scouts, and when he paused, Yahusharar turned to Nepheret. He had been scrutinising both of them while Damariel had spoken.

"Perhaps you have not come down from the north like these others have?"

Nepheret glanced at Damariel. This was no part of the plan they had made concerning the conversation, but having heard the singing in the camp she felt on solid ground.

"No, honoured sir. I came out of the land of the Mitsriy as a slave, and now I am a free woman and seer, married to Damariel here. Perhaps we share a common past."

The older man smiled slightly.

"Perhaps we do. But glad as I am to be greeted so courteously by you both, I do not yet see what we have to do with each other."

Nepheret and Damariel exchanged glances, before Nepheret spoke again.

"Sir, I think your people want to abandon these tents and build houses and villages instead. We can help you to choose the best places to live, the springs and wadis that do not dry in a long summer, the hillsides where the land is best for terracing. We can be your allies as you settle."

"Do I need allies? Damariel, tell me who lives there that would mean I need allies."

"That depends where you intend to settle and how wide an area you intend to spread into. There are a few towns in the hill country, north and south of here, and there are larger ones as you descend the other side into the lowlands. In the several generations we have been here we have made some friends in the hill country, but have not usually been on good terms with the lowland towns. Up the Valley is Bayth Shean, with a considerable Mitsriy occupation. Another garrison down in Gedjet, near the coast. Other towns here and there have garrisons. All this we can tell you in detail, as well as good places to live. We have heard of your victories in this land so far, and while they are striking, they are haphazard. We can help you to make them great."

The other man thought for a while.

"So you have been in this land for several generations. Not so recently arrived from the north after all. Perhaps you want to ally with us so that we do not defeat you in battle instead. Are you simply afraid of us, and hiding your fear in pleasant words?"

"Should I be afraid of you? Or should I instead welcome your arrival as an opportunity to make new friends?"

Yahusharar nodded, slowly.

"Do you speak for your entire people? There are just two of you here, both from one town, but there are four towns full of your people. Perhaps not all of them think the same as you?"

Damariel hesitated, and seeing this, Yahusharar leaned back and watched him closely, waiting. Nepheret spoke into the pause.

"Sir, like all people everywhere, we do not always speak in a single voice, any more than all of your people agree on the best way to settle in the lands you come to. As seers and priests, we can speak for the greater part of our people. But your question touches on the very reason we have come. There is a man who has been our chief, and he has been consumed by the lust for power. We cannot speak for him. He is an ambitious man, and a greedy one. He has greatly increased the wealth and produce that he takes from us. He has lost the hearts of most of us in the four towns, even many who once embraced him with enthusiasm, and he keeps his power only because he has more swords at his command. Where he can no longer persuade, then now he compels."

She paused, and caught his eyes as he glanced up at her.

"He is wanting to become king instead of chief, and to rule with a powerful arm and an outstretched hand. You know what that means. I know that you do. An alliance with you will give heart to our people to drive him away."

Yahusharar looked down again. There was a long silence, with the camp noises clear outside the tent. Somewhere close by, a group of children were playing. Damariel nodded with relief at Nepheret. They both waited patiently for the leader of the Ibriym to speak, conscious that this was a delicate moment. Eventually he spoke, and the outside sounds receded into the background again.

"I have no great love of kings. A people should not need a king so long as they have love for their chief and their god."

He nodded decisively.

"I think we could do with at least one friend up there in the hill country. So many of our encounters have ended in conflict, and I suspect there will be more before we are done. We will not be treated badly by others without seeking restitution. But I do believe that an ally to stand at our backs up there would be a good thing. But tell me. You say you are seers and priests for your people?"

"For Kephrath, yes, There is another married couple in each of the towns."

"And can you eight reach agreement over this?"

"Here and now today, I can speak for six. The remaining two are uncertain but their loyalty to the chief wavers. It will take only a little thing to bring them across. Then the eight of us can speak with confidence for two families out of every three in the four towns. A small number will follow the chief come what may, and the rest are undecided."

"It will be enough for me if you secure the allegiance of these last two priests, if it is as you say for the people at large."

Damariel nodded in relief.

"I am sure these two will join us very soon."

"So tell me, then, what is the nature of the agreement between us?"

"What do you mean? Our custom is to swear an oath at a sacred place, make a sacrifice to show our commitment, arrange regular times to renew the oath, and then agree how and when we will come to each other's aid. And other benefits we promise each to the other."

"Yes. All very good. But that is not what I meant. What is the benefit to my people of this arrangement? The idea of having friends in the hill country is a good one, and I can easily see the advantage of it, but the heads of each of the families will be looking for a more tangible harvest."

Damariel and Nepheret looked at each other. Yahusharar continued.

"Let us say you expel your chief. A few will follow him, most will not. But perhaps he gathers his support, and then in a while comes back to cause trouble for you. By now you have a new chief. Let us say he comes from your town. You would know better than I about this. What do you think? Will the other towns rally to his call when he needs help against the old chief or not?"

Damariel thought about it.

"What are you proposing?"

"Perhaps your new chief will need to be sure we can come to his help. But my people have their own plans for settling in the land. Perhaps we are busy elsewhere, and all unwittingly fail to come to your help until it is too late. But if, say, there was an agreement to provide us with the needful things of life, just a little each month, why then you would be fresh in our minds, and we would be swifter to come."

Nepheret nodded.

"I understand. You would be like the district mayor, supported by the people and upholding them in their needs."

Yahusharar beamed at her.

"Exactly so. Now of course I must talk of this with the families, and you must talk with your people. We must ensure we are of one heart and one mind in all this. But it seems to me better that one of us would be placed in authority over your chief. You would remember him with regular provisions, and he would remember you with regular support."

"And the Mitsriy governor?"

"How do you mean?"

"At the moment our chief is held accountable for providing the Mitsriy with tribute twice a year, spring and autumn. We provide to him, he provides to them. Perhaps you would now take on that responsibility?"

After a pause, Damariel continued Nepheret's thought.

"Mahur-Baal, the chief for now, believes that the Mitsriy will abandon the hill country soon, at least for a while until they resolve other matters. Now, he tried withholding goods last autumn, but too soon. They were vigorous in their response, more so than he had expected. But perhaps in this he will be proved right in the end. If you were the means by which their demands were met, then a time might come when the wealth would stay in your hands. Who can say?"

Yahusharar nodded slowly, absorbing the information.

"I think we have come as far along the road as we can for today. I cannot promise more without speaking with others, and nor can you. But as token of the words we have spoken today, and in expectation of a binding promise between your people and mine, let us eat and drink together before we part. Is this acceptable to you?"

It was, and they shared a brief meal of bread and beer before Nepheret and Damariel threaded their way back through the tents into the wooded ridges. The time passed swiftly as they walked, talking of the encounter. They climbed up the ridge in shadow, but emerged into the late afternoon sunshine at the top, and the sun was still above the horizon as they joined the main track and wound past the caves of the ancestors to the town gate and high place of Kephrath.

The light of an oil lamp showed from inside their house, and the door was standing slightly ajar. Inside, Kenizzi and Sallarsheh were sitting waiting for them. Kenizzi stood as they came in, while Sallarsheh, heavily pregnant, remained seated.

"Damariel, Nepheret, forgive the intrusion."

"You must consider the house as your own."

"Sara said you would be back this evening, and welcomed us on your behalf. We have not been here very long."

Nepheret went over to the table and picked up a wax tablet that Eli had written. It had not been there in the morning. She glanced at the first line or two of writing and saw that it began "your chief is looking for another gift from his people". She sat down beside Sallarsheh.

"Did you bring this down?"

"Not at all. Runners from Giybon sent ones like it to each of the towns. Ours too, and that is why we have come here today. Nepheret, it is another demand, another demand for more tribute."

"So soon after the other?"

"So soon, Damariel, and not paying any attention to any of the things we said last time about what the people could afford. Damariel, Nepheret, I tell you he has gone too far this time. Much too far."

"How do you mean?"

"Meaning he is asking for a full half year gift now, before time, and so soon after the last two collections. And rather than keeping the amount the same, he has increased the demand, taking no account of all that has been given since the autumn. Damariel, my people cannot do this. It is too much for them."

Nepheret had been skimming through Eli's writing.

"It is the same here, it is just the same here for Kephrath."

Damariel shook his head.

"I do not think that Kephrath can sustain this giving either, not without great hardship."

"There is more. Not written down, but Eli met me and told me mouth to mouth. If the full amount is not collected and brought in to him at Giybon within a month, the chief will hold the seers responsible, all of us, all responsible. It is a pretext, Damariel, and he means to be rid of us. If by some miracle we gather all this together for now, there will be another demand in another month. And another. At some point the towns will fail, and he will remove us from our place."

Sallarsheh was nodding as he spoke, both hands cupped around the swell of her unborn child.

"I do not know what he might do to us."

Damariel looked at Kenizzi.

"I thought at one time you were in favour of what he was doing here in the four towns."

Kenizzi nodded.

"At one time I was. Until he tried to cheat the Mitsriy. That was a step too far. And now all this. It came to me that my loyalty was first to Meyim, not to him. I believed for a long time there was no conflict between the two."

He paused, and looked embarrassed.

"And the thought of having a wider ministry was exciting. But not at this cost. I will not be party to this. Now, Eli indicated that you might have a plan. I hope so, for if not what will any of us do?"

Damariel and Nepheret exchanged glances, trying to decide whether to tell the others about the arrival of the Ibriym. The pause stretched out, and Kenizzi's expression deepened from embarrassment to shame. Sallarsheh, hands still pressed against her womb, looked down at the table.

"Look, I can understand your hesitation. I have not stood properly side to side with you other seers this last year and more. But things have changed. This new tablet has put everything beyond doubt for me. I would like you to accept my apology and restore me to your confidence."

There was another pause, then as Damariel was still hesitating, Nepheret, weighing up the mood of the other pair, took it upon herself to decide.

"Yes, Kenizzi, Sallarsheh, there is a plan. We have been away even today trying to grow the plan from scattered seed to implantation. And in truth it can only come to birth if all eight of us stand as one in this. If we are divided amongst ourselves we will not be helped by others. So your arrival today is very timely. See now, it is late for you to take the track back to Meyim. Stay here tonight and we will say all we know about it. Then tomorrow we will talk to Saniyahu and Halith, and you will talk to Eli and Birketh. All without the knowledge of Mahur-Baal as yet."

Resh

HIYARU – NISAN YEAR 25

YAHU THE GREAT GOD is with him,
the shout of the King is in him.
El brought him out from the Mitsriy,
he bears the great strength of the Bull.

About two weeks after that, Damariel had called for another assembly of the townspeople. Indeed, each of the four towns was having its own meeting at the same time. Mahur-Baal was away with Yaraq and a couple of others, down in the lowlands at the town of Laksh, and it was no accident that the meetings were timed to coincide with his absence, He was not expected back for about a week, and on his return the deadline for the ingathering of goods would nearly be on them all. One way or another, a resolution had to be found.

Like the previous meeting, the people were gathered up at the high place. This time, so far as Damariel could see as he looked around, everyone had come. Parents had brought young children along rather than miss the meeting, and there were a lot of young people there who strictly speaking were not old enough to participate. Nobody objected. The lives and livelihood of everyone in the town was at stake, young and old alike.

He began by reading out in everyone's hearing the message the chief had sent, though by now he was fairly sure that everyone already knew the content. Then he placed the writing on one of the flat stones in clear view of everyone, the living and the dead.

"Each of the four towns has had the same message. Each of us is holding a meeting today to decide what to do about it. Nepheret and I have talked with the other seers already, at great length. We have had ideas about it, many of them, but first we would like to hear your thoughts."

"Damariel, you know we cannot do this. There is little enough in reserve after the half year and the other two collections just recently. There is not enough to meet this. You know that."

"Yes, Abiram. I know that very well. We have talked with many who are already in difficulty over the last few weeks, even before this latest message. Each of the towns is in the same position; none of us has any more in reserve to meet this."

"Nepheret, what happened to your plan to give only one part in three of the whole?"

She stood to speak.

"It was a fair plan, I think. It was a good plan at the time. But the chief has rejected it. Now we stand at a new turn in the river and must decide what to do next."

Yusuf jumped up as she sat down again.

"If he will not listen to his people, if he rejects what we say after we gave it a fair hearing, then I say that we should reject him. We have given to him over and over again these last few months. You all know that. What has he given in return? When has he even given the time to come down the track to be with us? Where is he today? Where has he been all these months? I say we give him nothing, and instead we take back from him the trust he does not deserve and has not earned."

Danil was shaking his head.

"He is the chief. What does it matter that do not understand what he does? We should trust him. The lowland kings do not explain themselves to their people. Why should he?"

"Because we have never done it that way up here in the hill country. If he wants to live like a lowland king, let him go and live in the lowlands with them now. Let him be king there, if they will have him. I say we will have no part of him."

Kinreth, across the circle from the two men, stood up.

"The chief has fighting men. To be sure he has paid for them with the wealth that once was ours, but just now they are by his side and at his command. What do we have here in the towns to match that? Here in Kephrath? Danil, last time you said that you would side with the chief if it came to a choice. Is that still true?"

"It is. I trust him even if I do not understand what he is doing just now. That is what loyalty means."

Tamguta stood.

"I will not side with the chief. I said it last time we gathered, and I will say it again now for everyone to hear. My loyalty is to my kinfolk and to my neighbours."

Several of the other raiders nodded as he said this, but others were evidently siding with Danil. Little individual clumps of conversation were springing up all around the circle, when Danil suddenly jumped to his feet and pointed at Damariel.

"This is all your doing. You just want revenge because Qetirah died that day. You'd do anything to get rid of him. This has nothing to do with what is happening in the towns."

He stared defiantly around the circle.

"Don't listen to him. It's all just his own personal thirst for revenge. Nepheret, I'm sorry that you have to hear this, but this is all about his first wife. Maybe you didn't know that."

Damariel looked pained and turned his face away from the circle to where the rock faces of the tombs loomed against the hillside. Kinreth and Caleb were talking together, Kinreth clearly very angry. Nepheret stood and confronted Danil.

"Danil, I know all about Qetirah that was the daughter of Kinreth, and who was married to Damariel before. I have no guilt and no shame about my life and my new home here in Kephrath with you all. None. And so I can tell you all here today without a shadow of doubt that the matter before us today has nothing to do with Qetirah. Even now she walks by the pools and in the fields on the other side with the blessed dead. She rests in the tombs of her ancestors and is not with us today so that we might hear her voice. But today all this has to do with your chief Mahur-Baal, who is very much among the living and is squeezing all of us in his hand to crush our spirit. All of us, whether born here, or in the lowlands, or in the Beloved Land. We are one community, and we are here today to decide what to do about him."

She sat again. Damariel reached over and took her hand. Kinreth held her gaze for a long moment and nodded her thanks. Danil wavered. He sat, his confidence ebbing away again, muttering something about the duty to remain faithful. Caleb stood up.

"In any case, questions of loyalty are a very poor second here. None of us here in the towns have the goods to bring along to him even if we wanted to. Danil, do you have enough in reserve? I think you do not, any more than the rest of us do. Talk about loyalty all you like, but you are no more able to contribute to this demand than any other household."

Danil looked this way and that and said something very quietly.

"I did not hear that, Danil. Tell us now, can you meet this demand any better than the rest of us? You are in exactly the same position, and are just making empty noises about loyalty."

Danil shook his head. Caleb sat down, a look of scorn on his face. Yeresheth stood, one hand resting on the shoulder of Tobiaz.

"Damariel, let us leave aside for a moment the matter of tribute. We all know we cannot afford what is asked of us. Not one of us here can do that. Clearly not even Danil. But before I choose what to do, I want to hear more about his other plans. Tell us now, is it true that he wants us not only to give him more by way of tribute and gifts, but he also wants us to change our ways."

Damariel nodded.

"He wants to be king over us instead of chief among us. He wants to maintain a body of men to one side ready to fight at any time instead of working on the land or at a trade."

"But that does not touch my life from one day to the next. Some of us have already lost sons in raids and fighting, and no doubt others will in time to come. You know that this is true. What of my life as mother of a household? What of my daughter's life? What does Mahur-Baal plan for the women he keeps close to him?"

"His wife Asherith is forbidden now to leave the house he has appointed for her, except on such rare times as he chooses. She is out of his favour for giving away a piece of jewellery in a way he did not want, and this imprisonment followed soon after. He takes other women into his house as he sees fit, for a longer or shorter time as occasion arises. Some of the households in Giybon have set aside the transfer of house from mother to daughter and agreed that when the time comes he may decide who will inherit. He has said he wants to extend this to the other towns before long - a daughter will be provided for him, and in return he will give the assurance of the support of his lineage to them. The future of the household will be in his hands, not those of the mother of the house."

Yeresheth looked around the circle.

"I will not be diminished into a shrunken state where all I am expected to do is light candles in my house while another decides for me in anything that matters in this life and the next. I am mother of my household, and in time Sosanneth will be mother after me. I will have no part in anything that diminishes who I am in my own home."

Again, little circles of conversation spread around the circle, seeking a focal point to gather around.

Caleb called out again.

"Danil, perhaps you have already decided which of your daughters you are going to give away up the hill?"

Kalita stood.

"Damariel, Kinreth asked earlier about the fighting men that Mahur-Baal has even now following along behind him. If we are to stand in any way against him, we need to know what will happen about this. We know already that not all of our own men will stand alongside us. We have heard that again just now from Danil."

Danil pulled a face and shifted from side to side, but said nothing. Damariel stood and took a deep breath. It was time. He told them about the arrival of the Ibriym, starting with the first reports they had heard from the trader, through to the meeting he and Nepheret had had recently down by the River. He explained about the outline of agreement they had reached with Yahusharar, and what signs and tokens of good faith he was looking for in order to complete the covenant.

While he spoke there was a listening silence, with little expressions of hope, reservation or anxiety crossing faces as they heard what he had to say. When he had done, he sat down again and waited for a reaction. Tamguta was the first to speak.

"Can these people be trusted, Damariel? I believe from what you say that they can help us in a fight, but will they help us in the peace that follows? We need friends just now who know when they can come into our house, and know too when they should leave and go back to their own."

"I think so, Tamguta. At least, that was the impression that I was given. They hope to settle themselves in the hill country, mostly north of here towards Sychem, I think, and they will be busy enough establishing their new homes for a time. Just as our own ancestors spent two or three generations settling here after journeying from the north all those years ago."

There were other questions, all circling around the main issue without ever tackling it directly. Eventually Labayu, standing slowly and leaning on Kothar, voiced it.

"What must we do next if this is to happen, Damariel?"

"Labayu, we need to know for sure that all four towns are willing to do the same. I would like to think that each person in each town will feel that this has gone too far, and we can stand together as a single person, body, heart and will. But it is enough for the agreement that the towns stand together with the seers as majority, even if we are not in complete unity. If that is the case, Nepheret and I will go down and cut the covenant with Yahusharar of the Ibriym, and we all proceed from there. Their encampment is not far from here, less than a morning's walk into the Valley even going at an easy pace. And I think we will be in a hurry to conclude this if we can."

He looked around sombrely.

"As soon as the covenant is cut we can call on their protection if need be. My hope is that, faced with a single voice here, and with the support of our new allies, Mahur-Baal will recognise he has no place here among us any more and will leave. Perhaps there will never be a need for the Ibriym to send us along some of their fighting men. In which case we will provide them with some food and the other necessities of life on a regular basis, but very much less than what has been given this last year to Mahur-Baal. They are superior to us in fighting and battle, but they need the stability and good will of this land. We can give them that."

There was a general air of approval around the circle, with people nodding and turning to one another in relief and assurance. For a moment Damariel thought that the town had reached the unity of response he had been seeking, but then Danil got to his feet again, flushed and angry.

"I will have no part of this. This is just treachery you are speaking while the chief's back is turned away. Here he is trusting you, and you betray him. Even now he is finding kings to ally with in the lowlands, down at Laksh, and you whisper these words that he cannot hear. Well, I will not hear them either. I will side with him in this, not with you. I know how to stay loyal even if not one among the rest of you does. Look now, all you who have followed me on raids down the hill into the lowlands all these years, if you side with me and with our chief now, we can put an end to this rebellion here in this place today. There are enough of us to do this."

He looked around to where the raiding men were sitting, here and there scattered with their families around the circle. Tamguta pursed his lips, then shook his head decisively. He stayed sitting down in the circle at his place. Two or three others did the same. Rivkah reached up, pulled at Danil's sleeve, shook her head at him, but he pulled away from her and kept standing, looking to see who of his people had not yet refused, hoping for at least some support.

"Dadua, come on. I know you. You'll keep loyalty to me and to our chief."

There was a pause. Dadua got up slowly, took a long look at Tagi where she still sat by one of the stones, and went to stand behind Danil. Two others joined them, then two more that had never been part of the raiding group. All together there were six of them. There were looks of distress on different faces around the ring of stones. Danil waited to see if any more would come to join him. Nobody else moved. He looked around again at the little group. Judging from his reaction, the number was much less than he had hoped.

He swallowed, knowing that he was committed now to the course of action but with far too little help to make an issue of it that day. Six of them could not possibly try to take back the meeting and the town on behalf of the absent chief, and he knew it. He looked around again, defiantly, unwilling or unable to back down again from the position he had taken.

"Danil, you don't have to do this. Sit down again with us."

Danil shook his head again.

"So, then we are the only loyal ones. The rest of you are oath-breakers. We will go to find Mahur-Baal down at Laksh and bring him back, and when he comes back here his retribution will be swift upon all the rest of you. Every one of you will wish he or she had honoured his request by providing the extra gifts. He will take them from you anyway, and when he has finished in this town you will long for the day that you had never listened to this man."

He turned on his heel and left, the other five behind him. In the silence that followed, several people looked at Damariel to see what he would say.

"Perhaps it was too much to hope that we would all stand together in this. But I am sorry to lose anyone at all. As for the rest of us, there is no truth in what he said, and I lift from each of us every evil word that has been spoken here today. There is no oath that we have broken that has not already been trampled on and cast aside by the chief himself. Now, if the rest of you are in agreement, Nepheret and I will go first to the other towns, and then, all being well, down to the Ibriym camp to secure the agreement with Yahusharar."

There was agreement, and the other towns had reached the same conclusion. In each of them, a few people had left just as Danil had done, but there had been active conflict in none of them. Damariel assumed that the four small groups would gather together somewhere, and would then go to find Mahur-Baal in a group before trying to get back into any of the towns. In each town there was a mood for haste, and so before long he and Nepheret had gone down into the Valley and were again being invited into Yahusharar's tent. He listened to their account and was satisfied. Indeed, to Damariel's surprise he was delighted at Danil's reaction, and especially at his departure to find the former chief and bring him back.

"That is the best of all news. If he had not done that, we would have to wait who knows how long for a resolution. This way your former chief will force a crisis at once. Perhaps he thinks the towns are still wavering, or that we are not ready to help, in which case his best plan is to attack at once. And from what you have said he is not a patient man. That is excellent. We will not be waiting long at all before the encounter that will decide all of this."

"So let us cut the covenant between us here and now."

"Yes indeed. Let us do that."

He stood up to go outside, then stopped and sat down again.

"It occurs to me that I have not told you of the debates that have gone on down here since you left the other day. I gave them a most thorough account of all our conversation, and all that I had learned from you. The family heads were pleased with all our plans, and very eager to proceed with the arrangement we set out in this tent together. But there is a little detail that they insisted on. Instead of your new chief being appointed there in one of your towns, and being accountable to one of us, why, they felt it better if we simply provided the person who would be chief. Instead of two people, one above the other but in different places, just one person."

Damariel frowned.

"That was not part of what we talked about. I think my people are expecting the chief to come from among our own."

Yahusharar spread his hands out.

"Just what I said to the family heads. But they persuaded me otherwise. Listen, Damariel. You say you want the chief to be from your own people. Perhaps there is some person in your own town of Kephrath who has a family claim on the title."

He looked enquiringly at the two of them. Damariel nodded.

"Yes. So this person believes they should be chief. But perhaps there is another person in one of your other towns who has a similar claim. Better or worse, who knows? Then perhaps as well as those two there is some distant relation of this Mahur-Baal who has felt pushed away from chiefdom for years and now sees a chance to step into that empty place. You can see what would happen. At the very time that you most need to be standing together, and moreover standing together with our strength at your side, you are divided into little squabbling pieces. People who now are happy to support you - and us - will become weary of the arguments. They think that perhaps it was better during the older time with Mahur-Baal. The former chief returns, he finds chaos instead of order, and he seizes power again with hardly any difficulty. I do not think that any of us want that, neither you nor I. So you see, the only way to avoid that is if the chiefdom is placed in someone else's hands."

There was a long pause. Eventually Yahusharar spoke again.

"Of course, if you feel that this new situation must be taken back to your town assemblies for public consideration, then so be it. We are not in any danger down here, and we can wait until your decision is made. But of course Mahur-Baal may not wait that long before returning with armed men at his back. Half a dozen from Kephrath, I think you said, and a similar number from the other three towns. Perhaps more will slip away at night and join him. Then he will have paid his allies for some support. And there are always scoundrels and outlaws that will join in any fight in the hope of finding some personal gain. But if you would prefer to take the extra time to debate the matter, we will simply wait for you and honour the agreement once we can both assent to it."

There was another pause. Damariel knew, as indeed they all did, that he was trapped in a corner. There was no way that he could afford the extra time to arrange another series of town assemblies, not with the former chief only a short distance away and presumably eager to strike back swiftly.

All of a sudden he was gripped with a gnawing anxiety. Was this the right choice? Had he, after all, been led into a trap instead of finding an escape route? Was this a plan that Yahusharar had made right from the start, and had simply waited patiently until the four towns had no choice in the matter? He looked at Nepheret, hoping for inspiration, then back at Yahusharar.

"Does this mean that my people will become vassals?"

Yahusharar seemed surprised, taken aback by the idea.

"Not at all. If anything, it means the reverse. It means that we are willing to open our arms fully to you and embrace you as though you were already one of our own families and clans."

He paused.

"Do you think your own people would see it as a loss of freedom, then? Perhaps it would be wise to delay cutting the covenant until we are sure of this?"

Nepheret leaned forward.

"No, honoured sir, I think there is no need for that at all. But perhaps the words you use here in this tent should be moderated a little before we speak them up at the four towns. Damariel and his people may hear in them a different meaning than your intention. I realise that you are offering a place under the cover of your own shield and the awning of your own tent. And perhaps, in time, a place as clans and families alongside your own."

"Yes, Nepheret, though that last will take more than one year. Indeed, more than one generation according to our own customs. But yes, in time to come, most certainly you are right."

Damariel began to feel some relief, though still feeling the weighty burden of doubts in his heart.

"So the chief will come from among your own people."

"Damariel, answer me this. In recent times, have your own people produced such magnificent chiefs that you would prefer them? If so, then perhaps your people should provide a chief who will serve my people as well as yours."

He smiled, and Damariel felt able, at last, to join him.

"Yahusharar, I hear what you are saying. I apologise for my misunderstanding. I do not need to discuss this with the towns."

They went outside, to the edge of the meeting area with the curtained tent. Yahusharar kept them well away from that, and led them over instead to a free-standing stone used as an altar, calling over a man nearby who was serving as lay priest for the day to be witness.

They each killed a pigeon, mingled the blood of the birds together with a drop or two taken from their own veins in a shallow bowl on the altar, then burned the carcasses and blood together with some oil in a fire that was already kindled in a metal stand nearby.

Damariel and Yahusharar knelt down together, and Nepheret and the priest stood behind them listening to the words of the promises each made to the other. It was a solemn moment, and there was a little pool of silence around the four of them as the ceremony unfolded, a still place of rest in the centre of the busy community. One or two people stopped nearby for a few moments to watch the vows enacted, before moving on again about their business. Eventually the two men rose to their feet again and embraced one another.

"The wealth of the hill country that is ours to share: we share it with you."

"The strength of the clans and the promises of our god; we share them with you."

They went back to the tent, still locked together in the sacred silence of the other world. After a while Damariel took a deep breath and turned to face Yahusharar, mouth already open to speak. To his surprise, the leader of the Ibriym had tears in his eyes. He stopped.

"Ah, me. These encounters with the other world always leave me this way. I find it a fearful and most moving place to pass through. I can face a hundred men in battles without flinching, and lead the families through all manner of hazards on the journey, but I am undone by meeting what is on the other side. I have no idea how it can be for you to meet it one day after another. Give me a battle and a sword in my hand any day instead of that."

Damariel said nothing, but placed his arm on his shoulder to affirm their companionship. After a few moments Yahusharar recovered himself, and nodded to Damariel to continue.

"I was going to say, that when all this is done, I would like to invite you to come up to Giybon and sleep one or two nights on the great stone at the high place there."

"Why?"

"People have travelled from far and wide to ask the seers if they can do that. Chiefs, priests, and those of no rank alike. It has a reputation that the dreams that a person dreams there give true insight into the things ahead. Since you will be settling your people here in this land, perhaps it will be a good and godly gift that we can give you on behalf of the clans and families you lead. Eyes to see what lies on the road ahead for your people. Or perhaps for yourself. Who can say? But it is a gift we can give to you out of our heritage that has nothing to do with barley, lentils, or grapes. You might find it to be a precious time that will stay with you for the rest of your life here in this world."

Yahusharar looked down at the ground for a time, breathing in and out, considering.

"If I am brought to tears by the cutting of a covenant, will I find this dreaming stone to be too fearful?"

"Who can say? But even if it is fearful, it may be worth the hazard anyway. I offer it to you as your choice to make when your people start to settle in the land. Even if that is some years from now. We will not forget or withdraw the offer."

The stocky leader of the Ibriym, his face still troubled by the nearness to the sacred, clasped Damariel's hand.

"I am afraid of it, but you are right. That should not make me shrink away from the possibilities it holds. But not yet, not for a while, I think. First we have tasks at hand that I understand better and which hold no fears for me. You must find out for me what this Mahur-Baal plans to do. I suppose you have lads you can put out to scout around to find out where he is?"

"We do. And as well as that, I know some of the seers and priests down at Laksh and the towns between there and Kephrath. Like Ayaluna. I should be able to find out for you by late tomorrow whether he has moved on from Laksh or is still there. We will know if he has already moved on. But they will not be able to tell us if he has camped out beyond the sown land or is marching on the road. We need scouts for that. But my guess is that just now he is still with the king of Laksh, and will wait there to gather a force of people before making his attack."

"Which way will he come?"

Damariel shook his head.

"How should I know? There are several ways that a man might travel between here and there. But I suppose some of them are fit only for one or two people travelling together. Some would not be at all suitable for a large group. I really have no idea about that."

"I think they would come up the track past Ayaluna. I remember the men in the stables at the master's house at Gedjet speaking those names. I think they meant it was a good track for baggage animals."

"What about the way around Bayth Shamsh?"

"Is that fit for a group of men?"

Yahusharar was amused but patient.

"In short, neither of you know."

They looked at each other, then back at Yahusharar, shook their heads. Damariel shrugged and looked blank.

"I have never in my life led an army. Not even a group of raiders. At most one or two people with a couple of baggage donkeys."

"Then take me now up to your town and let me meet someone who can tell me this sort of thing. I need to know what the tracks are like between Kephrath and this Laksh place, so that I can choose the place of battle in the way that suits us best. Somewhere where we can surprise them."

"Will you not meet them head on?"

He laughed.

"Whatever for? We will find a place to fight where the balance is so in our favour that your former chief could have four times the men he has and we would still defeat him. We have not come this far along our path by running around in the open, like foolish men inviting a battle on equal terms. But you will see all this soon. Also, be sure that your townspeople know that I am the warleader of the Ibriym, if they do not work it out from my questions. Let us not for the time being raise the question of who might be chief in time to come. We need to make sure that your people are most thoroughly concentrating on removing the man who was chief, and not spending time and effort on questions of the future."

"Someone will ask."

"Perhaps they will. And we will not deceive anyone. But I think it is more useful for the time being to steer conversations away from that topic if we can. I am not going there today to claim any rights, or to walk the boundaries of your community, or anything like that. Take me to your house as a guest, and we can invite into that house those people who can be helpful in planning what comes next. The more that your people see me today as warleader and the less they see me as possible chief, the better. In any case, it is not likely that I will ever become chief. By the time we have built new settlements and fought whatever battles lie ahead, it will need a younger man than I to fill that place. I shall be content to sit under my vine in the house they build me, and look out over the hills that you have helped me call home."

Some time later, once back at their house at Kephrath, Nepheret went off to find Kothar, Tamguta and Yusuf while Damariel set out sweet bread and mint tea for them all. Yahusharar looked around the room while the water was coming up to the boil, peering closely at the table of musical instruments but carefully not touching any of them. Damariel watched his new ally curiously, keen to see where he set himself internal boundaries within his host's house. Yahusharar turned suddenly, catching Damariel with a smile.

"You leave all these things out here in plain view?"

"Those, yes. There is nothing unusually sacred about them. Play one if you like. There are other things that are hidden away from everyday use."

He shook his head.

"I do not think that the noise would honour your house. I have never played pipes or a lyre. But I do know these. This might not be so bad."

He picked up one of the timbrels carefully, shook it to hear the little bells tinkle, tapped gently on the taut headskin. Hearing voices outside he quickly put it down again and came to stand beside Damariel. Nepheret came in with the three men and there was a brief, awkward silence. Yahusharar took the initiative and bowed his head to them all.

"I am Yahusharar, warleader of the Ibriym and now, just today, your brother by virtue of a covenant cut between us. I am pleased and honoured to be here with you in Kephrath and meet you. I wish we had more time to become friends, man to man, but I have heard from my brother Damariel that your former chief may arrive here in Kephrath with his fighting men any day. Now, when all this is done and our new chief holds the land in peace for us all, why, then we shall sit together in peace, you and I, and tell each other of our lives. But for today we are here to take counsel and decide how we can best meet this threat to us all."

The room relaxed. Damariel was struck, as he had been before, by Yahusharar's ability to win people over. The earlier anxiety welled up in his mind again, as he wondered whether he too had simply been taken in by the man's charisma. What if the end of the trail they were now walking with the Ibriym was betrayal? But the other three men were sitting at the table with Yahusharar now, sipping mint tea and sharing broken sweet bread together. Even Yusuf, whose sensibilities might have been triggered by the mention of a chief, was talking and laughing with Yahusharar as though they were old friends.

How quickly, how easily they were all slipping into this new alliance. Suddenly realising that Nepheret, already sitting with the others beside Kothar, was watching him curiously, he wondered how much of his inner thought had shown on his face. He smiled at her, acknowledging the mild reproof, and sat in the empty place between Tamguta and Yahusharar. They looked at him.

"See now. We are here today so that Yahusharar can understand the lie of the land, and the path that Mahur-Baal is most likely to choose when he comes up with his men from Laksh. I was not able to tell him anything of use, because I have never tried to lead a group of men along any of the tracks. It seemed to us that you three are the best to help him with this."

There was a lot of discussion, circling round unknown factors like how quickly the former chief would want to advance, and whether he would want to approach from along the ridge or up the valley route. In the end they decided that the most likely choice was up the main track from Ayaluna, but there was also a small chance that he would head first across to Shalem, and then follow the ridgeway past Meyim.

He would not attack Giybon first since his own home was there. Rather, Kephrath was the obvious first target. If that fell, then the smaller settlements of Meyim and Jarrar's town would soon follow, and with those three in his hand Giybon would almost certainly yield without a fight. And, of course, Damariel was here, and Mahur-Baal now saw him as the main adversary.

For Damariel's own part, he found it profoundly difficult to sit in his house planning how best to repel an armed assault from his own countrymen; there was an air of unreality about the process. He could not imagine Mahur-Baal marching in to Kephrath, burning and seizing goods as he came, killing those who had defied him. The other men seemed to be able to contemplate and plan for the possibility better than he. The action seemed either impossible or unthinkable, and he could not work out a plan in either case.

Finally, Yahusharar summed up their thoughts.

"So the thing we need to know first is which of these two paths he will choose. I can send out my own scouts for this, but they do not know the land as you do. Perhaps it would be best to pair up one of my men each with one of yours. We will send out two pairs to watch over each path. The sooner we know his choice one way or the other, the better. And today, as soon as we are done here, one or two of you must take me a little stretch along each track, so I can decide where we will set the trap for them."

Shortly after, Kothar and Tamguta set off with Yahusharar. They headed along the ridge to the south first, as that was the less likely choice, with the intention of swinging back down towards Ayaluna and the lowlands later in the day. Yusuf waited until they had gone, then sat down again at the table. He looked very solemn.

"Damariel, we are not brothers to each other, except perhaps by grace of living together in this town of ours. But you are priest and seer among us, and I would like you to answer me this truthfully, as though we were indeed brothers. Will the Ibriym choose one of their own to be chief over us, or are we going to choose for ourselves as we have always done?"

Damariel sat opposite him and nodded acceptance of the question. He took a deep breath before answering.

"Yes, they will choose, Yusuf, though for a while they will be too busy to exercise any great control over us. They will be settling for themselves in their own towns, and will have plenty to occupy them. The new chief's hand will be very light on us. But yes, part of the agreement is that they will choose who is chief over us."

He stopped to gauge Yusuf's reaction.

"Do you think Kalita will object?"

Yusuf thought about that for some time.

"Well, she still holds family dreams of restoring some former grandeur. You know the past of her family. But in truth neither of us knows how to fulfil such a calling. It has been several generations since that was truly in her family's blood, and it has never been in mine. Who am I? I can see, we can all see, what Mahur-Baal's greed has brought us to. But who among us might have done a better job?"

He stopped for a long time, frowning in consideration. Damariel was about to speak, but Nepheret put her hand on his and shook her head. Eventually Yusuf continued.

"I think that whoever becomes chief after this will be surrounded by people who will watch his every move. It will be a difficult time to be chief. Perhaps after all we will be better served by someone from outside the four towns. Then we can all feel that we might do better than they can, and that will draw us all back together again. I can despise what Mahur-Baal has done in these towns to us all, but perhaps none of us would have done any better. Now I would like to think that in a little while we can repair the harm."

He stopped again, this time with an air of finality. He looked up at the two of them to see their reaction to his words.

"Yusuf, I think that too. But you know Kalita better than we do. Will she accept this in the way you have said? Can you explain it to her with the same conviction you feel talking with us?"

"I think so. I will try. In truth, we have plenty to do with three children in our own home without having the burden of all the other houses too. How many children can one couple carry?"

Yusuf left them after that to make his way back to Kalita's house. The next few days were a time of great anxiety for Damariel. He had heard indirectly from a priest he knew down in Laksh that on that day Mahur-Baal was still resident in the town. But he could not ask the man every day for news, so the reassurance of the original message soon faded into the background. Then for some time there was no word at all from the scouts sent out along the trails. Who could say for sure that Mahur-Baal had not eluded them and be even now on the track somewhere, about to round some final bend in the path and come in sight of the town gate?

The everyday tasks of life in the town went on, but it was hard to concentrate on them with full devotion. The time for the weekly celebration was rapidly coming around again, and he had no idea how to prepare for that.

But then, shortly after noon on a day when the sky was mottled with puffy clouds, before the time of the weekly celebration came around, two of the scouts came up the track from Ayaluna. They had moved fast over the land, skirting the roughest terrain and cutting straight across places where the road took a more leisurely bend. The former chief had indeed chosen to come by that route and was not going to go up to Shalem first. As soon as they arrived, two more men were sent straight down into the Valley to the camp of the Ibriym to pass on the word.

The rest of the day passed anxiously again. Although there could be no chance that Mahur-Baal and his men could arrive until the next day, Damariel felt himself and his whole town to be horribly exposed and vulnerable. Ordinary life and work was impossible. After darkness had fallen, he and Nepheret spent a great deal of the night in prayer outside the house among the stones of the high place, kneeling or prostrate beside the great altar stone.

But with the early morning came Yahusharar and three others up into the town, having left their camp well before dawn. The rest of the Ibriym fighters had taken little individual routes around the outskirts of the town and were going to regroup where the main track curled around near the children's stream. Yahusharar had decided that to have his own men march through Kephrath before the battle would be too provocative, and too revealing of his own strength in case there were some who even now might pass word on to the former chief. The less known, the better in this case, he thought.

Kothar and Shaharti had come up to join Damariel at the high place when they heard of the arrival, together with about a dozen men of the town who would come down the track with them. Kothar was under instructions to stay beside Damariel throughout the day. As many of the other men as possible were staying in the town as a last line of defence. Looking at them, Damariel prayed that their ill-disciplined and scarcely armed courage would not be called upon.

The men were waiting. Yahusharar was waiting. There was no time. It was time for him to go with them down the track. He took Nepheret into his arms and held her for a long moment, feeling the pulse of her heartbeat against his body and the dark curve of the edge of her hair spilling out past her kef against his cheek. Then he released her and turned to Yahusharar, trying to appear bold.

"Well then. We had better go."

Yahusharar grinned, eager for the day's work.

"Yes indeed. Down to gather the men first, then along the track to the place Kothar and I agreed."

Damariel led them along the familiar ways of Kephrath, part of him wondering if he would ever again see these houses with the eyes of the living. They went by Yeresheth's house. She was outside, under her mimosa tree, leaning on Sosanneth to watch them pass. She had chosen to wear a sleeveless smock that showed, vivid on her arms, the scars of the wounds she had cut into herself in the spring eight years ago, on the day that Baruk and Bashur had died. It was very close to being the same day of the year.

Damariel held his mother's eyes for a long moment as they passed by the house, wanting to reassure her that he would return home at the end of the day. Surely he would return at the end of the day. Then they were past her home, beyond the last of the houses and dropping down among the terraces stepping down the steep hillside to the stream. There among the low trees and the bushes coming into leaf they joined with Yahusharar's men, crossed over the open space to the trackway and set off all together towards Ayaluna.

Shen

NISAN YEAR 25

SEE A PEOPLE who like a lioness arise,
and lion-like lift themselves up.
Who will not lie down until their prey lies dead,
and the blood of the slain runs like wine.

DAMARIEL HUDDLED DOWN in some scrubby undergrowth on the hillside by the main track from Kephrath down towards the town of Ayaluna, and the lowlands in general. Kothar was on his right. This was the place he had recommended to Yahusharar as being all but invisible to anyone approaching from below. The track curled up and over a little ridge here on its way up the valley, so Mahur-Baal and his men would have to come from the lowlands into the bowl of the valley with no line of sight ahead.

It was rather too close to Kephrath for Damariel's peace of mind, but Kothar had assured him it was far and away the best location for an ambush along the whole route. Damariel had no choice but to accept his decision, though his home was only a short walk back up the track behind.

If he turned round, he could see already the ridge next across from Shomal's olives, and the cleft where the stream tumbled out and the children played. But looking ahead, he could understand Kothar's reasoning, since the approaching Kinahny could not possibly see into the bowl of the valley until they had crested the lip. Heavy clouds were over the valley lower down, but the spring sunshine still shone where they were.

Yahusharar's men had taken up positions either side of the road. Well over half of the Ibriym, including all the men with missile weapons of any kind, were on the northern side, spread out in a thin line on slightly higher ground where a low ridge flanked the track, just before a boggy tract of land which pinched the track from either side. The rest were in a compact group facing them, tucked away and concealed in slightly denser foliage. Even knowing where most of them had positioned themselves, Damariel could hardly see any of them, with only little metal glints or movements here and there in the brush as they waited at ease.

The jaws of the trap were set. The plan was for the smaller group to remain hidden at first. The more numerous northern group would break cover, shower the approaching force with missiles, and make use of what they expected to be complete surprise to disorder their enemies. After that, there were two possibilities. The enemy might fall back away from the hail of missiles, in which case the hidden group would spring out at them in their discomfort and finish the attack. Or they might try to counter-charge up the slope, in which case the southern group would pursue and attack the remnant from behind. Either way, the final effect was intended to be like crushing grain between a pair of millstones.

Kothar settled more comfortably into his place beside him. There was still some time to go before the chief and his men climbed up along the road to the place where it came over the scrubby ridge ahead. Yahusharar had already reported back to them that there was no advance guard of scouts, and that they were coming in a single compact group up towards Kephrath.

Damariel looked back again towards where his home was concealed by the rise of the land. If the plan miscarried there was nothing to stop Mahur-Baal and those with him from going directly in among the houses and doing whatever he pleased, exacting whatever revenge or recompense he chose. Every time this thought invaded his soul, he felt his skin turn clammy and his heart start to race. Everything that was dear to him, places as well as people, the living and the dead, would be exposed and, most likely, torn apart.

The men from Kephrath were stationed in a loose line behind them, this side of the next ridge, but although highly motivated in defence they were poorly armed. Qeren was among them, and Yusuf, and others he knew. It had been decided they should play no part in the first assault on the chief, in case conflicts of motive and the sight of friends on the other side weakened their resolve.

The townspeople were ill-schooled in the art of war. The town gate had no defensive strength or purpose at all, being only a symbol of trade and peaceful authority, and the Mitsriy had never allowed the construction of any kind of defence wall. Only the older towns that could claim history before their occupation of the land were permitted this. Kephrath had not even the sort of loosely secure perimeter that Damariel had seen elsewhere, where blocks of houses on the outskirts were joined together with doorways facing inwards to serve as a way to restrict access. Gilem's house at Yabneh was one of these, but Kephrath had nothing like it.

There was a rustle of vegetation behind them, and Yahusharar, bent low to the ground, came over to them and squatted beside Damariel and Kothar where they were lying down. He had an eager, expectant air as though he could barely restrain his vigour. Like the other Ibriym, he had tied his kef around his neck to ensure nothing restricted his sight, and his greying hair ruffled in the growing wind.

"Not long now. Natan has just signalled that they are at the foot of the rise."

Damariel had seen the signal Natan-netjer sent, a quick flap of a square of yellow cloth from his position beside the road just at the curl of the ridge. He had not understood its significance. He swallowed, and felt again his insides clench with fear and anticipation. There was no time left for a change of plan. Yahusharar, looking across the bowl of land, grinned.

"You know, the Mitsriy kings say on their monuments that a day of slaughter of their enemies is better than a year of feasting. I think this time they are right."

He paused, and laughed quietly.

"They're not right about very much else, I think, but they are right about this. So maybe you could pray to the gods of this land to give us a double-length day to finish the fight."

Damariel looked at him, a rather foolish grin on his own face, and then suddenly found the voice that sometimes welled up from somewhere inside him like a living spring of water.

"Then sun stand still over Giybon, and moon hold high above the Vale of Ayaluna."

Then he turned to Kothar and said in a low voice that quavered more than he expected.

"It's nearly upon us, Kothar."

His friend nodded, slipped his long hunting knife from its sheath and placed it in front of him, pulling some loose leaves over it to ensure it did not glint in the light. After that he turned to look at Damariel and appraise his mood.

"All well with you, brother?"

Damariel nodded, then clasped his hands together to stop them from trembling. He loosened the strap of the bundle he carried over one shoulder and took a very long breath. Kothar and Yahusharar exchanged glances with each other over his head, then Yahusharar put one hand on each of the two before slipping away into the scrub, bent low as he moved.

"Keep out of sight, both of you. Nothing to fear here. My men have done this sort of thing before, many times. Kothar, stay with your priest and keep him safe. We'll need him later."

They caught glimpses of moving vegetation as he worked his way round from them to join the larger group north of the track. There was a silence that seemed to stretch out for a long time. Then Natan-netjer flapped his square of cloth three times, and rolled off to one side to fully conceal himself.

Kothar put his hand to Damariel's shoulder to ensure he kept low to the ground. Several more heartbeats passed.

A group of five men appeared over the ridge, cautious heads showing first, and then all together in a sudden move. They were clearly as aware as anyone else that the terrain was not in their favour.

They stood there at the lip for a time, looking all around the hillsides on either side. Damariel hardly dared draw breath, lying prostrate and peering between the lower branches of a young tree.

The little twigs in front of him, and the veins on the leaves, opening now with the spring warmth, stood out for him with a peculiar vividness.

Kothar's hand was firm, solid on his shoulder, but his own body shivered from time to time with little tremors. The sun disappeared behind the edge of the cloud bank coming up from the west, and a few drops of rain spattered on the ground, like heralds before an army.

Apparently satisfied with what they saw, one of the five men turned back down the track and called out something that none of them could hear. There was another pause, and then the rest of the attackers appeared. They moved along the road together in a solid block. Damariel could see Mahur-Baal in the middle of the group, walking beside the eldest son of the king of Laksh. He spotted Danil in amongst the others, and with them, he thought, a few others from Kephrath, but he could not be sure.

He knew that there were about a hundred men in total, though in the poor light at that distance he could not count them. According to what they had been able to find out from scouting at a distance and rumours from Laksh, just over half were from the four towns, with most of the rest from several of the nearby towns including Shalem and Laksh. A handful of townless individuals willing to join in for whatever reward they could glean made up the balance. Together they outnumbered the Ibriym and men from Kephrath by about three to two.

The prince of Laksh turned to Mahur-Baal. In reply the chief pointed up the ridge, and Damariel realised with a sudden grip of fear that they were talking about the approach to Kephrath. Little prayers crossed his heart and lips as his imagination dwelt again on what might happen there. Mahur-Baal looked around him, up and down the valley. Damariel felt that he was looking directly at him at one point, and tucked his head down into the leaf litter, closing his eyes, wishing that the chief's gaze would turn and look elsewhere.

Kothar's hand squeezed his shoulder suddenly, eagerly. He looked up. The group of men were coming up level with the low ridge where Yahusharar and his men were spread out lying in wait. Watching the marching column, Damariel thought how small an impression a hundred men make on a whole landscape. The slopes of the hills on either side diminished them into a little clump of purposeful movement amongst a wide span of leaves tossing to and fro.

The main edge of the rainstorm had reached them at the same time that the warband had come up level with the ridge, and the patter of heavy raindrops was loud on the leaves and dark across the dry ground. The rain had turned swiftly to a spring downpour.

The prince of Laksh was once again turning to the chief when Yahusharar sprung his trap. A wave of arrows and sling-stones descended from out of the bushes, and then the Ibriym rose out of their concealment. A number of the attackers fell in that first assault, while others turned towards the threat, fumbling with weapon straps that were slippery with rain. There was complete confusion among the Kinahny, as most of the group were turning this way and that to try to see what was happening. Two more showers of missiles rained down, then with a shout the Ibriym were rushing down from their higher ground towards the track.

A couple of men furthest back in the column turned and ran back along the track towards Ayaluna, where Natan-netjer and two men with him leapt from their place in the bracken in front of them. They stopped and threw down their swords, still tangled in straps and sheaths, but the Ibriym cut them down where they stood. Damariel winced; it was too far away to tell for sure, but there was a good chance he knew the men. The prince of Laksh, surrounded by a small group of men, ran off to one side to try to reach a raised hillock, and Yahusharar, seeing the move, set off with a group to intercept him.

Kothar pointed to where Mahur-Baal, with another group close around him, was restoring some order and moving away from the track, starting to form into a defensive block as they did so. Unlike the prince, he had decided that the best plan was to break away from the attackers, gain some distance, and slow the action down from its current pace. By now he had probably worked out that he had superior numbers, so it made sense to hold back until the weight of this began to tell.

Some of the men with him had bows of their own, and Damariel saw Ibriym here and there fall to the ground or back away from the fight, unsure how to proceed. Beside him, Kothar was taut, stretched tight by the conflict between the desire to be in the action and the promise to stay with Damariel.

Yahusharar, leading the group of men who had been unable to head off the prince but had now encircled them, looked about to gauge the situation, then led a dozen or so men off towards the place where Mahur-Baal was making his stand. Natan-netjer and the others were still at some distance, waiting to deal with stragglers. The Ibriym he had left surrounding the prince made no effort to close in for a fight, but were content to ensure that they could not reform into a single group with Mahur-Baal, by containing them north of the road. Each time the Kinahny tried to move back southwards there was a brief skirmish, leaving a man from one group or the other on the ground or off to one side.

Mahur-Baal turned his men in a tight wedge to face Yahusharar, getting ready to countercharge and seize back the advantage. But before he could do so, Yahusharar gave a great shout and his last group of men emerged from the bushes behind Mahur-Baal, not many paces away. The second ambush came as a complete surprise, and Damariel could see the neat formation around the chief unravelling around the edges like a fraying piece of rotten cloth as one man or another turned to face the new threat, or tried to make a lone dash for safety.

Seeing that his men were starting to fail of heart, Mahur-Baal led the dwindling group in a wild dash for the gap between the two groups of Ibriym. It was the only remaining escape route. There was a wild noise of shouting and the three groups came together in a rush. The fighting turned into a fierce, confusing turmoil, like water seething on a red hot iron, then abruptly it was over and individual Kinahny were running here and there to escape. Damariel saw Mahur-Baal and two others force their way through a gap, saw one of the three cut down from behind, saw the chief stagger as though from a weapon strike but then get free.

He disappeared into a little wadi cut into the side of the valley, out of sight, one other person with him. Belatedly, two of the Ibriym set off in pursuit. Kothar cursed and nearly leapt to his feet, but then stayed crouching beside Damariel. The heavy rain abruptly turned to hail, lashing hard pellets down on them all.

Yahusharar brought about half of his men back towards the prince of Laksh, where the struggle was still in the balance, leaving the rest to pursue the remnants fleeing here and there. They were moving more slowly now, with the fatigue and wounds of battle starting to tell. The prince saw the group approaching and looked around at his diminishing forces. There was no possibility of victory, and he held up his hands and threw his sword onto the ground in front of him. His bodyguard did the same, and the two stepped a pace or two forward towards Yahusharar.

The others in the group suddenly scattered in every direction, running for the edge of the valley bowl and safety. Most were cut off by the Ibriym nearby, but a group of four, running as fast as they could, eluded their captors and headed directly towards where Kothar and Damariel were hiding in the bushes. Yahusharar set off with some others in pursuit, but they were slow with battle weariness and had little chance of catching up. Kothar gripped at his elbow.

"Stand up, Damariel, stand up and face them."

"I have no weapon, Kothar."

He looked around. The thin line of men from Kephrath was too far back to make a difference here, and had not yet even started to respond to the threat.

"I know that, but they do not. As you love me, brother, stand up with me and act as though you were ready to fight them beside me."

Damariel's legs felt strengthless, and his innards crawled with fear, but as Kothar pulled at him again, urgently, he pushed himself to his knees, then stood upright facing the oncoming Kinahny. Kothar was already on his feet, brandishing his hunting knife and roaring as though at the head of an army of men and the whole host of heaven. Damariel waved the bundle he carried and shouted alongside him, his face rigid with tension.

Out of the corner of one eye he could see some of the Kephrath group running down the hill, but they were too far away, much too far away. The four Kinahny were much closer, pelting towards them with heads down and desperate to escape, half-blinded by the sheets of hail. Suddenly they saw, or perhaps heard, Kothar and Damariel ahead of them. One of them stopped short and pulled at the others. Two lost their footing on the ground, slippery with hailstones. One fell over, fumbling with the sheaf of a knife.

Yahusharar and his men caught up with them, and there was a brief, vicious flurry of sword and knife strokes. Damariel was breathing hard, his fists clenched around the cloth bundle. The men had been no further from him than the distance across the sacred stone circle.

Yahusharar ran up to them, face flushed and a fierce wildness in his eyes. He had little cuts across his face and shoulders, but most of the blood on his clothing belonged to other men.

"Ha! Good work, priest! We will say that you killed those men."

Damariel shook his head, tingles of visceral excitement still shaking his limbs. He held on to Kothar for support.

"The hail killed them more than I did."

Yahusharar gave a great bellow of laughter.

"Then when we go back to our tents, our women will sing that the hail of Yahu that he sent from above was the greatest warrior here today."

He looked around, saw that his men were scattering across the hillside in pursuit of individual Kinahny, and that a larger group was trying to make an escape down the track towards

Ayaluna. The group from Kephrath was blocking escape up the hill.

"I must go and finish this. Wait here until I get back, then we will enter in triumph into your home town together."

Kothar caught at his arm as he turned.

"The former chief got away, we think, into that wadi there. Two of your men were in pursuit but we lost them from sight."

Yahusharar paused, clearly in two minds. Damariel spoke, his voice now back under his control.

"You lead your men. We will find him."

Yahusharar nodded.

"Find him. Kill him."

Then he and his men were running down the hillside, skidding here and there, shouting to others to join with them in pursuit of the group trying to escape away down the track. By now they were almost at the lip of the bowl, about to drop out of sight.

Damariel and Kothar made their way diagonally across to the mouth of the wadi, going as quickly as they could across the uneven terrain, skirting the worst of the boggy ground. It was still slippery and white in patches with hail, but the storm itself was easing away. Little gusts of wind now blew rain rather than hail at them from every side, and the full strength had now ebbed away.

At the mouth of the wadi they passed the Kinahny they had seen fall. It was Yaraq, his dead body contorted around the thrown spear that had struck him low down in his back. They ran on along the flat wadi base as it wound up the hillside, the tracks easy to follow here. A bit further, one of the Ibriym sat propped up against a rock, holding closed a great gash down his right arm. Seeing them as they rounded a corner unexpectedly he flinched back and tried to reach a knife with his left hand, but Damariel held up both hands empty.

"We are with you. I am the priest Damariel of Kephrath."

The man nodded in recognition, slumping back in relief, then gestured up the track.

"Up that way. Two of them, one badly injured. Tsuriy was after them but he has not come back down yet."

They ran on. Round the corner where the wadi widened briefly the tracks became confused and scuffed, as though there had been another struggle, but they cleared again as they went further. The sides of the wadi were becoming lower as they climbed, and were now no more than waist height to their left. They were not far from the top of the valley bowl. With a sudden shock of recognition, an unexpected familiarity in an alien terrain, Damariel caught sight of Shomal's olives, clear on the ridge above them. The rain had almost stopped down where they were, and the slopes above were already gleaming in the sunshine again.

Around another corner, and a body was thrown to one side amongst a great confusion of turned up ground, broken twigs and bloodied leaves. It was Kinahny, judging by the clothing, and Kothar cautiously turned it over with his foot so they could see the face. It was Danil. His expression was curiously peaceful above the great wounds around his chest and neck. Damariel shook his head.

"Never thought to see this, Kothar. This man has cost my family so much. I hold him accountable for Baruk, Bashur, Ketty. And he split the village by going with Mahur-Baal. But I never thought to see him dead on the ground like this. He could have been a good man if he hadn't been so weak. Easy prey for Mahur-Baal. What a waste."

Kothar, still wary and with knife drawn, tugged at him.

"Leave that, Damariel. We must find Mahur-Baal."

They ran on, and around the next corner was the remaining one of Yahusharar's men, propped up against a boulder that was the last remaining vestige of the wadi they had been following. There were signs of another fierce struggle.

"He was the last one in pursuit, Damariel."

They both looked up at the nearby ridge, aflutter with the opening leaves of Shomal's olives. At a fast pace it would take hardly any time to reach it. Damariel shivered.

"Tell me that he did not get away to go up there, Kothar."

Kothar pointed ahead to where a single set of tracks stumbled across a bare patch of soil. The steps were clearly ragged and uneven now.

"He is not moving quickly any more, Damariel. We may yet catch him."

Damariel nodded, his features grim and his heart painfully full of all his undefended love residing up the hill. They set off along the trail of footsteps, pushing through a little stand of low bushes where spring flowers were sparkling among the small pale leaves. The rain had completely stopped now, and the fresh wind was breaking up the clouds and starting to dry off the land.

On the other side of the bushes was Mahur-Baal, blood ebbing from a gash in his side. Seeing them, he tried to pull out his knife, but Kothar seized his arm and then kicked the blade away into the bracken nearby. Mahur-Baal groaned and lay back again.

"I thought I might just get up there. No chance now. Those cursed new friends of yours have ruined everything."

Damariel sat on a boulder beside him and started unwrapping the bundle he had carried over his shoulder all this way. He was all of a sudden quite calm. This was a moment he had imagined many times, though always with slightly different details filling the scene. His mind's eye could rest easy now, for this was true seeing and not vision.

Kothar watched him curiously, still keeping a wary eye out for others that might approach. Mahur-Baal closed his eyes, shifted position again with a groan, and tried to hold the edges of the wound together against the steady flow of blood. He looked up again suddenly, directly at Damariel.

"I suppose your allies have won back down there. They'll betray you in the end, you know. They're not like us. Different ways, different gods. They'll just look out for themselves. They'll take your land away one day, push you out of here. A time will come when you'll know I was right."

"I don't think so."

The chief closed his eyes.

"One of us will be proved right in time."

"But not in my lifetime, and certainly not in yours."

Kothar, apparently satisfied that the surrounding area was safe, walked over and stood beside Damariel, looking at the chief with distaste.

"What are you going to do, Damari? What do you want me to do?"

"Yes, priest. Are you going to kill me yourself or make your friend do it for you?"

"Mahur-Baal, victorious over his enemies and glorious in battle. Neither of us is going to kill you. It won't need either of us to do that. You have only a very short time left before the wounds you have already received will take you across to the other side. But before that, I want you to know something."

He had finished unwrapping the bundle. Inside it was a kef, with a silver brooch pinned to it, and a small lump of squashed, shapeless gold.

"Do you know what these are?"

Mahur-Baal opened his eyes, looked vaguely towards the things he held, shook his head.

"Nice. You brought your old discarded rubbish to show me as I die. Have you no prayers for me instead?"

"The kef belonged to Qetirah. The gold was a brooch you sent down after you took her. Before she died. The silver was a thing I had found for her up at Hatsor, just before I set off home again."

Mahur-Baal tried to laugh, choked and stopped abruptly. His face was very pale.

"All this is about that woman? About the one night I spent with her that time? About the fact that you couldn't give her what she wanted and I could? I could have given you ten women if I had known that was all you wanted. Bad choice, priest, betraying your own people for a desire for vengeance over a woman."

Damariel leaned forward and placed the ruined gold brooch on his chest. Mahur-Baal, without thinking, picked it up in his free hand and looked at it. He coughed again, and a little more blood seeped out from behind his hand.

"I thought I gave her something better than this. This was good once. Like her. Pity you couldn't give her what she wanted. It was a good present I gave her. She was weak, that's all, chief's seed was too much for her."

He looked up at Damariel, a mixture of triumph and acute pain on his face. Kothar started forward, knife at the ready, but Damariel held up his hand.

"No, Kothar, all he wants is a quick end now. Let's not be so quick to satisfy him. If you like, go back and help that man of Yahusharar's we passed on the way up. I'll be a little longer here."

Kothar stood and leaned over the chief before going.

"If I had my way you'd find a lot more pain before leaving this life."

Then he turned away down the wadi. Mahur-Baal grunted and looked back at Damariel.

"So you have given me back the brooch, though hardly in the condition that I gave it to the woman. Is the kef going to be my shroud?"

Damariel shook his head.

"After you are dead I shall bury this up at Kephrath somewhere, and give Ketty the peace in death she deserves. I never got to be with her when she was put into the ground, and this will have to suffice for me. But before that, this kef here is a witness to all these things."

"Hardly my fault you were not there."

There was a pause, broken by the ragged, laboured breathing of the chief, who spoke again with an effort.

"I think you might pray for me now, priest."

"Never. Not even once since you turned thief. And you will never rest with your ancestors. I have no idea what Yahusharar and his men plan to do with your body, but I shall conduct no service up at the stones. As far as I care your carcass can feed the carrion birds and be torn apart by wild beasts."

"Will that make any difference to me? Hard to believe that just now."

"Your ancestors will despise you. Go to them when you cross over and they will turn you away."

Mahur-Baal leaned forward against his pain. He was genuinely angry with Damariel.

"Don't you understand, priest? Everything I did was for my people, and I did it to keep our way of life. Yes, it meant I had to gather more wealth from the four towns than they wanted to give, and yes, Yaraq and his men were standing ready all the time to make sure it came in. I suppose he is dead too."

Damariel nodded.

"Ah well. He never understood either. But at least he knew how to stay loyal even when he didn't see all the reasons. I'd have been king by now, and Kenizzi my high priest if only you lot had seen the good sense in it. Selfish, the lot of you. Only out to look after yourselves. If that Mitsriy officer hadn't come up the track that time I'd have done it, too. Never thought they'd bother."

He trailed off again and sagged back against the trunk of a small tree. Damariel unfolded Qetirah's kef and spread it out over his legs, then leaned forward.

"I told them that."

The chief shook his head in disbelief.

"Yes. I told them that. Nepheret taught me what to say and I wrote it. I wrote to the governor and told him what your plan was before ever you did it. He was all ready for your little attempt at treachery. I'd hoped he would throw you out then. But it's better like this, I think."

"So. Well, you've ruined it for all of us now. The Mitsriy are falling back to their own borders. They'll be gone in another few years, all bar a few soldiers and traders. Even if they try to come back it won't work. They're weak now, priest. You seem to have a fondness for weak people. Now there's this new lot you've gone in with. Might be anyone. You didn't care. Just because of that woman. But we'll be the losers in the end. They'll take our land and make us live in little camps here and there. Everything we now have will be gone. I'd have stopped that if I was king. It was the only way to keep all we have."

"You don't know how to keep. You only know how to take. As if we ever needed a king before. You should have stayed a chief and kept all of us with you. You know, when you were first anointed chief I thought you'd be good for us. I said as much to Kothar one day. But then you turned greedy, turned to thieving. What has it brought you now? We have a covenant with the Ibriym now – they get to provide the chief and we get to keep our way of life."

"It won't last. You can't trust them."

"It will last long enough. For sure there are good men and bad men among them, those who are sound of heart and those who are greedy. Is that any different from now? From the four towns?"

"Your name will be forgotten. Your lineage will die out and be forgotten."

Damariel laughed.

"I have never wanted my own name to be remembered. But because of today, my people will be remembered. People will remember what we did here today. And chief, I say to you as seer of my people, that the words I bring to life in song will be sung long after all of us are dust. And if it should be that I never father a living child in this land, I shall have given birth to something else that will outlive me."

The chief slumped, exhausted from speaking and barely clinging to life. The flow of blood from his side had slowed to a feeble trickle. Damariel watched him in silence as this happened, his hands stroking the kef as he might once, long ago, have caressed Qetirah's hair or cheek. After a long pause the chief spoke again, his voice very quiet, quite broken.

"It's cold."

And then, after another pause.

"Pray for me, priest."

Damariel got up, knelt down beside him, leaned his head very close to the chief and looked directly into his eyes.

"Never."

They remained like that for a long moment, then the chief gave a great shiver and went still. The hand that had been pressed against the wound in his side slipped loosely down. His eyes were still open, but now were looking at nothing. Damariel nodded to himself, moved to close the chief's eyes, then stopped and left them open in their empty stare.

While the fingers were still easy to move, he unclenched them, wrapped them around the gold that had been a brooch, and closed them again. Then he stood up, carefully folded the kef with the silver wrapped up hidden inside it and put it away. Looking up at the ridge that marked the start of Kephrath, he took a long breath of relief and completion, and started back down the wadi.

He passed the bodies of Danil and then Yaraq, but the Ibriym were no longer there, neither the dead nor the living. Coming out of the mouth of the wadi he looked around. About half the Ibriym were stripping Kinahny bodies and caring for their own wounded.

Kothar was helping them, and was now talking with Yahusharar's second in command, a man called Caleb, just like Kinreth's husband. The prince of Laksh and his bodyguard had been made to stand on a rocky outcrop with their feet tied together to prevent escape, and their leather jerkins and helmets had been taken away together with their weaponry.

Yahusharar was nowhere in sight. Kothar had also been organising the little group of men from Kephrath, who were now in a light screen of lookouts, stationed on the lip of the path where it disappeared down towards the lowlands. Damariel approved; it helped the men feel that they were participating, but kept them away from suddenly coming across the corpses of former friends and neighbours.

As he made his way across to Kothar and Caleb, he heard a voice he recognised, Yusuf, calling out. He was pointing down the track. There was a moment's tension among the men scattered around the bowl, then Yusuf waved his kef three times from side to side. Friends then, and most likely Yahusharar returning from the pursuit.

As he came near, Caleb looked questioningly at him.

"The one who was chief?"

"Dead. He died of the injuries your people gave him."

"Good. Now look, Damariel, we are nearly done here stripping the bodies. Some of it rightly belongs to you and your people. Your town and the others. You must decide what is yours and what is ours. And also you must tell me what do you want done with the bodies."

Damariel stood and thought about this. Previously he had not dared to think his way through what would happen in the case of victory, so he had no plan. He looked around. About five or ten from Kephrath, and much the same from each of the other three towns.

"We will bury the dead of the four towns together here to prevent dishonour and give them rest. I will take something small from each to give to their families and to lie with their ancestors. But we will make no effort to return anything to the rightful family. It is enough to take it back to each town. Share whatever other wealth you find among your own men as you see fit, for you have carried the weight of this day and some will never return to your camp."

Caleb nodded and turned to go, but Damariel continued.

"But there are two men up the track who must receive no honour. Strip the bodies and leave them exposed like carrion. I want nothing of whatever they have."

Caleb shrugged.

"Will their women not want something to grieve with?"

"I think the chief's wife will not be grieving much at his death."

At that point Yahusharar and the others appeared up from the lowlands, and they congregated into one group. Damariel could now see that only a handful of men had been lost. It was as Kothar had said; fatalities during the battle itself were slight, and it was during the subsequent rout that most were killed on the losing side.

He grimaced, thinking of the loss of men from the four towns. Five or ten men less at Kephrath would make for difficult growing and harvesting seasons for the next few years. It would be hard at each of the four towns for a while, but they would recover, especially with Mahur-Baal and his demands now gone. He was quite sure that, for the next couple of years at least, the Ibriym would be too busy and too disorganised to think about consolidating their territory.

He was pulled from his thoughts by Yahusharar's approach. He came up to him and embraced him vigorously, sweatily. The wild enthusiasm for battle had gone, and he was once again in calculating mood. He called to the men guarding the prince of Laksh and his bodyguard to bring them over. As they came, he conferred briefly with Damariel.

"This man is a chief's son, they tell me?"

"They call him a king's son, now."

"What town?"

"Laksh."

Damariel pointed down the track.

"Down to Ayaluna then south, perhaps a day or so from here walking quickly. It has a wall from the time before the Mitsriy ruled here. A fair-sized town, quite wealthy."

"Allies of yours?"

"No. At least, not until Mahur-Baal negotiated with them. We have no ties of history or family with them."

Yahusharar nodded and turned to the prince.

"You choose your friends poorly, king's son."

The other looked around.

"This battle is lost, but we will win the next. We will choose the battleground better another time. My father will pay the ransom and in future he will plan his covenants more carefully. Name your price."

"Would you ally with us, as this priest has done on behalf of his people? Would your father the king honour such an arrangement?"

The prince looked at Damariel and pulled a dismissive face.

"He might well need your help. Little villages up here in the hills might well look to tent dwellers and lawless criminals for their allies. Down towards the coast we have different standards."

Yahusharar nodded and grinned as though amused. He took the prince's sword from the man who had been guarding it and looked it up and down carefully as though assessing its worth. Then he stepped up very close to the prince, who held his ground with an effort.

"I think, prince, that I prefer little villages in the hills."

With an unhurried move, still eye to eye with the prince, he thrust the sword into his body. The prince choked, fell first to his knees and then full length on the ground, and writhed for a short time before lying still. Damariel struggled to catch breath, taken aback by the sudden action. He had seen death many times before, both natural and the result of passion, but he had never before witnessed an execution.

Yahusharar pulled back the sword and then turned to face the bodyguard, who straightened his back and waited, clearly expecting the same treatment. Yahusharar threw the weapon at his feet.

"Take the sword back to this man's father and tell him everything that happened here today. Omit nothing. Tell him that if he is wise he will leave us well alone, in case we decide to visit the lowlands as well as the hill country."

The man swallowed, looking around. He bent to pick up the sword. The Ibriym parted left and right to make a passageway for him. He walked along it slowly and carefully, being careful to look at nobody as he walked, then set off down the track without ever turning round.

Much later that afternoon, when the sun was low on the horizon, they walked in to Kephrath together. Damariel had led them around in a loop so they could enter the town in the proper way, along the main track and through the town gate.

He had sent Qeren back long before to pass on the news of victory. As they approached, the women came out of the gate to meet them, singing as they came, Nepheret leading them and the other women responding line after line.

At first they sang the old song of Anath stalking the land, slaying her enemies while her people followed in the shelter of her shield.

Then the song changed to a new song that Damariel had never heard before, and he laughed to hear how words from the morning's work were already being sung. So now still stood the sun and the moon had stopped, and the storm of Yahu took the place of the sword of Anath.

The beat of the song shaped the tread of their feet, and the heartbeat of the new song, the long and short pulse of the Mitsriy way, ran around their bodies like lifeblood. The Ibriym loved the song too, and they clapped and sang along with the women around the gate.

The sun stood still over Giybon and the hills,
  And the hail of Yahu cut them down.
Ayaluna quaked at the high hanging moon,
  And the hail of Yahu cut them down.
A double-length day, a day for winning wars,
  And the hail of Yahu cut them down.
The hearts of the enemy all melted like wax,
  And the hail of Yahu cut them down.

A child brought out flowers woven into a necklace for Yahusharar, and he bent his head low down for her to place it around his neck. Damariel turned in order to formally welcome Yahusharar and his men into Kephrath, and then realised Asherith was standing in the shadow of the gate.

She was wearing the plain white kef of a single woman, and conspicuously not wearing any kind of mourning attire. She stepped forward like a queen and came over to Yahusharar. A silence fell. Yahusharar looked at her, clearly not quite sure who she was, and waited for her to speak first.

"Yahusharar of the Ibriym, I am Asherith, and I was chief wife of Mahur-Baal who you killed. I am here to offer you welcome in the four towns."

He looked at her, weighing up the situation.

"I regret any grief that his loss might bring you."

"Do you see me grieving? That man took away my dignity as a woman, and my honour as mother of my own household. He lost what had been his, and trampled on what had been mine. I have no wealth to bring to honour you and your people, because of all that has been squandered. All I offer is my word alongside that of Damariel that, so long as you and your people stand with us and defend us as you have done today, we will serve you faithfully and do all that a people ought to do for their chief, even if it be the chopping of wood or the drawing of water."

She stopped and waited, pride holding her head up as she held his gaze. Yahusharar suddenly, unexpectedly, knelt in front of her and kissed her hand before rising to his feet again. He stood beside her, took her hand in his own, and then turned to address his men standing all around the gate.

"When we are secure in this land and are settled with our women and children in our own towns, we will provide a chief who will rule these families and clans alongside our own. We will honour the covenant we cut with Damariel, and these people will serve the new chief we appoint, as a people ought to serve their chief. But I say to you here that this woman, whose dignity was lost to the man we defeated today, and whose honour was taken away, shall have that honour and that dignity restored to her by me. Since she lost a place as mother of a household, we shall name her as mother of these four towns. Until that day when we parcel out the land and appoint chiefs, she shall speak for the wellbeing of her people as though she was chief, and Damariel and the other priests with him will uphold her as they minister to the people."

He took Asherith's hand and passed through the town gate into Kephrath to begin the formal circumnavigation of the boundaries of the community. In a short time he would do the same for each of the four towns. Damariel, following the couple with Nepheret beside him, reflected on the exchange. Earlier in the day he had seen that Yahusharar could be brutally ruthless to a defeated enemy; now he had seen him act with devastating, disarming kindness.

Asherith was won over, and with her most of the people within earshot, even if they had lost family members this day. Indeed, there were probably few present who were not expecting a sharing of beds to follow soon after the sharing of land and power they had witnessed. He wondered if both faces of Yahusharar's character were, in truth, equally detached and calculating. Which face would his people become acquainted with in the longer term?

What would the dying Mahur-Baal have made of this, he wondered as they passed the high place and the house he shared with Nepheret now. Would it have confirmed his bitter accusation that one day the Ibriym would betray them and push them out to the margins? Or his own confidence that the covenant would be upheld? As they passed the house where Danil had lived, where Rivkah was wearing a mourning kef and had new cuts down her arms, he found himself pursuing an inner debate with the dead chief.

Passing Kalita's house, with her own dreams of chiefdom now silenced, he pointed out where the words and deeds of Yahusharar and the other Ibriym gave proof that all would be well, and that their way of life would survive. Finally on the way back towards the high place, close to Yeresheth's house, with his own family gathered at the door to watch the newcomers walking the streets of Kephrath, the internal conversation ceased.

Whether eventually, in long years well beyond his ability to foresee, the chief would be right or wrong had never been the issue; he was sure they had chosen the right alliance for the next few generations. After that, who could say?

Taw

Matan Year 25 and after

My heart still reminisces on this love –
how with half my head unbraided,
I went running, chasing after you,
my crown of curls quite out of mind.

Now unravelled and redressed are all my braids,
completed from today forever.

THE MONTHS FOLLOWING THE DEATH of Mahur-Baal had been a busy time for Damariel and Nepheret. They sought to heal wounds and rifts in their own community, rebuild broken links with the other three towns and the other nearby communities they normally traded with, and also to forge a more substantial relationship with Yahusharar and his people. The last of these was particularly slow, as the Ibriym were busily trying to secure land in a wide belt north from Kephrath and Giybon up to the hills around Sychem. Yahusharar had decided that the four towns would indicate their southern border, at least for the time being.

From what Damariel had been able to glean from a variety of sources, the newcomers were happy to settle peacefully where they could, but fought eagerly when they appeared to have no other choice. Indeed, if they were blocked or challenged, and especially if they were attacked and lost members of the tribes, they were ruthless in exacting revenge and felt entitled to take five, seven or even more times the number of their enemy to account for the loss.

It was as the warleader had told him – their style of fighting was to completely avoid direct assault, and instead to defeat their enemies by a mixture of ambush, night attack, or swift marches to approach from an unexpected direction. It seemed to work for them, and in terms of territory they were securing a place for themselves quite rapidly. They had, however, no real knowledge of working the land, and people from the four towns found themselves in considerable demand for passing on skills of terracing, storing water, and choosing crops that thrived in the hill country.

Once or twice Damariel had heard of less happy incidents. Some of the Ibriym seemed unable to make a distinction between his own people as their ally, and some of the other towns in the region as their enemy. It was as though the word Kinahny, which to Damariel always signified a rich and diverse collection of clans and tribes, friends and rivals, had become for these few nothing except for a term of abuse. It was disquieting, but Yahusharar always acted swiftly to resolve the situation amicably as soon as he heard of it. In any case, the number of people that thought that way was small, and mostly found amongst those of the Ibriym trying to push up further north.

Most of the former nomads were happy enough to build settlements, make friends, and even establish intimate relations with the current occupants of the land. Damariel suspected it would only be a short time before the first intermarriages took place, and the first children of mixed unions would be born into the hill country. So far as he could see, this could only help to strengthen the covenant relationship he had made with Yahusharar on the eve of battle.

And in fact connections in battle were another way of integrating. Perhaps it could be seen as another form of intimacy. Yahusharar had come around each of the four towns only a couple of weeks after the battle against Mahur-Baal with a group of his fighting men, asking if anyone wanted to go with them. They would teach them to fight in the Ibriym style, by stealth and sudden strike, and then help to defend the hill country against another incursion from the lowlands.

Another attack would follow very soon; news had reached them of this from several different sources, and the rumour seemed reliable. Yahusharar saw this as simply a continuation of the first skirmish against the former chief. Indeed, to his mind it would be the crucial one, whereas Damariel saw the resolution of the local problem as more important. In the future, when they told about this in story and song, it would be presented as a single decisive event.

The king of Laksh, incensed by the execution of his son, had called on some of his allies to arise with him and seek revenge. Yahusharar planned to meet them somewhere suitably unexpected, probably not all that far from the place where they had set the former ambush. All being well, this should settle the matter permanently. From his perspective, it would be particularly fitting if the same battleground were to be used this time around as well. Seen in that way, he was offering the young men of the four towns a great opportunity to be part of the resolution.

As an added motivation, if things did not go well then the invading force would bring war up to the doorsteps of Kephrath and of Jarrar's town.

A little to Damariel's surprise, a couple of dozen men from the towns had responded to the call. They were away for a while preparing, then one day arrived back in triumph, passing through Kephrath first and then the other towns in turn. The invaders had again been taken by surprise, a little further down the valley towards Ayaluna, completely put to rout, and the lowland kings and city leaders who had marched with them put to death.

Yahusharar was pleased; this would secure the southern and western borders for some time to come, and allow his people to concentrate on their northern perimeter. So far as Damariel could tell, matters there were not so clear cut as in the south. Internal divisions within the Ibriym tribes were causing difficulty, and although there was some mixing with Kinahny groups, for trade or mutual help, they had not found a group that would make formal covenant with them.

In some areas the clans concerned had become very much the lesser partner in the relationships, so that they were more or less vassals of Kinahny leaders. At any rate, Yahusharar was pleased with the four towns, and in recognition for the help given had declared that there would be no work levy requested from the towns for a full year. It all meant wealth flowing back into the towns.

The monthly provision of supplies which had taken the place of the twice yearly provision of gifts was not a burden at all, and the men who had gone out to battle with the Ibriym had brought back goods they had stripped from the bodies of their enemies. They were enjoying covenant life at a level far above Asherith's promise that they would be loyal even if it should involve cutting wood and drawing water.

On this particular day he was passing Yeresheth's house, and seeing the door open he called out and went in. Sosanneth was nowhere in sight. Yeresheth had Sophireth on her lap and was trying to organise pieces of woven material into piles; not an easy job as her daughter's daughter had her own ideas about the arrangement.

Tobiaz and Qeren were at the back wall, measuring out a large rectangle on the stones with a wooden stick. Labunasi was standing between them, looking up at each of them alternately. They were finishing one more measurement as he came in. Yeresheth pushed fabric and needles out of reach and put Sophireth down so she could toddle over to him. He picked her up and settled her on his hip with one arm while hugging his mother with the other.

"They're going to build me another room, Damari, they're going to take part of that wall down and build out just there, from that side. We've all decided it's too full in here now with everything in the rooms we've got. So they're going to build out, so we can put the hand loom in there, and some of the other bits and pieces. What do you think, Damari, my family home needs more space."

He laughed and hugged her again.

"And may you need many more rooms many times over."

He squatted down by Labunasi who was holding out his own measuring stick for him to see, then let Tobiaz and Qeren explain how they were going to add the extra room on with pillars to hold up the roof. All being well, it would all be done before the end of the summer. After that they were sitting down together around the table, when Sosanneth came in and it all had to be said again. After a while Yeresheth took him up onto the roof on pretext of seeing how the new room would fit on to the house when seen from above.

They sat together in the lee of a wattle screen, looking out over the mimosa tree and the wooded ridges of the hill country and listening to the family noise drifting up from below. She leaned back against the stone parapet bordering the open part of the roof, tucked her arm through his and gave a long wordless sigh of contentment. He smiled down at her.

"So, mother, you need more space."

"Yes, I do, Damari. Isn't that something?"

She fell silent again for a while, leaning her head against his shoulder.

"A daughter and a daughter's daughter to carry the household forward for generations to come, men around the house again, and fruitful work for my hands to do. And my firstborn son able to rest again easy at night after all that he has accomplished for his people this last year or so."

"You wouldn't call it resting easy if you had to sit beside Nepheret and I, with most of Kephrath at one time or another, and hear what they have to say. Several times over, usually, not just once. And then some people from the other towns who want to talk to us, as well as their own seers. And then Yahusharar comes down quite often, and he sometimes brings others of the Ibriym along with him. And this firstborn son has still never given you children."

She shook her head, so that the fringes of her kef seemed to dance in the air around her face.

"You have given a future to this whole town, Damari. And you chose well with Nepheret. She has worked hard to win approval and standing among all the people of the town. Not an easy task for any of us, and still less for someone born in another land. She has made as great a journey as any of us. You have both given us songs that I think we shall be singing for generations to come. You have made allies of these newcomers who, from what I hear, might otherwise have been quite fearsome adversaries. Isn't that a future for all of us?"

He shrugged.

"I suppose so. Yes, of course it is. And most of the time it is enough for me. But not all the time."

She looked very sternly at him.

"You must not waste your time on things you cannot solve. Let all you have done for us, and all that you are among us be enough. Do you see any of the people of Kephrath expecting more from you?"

"They used to."

He looked down at her defiantly.

"When Ketty was alive, and before everything that happened with the former chief. They used to expect more of me. You remember what used to be said."

"But do they say that now? Do you ever hear that now?"

He looked away again, across the windy moving trees.

"Well, in truth, no."

He looked for a moment as if he was going to continue, but then remained silent. After a while she spoke again.

"Look, Damari, do you grieve for Qetirah still?"

"Of course. Every day."

"But life with Nepheret is good? How does she say it? Does she make your heart happy?"

He replied in scarcely more than a whisper, his eyes wet with sudden tears as he looked out from the village.

"More than anything."

"So that is how it is. You have lost and you have gained, and they do not cancel each other out as though neither was true. The loss and the gain live side by side in your heart. You have built another room onto the house of your heart to hold the joy that you have gained, without knocking down the room where your loss lives."

He nodded, not quite able to speak.

"And so it is for me. I have lost two sons, and the family you grew up in as a boy is no more. It has gone forever. But I have also gained - well, you know all that I have gained. And although we are building an extra room to contain everything that I have gained now, I will not allow the kitchen area to be knocked down where on that day I thought my life had ended, and where one time after another I was broken apart by things I was told. In my house I will have both rooms. And so it is with the whole town of Kephrath. We have lost people, we have lost the right to appoint our own chief which we have had to ourselves for generations. Perhaps if what we hear is true, we have also lost the abiding protection of the Mitsriy that has been over us all these many years. But look at what we have all gained by way of a future. Can you measure the one against the other, as though one generation yet unborn should be set against the lives of two lost men?"

He stayed silent for a long time, still watching the ridges to the south. She nudged him.

"Well, can you?"

"No. No, of course not."

"Then hold them both together. Look now, every morning that I dress I see all over again the wounds I cut into myself that day in Matan."

She ran her hands down the old white knife scars on her arms, gestured down her body.

"These make sure I do not forget. As if I could. And the same for you. Every night when you share Nepheret's bed she holds against her the wounds that you made to mark Ketty's death. Every one of us in this town sees how they are cut into you whenever you lead the celebrations and the festivals. And we have left the foundations and a few stones in place of Isheth's house where Ethan lived, to hold in the memory of the whole community the thing that we shared that day with them, and with Iqnu and Qerith too. That is who we are, Damari, who your people are that live here in Kephrath. I don't know if our new friends do the same, but they will have their own ways of remembering, and perhaps we can teach them this."

He nodded absently, recollecting things he had heard.

"The people do. I think their priests are not supposed to, but some do anyway. One of them told me that these things should be cut on our hearts rather than our bodies. But I don't know how to do that. If they are not cut into our hearts already, how would cuts on our body do anything to help? But you were not really talking about them, were you?"

"Not really, no."

He nodded.

"I suppose that sometimes I cannot really believe it is all over. All of a sudden there we are on a different path. Do you think I was right to cultivate this covenant with the Ibriym? Sometimes I wonder if we are right to trust them."

She looked at him.

"If you do not know, then surely I do not either. Are these real doubts or just ideas that come upon you in an anxious moment in the dark?"

"I wish I knew. I trust Yahusharar as a man, and as an ally, now that I have come to know him. I think he is quite straightforward in his dealings. Either you are his friend or his enemy. It's all quite simple from his point of view. We are allies, and so he will stand by us, come what may. And most of the others I have met are like that. But there are others who do not share that view, and I suspect they would rather we were not living here. I do not think they are used to having allies and having to share a land with them. With us. Sometimes my heart has misgivings about this alliance. Perhaps that misgiving is true seeing from the other world, and in time what I have done will lead to betrayal. The former chief thought so. He told me as much when he was dying, when he had nothing more to lose and might as well tell me what he really thought."

She made a dismissive gesture.

"Take no notice of him, Damari. All that he said and did was for his own gain and his own advancement. If he said that to you it would have been to win you over to his schemes, even in his last moments. Do not give his dead spirit any consolation by yielding to those thoughts."

"I hope you are right, mother. But my whole life circles around trying to hear what the other world might be whispering into my heart. I cannot ignore it just because I find it uncomfortable. I wish I could see generations into the future, to know for sure that what I have done is for the best. I believe that I have done all this so we will remain in the land, will continue to have a place in these hills that will endure. I think I need to cling on to that belief like a man on a windy cliff hangs on to his rope."

She nodded again. "Without what you have done, none of us had a future."

At that point Sosanneth called up to find out what they were doing. They went back down into the little house, into the midst of family life.

About a week later Damariel was heading back towards his home from speaking with Rivkah, who was still wearing mourning kef and clothing. The time seemed to have been spent well, and he was satisfied that she would soon feel able to regain a place in the town. As he crossed over one of the main paths between the houses, he heard his name being called out. He turned to see Kothar, accompanied by his dog, heading back towards his own home from the ridgeway track. He turned back and joined him, and before long they were outside Shaharti's home.

"And you will come in, brother, so I can tell you about my journey. You must come in now you are here."

"If Shaharti does not mind."

She was opening the door as he spoke, having heard the voices outside. Damariel looked around at the other houses and let them go in and have a brief time to themselves before following. Kothar still had his arms around Shaharti and both children at once.

"Seer, you honour our house. Please accept some refreshment."

"Just some water, if I may, Shaharti, and that would be a great gift to me today. Like spring rains on the fields."

Kothar took Damariel into his work room and they sat together.

"So you have been away?"

"I have. Yahusharar asked me to show some of their lads where there were good places to hunt along the ridge north from here. And they really know nothing about how to track game in the hills so I showed them how it is done up here. They're used to life out in shabby scrubland, or even proper desert. They might be quite good there but they need a lot of help here."

"I hear the same is true about farming."

"Oh yes. Most anything, really. They have very little idea at the moment how to work the land, either to cultivate or to hunt."

"But it sounds as though you like them."

"Oh, they're alright. Yes, I think I do like them. There's some that don't know how to make friends or show their appreciation. Reckon the whole land owes them a debt, I think. But the ones I've been with, they're fine. I do like them. Some of them wish they were still on the move, don't really want to settle anywhere at all, but others are very happy to be making a home up here with us."

"And you've been up there a lot?"

"Three times in the last few weeks. And another of their families asked just today as I was leaving if I'd go back and teach their sons the same thing. I'm doing more up there with them than out along my own traps and snares at the moment. That'll come to a close at some point, I think, but it's all bringing back food and gratitude gifts into the house just now. After all that the old chief took away from us, it's good to be having a bit of wealth coming back in now."

Shaharti, bringing them a refill of water, heard the last few words as she came through the door, and nodded vigorously.

"He's right, seer. Life is much easier now. A woman can feel that her household is growing again instead of shrinking. And Kothar tells me always that although these newcomers are hard bargainers, they give fairly once they've made an agreement with you."

Kothar laughed.

"It's just getting them to the point of agreement that is hard. I find that quite wearying, and am always happier once it is behind us and we can get out among the hills."

"I am very glad to hear that, Shaharti."

As she left again, he turned to Kothar and continued.

"Truly, Kothar, I am most sincerely glad to hear that. I have been very burdened with worry since the spring. I am very happy with our covenant with the Ibriym, and I hear from other people similar words to those you have spoken. Just as you have both said, they are exhausting negotiators, but they seem to keep their word once they have given it."

"Why burdened with worry, then?"

Damariel shook his head.

"I was suspicious of Yahusharar at first. There was a time as we were negotiating that suddenly filled me with fear. I wondered if he would turn against us as soon as we had kept our word to them and they no longer needed us. I felt all of a sudden like a man who had been pressed into a corner. All said and done, we know very little about these people still. And then as he was dying, the former chief spoke words to me about this alliance that worried me. He thought it would be ruin for our people in the end."

Like Yeresheth, Kothar was unimpressed.

"I would give no place to that man's words in your house or your heart."

"But sometimes the dying speak truth, Kothar. They are so close to the other side already that sometimes true words speak through them, without them even knowing what they say. But anyway, whether true words or lying ones, they have stuck inside me and disturbed me sometimes, both by night and by day. So every time I hear a person speak of how these people are inclined to stand beside words and promises they have made, it eases my heart. I want to trust them, Kothar, I want there to be reasons for trust. I want to have reasons like a great heap of stones under which I can bury the chief's words forever."

"Then let them be buried, Damari. I have seen nothing in the Ibriym that would make me regret the vows we each made to the other."

On the way home he diverted off to one side of the high place. He felt that what he needed was a wider perspective on the village, and the place that came to mind was the lookout rock on which he had spent time with Qetirah long ago. But when he scrambled up onto it, it seemed very small. Where once it had assumed a stature in his mind quite appropriate to all the beginnings of relationship he had shared there with her, now it seemed quite a small and isolated outcrop standing out on a limb.

He sat on the top for a few moments, looking down at the high place, then scrambled down again and climbed instead up around behind the tombs of the ancestors. From here he really could look over most of the village, and it was altogether more satisfying for what he wanted to see.

The life of Kephrath washed to and fro along the tracks between the houses. For a while it had seemed that that life was ebbing away, gradually leaving empty houses behind as the living occupants moved elsewhere and once-important families dwindled in numbers and vigour. Even now, the scattered collection of houses beyond the liminal marker of the town gate stood mostly empty. The community had, for a while, shrunk back inside itself. Now, he hoped, a new time of growth and fullness might be coming again.

Could he foresee those same houses thriving again, full of family life and adorned with doorway plants for the women who lived there? Many years ago now, Saniyahu and Halith had warned him about not seizing too quickly on a vision that seemed to fit a situation too perfectly.

They were right, of course; it was all too easy to turn wishes into dreams, and dreams into visions, and then present them to his people as though they were engraved in the rock of the future in writing that could not be erased. But he did have, if not a true vision, at least a profound wish that the borders of his town would spill out beyond an imaginary line drawn through the town gate.

Of course that was all in the future. Just now numbers were at a low point, with the deaths of those who had sided with the former chief. That conflict, however necessary it had been, had led to more widows and orphans in Kephrath, and the additional wealth that the town was now generating could only address their material lack, not the absence in body and spirit that came along with it. He could console himself with the fact that in another few years the town would be a stronger and richer place, and one that had a more secure future, but he would not attempt to console bereft wives and children with that. Nevertheless it was true. If he, and others, had not done what they had done, the town would have bled to death like an exposed infant on the open hillside.

But the vision he most longed to see, the unwrapping of the veil over the years of the future, was not one of a few years hence, but of many generations. For the time being, and in conversation around the four towns, he was content to accept the assurance of Yeresheth, Kothar, and others, that the chief's opinion was worthless. He hoped that the word of the Ibriym would be with them as a shield and a stronghold far into the future, as many generations ahead as the great migration down from the north was in the past.

He longed for the veil of years to grow thin for him, and for the other world to invest in him complete assurance that all would be well. So far it had never come. Every now and again he knew, as he had down on the trackway on the day of battle, that words were coming into him that were more than just his own. But never once had those words given assurance of the kind he wanted.

He sighed to himself, looked around at the friendly houses of his town, and climbed down again. Crossing the high place, he went back into his own house, where at least he had the assurance that Nepheret would be there beside him at sunset and at sunrise. Two months previously, not long after the defeat of Mahur-Baal and the foundation of the covenant with the Ibriym, Damariel had asked Nepheret one evening whether she was sure that she was happy to stay with him in Kephrath.

He had meant it as a sincere offer of release for her if she had wanted to go back amongst her own people, in case hill country life had proved not to her taste. But his intentions had not been fulfilled, and instead, she had at first heard his words as a rather cruel rejection of all that she had accomplished so far in Kephrath, with him and among his people. The resulting argument had been lively, and had left him in no doubt as to her intention to live her new life to the full.

More months rolled by. The time of the autumn festival was rapidly approaching, and the town was alive with anticipation. Every festival this year was seen as the first one since the old chief had been thrown down, and was an occasion for particular celebration. Damariel had spent almost all of the day going from one house to another, arranging who would provide what. It had been a long day. Eventually he came back to the house beside the high place. All of the visits he had made had taken longer than he had expected, but they had undeniably gone well.

After all this time it did seem that the community was settling down into the routine of everyday life. So perhaps there would be a new chief, and perhaps in time he would want to play a more active part in the life of the towns, but after all things were not very different. Whoever it was, he would want very much the same seasonal dues as Mahur-Baal had done before his unfortunate brush with kingship. So far as anyone could tell at this stage, the new chief of the Ibriym would be no different.

No doubt when the current excitement regarding their new covenant allies had waned a little, the townspeople would be seeking to hide a little of their true wealth from him in the same way they always had. The newcomers were divided into families and clans just like Kinahny, their men and women shared much the same joys and travails as people did in Kephrath and Giybon, Woodlands and Meyim.

Just now the Ibriym needed the support and covenant loyalty of his people, and the four towns were valued, necessary allies for these new arrivals. As the time had passed by, he had become more sure that the gloomy defiance of the chief before he had died was no true prophecy, but was no more than mean bitterness in the face of his own ruin.

He opened the door of his home. With him being later than he thought, Nepheret had already settled most of the house down for the night. The fire was out and the embers covered, kitchen utensils were put away, drapes pulled across windows. One oil lamp still burned in the kitchen area for him, its flame tossing slightly in the draught from the door, and another burned steadily beside Nepheret in the room where they slept together.

She was sitting on a stool beside their bedroll, a clay tablet propped up in front of her while she cleaned and overhauled the little flute she had played earlier in the day at the weekly time of celebration. He snuffed the light in the kitchen and joined her. She had left the drape open at the window in that room, and a nearly full moon was shining over her shoulder. She looked up at him and set the flute aside, her expression hard to read in the shifting mixture of moonlight and lamplight.

He sat down on a stool beside her. It was only three weeks since they had joined together in formal marriage beside the stones of the high place. Saniyahu and Halith had come down to witness the act, but they had asked Eli and Birketh to actually conduct the ceremony.

Damariel had been surprised at first, but after a time had decided that the decision was right. For families in Kephrath, and especially for Kinreth and Caleb, it would be difficult to manage too many echoes of the previous wedding to Qetirah. Eli and Birketh had played no part in that ceremony, and so trailed no history into the event.

Nepheret, of course, had no family to bring her to the stones and then stand beside her, and no kef from her adolescence to be torn in half during the wedding. They had talked at some length about what would be suitable. In the end she had asked Kothar and Shaharti to stand with her, and they had been very willing.

When the right time came, she had given over, to be torn from top to bottom, the plain linen dress that she had worn when she left Gedjet. It was the last piece of clothing she had from that life, and now only the sistrum and wood-blocks remained from her time living in Senenptah's house.

Then there was the dancing and the communal celebration. Yeresheth and Shomal were both there, and managed to successfully ignore each other the whole time, an achievement that Nepheret had found quite entertaining, especially as Aliyna and Tobiaz evidently felt themselves under no such constraint.

Finally, when all was done, Nepheret and Damariel were ushered between two long rows of the people of Kephrath back into the house they had already been sharing together all the recent months.

As they went towards the door, Damariel overheard some of the people in the crowd making witty suggestions about the forthcoming union, and speculations as to whether the couple would manage to find anything to surprise each other. He was happy. If the townspeople were not making those jokes, then he certainly would have been worried about their mood.

That had been three weeks ago, and so far their life together had not changed in any appreciable way. Damariel was not sure if he had expected any great change to have occurred from that day. Before that day, they had started to learn the process of living under the same roof, and they would both, no doubt, continue to learn it for a long time to come. As seers in

Kephrath, they had already been learning to stand up alongside each other, as well lie down facing each other.

Perhaps there was a greater sense that each was committed to the other, a sense of willing abandonment of other possibilities. Before that time, the question he had asked about whether she wanted to leave the town had seemed quite natural to him; after the wedding, it was no longer thinkable. Their lives had been joined not only to one another, but also woven into the fabric of the life of the town. It all made for a more complete sense of partnership; each with the other, and both within the community as a whole.

Like so many other evenings, they sat together and talked about the different people that each had met, spoken with, and prayed with. It was a comfortable, satisfying habit to have cultivated, but on this occasion she had an elsewhere feel as she listened to him. There was a sense that she was inhabiting some inward place that he was not sure had been shared with him yet. As he continued to talk, he wondered what was passing through her heart and mind, but did not ask. In the end the day was done. He got up and went to pull the drape across the window.

"Can we leave it open tonight, Damari?"

"Of course, if you like."

"The moon is nearly full tonight, and I want to see it when we lie down."

He nodded and let go of the drape again. When he snuffed out the wick of the oil lamp, the brightness of the moon still filled the inside of their room.

He leaned out of the window for a few moments, drinking in the beauty of the view across the trees growing in waves to the north of them. She came over to join him and tucked her arm through his.

"It is lovely, isn't it? Who would have thought it, that I should be living in a place like this? I have come up from the Beloved Land into the hills of your country, and do not feel any regret that the way has sometimes been steep."

Soon after they were lying side by side, a thin woven blanket over them although the air was warm. She was looking over to one side, through the window still where the undrawn drape flapped lazily, beyond to the moon hanging high over the ridges of the hill country. He turned on his side to face her and touched her cheek with his hand, finally allowing his anxiety to find a voice.

"Nepheret, is everything all right? Are you well?"

She smiled slightly, kissed the side of his hand where it brushed her lips and then pressed it with her own hand to cup her cheek.

"So tell me again, is our home safe now, Damariel?"

"Yes. Yes, I think so. I believe it is now. Yahusharar and his people will keep their covenant with us. I am sure of it. Families who followed Mahur-Baal are accepting his defeat and death. Wounds are healing. Why ask? You know all that, and my news from today has not changed it."

She nodded.

"I know."

There was a little silence while she caressed his hand with her fingers. He waited for a while for her to make more of her reply. But she remained silent beside him, and finally he spoke again.

"So why ask tonight?"

She turned her head to look at him, with as enigmatic a look on her face as there could be between a Mitsriy woman and a Kinahny man. Her dark eyes, and the dark wing of her hair that was spilled across the pale bedroll filled his world.

Then she took his hand from her cheek, squeezed it, pushed back the light blanket to uncover herself and held the open palm of his hand against the curve of her body below her ribs. He was perplexed for a moment, keeping his hand on her until realisation came, and with a thrill that ran all through him he was filled with a sudden surmise. His eyes ran with tears.

She kept silent for several heartbeats, holding his hand still against her, then spoke out four lines in the Mitsriy language, as though not trusting herself to speak except in her own tongue. He closed his eyes briefly, listening to the pulse of her poetry and feeling the flutter of her heartbeat through her body, pulling the Mitsriy words he had learned out of his memory and piecing together the meaning. Then he looked back into her eyes and spoke the lines back to her in Kinahny.

"Your love, my brother, has filled up my body,
like new seed sown on the flooded fields,
like vine fruit and yeast, transforming to wine,
like honey-drops mingled with dates."

She nodded, waiting for his response. He kept his hand cupped over her womb. She felt no different yet to his touch, but before too long he knew his hand would start to feel her body swell out and fill with new life. He leaned down and kissed her twice, very gently, once each for mother and infant, then gathered her full length into his embrace. There would, after all, be another round of childhood in the hill country.

Coda

WHEN IT IS TIME, I shall rest in the tomb of my ancestors, along with those of my family who have gone before. Not with Qetirah daughter of Kinreth though, for she rests in her family's cave where her mother laid her down after that day, so very long ago now. Qetirah was the incense of my youth, but that incense was taken by the winds that sweep across our land and blown away from us all.

But Nepheret-er-sefet-Tefnut, the abiding fragrance of my life, will lie beside me in death as she has in life. It will be easy to go on singing with her. At one stage the thought of resting so far from her Beloved Land was difficult for her. The great river that flows from end to end of it, and which gives life in its own cycle of breathing in and out through the year, seemed very far away.

I saw that river once, in its placid state having flooded the land with richness and then returned within its banks, when she and I journeyed all that long way to see it. I can understand how a soul might long for it. But here, as a Mitsriy scribe once said to us down in Shamsh when we met one day trading for amulets, here we have a river that runs from the sky. It has been enough for Nepheret in life, and it shall be enough in death. She brought the fragrance of the lotus and the acacia into these hills, and it will linger yet a while after she and I are both gone.

Kephrath will remain, though. I am sure of that. It will not, perhaps, be the same as the town I have known, but it will remain. It is changing along with the whole hill country. Little hamlets and villages are springing up all across the land, and trees and groves are being cleared in great blotches around them. The hill country is changing, the land itself and not just the patchwork of people who live upon it. Who can say if it will ever change back again?

Customs change too. I think perhaps that not so many of my people will be laid to rest with their ancestors as the next generation comes and goes. I shall, and they will honour me in that because of all that has happened. But our children, and the children that come after them, will find a different way to honour their dead. Some have already done that, in imitation of the Ibriym who have established themselves in a great swathe north of us.

I would like to think that we are able to reshape some of their customs too. Their worship is full of the vigour and violence they have had to endure from others, and to practice on others.

Perhaps we can convey to them some of the gentler qualities of the land we live in and love. I heard some of them singing a song of liberation of their own, and then sang it back to them with a little more of our own style woven into it. I think they liked it. Perhaps they will keep singing it that way.

The story they tell around that song is full of the visceral struggle of labour, but, to my ears at least, it lacks recognition of the wonder of pregnancy and the nurture of infancy, when milk and honey drip from all around. Perhaps I shall talk with some of them about how together we can bring something of a more motherly quality into the telling of their birth.

There is no great rush. I think they are here to stay. They are very determined to stay, now that they have arrived here. Although Yahusharar no longer leads them in war - and they honoured me by asking me to sing at the assembly they held after his death - they are still very determined.

Like any group of clans walking along a track together, they do not always agree. But when they can bring themselves to act in concert, they show the same mix of winning charisma and ruthlessness that I first saw in the war leader who protected our four towns. I still find it difficult, just as I did when I saw it in him.

Most of them now see us as just another of their own family groups. Yahusharar once talked of a generation or two before that might happen, but we have proved ourselves valuable to them, and formalities have a way of being overlooked by gratitude. I think in time that our different origins might be forgotten, and we shall be remembered as though we were just another Ibriym clan.

That thought has stuck like rotten meat in the mouths of some of the towns nearby to us. Places that were once friends and allies now look at us askance. Have we betrayed them? Have I betrayed the heart of what my people once were? Some say yes, and have severed all relationship with us. Others waver in doubt, pulled in both directions at once like a moth between two flames. I am at peace. If I had not led my people thus, we would have dwindled and perished, been beaten down and left for dead by the side of the track by the man who was chief. As it is, we have a future, albeit not the same one that we had expected.

The future that waits for us outside the open door of tomorrow as one of the Ibriym clans is indeed very different. But once we have been accepted and grafted in, does our former lineage matter? Already from time to time when I listen to someone around the hearth fires, or up at our high place, or in the assemblies of the Ibriym, I hear different tales of our family connections being told. It is a remarkable thing, to see how creatively people set to work to find links with distant kindred in the most unlikely places, once they are motivated to look.

I think in time to come our northern origins might be overlooked, and a new family heritage will be told that unites us instead with some suitable branch of the Ibriym. I would like that. I would like it to be told that I was close kin to Yahusharar.

But most of all, I should like to think that my people will go on living in this milk and honeyed land.

Notes

About the author

Richard Abbott has visited some of the places that feature in this story and others set in broadly the same region. As well as writing fictional accounts of the period, he has also participated in the lively academic debate surrounding it.

Richard now lives in London, England. When not writing he works on the development and testing of computer and internet applications. He enjoys spending time with family, walking and wildlife – ideally combining all three of those pursuits at the same time.

Follow the author on:

- Web site – www.kephrath.com
- Blog – richardabbott.datascenesdev.com/blog/
- Google+ – google.com/+Kephrath
- Facebook – www.facebook.com/pages/In-a-Milk-and-Honeyed-Land/156263524498129
- Twitter – @MilkHoneyedLand

Look out for his other works, which include the following.

Fiction – full-length novels

- *Scenes from a Life*, available from most online retailers, and general booksellers in
  - soft-cover – ISBN 978-0954-5535-9-3
  - hard-cover – ISBN 978-0954-5535-7-9
  - ebook format – ISBN 978-0954-5535-8-6

  In case of difficulty please check the website http://www.kephrath.com for purchasing options.
  Feedback for this novel includes:
  "The author is extremely knowledgeable of his subject and the minute detail brings the story vividly to life, to the point where you can almost feel the sand and the heat..."

  Historical Novel Society UK Review

  "... lovely description – evocative sentences or phrases that add so much to the atmosphere of the book"

  The Review Group

  "The striking thing about 'Scenes' is... its sensitivity: its assured, mature observation of people"

  Breakfast with Pandora

- *The Flame Before Us*, available from most online retailers, and general booksellers in
  - soft-cover – ISBN 978-0993-1684-1-3
  - ebook format – ISBN 978-0993-1684-0-6

  Feedback for this novel includes:
  "Wide in scope and rich in detail and plot, this is an accomplished illustration of this era in the region: complex, informative, enjoyable and skilfully put together."

Historical Novel Society UK Review

"...A surprising tenderness in the face of brutality, loss, and displacement is the emotion that underpins the action..."

Breakfast with Pandora

Fiction – short stories

- *The Man in the Cistern*, a short story of Kephrath, published in ebook format by Matteh Publications and available at online retailers, ISBN 978-0954-5535-1-7 (kindle) or 978-0954-5535-4-8 (epub).
- *The Lady of the Lions*, a short story of Kephrath, published in ebook format by Matteh Publications and available at online retailers, ISBN 978-0954-5535-3-1 (kindle) or 978-0954-5535-5-5 (epub).

Non-fiction

- *Triumphal Accounts in Hebrew and Egyptian*, published in ebook format by Matteh Publications and available at online retailers, ISBN 978-0954-5535-2-4 (kindle) or 978-0954-5535-6-2 (epub).

About Matteh Publications

Matteh Publications is a small publisher based in north London offering a small range of specialised books, either in ebook or softback form. For information concerning current or forthcoming titles please see http://mattehpublications.datascenesdev.com/

Some Background and Glossary

The Background

A rather curious episode is related in chapters 9 and 10 of the book of Joshua in the Hebrew bible. It describes how four Canaanite towns – Gibeon, Kephirah, Beeroth and Kiriath Jearim – decide to trick the oncoming Israelite army, with a tale of having travelled huge distances specifically to establish a treaty. The nearby Canaanite towns see this, with some justification, as a betrayal of local solidarity and march against the four towns, who then appeal to Joshua to rescue them.

A battle follows in which various miraculously arranged natural phenomena including a hailstorm help the Israelites to achieve complete victory. Unsurprisingly, the bible tells the events solidly from the Israelite perspective and does not explore the preceding actions or motives of the Gibeonites, other than to suggest that they feared the approaching invaders.

The episode leaves a lot of loose ends. Why would the inhabitants of these four towns take the initiative to arrange the peace treaty? Why not remain in league with their former allies? Why would the Israelites believe this rather improbable story and go into the alliance, if they were as confident of victory as they claimed? Scanning through later books and chapters of the bible reveals that these Canaanite towns, especially Gibeon, were to feature prominently in Israelite religious life over the next few centuries. For a long time, Gibeon was a more important holy place than Jerusalem.

Clearly a fascinating untold story lies largely hidden behind the rather brief account left in the book of Joshua. This book attempts to recreate this hidden story. Unlike Joshua, it is written taking the perspective of the inhabitants of the towns, and in particular those in Kephirah – Kephrath. It is not written to defend the Hebrew bible in general or Joshua in particular, nor with the assumption that the bible account is necessarily accurate. It is an attempt to look at the Israelite arrival from the opposite perspective. The two accounts overlap in places, like two very different views on a complicated and confusing sequence of events.

For those interested in the historical and cultural background to these events, here is a very brief overview. The story is set around the year 1200 BCE. There is a great deal of currently unresolved scholarly debate as to when and how the Israelites became the dominant force in the hill country. This story simply short-circuits this whole fascinating and lively debate, and picks a date that has quite good evidential support.

Archaeologists call the thousand years leading up to that time the Bronze Age. After that comes the Iron Age, though in fact for a great many years bronze remained the preferred metal of choice. During most of the Bronze Age, especially the last three or four centuries, large and powerful states such as Egypt ruled the region, controlling by treaties a collection of vassal buffer states adjacent to their borders.

Early in the Iron Age many small local states and kingdoms sprang up to challenge and in most cases replace the former system. There have been many explanations offered as to why this happened, often with contemporary echoes – new military technology, displaced groups of refugees, social disintegration, and climate change have all been suggested. This story is set at a time when the old social order is still very vigorous, but the winds of change are starting to blow with increasing strength.

During what is called the New Kingdom, from about 1500 BCE or so, Egypt controlled the region from her own borders all the way north to what we now call Syria and Lebanon. North from there was under the control of the Hittites, whose homeland was in modern Turkey. Egyptian control was focused almost entirely on the wealthier regions along the coast road and valley routes, and the hill country was largely neglected except for collection of tribute and occasional armed raids to enforce loyalty of local rulers. The Egyptians seem to have had very little interest in the land east of the Jordan River. Their political strategy was largely based on the principle of ensuring that separate towns and cities did not combine into larger or more powerful groups, and prohibiting towns from building serious defensive structures.

This period of Canaanite life reveals fierce competitiveness between different groups, and a persistent habit of gaining favour with the Egyptian overlords by denouncing actions of other rulers that could be seen as treacherous. The most important documentary collection is a group of letters written from various rulers in Canaan and beyond to the Egyptian Pharaoh around 1350 or so, revealing a constant turmoil of intrigue and inter-city conflict. These are collectively called the Amarna Letters, from the location in Egypt where they were found.

Canaan, then, was a patchwork of small-scale cities and regions unable or unwilling to establish successful long-term relations with each other. It was also a place where people of quite different origins had come to live. Some groups had been settled in the region for a long time, and many settlements show great cultural continuity over hundreds of years. However, other groups had come into the region from the north. In some cases they formed a ruling elite that simply took control of cities by force of arms. In other cases whole tribal groups seem to have migrated together. We can trace these movements by noticing the use of names that are not Canaanite in origin, but reveal a different heritage.

Gradually these differences disappeared, so that by the year 1000 or so, use of the distinctive northern names had almost vanished, either dying out or being absorbed into the mainstream of Canaanite life. This story adopts the theory that the inhabitants of the four towns were one of these migrant groups, and retained a memory of this in their collective memory and in some family names.

In this novel, the names of groups of people have been deliberately chosen as close imitations of the ancient names, rather than their modern equivalents. This is intended to help the reader meet these people on their own terms rather than through other lenses, whether modern ones or out of the bible. So the Canaanites here are called Kinahny, the Israelites are called Ibriym, and the Egyptians Mitsriy. Anyone familiar with the modern middle east will find many of the personal names of men and women in the story recognisable. The major liberty that has been taken is with the Ibriym, who have been given names that blend Egyptian and Hebrew elements. The bible suggests that the Israelites had been living in Egypt for many years prior to their arrival in Canaan, and it seems reasonable that they would have absorbed some Egyptian habits of speech.

So, one of the Ibriym is called *Natan-Netjer*, blending the Hebrew name *Natan* ('gift') with the Egyptian word *netjer* ('god'). So the name as a whole means 'gift of god', rather like the later Hebrew names *Nathaniel* or *Natanyahu*. The Israelite war leader is not called *Joshua*, nor the closer version *Yehoshua'* (which means 'Yahu is salvation', *Yahu* being one form of the divine name used in the bible). Instead he is called *Yahusharar*, blending the same divine name with the Egyptian word *sharar*, meaning a son or small copy; the name as a whole therefore means 'son of Yahu'.

Short glossary of words and customs

Most terms and phrases used will be quite familiar to readers. One that probably will not be is the word *kef*, used here for the headscarf worn by both men and women from childhood onwards. A person's *kef* signals their social and family status, in ways that would be easily recognised by people from the same community. Wearing head coverings of different kinds is still an important part of middle eastern life, and pictures from ancient Egypt and elsewhere show that this was also the case in the past.

Coinage was unknown at this time, with trade and other transactions usually managed by the transfer of weights of silver. Indeed, many of our terms for coins originated as descriptions of particular weights. Within a small community, just as within an extended family today, most exchange would be by barter, or by mutually satisfactory exchange of obligation. Silver would only be used where the participants in the trade did not know, or perhaps did not trust one another.

Within most towns and cities, standing armies were unknown except perhaps for a small retinue personally loyal to the chief or king. The economic base of communities was agriculture, and most small states simply could not afford for much of the population to be away from the land for very long. If for some reason a body of armed men was needed – and was allowed by the overall regional ruler – then it would be called up at need and disperse as soon as feasible. Similarly, work on what might be called civic projects affecting more than a single village relied on a system of labour called up by the local leader. In many parts of the middle east this tradition persisted until very recently, and often goes under the name of corvée labour. It is generally agreed that the limitations of this system meant that projects lasting longer than a month or so at a time could not realistically be undertaken.

Poetry

The portions of poems and songs scattered through the book are all either translated by the author from various Hebrew and Egyptian originals (often with minor changes such as personal names), or else are new compositions using the same kinds of style and convention as the original works. The translated snippets from the Hebrew bible are mainly but not exclusively taken from items which scholars consider to be early compositions. It is most likely that, like the creative works of art of any nation, the style of poetry found in the bible can be traced back to earlier origins. The Israelites would have absorbed, and transformed, ways of writing and singing from other people they encountered around them.

The extent of Egyptian influence, which in the story features as a key creative spark between Damariel and Nepheret, is less certain. There has been a great deal of debate as to what kinds of creative designs Egyptian and Hebrew poets and song-writers used. So far no consensus has been reached. A casual inspection of poetry of any of these ancient languages shows that there was no attempt to create lines of consistent length within a poem. However, there is good evidence that, at least for the bulk of later Hebrew poetry, there was an attempt to keep lines more or less the same length, so that the average lengths of lines across different poems work out pretty much the same.

Recent research carried out by the author under the supervision of Trinity College, Bristol confirms the existence of a "popular" style of New Kingdom Egyptian poetry, in which as Nepheret explains, the first line of a pair comes out longer than the second. The very earliest Hebrew poetry seems to share this pattern. A different style was used in Egypt for royal and official temple poetry and music.

If Nepheret and Damariel were instrumental in introducing this style into the hill country, or indeed if the early Hebrews were familiar with the style because of earlier encounters, this injection of new life into the poetry did not last more than a few centuries. Of course a few centuries would still be a substantial contribution to the artistic life of the region! Later Hebrew poetry shows no real signs of Egyptian influence, either because of deliberate rejection of past influences, or else the natural result of developing new styles and tastes.

It seems altogether likely that the first settlers that archaeology recognises as Israelite, responsible for the sudden increase in small villages and settlements in the central hill country, sang songs that blended both Egyptian and Canaanite styles along with their own traditions. As time went by and they came to dominate not just the hill country but the adjacent valleys and lowlands, they developed their own distinctive national style, often rejecting the thought of any prior influences.

This story is set at a time when the mixture was very much on the surface, and suggests that a few individuals might have been responsible for bringing about the particular mix of ideas. We have no way to know how these different influences were blended into a single creative whole, but it is possible that such a combination of individual talent and background was crucial. This particular time in history presents an ideal opportunity for these people to have met and changed each other's thinking.

The chapter names are taken from a fair guess at the names of letters of the alphabet used by the Canaanites. They are similar in name to later Hebrew and Arabic letters but differ in details. So far as we can tell, this alphabet was invented as a variation on older Egyptian forms some five or six hundred years before this story is set, either in the Sinai or else near Karnak in Egypt. This alphabet, which seems easy to learn and natural to us, was not used for serious large-scale inscriptions or monuments for about a thousand years after its invention, though there are plenty of examples of short pieces of writing, often to indicate ownership of small items.

In a few places the story touches on items that are genuinely linked to the area. There was indeed a woman who wrote to the Egyptian pharaoh in the way that Damariel tells Baruk. It is probable, though not certain, that she lived in or near Kephrath, and her two letters are now known as EA 273 and 274. She identifies herself in the letters as *Nin-Ur Mah Mesh*, "the Lady of the Lions". The letter that Damariel and Nepheret wrote for the Egyptian governor at Gaza has never been found, but the style in which it is written mirrors many Egyptian letters where a person writes to their superior.

If Damariel ever did write out the agricultural calendar for Baruk, the copy has been lost to us. The version that we do have was found near Gezer, a little over ten miles down the track towards the coast, and so is known as the Gezer Calendar.

The tablet that Kothar acquired for Damariel at Bayth Shamsh, which Damariel identifies as part of the tale of Gishgimu, is better known to modern readers as Gilgamesh. Although this originated far to the east, it was a popular story and partial versions have been found at many different locations. The closest that we know of so far to this story is from Megiddo, about 50 or so miles north of the four towns, from a few generations before this story. There really was a scribe called Ilimilku, whose name appears on some of the most important religious tablets from the city of Ugarit, on the coast of modern Syria, but we do not know if he ever copied out the story of Gilgamesh.

The joke that Kothar learned is one of the oldest pieces of humour we know.

The Months

Hiyaru... February-March
Nisan... March-April
Matan... April-May
Dabah... May-June
Kiraru... June-July
Tsah... July-August
Mepagh... August-September
Etanim... September-October
Bul... October-November
Merap... November-December
Pegerim... December-January
Ibalatu... January-February

Families and Individuals

Kephrath

Yeresheth = Shomal (later Yeresheth = Tobiaz and Shomal = Aliyna)
- Damariel = 1) Qetirah, 2) Nepheret
- Baruk
- Bashur
- Sosanneth = ?
  - Labunasi
- Sosanneth = Qeren
  - Sophireth

Nerith = Adonilanu

Kinreth = Caleb
- Qetirah = Damariel
- Laylah

Tamar = Labayu
- Kothar = Shaharti
  - Labayu
  - Yasmit

Tabiya = Ethan
- Ayala
- Qeren = Sosanneth

Binti Rahmay = Tobiaz (later Tobiaz = Yeresheth)
- Kunor
- Gazala = 1) Uzziel, 2) Yosheb

Ayala = Emeq
- Uzziel = Gazala
- Shaharti = Kothar

Asherith = Issi
- Sepheret
- Yusuf = Kalita

Shelomith Rahmay
- Kalita = Yusuf

Hinnah = Nawar
- Ethan = Isheth

Mahiram
- Danil = Rivkah
  - Hannah Taliy

Tamguta
- Nikkallia

Niri-Shadday = Nesher
- Tagi = Dadua

Sara = Abiram
Putiheba = Pirigalla
Aliyna = Shomal
- Mahir

Alloni = Aniyt

The seers

Kephrath
    Iqnu = Qerith
      - Asherith
    Saniyahu = Halith
    Damariel = 1) Qetirah, 2) Nepheret
Jarrar's Town or Woodlands
    Adonibaal = Iliuri
    Saniyahu = Halith
Giybon
    Eli = Birketh
Meyim
    Saniyahu = Halith
    Kenizzi = Sallarsheh

Other towns

Yad-nesherim (Giybon)
  - Mahur-Baal = Asherith

Ben-bamah (Giybon)
Yaraq (Giybon)
Zakarabi (Woodlands)
Rakham-Taliy (Woodlands)
Shelsheth (Woodlands)

Gilem = Beliniri (Yabneh)
- Kinor

Towns

The names of towns reflect, so far as we know, the old names given in the Bronze Age. Modem equivalents to these places, where they differ from those used in. the story, are:

In Canaan:

The Four Towns

The four towns are close to the modern highway 1, running from near Jerusalem down to the coast, and itself following a very ancient trackway. Several modern settlements are in this vicinity, although we do not know the exact locations of the original places.

Kephrath – Kephirah in the Hebrew bible
Giybon – Gibeon in the Hebrew bible
Jarrar's Town or Woodlands – Kiriath Jearim in the Hebrew bible
Meyim – Beeroth in the Hebrew bible

Other key places

Shalem – Jerusalem
Bayth Shamsh – Beth Shemesh
Bayth Shean – Beth She'an
Gedjet – Gaza
Ayaluna – Aijalon
Laksh – Lachish
The Valley – that of the Jordan River

In Egypt

Pa Yam – the Faiyum
Waset – Thebes/Karnak

Later history of the Gibeonites

The later history of the four towns can be deduced from two sources – results from archaeological digs, which are only available for some periods of time and small parts of the area, and accounts preserved in the Hebrew bible, which by nature only cover a limited range of topics and are presented from a single point of view. Of the four towns, we can be confident of the location of Gibeon, cautious about that of Kiriath Jearim, and have only a rough idea of the other two.

Archaeology confirms that Gibeon was a place of major importance from about 1200 BCE onwards, with substantial water supplies and a thriving wine industry to generate prosperity. Since the nearby track down to the coast has always been an important arterial route, it is likely that trade has always fed wealth into this region.

The bible records that various people in key military and religious positions in the early stages of Israelite history came from the four towns, so the inhabitants were evidently trusted with high rank in spite of being of foreign origin. Perhaps even more surprising are the times when the towns played a key role in the religious life of the nation. The ark of the covenant, at one time the most sacred relic, was stationed at Kiriath Jearim for a number of years – possibly even a number of decades – before being moved to Jerusalem.

When Solomon succeeded to the throne and wanted divine confirmation of his fitness for the post, it was to the great high place of Gibeon that he went to seek a prophetic dream. We do not know if Joshua – Yahusharar – ever took up Damariel's similar offer, but it is possible. Over time, Gibeon and the other three towns became more completely integrated into the nation, and we read less about particular events that took place there.

As for Damariel's hope that he might one day be counted as a relative of Yahusharar, this was fulfilled in part. Although the inhabitants of the four towns are clearly identified as foreigners, and some of them have names of northern, non-Israelite origin, some of the later genealogies connect them with the Israelite tribes of Judah and Benjamin. This probably has more to do with geography than blood relationship, but also shows a willingness to grant the Gibeonite people a legitimate place in the hierarchy of the Israelite nation.

Whatever the true history of the four towns in this era might have been, the inhabitants were evidently much more than the enslaved wood cutters and water carriers which is how they are left in the book of Joshua. In both religion and poetry, they have left a lasting Canaanite impression on the ancient middle east.

Scenes From a Life

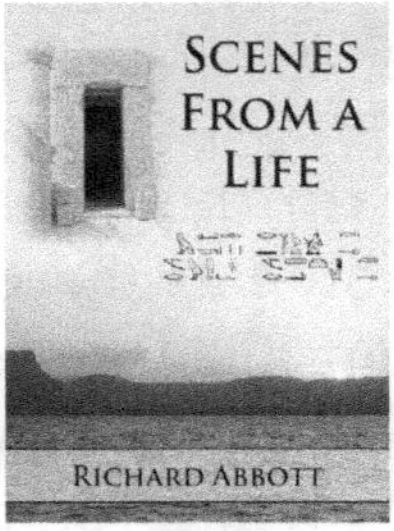

An extract:

HOW SHOULD THE PATTERN BE FINISHED? Makty-Rasut leaned back against the tomb wall, rough and unsmoothed as yet, and nowhere near the full length it would extend out to.

The courtyard designs were all complete, but the details for the transverse corridor had only been recently agreed with the senior priest whose eternal home it would be. Only a few of the key highlights of the main approach had been roughed out. In any case, these were just designs at this stage. They had not been called out of their potential to be created in sculpture and paint.

The man had insisted on one of the less common variations of the scene where his heart was being weighed. He had good reasons from his own religious experience, and Makty-Rasut had readily agreed once the request had been made. But in other things the old man was willing to be flexible. They had sat together while the priest told him something of his life's endeavours, and they worked together on the ideas that emerged.

Makty-Rasut marked two deep parallel lines on the pottery sherd he had brought, to represent the walls of the corridor. He had sent the rest of the team home early. It was a festival day tomorrow anyway, and he wanted the time to himself to think, alone in the tomb. It was easier. He wanted to have some ideas to show the priest when they next met, and he could not think clearly when the area was full of his team working and jibing.

Dreams had steered much of the old man's life. A dream had first sent him out, years ago now, into the provinces. Gedjet mainly, with a short spell up in Beth Shean at one point, and other brief sojourns elsewhere. Another dream had called him back to Waset. Other dreams, too, at different times, held less profound significance but were still vivid in the priest's memory. So dreams should figure prominently on the chamber walls. The journey out to Gedjet was a focal point. It could blend several traditional elements with some unique ones. That should please the old man, whose words often betrayed the same mix of past and future, convention and innovation.

He sat there for a while looking at the space available, working out in his mind where the main pictures and writing should go. Finally, happy that he had something definite to present to the priest at their next meeting, he added the ideas as rough notes scratched onto the sherd. He packed everything away. He would do a neat copy tonight, back at home with better tools and more light. For the time being he was content, and sat back again against the end wall.

He was very tired. There had been a series of long days. He had never worked with some of this team before, and he had wanted to be first in the workings every day and last out. It set a good example, and also gave him a good sense of the new men's attitudes. It was as usual: some good and some poor.

His second man, Sanedjem-Keni, was an old colleague, and Makty-Rasut had had no hesitation in choosing him. He had worked with him before, both recently here and also longer ago elsewhere in the land. For the first few weeks Sanedjem would lead the left side while he led the right himself. Then when the team came up to full strength he would move Sanedjem onto the right so as to be able to concentrate on the overall design and finishing.

He had no idea yet who would lead the team on the left. He was short of good draftsmen, who could take a plan and a blank wall and rough out the designs well enough to be ready for the painting. Several of the workers he had wanted on his team had moved up from working in the tombs of nobles to those of royalty.

Let them, he thought. The nobles' tombs were more interesting, and more diverse, than the eternal homes of those who were of higher rank. In them, the same religious motifs had to be portrayed in very much the same way, with very much the same words, over and over again. And they took so much longer. Years even. His work for the nobility suited him perfectly – a few weeks, or a few months, maybe a season or two, then the job was done and he could move on to the next one.

In fact, he thought as his eyes blinked shut, perhaps it was time to think about moving on from Waset altogether. It was considerably more than two years since he had come here, bored with the trips out into the eastern desert overseeing the gold mining. It had been a good couple of years, but perhaps it was getting to be time to move on again.

South to where the River turned turbulent, perhaps? That sounded very promising. He had no particular desire to head downstream again, back towards former homes, but there were enough places to ply his trade further up the River to keep him in work for a long time to come.

He caught himself falling asleep and sat up straight again. He would just wait a little longer in case some further inspiration came to him about the patterns. He really was extremely weary, though. His thoughts were flitting about like dragonflies, hovering here and there over the stream with constantly moving wings, unable to settle. For a little while he daydreamed about a woman he had seen briefly in the marketplace over at Waset last week, a junior singer at one of the temples from her dress. But she seemed very remote, separated from him by the width of the River as well as profession.

He sighed. He could not even remember her appearance well enough to conjure it in his mind's eye, and the daydream kept slipping back into an everyday fantasy, with nothing to distinguish her imagined body from that of any other woman. It was hardly different from reflecting on occasional nights spent at the houses of pleasure over on the east side of the River, although some part of his soul wanted the experience to have more meaning. The brief glimpse had not been enough to feed him with anything substantial.

He bundled the headscarf that he had needed in the cool of the morning behind his head, closed his eyes and leaned back against the wall, rough but solid and secure behind him. Perhaps he would think better like that. But in fact he must have fallen asleep, because all at once the dream came to him.

It was a familiar dream. He had had similar ones several times before, each time with minor variations.

He was inside a darkened boat, somewhere below decks where the light of moon and stars would not reach. He was rocking in little waves, as though the boat was crossing gentle ripples as it drifted downstream. It was warm, and his body was cradled in a nest of soft fabric, dark and red all around him. The boat had eyes on the prow that watched out ahead, he knew, though he could not see them just now. The boat contained ample nourishment to satisfy him, though just now he did not need it. The boat had a wide beam that made her stable in the water. It was all deeply pleasant.

He looked down, still in the dream. He was wearing a pair of startlingly white sandals. The sandals were of a style and an extravagance that he would never think to wear in waking life, but here it was fine. More than fine: just right, in fact.

But then all at once the boat and the warmth, the eyes and the provisions were gone, and he was plunged in the cold water, tumbling in one of the River's turbulent places. The current pushed him away. He could not reach the banks of the River, could not see them in the windy mist that clung to him. He felt coldness everywhere, coldness throughout his body, clinging at him, and his mouth was filling up with water. He was still wearing the sandals, and they made it just about possible to remain at the surface.

He woke all in a rush, pushing away the scarf that had now tangled itself around him. He sat there for a while to allow his racing heart to return to a normal beat, trying to root himself back in this world. His oil lamp had long since gone out. Finally he got up, felt for his bag of tools, and walked slowly along the corridor from memory with his left hand trailing along the wall to guide him. Looking out from the courtyard, east towards the River, he found that the sky was starting to fill with stars, like jewels adorning the clothing of night. There was a sharp scent of a nearby herb, clinging to a crevice in the rock. No-one else was anywhere near him.

How long had he been asleep? The air breathing down the hillside from his right, down from Meretseger's peak, was cool against his skin. He held on to the upright timber of the door-frame and steadied himself. Eventually he walked home, offered a pinch of incense and a brief prayer at the little shrine to Seshat that he kept, pulled at some bread and dried fish without really tasting either, and finally settled himself on top of his bedroll, tossing his unwanted clothes into a corner. He lay there for a while alone in the dark, feeling dislocated, and finally fell asleep again.

The Flame Before Us

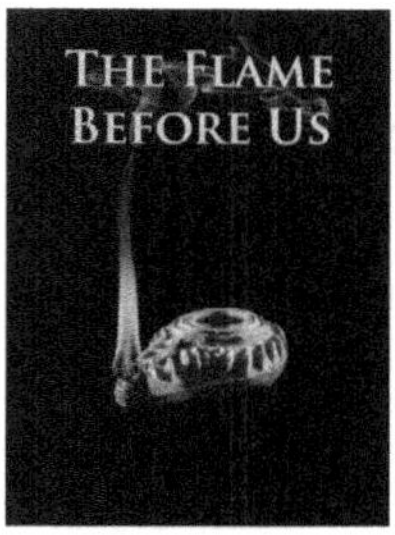

An extract:

BUT FATHER WILL BE BACK from the north before we have to leave?"

Anilat looked carefully at her mother, hoping to see some sign of the truth of the matter. But the old face, schooled in a great many years of diplomacy, was giving nothing away beyond the essentials, and the old voice did not directly answer her.

"You will be leaving as he instructed, a half-month from now. I will wait for his return and follow on after. He has been called to attend to the wishes of the King of the North even now."

The last was, surely, a simple guess, perhaps even a needy wish. Anilat nodded slowly, wondering if, after all, her mother had no more information than she had already shared. All that she herself knew came from the brief report delivered by the weary rider as he passed by the envoy's house on his way to the royal palace of Ikaret.

Not long after his arrival, the city gates had been closed, and the priests were called out from the temple to bless and prepare the few city guardsmen who remained. Most of the army had already been sent north to join the collected forces of the great King of the North, assembling somewhere in the vassal territories along the coast. As well as force of numbers and weapons, they had taken wagon loads of supplies, honouring the requirements of the treaty.

A little over two years ago the first stories had reached the city, of raiding groups harrying the fringes of the settled lands, a long way north and west of Ikaret. They were from island settlements mostly, or very remote coastal towns which could not be easily reinforced. Rumours of troop losses had spread, and the great king had been swift to silence the more vocal of his critics. But the reports were still carried, by traders and officials more concerned about the immediate risk to their life and livelihood than the king's displeasure. Then there had been a lull for a while, and it seemed that peace had returned.

But as the weather turned colder and winter drew close this year, groups of forlorn homeless had started to come down the Sea Road. The first few dozen of these were treated with kindness and a spirit of welcome. But dozens swelled to hundreds, and generosity could only stretch so far. Some of them stopped around the outskirts of the city, clustering in great tented pools around the streams and wells. Others moved on again, southwards, hoping to find better favour among the Fenku, or even the Mitsriy. They would have a long journey ahead, but perhaps the effort would be worth while.

"Are the children ready to leave? Yours and your brother's?"

Anilat brought her thoughts back into the room and nodded firmly.

"Indeed yes, mother. Provisions are ready for all of us. All three of my little ones are with Auntie now and she is preparing them with tales of journeys."

She stopped, hesitant. How could she speak about her older brother and his refusal to leave the house? Her mother waited, her face shrouded by the hood she wore. She had never liked the climate here, and found the winter air far too cold for her southern body. Anilat had become used to it as she had grown up, and earlier today had relished the freshness of the sea breeze drifting in over the land.

"If User-Amun will not leave, you must be ready to take his children as well."

So she did know after all. If events took this turn, Anilat and her husband Tadugari would be taking five children when they left. But her brother's daughter and son were considerably older, and they should be able to help make the journey easier.

"Mother, when you leave here, where will you go? All the way back down to the Beloved Land?"

Her mother sighed. "It is so many years since I was last there. So many years during which your father and I have moved from place to place at the bidding of the king. It would ease my heart to see it one last time. But it is a long way, and I am already old. Listen now. You must take the children from here when the time is right. Your husband will wait too long: you must be ready."

"I will not leave him. If he stays, I stay, and the children with me."

"All of the fruit of my body is in this one city together. In times like these, that makes me afraid. Shall I see all of you taken together? The good of the family requires you to leave when the time is right. I will not hear argument about this."

The two women were silent together for a while. Finally the mother spoke again. "And what of your sister?"

"She says that she will follow whatever the great priestess decides. She says that for her, it is as though she was a chantress of the kind you used to talk about when we were young together."

"The more fool her to think so. The priestess is not so high, nor the temple so grand, that she should do that. And her with child as well. You see, Anilat? You must take the lead here and ensure that the children are safe."

"Why should she hurry? She has confidence that even if some remnant of this enemy should escape destruction to the north, our own city guard will hold the walls and gates."

"Could the King of the North hold Taruwisa? Could his army hold his southern coastal towns? Do you think our soldiers have held the northern border?" There was a silence in the chamber. Her mother's breathing was rough, laboured in the damp air. "Well, how can I blame her? I sit here and wait for my own husband to come back from the north. Am I so different?"

"What about Taruwisa and the coastal towns? I had not heard anything of them?"

The old woman, eyes shrewd and bright in her lined face,

made a little move of her hands. Anilat, understanding it as dismissal, gave a little bow and left the room.

The Man in the Cistern

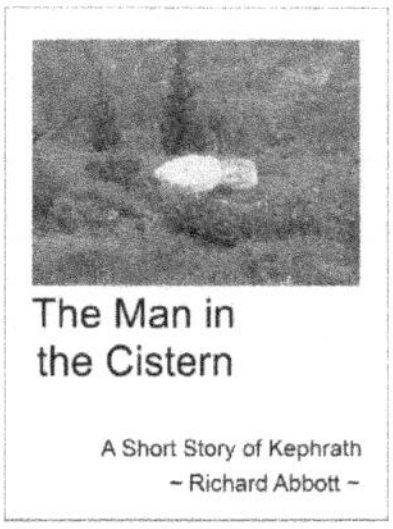
The Man in
the Cistern
A Short Story of Kephrath
~ Richard Abbott ~

A short story of Kephrath
Set about ten years after the conclusion of the full-length novel *In a Milk and Honeyed Land*, this short story follows Damariel and Nepheret as they tackle a new challenge to the four towns. A group of migrants has set up an encampment just down the trackway towards Shalem. What are their intentions? Do they come in peace or war?

The Lady of the Lions

The Lady of the Lions
A Short Story of Kephrath
- Richard Abbott -

A short story of Kephrath
Set about one hundred and fifty years before the full-length novel *In a Milk and Honeyed Land*, this short story is based on two historical letters written by a Canaanite woman to the great king in Egypt. The people of the four towns are being threatened by a band of rebels disdainful of the provincial ruler. Kephrath and her sister towns are outmatched by the raiders - can they secure help before their deadline runs out?

Triumphal Accounts in Hebrew and Egyptian

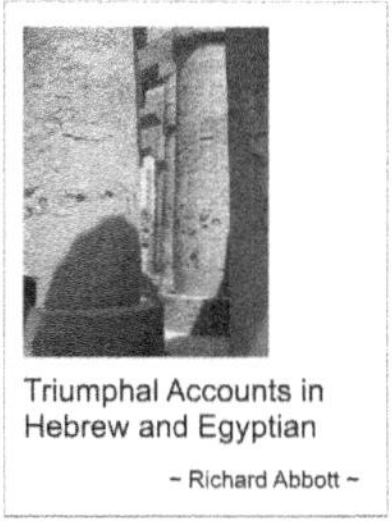
Triumphal Accounts in
Hebrew and Egyptian
~ Richard Abbott ~

An academic thesis

This ebook contains the text approved by the external and internal PhD examiners for a thesis carried out under the supervision of Dr John Bimson at Trinity College, Bristol, England. It will be of interest to those who wish to explore cross-cultural connections between early Israel and New Kingdom Egypt, as expressed in triumphal literature. The thesis looks at issues to do with the creation of poetry in each of those cultures, and the links between them, as well as investigating when appropriate cross-cultural contacts might have happened to forge common links between them.

www.ingramcontent.com/pod-product-compliance
Lightning Source LLC
Chambersburg PA
CBHW051928020726
47501CB00001B/33
9780993168420